D0177393

Praise for Lulu Taylor

'Don't you just want to grab this, switch off the phone and
curl up on the sofa? Winter bliss from Lulu Taylor'
Veronica Henry, top ten bestselling author of
Christmas at the Beach Hut

'Pure indulgence and perfect reading
for a dull January evening'
Sun

'Told across both timelines,
this easy read has a sting in the tale'
Sunday Mirror

'Utterly compelling. A really excellent winter's story'
Lucy Diamond

'I raced through this gripping tale about secrets and lies and
long-buried emotions bubbling explosively to the surface'
Daily Mail

'Wonderfully written . . . this indulgent
read is totally irresistible'
Closer

'A creepy story of obsession and deception. Very chilling'
Irish Sunday Mirror

'A gripping psychological thriller'
Essentials Magazine

'This is a fantastic, all-consuming read'
Heat

'[A] gripping story'
Hello!

'The cold, snowy cover and winter setting make
this a great stocking filler for your mum or sister'
Thelittlewildwoodkitchen

'The book is full of mystery and intrigue, successfully
keeping me guessing until the very end . . . An evocative
read, full of dramatic secrets that will make the reader gasp'
Novelicious

'A poignant, sophisticated and romantic love story'
Handwrittengirl

THE
FORGOTTEN
TOWER

Lulu Taylor is the author of thirteen novels including six *Sunday Times* bestsellers. Her first novel, *Heiresses*, was nominated for the RNA Readers' Choice award. She lives in Dorset where she continues to find inspiration for her stories of families, secrets and the mysteries of the past.

THE FORGOTTEN TOWER

LULU TAYLOR

PAN BOOKS

First published 2023 by Pan Books
an imprint of Pan Macmillan
The Smithson, 6 Briset Street, London EC1M 5NR
EU representative: Macmillan Publishers Ireland Ltd, 1st Floor,
The Liffey Trust Centre, 117–126 Sheriff Street Upper,
Dublin 1, D01 YC43
Associated companies throughout the world
www.panmacmillan.com

ISBN 978-1-5290-9397-1

Copyright © Lulu Taylor 2023

The right of Lulu Taylor to be identified as the
author of this work has been asserted by her in accordance
with the Copyright, Designs and Patents Act 1988.

All rights reserved. No part of this publication may be reproduced,
stored in a retrieval system, or transmitted, in any form, or by any means
(electronic, mechanical, photocopying, recording or otherwise)
without the prior written permission of the publisher.

Pan Macmillan does not have any control over, or any responsibility for,
any author or third-party websites referred to in or on this book.

1 3 5 7 9 8 6 4 2

A CIP catalogue record for this book is available from the British Library.

Typeset in Sabon by Jouve (UK), Milton Keynes
Printed and bound by CPI Group (UK) Ltd, Croydon, CR0 4YY

This book is sold subject to the condition that it shall not, by way of
trade or otherwise, be lent, hired out, or otherwise circulated without
the publisher's prior consent in any form of binding or cover other than
that in which it is published and without a similar condition including
this condition being imposed on the subsequent purchaser.

Visit www.panmacmillan.com to read more about all our books
and to buy them. You will also find features, author interviews and
news of any author events, and you can sign up for e-newsletters
so that you're always first to hear about our new releases.

To Amber, Matthew and William
With lots of love

Prologue
WAKEFIELD CASTLE
1939

'What time are we going to the fair?' Rosalind asked, directing her question at no one in particular, but sending it out over the breakfast table for anyone to answer.

Miranda, who sat opposite, was her mirror image: fair curls that frizzed when not brushed and tamed, and wide blue eyes that seemed to take over most of her face. The twins were the fairest in the family, but their semi-angelic appearance was at variance with their reputations for obstinacy and, in Miranda's case, mischief. Now she made a furious face at her sister.

Their younger brother Toby looked over, munching on his cold toast. 'I think we should go early,' he said indistinctly through a mouthful of bits. 'I need to get there before the man on the hook-a-duck runs out of goldfish.'

'Toby, *mouthful*. Please. *Please!*' Great-Aunt Constance held up one hand as if she could fend off the noise of Toby's toast. She was very sensitive to the sight and sound of people eating, and talking while doing so was particularly irksome to her. 'Any more of these bad manners and you won't go to the fair.'

Toby looked stricken and closed his mouth at once. Archie, the very youngest at six, was lost in his comic, but at the threat he looked up with frightened eyes, nervous at the treat being taken away. Both boys, alike with their light-brown cowlicked hair and freckles, looked fearfully over at Imogen, their eldest sister, who was busy buttering toast for Archie.

'I'm sure Aunt Constance doesn't mean it,' Imogen said hastily. 'But do eat quietly, won't you, Toby?' She smiled kindly at her brother. After Nanny had left in the spring, Imogen had become a mother figure to the two youngest children; she was soft and gentle where their great-aunt was spiky and distant. Small boys were like a different species to Constance, but Imogen was a natural clucking mother hen, gathering them under her wing.

'No wing nuzzling for me,' Miranda would say. At sixteen, she considered herself a grown-up and perfectly independent.

'Don't be mean about Immy,' her twin would beseech her. 'She's doing ever so well, considering.'

'I'm not mean. She's wonderful with the little ones. She just better not try mothering me. I don't need any,' Miranda would say brusquely. And she thought that she meant it.

Imogen said now, 'Well, I think we should set off as soon as we can after breakfast. Toby's right, it is best to get there early.'

'We can't come,' Miranda announced firmly.

'We can't come?' echoed Rosalind, as if mystified.

'No,' Miranda said, giving her a meaningful look. 'You're not feeling well, remember? And neither am I.' She adopted a suffering expression. 'We both have the most awful headaches.'

Rosalind quickly took on the same expression of woe. 'You know how twins are, feeling the same things.'

'I'll have to take your word for that,' said Imogen. 'But you love Bell Friday!'

The Bell Friday Fair was held each year to mark the arrival four hundred years ago of the great bell in the abbey, the largest for five counties, and workers were traditionally given the day off to go. Local ladies and storekeepers were known to groan with dread at the thought of Bell Friday, when they'd be left without housemaids and shop assistants for a whole day.

'Not really,' Miranda replied. 'It's got awfully boring lately.'

Toby looked at them, astonished. 'Boring? It's the best thing that happens around here by miles.'

'I prefer the village fete,' Miranda said primly.

Toby stared. The fete was no match for the fizzing excitement of the fair. There was a firing range where you got to shoot an air gun and actually win something decent like a model car or a Meccano set; a toffee apple stall; another where fresh doughnuts were served hot, rolled in sugar and cinnamon and tasting of stale oil. There were bottles of orange pop and the heady scent of mulled cider. There was nothing to choose between them, that was obvious.

'If you can't go to Bell Friday,' Imogen said, thinking it through, 'that means I'll be taking the boys on my own.'

Her sisters said nothing but gazed at her from wide china-blue eyes. 'The power of silence' Miranda called it. It was somehow more effective coming from two identical faces, each with a clear, blank stare. It seemed to overcome most resistance, and Imogen soon dropped her own gaze back to Archie's toast.

'Oh, all right,' she said weakly. 'If you really don't want to come, I suppose I can take them on my own.' She looked unhappy at the prospect.

Miranda felt a twinge of guilt. Imogen's life was being sacrificed to their little brothers. She might be motherly, but she wasn't actually their mother. When Miranda had once asked her if she minded, Imogen had just said, 'I know it's what they would have wanted, and that's that.'

Miranda found it far too painful to think about what *they* might have wanted although she knew Imogen believed it. *Perhaps I would do the same if I was the oldest*, she thought. But she wasn't sure.

Despite being glad that her sister was prepared to take on the mantle of substitute mother, she found Imogen's lack of spirit aggravating. No one seemed to fight back any more. Even the boys were quiet, obedient little things. Once they'd been bundles of energy and noise. Now they were solemn and restrained.

Aunt Constance had been sipping her milky tea, apparently lost in her newspaper, but now she looked up suddenly. Although she had completely missed the last minute or two of conversation she had somehow heard a familiar noise on the stairs outside. 'Ah, here's Leonard,' she said gratefully. 'He can take over. Are his kidneys ready?'

'In the warming dish,' Imogen said, nodding over to the sideboard. 'Mrs Graham put them out earlier.'

Aunt Constance shuddered. 'How . . . lovely.' She stood up. 'I will see you later, my dears. Enjoy the fair, won't you? I'll be spending the day with Miss Roberts. The mobile library is coming through today and we particularly want to change our books.' The breakfast room door opened and Grandfather came in, limping slightly. In his scratchy tweed suit and with his bushy white moustache, he looked like any other country gentleman except for the black eyepatch which covered a socket made empty during the Great War. 'Good morning, Leonard, enjoy your breakfast. And girls . . . ' – she paused as she went past the twins' chairs – '. . . as you've both got headaches you'd better go back to bed for the day.'

'Yes, Aunt Constance,' Rosalind and Miranda murmured obediently, but when she'd passed, Rosalind shot her sister a cross look and Miranda stared meaningfully back. Then she mouthed, 'Trust me,' and they went back to their cold toast and marmalade.

Miranda said that Wakefield Castle sometimes felt more like a wind tunnel than a house, it was so draughty. The ancient stone walls were never warm, and the mullioned windows seemed designed to let as much of the outside in as possible. The feeble fight against the pervasive cold consisted of thick curtains at every window, tapestries on the walls, fires burning most of the year and tepid radiators, installed ten years ago, that couldn't cope with the vastness of the house – the boiler heating the water for them was miles away in the cellar.

'Remember the old house in Kensington?' Rosalind would sometimes say. Four years ago, they had lived in a narrow townhouse, with a staircase that went on forever, up and up. The house had been light, and cheerful, full of colour and fresh flowers. From its glossy black front door, they had walked to school, to the park or to the museums and life had been safe and predictable and they had been protected. There had been a nice nanny and housemaids, a cook and even a lady's maid called Whittaker who looked after Mother with almost religious devotion.

'I don't want to talk about the old house,' Miranda would say crisply. 'They said we shouldn't think about any of it, and that includes the house.'

Rosalind would look unhappy. Miranda knew that her sister really did want to talk and remember, but she could not. It was too hard, even though there was no one else for Rosalind to talk to. The little boys were too young to remember, and Imogen, now so grown-up, had become one of the triumvirate of guardians with their great-aunt and grandfather, so that she was almost not really one of them any more.

Life had grown cold in so many ways. The warm house in Kensington was gone and now they lived here, in the freezing castle with their grandfather and his elderly spinster sister in place of their parents. What was the point of remembering what they could no longer have?

*

The only place in the castle that was reliably warm was the kitchen. In the great fireplace, the old iron range burned away day and night, filled with wood brought in by Alf, the slow son of Carter, the last of the old indoor staff who was now butler, driver and sometimes valet to Grandfather. Alf was twenty-five now, but everyone treated him like he was a child of eight, and he was kept busy all day splitting logs and bringing the results to the kitchen to feed the range and the boiler. The range burned high and hot all day, and then ran on the heat of the embers until the following morning when they were prodded back to life with more wood by Alf. The range was large but looked small inside the cavernous fireplace, where cooks in past centuries had roasted joints on spits over open flames and baked bread in the cubby holes hidden in the back of the fireplace. Inglenooks on either side showed where boys had once sat to turn the great spit to cook a carcass evenly.

The kitchen, though, was toasty warm, which perhaps explained why Mrs Graham, the cook, was always dripping sweat from her red cheeks while the rest of them were shivering with cold upstairs.

'Disgusting,' Miranda said sometimes. 'Imagine if she drops that sweat into the soup!'

But she only meant it as a joke to put the boys off. It didn't work. Although she was rather scrawny and mean-looking in herself, Mrs Graham's cooking was very good, and if that included her sweat, so be it. There was no way the colonel, their grandfather, would have allowed anything other than a superb cook in his kitchen. He was most particular about his food. In the trenches of the Great War, he had taken receipt of parcels from the Officers' Department of Fortnum and Mason. 'Foie gras,' he said wistfully sometimes. 'I can taste it now. Ambrosia. And the marmalade and crystallised plums . . . My batman made me coffee each morning with the home blend. It was when I truly learned to love food.'

Life in the castle revolved around meal times, which punctuated the day as regularly as a railway timetable, the chafing dishes in the dining room filled with the plain fare Mrs Graham served up for ordinary days. The days were mostly ordinary now. There weren't the great parties there once had been, before the disaster. Grandfather had a shooting party once or twice a year. Aunt Constance sometimes had her friends to stay, the ones who had helped her in the struggle before the war, or the political ladies whose causes she supported these days. They weren't interested in food, however, but in talking.

For the children, though, food was always very interesting and a highlight of their days. Breakfast was eaten downstairs, the venue for lunch depended on the day, and supper was upstairs in the nursery. In the glory days, when there were footmen, eggs for the children's tea were placed in a saucepan of boiling water in the kitchen and by the time they arrived upstairs, they would be perfectly soft boiled, while toast was made on the fire under Nanny's very watchful eye. Nowadays, Imogen made eggs and toast herself in the small nursery kitchen, little more than a hot ring and a tiny sink in a cupboard. Many of the staff had left over the last few years and most of the rest had given notice in preparation for war.

Mrs Graham had said that if it did happen, she would go to her sister in Bournemouth for the duration and no one knew what would become of meals then. It was a terrible thought.

Now the girls crept into the empty kitchen. Mrs Graham and Lottie, the girl from the village who came in to help, had gone to the fair. Imogen had taken the boys on their bicycles. Aunt Constance had headed off in her little pony and trap, clip-clopping away down the drive. The coast was clear.

Miranda got straight to work in the pot cupboard, while Rosalind was drawn to the windows. She climbed up on one of the long wooden counters and sat there cross-legged, gazing out of the window through the diamond-shaped leaded panes. 'It's the same colour as that tube in my paint box,' she said dreamily. 'French blue. Or is it marine blue?'

'What are you talking about?' Miranda asked breathlessly as she staggered back into the kitchen under the weight of a huge boiling pan. 'Help me, can't you?'

Rosalind jumped down from the counter. 'Course I will, no need to shout.'

'I'm not. And what's blue?'

'The sky, you idiot.'

'Ah, the sky is blue, is it? You truly are the towering intellect of our age. Come on, let's get this on the table.'

The two girls lifted the large pan onto the scrubbed wooden table in the centre of the kitchen that served as the workbench.

'Now let's see, what shall we do next?' Miranda didn't always have the answers, no matter how it looked when other people were around.

'Get the berries of course,' Rosalind replied.

They moved in tandem and fetched the buckets of blackberries they'd collected the day before, which had arrived early due to the summer being particularly warm. It had been a happy day in the hedgerows, using a couple of their grandfather's walking sticks to hook down brambles laden with the dark purple jewels of fruit. They'd filled two whole buckets.

'Have you got the book?' Miranda asked and Rosalind nodded.

'Right here.' Rosalind pulled out a battered book from under the table and put it on the table and opened it. It was very old, and written in many different hands; the later pages were filled with more recent entries.

'Here we are. Mother's recipe for bramble jam. It looks easy.'

They both pored over the page, reading the neat handwriting.

'I didn't realise we had to cook the jars,' Rosalind remarked.

'Just heat them.' Miranda read everything again. 'Well, let's get started. You get the jars from the pantry and I'll start sorting out the berries and weighing them.'

Rosalind turned to look at her. 'But what about our extra ingredient? Will that change things?'

'We'll see. I don't see why. Let's get started.'

They moved around in easy companionship, another sign of their twinnishness. They didn't seem to need to talk all that much as they worked and yet they were constantly in sync with each other. Miranda sorted the berries, removing twigs and the odd leaf or stalk, while Rosalind washed the jars in hot soapy water, put them in a tray and placed them in the oven. Then she came over to join her sister and continue preparing the fruit.

'I think,' Miranda said, 'we make mostly normal. And three or four special.'

'All right.'

'So we can explain what we're doing.'

'Of course.'

They poured the berries into the large brass weighing pan and set it on the cast-iron scales. Then Miranda tipped them into the boiling pot. Rosalind weighed out the sugar from the Kilner jar and they tipped that in as well.

When all was ready, they hauled the pot to the hotplate on the range and set it on.

'How long?' Rosalind asked.

'Two hours or so. We bring it to the boil and then let it simmer very long and slow until it's thick.'

'I'd better move the jars to the cooling oven.'

'Good idea. Then once they're full, we turn the jars upside down until they're cold. That keeps the jam from going off apparently.'

'Interesting. I wonder why.'

They stirred the blackberries with a long wooden spoon, watching the sugar disappear as it dissolved into the fruit. Soon the fruit was bubbling and popping as it came to the boil, roiling and spitting like molten lava. They moved the pan to the cooler plate and it subsided to a gentle simmer, the odd bubble bursting wetly on the surface as they watched.

'What now? Do we have to stand here for two hours?' Rosalind was gazing down into the dark purple mass below, where berries were gently releasing their juice.

'No. I suppose we can take it in turns to come back every twenty minutes or so to check on it.'

They slipped away, back to their bedroom just in case Aunt Constance returned early from her visit with Miss Roberts.

When they were sure the jam was ready – thick, glossy and almost black with only traces of the berries left – they took out the jars and Miranda began to ladle the mixture into them. It smelled delicious: hot, sweet and fruity.

'This makes me long for Mrs Graham's scones. Shall we ask her to make some?' Rosalind suggested, putting the lid onto each full jar and turning it over.

'Yes, good idea.' Miranda stopped when the jar she was filling was up to the brim. She looked thoughtful. 'Well, I think we've enough left for four jars.' She looked at her sister. 'Shall we?'

Rosalind was suddenly breathless, her eyes wide and scared. 'Well . . . that's what we decided. You think it's a good idea, don't you?'

'Of course I do. It's our duty. You know it is. Bessie Glanville told me that her mother is spreading the word all over. Lots of people are doing it.' Miranda looked decided. 'I'll get the stuff. I asked Alf to put it in the cold store.'

'Let's heat the jam up again.'

They hoisted the pan back to the range, then Miranda ran lightly over the flagstones and out of the kitchen door, through the scullery and into the cold store, a place of dusty shelves and tins, and abandoned boots and discarded household items not fit for the attics. Mrs Graham hated it. 'Nasty, dusty and dirty,' she said. 'Someone should clean it. But it isn't going to be me.'

In the cold store, Miranda found the tin she was looking for, the lid already prised off and then lightly replaced so that she could easily remove it. She picked it up carefully, nervous even to hold it, and hurried back to where her sister was waiting.

'Got it!'

'Do you know what to do?' Rosalind asked.

'Well, not really, but Alf said his dad puts down a scattering to kill dozens. So I'm sure we can guess.'

Miranda pulled off the lid and they looked inside. It was three-quarters full of small white pellets, quite dainty and attractive-looking. Miranda took the tin to the range, and tipped it slowly over the jam. There was a rustle, then a slide and the soft rattle of movement, and dozens of the pellets tumbled into the remains of the jam. Miranda tipped the tin back and the twins stared wide-eyed into the pot.

'Is that enough?' wondered Rosalind.

'I bet it's more than enough. But just a little bit more for luck.' Miranda shook a few more pellets in on top of the others, and then put the tin on the floor, pressing the lid back on. 'Time to stir.'

Rosalind took up the spoon. 'I almost don't like to. It feels wrong to use something Mrs Graham uses for soup and gravy and everything.'

'We'll wash it up. Or throw it away if it makes you feel better.'

Rosalind carefully put the spoon into the mixture and started to stir. 'I hope they melt.'

'I hadn't thought of that.'

They watched anxiously as the white pellets remained stubbornly whole and solid even if now stained a fetching pink. They decided hot water might help, especially as the jam was looking very thick now, and boiled the kettle so that they could pour some in. This seemed to work, along with moving the pan back onto the hottest plate. The pellets began to vanish, darkening in colour, shrinking in size and disappearing into the jam.

'There,' Miranda said happily. 'We did it.'

They ladled the jam into the last four jars. There was just enough. They turned the jars on their lids to cool down, handling them carefully with dishcloths, as they were scalding to touch.

While the jam cooled, they took the wooden spoon and the ladle and washed them thoroughly several times in the butler sink in the scullery, and scrubbed the boiling pan clean, rinsing it out with kettlesful of boiling water.

'I'm sure they're safe,' Miranda said, as they put the implements back in their rightful places. 'I couldn't be surer.'

'All right,' Rosalind replied. She'd been in favour of burying everything in the garden but Miranda said that while Mrs

Graham might put up with a lost spoon, a vanished ladle and boiling pan would certainly make her suspicious and some awkward questions would be asked.

When they had finished tidying up, the jars were cool enough for their labels. The four jars of rat-poisoned jam had carefully been put at a distance from the others. Rosalind produced the labels. They were painted by her: a picture of a bramble dangling some pretty, glossy berries. On almost all of them, sweet dormice were reaching paws for the luscious fruit. But on others, fleshy tailed rats were staring greedily at the berries, their long yellow teeth on show, and in a tiny detail, just visible under a bramble leaf, a dead rat lay on its back, paws hooked in stiff agony.

All the jars received their dormouse labels but for the last four, which had the dead rat labels instead.

'Your paintings are wonderful, Rosie,' Miranda said admiringly as they gummed them onto the jars.

'Thank you. Do we tell Mrs Graham?' Rosalind frowned. 'What if she uses one?'

The idea was too horrible.

Miranda said, 'We can't tell her. She'll throw them out and all our effort will be wasted. You know she will. But we can put them right at the back in the pantry. No one uses the jars at the back, they always use the ones at the front first. It will take months for her to get through our jam. And I'll check on the jars just in case.'

'I don't think that's enough,' Rosalind said. 'I shan't be able to eat a mouthful of it just in case.'

'All right. Look, I'll hide them and you and I will know

where they are, and if we need them, we can get them out. Would that make you happy?'

'It would make me less nervous.'

'Good. That's what we'll do. I'll hide them in the cold store, you know how much Mrs Graham hates it in there.'

'Yes. That's the place.'

'We'll do it now.'

When the poison jars were safely concealed on a high, cobwebby shelf, with some tins of nails in front of them just in case, and the good jars were stowed in the pantry, the girls took up the old cookbook that was still sitting on the kitchen table where they'd left it.

'It's funny to see Mother's handwriting again, isn't it?' Rosalind said softly. She touched it with a fingertip. 'It's been so long.'

'Yes.' Miranda gazed over her shoulder. 'She loved that book. She was always reading it, do you remember? "Listen, girls," she'd say, "what do you think of this?" And then she'd read out one of the old recipes, and all the exotic ingredients. How funny they were, weren't they? No proper quantities, such odd names.'

'Then she'd cook them. She was the only person Mrs Graham didn't mind having in the kitchen. Do you remember she'd make them for Father and Grandfather? Her tasting committee.'

'The gastronomes,' Miranda said. 'Remember? Every now and then she'd cook a feast and called it a gastronome night. I thought she meant actual gnomes. I was very disappointed when they didn't arrive for dinner.'

Rosalind laughed, though she'd heard it before. 'Father was nothing like a gnome. So tall and handsome.'

They were both silent, suddenly solemn. They rarely spoke of their parents. What was the point? Each knew exactly how the other felt, and how their brothers and sister also felt at the tragedy that had engulfed their family.

That was why Miranda had suggested that they do this.

'Don't you see, Rosie?' she had urged. 'It would be our way to get revenge. If it weren't for this war, it never would have happened! Mother and Father would still be here. But not just that. It's our duty!'

Everyone was trying to think of ways to aid a swift and total victory. One of their friends had actually made a jar of liquid concocted with anything toxic they could find – aspirins, cleaning powders, borax, boot polish, acid and laundry aids – labelled it 'This Is Not Poison', wrapped it up carefully in brown paper and sent it to Mr Hitler, The Palace, Germany.

'That won't work,' Miranda had said scornfully. 'Even if someone drinks it, it will be a taster, like in medieval courts. They won't let Hitler touch it. Especially if they see the English stamps. Besides, I bet it smelled foul. Our plan is much better.'

Delicious blackberry jam. The invaders would arrive, roaring up to the castle in their horrible cars, ready to march in and take over, in their jackboots and overcoats. They would be surprised by the warm welcome they received.

Miranda and Rosalind planned to let Imogen in on the plot at that point, and to persuade their sister – eighteen years old, as fair as they were, and very pretty – to use all her feminine wiles.

'How charming to meet you,' Imogen would say. 'Please come in. Do join me for tea.'

'She will have to wear lots of lipstick,' Miranda said, 'And smile beguilingly.'

When the Germans had relaxed, and were off their guard, Rosalind and Miranda, all smiles, would bring in a tray loaded with tea, freshly made scones, butter from the farm and homemade blackberry jam.

The German officers would greedily help themselves. A few bites and a moment later, they'd be lying on the floor, glassy eyes staring at the ceiling as they expired. Perhaps one would mutter, 'You English fiends! With this jam, you have defeated us!'

That was what Miranda predicted.

'And if Hitler himself comes . . .' She breathed out with suppressed excitement. 'Imagine! We would kill Hitler. I think we'd get a medal.'

'It won't be Hitler,' Rosalind said. 'Why would he come here?'

'Well, it doesn't matter, we can kill a decent amount of officers. Hide the bodies and deal with the next lot who come looking for the first lot the same way.'

They spent hours plotting their perfect jam murders, enjoying the sense of power it gave them. The truth was, everyone was afraid. No one was in doubt that war was coming, and that Hitler had his eye on Britain. There would be an invasion. Everyone needed to prepare for the day when the German army landed, and be ready to do their bit.

'We don't have guns and we're not grown-up and strong,' Miranda said, 'but we do have delicious food. So that's what we'll use. If we have to protect ourselves, we'll do it.'

And now they had done it. They had actually made the poisoned jam that was sitting right now in the cold store. It was almost deliciously frightening that they had dared. But the thought of disposing of even one of the enemy seemed to put right the dreadful wrong that had been done to them three summers before.

Chapter One

LONDON

Present Day

Georgie blinked at Caspar. 'This. Is. A. Living. Nightmare.'

'That's overstating it, isn't it?' He was always very pragmatic. 'But . . . granted. Not ideal.'

'Not ideal? It. Is. A. Disaster.'

'Please stop talking like that, Georgie. I understand you feel emphatic about this.' He shrugged. 'But this is the way the cookie has crumbled.'

'Honestly, Caspar! I mean it!'

'Okay. I understand. I knew this would be hard. Take a few minutes. Let me know when you feel calmer, so we can have a proper talk about this.'

Casper was hard to ruffle, but that was one of the things she loved about him. But right now, she wanted him to see how unhappy his news had made her.

They were sitting in the sunny kitchen of their little London flat. Caspar had come back late the previous night from a family meeting in a gloomy solicitors' office in a market town in Oxfordshire and then a family dinner. Only a fortnight before, Georgie and Caspar had driven through it on their way to St Jude's Church for the funeral of his great-uncle, Sir Archibald Wakefield. Afterwards they had gone to Wakefield Castle for cucumber sandwiches, fruitcake and tea, to reminisce about Uncle Archie, who'd lingered on to the great age of ninety.

The miracle is, Georgie had thought, looking about the great hall, *that he didn't die of cold before then. But perhaps . . . he had ways of keeping warm.*

She had glanced at Uncle Archie's widow, who was wearing a magnificent black coat, and a hat with a veil that swathed her face, only a pair of scarlet lips visible beneath. Occasionally a handkerchief was held up to dab at the veil as though soaking away tears, but Georgie suspected that it wasn't possible to do so without actually touching the face, which Viktoria kept hidden under her veil the entire time. Caspar went up to murmur his sympathy and she clutched his wrist with her black-gloved hand and said something to him, but Georgie shrank away from all that. She was painfully shy, and still found herself tongue-tied with all of Caspar's family. Even after four years of marriage, she found it hard to tell them all apart, and more children sprang up almost overnight, like snowdrops. The castle was thronging with Wakefields: dozens of them, from grey-haired elders down to the screaming youngsters tearing about the place, everyone talking at the tops of their voices and seemingly neither deafened nor freezing. Georgie had lingered by the fire, trying to soak up some of the feeble heat, but there were just a couple of logs smouldering in a fireplace that could have easily fitted an entire cow within it. Caspar's sister Alyssa had come up for a chat, and although Georgie liked her, she found it stressful that Alyssa had a squirming, moaning six-year-old hanging off her hand, and her voice was lost in the babble which bounced off the stone walls and made it impossible to hear. Georgie had tried to stay calm and concentrate but she became ever more agitated, until tears – foolish, silly, overwrought tears – had threatened. Fortunately Alyssa had finally given in to the whines of her youngster, made her excuses and wandered away in search of crisps. Georgie had been grateful when at last Caspar had sought her out to take her home.

The car was a haven of peace and quiet after the noise and chaos of the great hall. She liked the way they usually travelled in silence, sometimes putting on some classical music, but more often listening to the noise of the engine, and the sounds of the car – indicators, gear changes, windscreen wipers. It calmed her down.

'What did Viktoria say?' Georgie asked at last.

'She said, "Thank you, my dear, my heart is broken. I do not know how I will live without him. He was my sun, my moon, my everything."'

Georgie laughed because Caspar said it in an entirely flat voice. He was always fairly emotionless. He had proposed by saying, 'Apparently there is an excellent deal at the wine merchant's for champagne. I thought we might take advantage of it and have a wedding reception?'

Caspar slid his gaze away from the road and over to Georgie as she laughed, then back, his lips twitching. 'I'm glad that wasn't my response when she said it.'

'I'm not laughing at that, you know very well. It's the way you say it. Do you really think she's heartbroken?'

'I do think she's heartbroken, but not necessarily about Great-Uncle Archie. I mean, it can't have been a shock, not at his age. His ticker had been dodgy for a long time. Then there were the two types of cancer. And he was carrying most of his organs around with him in bags by the end.'

Georgie giggled again. 'No he wasn't. He had one, after his colon got taken out.'

'Whatever, he was hardly love's young dream. I should think Viktoria was more like a nurse than a wife by the end.'

'She hired at least two nurses, your sister told me.'

Caspar shrugged. 'There you are. Practically running a hospital ward.'

'What do you think she's brokenhearted about?'

'Perhaps she doesn't like change.'

'We're being very mean. She's probably very sad about your uncle dying. He was her husband, after all.'

'True. And what she, a forty-something divorcee, saw in a well-off old man . . . I have no idea.'

'Do you think he's left her money?'

'Bound to have,' Caspar said firmly. 'She'll have made certain of that.'

'Then I'm sure she'll be all right.'

'She's just sad her comfortable life with Uncle Archie is coming to an end.'

'It can't have been that comfortable at Wakefield,' Georgie said feelingly. 'I don't know how she stood it.'

'It looks like she mostly ignored it.' Caspar frowned at

the road, a touch of crossness in his eyes. 'The place is worse than ever. Some of it is on the brink of collapse.'

'Well,' Georgie said, 'thank goodness it isn't our problem.'

And she'd put the whole thing out of her mind as they headed back to peaceful, calm, quiet home.

'I suppose I'd better tell you,' Caspar had said that morning, after the meeting with his family and the solicitor.

Knowing his deadpan delivery and general lack of emotion, Georgie could guess nothing from this. She'd carried on making coffee in the glass drip jug. 'Of course you must tell me. Are we millionaires? Did Uncle Archie leave us all his loot?'

'Not exactly.'

'Did you get a book token wrapped round a cannonball?' There were cannonballs scattered all over the grounds of Wakefield Castle, supposed to look picturesque, Georgie guessed, but now that the lawns were overgrown they were terrible hazards, and on one visit Georgie had broken a toe walking into one concealed in a tuft of grass.

'Nope.'

'All right then.' Georgie leaned over the kitchen table and poured coffee into their mugs. She loved their Saturday morning rituals: coffee and papers in the sunny kitchen. A walk to the river. Brunch in the Duck Egg cafe – she always had the eggs Benedict – mooching around the shops, going to the market to pick up nice to things to eat over the week-end, and home for dinner and a movie. Caspar would open a good bottle, though Georgie didn't much care about that; she couldn't tell the difference between wines. Relaxing, ordered, calm. Just the two of them. The way she liked it. 'So. Come on then. Spill the beans.'

'You know Uncle Archie didn't have any children.'

'That was partly why he married Viktoria, wasn't it? To begat an heir.'

'Yes. As we know, the clinic did not make good on its promise.'

Georgie remembered the Christmas some years ago when Viktoria had bent over Great-Uncle Archie as he sat partially slumped in his chair in front of the dining table, his lunch cut up and mashed slightly with a fork. She'd grasped his raddled hand while he looked rather bewildered, and declared joyfully, 'We are going to be parents!'

Everyone had gone quite still with amazement.

'You're pregnant, Viktoria?' Alyssa had exclaimed. She was pregnant herself with her third baby, but she was in her mid-thirties and although Viktoria admitted to being forty-five, everyone was sure she was closer to fifty.

'Not exactly.' Viktoria had beamed. 'Nature needs a little helping hand now that Archie is getting on. We are having IVF.'

'That's wonderful,' Alyssa said in a strained voice and Georgie could tell that she didn't think it wonderful at all.

'They can work miracles these days. My little boys can't wait to have a baby brother or sister!' Viktoria declared with a girlish laugh.

Her sons, Siegfried and Wilhelm, were both at the table and Georgie glanced at them: large, silent, unsmiling and beetle-browed young men of twenty and twenty-two. Neither looked at all excited at the prospect. Everyone else murmured their good wishes and Caspar spoke up to change the subject.

Later Alyssa had told Georgie that it was outrageous. 'There are people who really need IVF! Cancer patients, people with fertility issues! Not an elderly couple like Viktoria and Uncle Archie. It's an absolute scandal.'

'I agree. But let's wait and see,' Georgie had said. 'I'd be surprised if it works.'

She was right. It seemed that nature had its limits, and was not prepared to be forced in that direction despite the very best and very expensive efforts of the fertility clinic. There had been no baby.

'It's for the best, I think,' Georgie had said to Caspar. 'And Viktoria has her two sons in any case. Imagine being born when your father is in his eighties! It isn't right.'

'No,' Caspar replied meaningfully. 'Babies should be born when the parents are in the prime of life.'

And Georgie had hastily changed the subject.

'So?' she asked now. 'I suppose Viktoria has got everything.'

'Not quite. It seems that blood is thicker than water after all.'

'Oh?'

'She gets a cut of the estate of course. And there are lots of bequests to nephews and nieces. So that will deplete what she gets.'

'And I suppose the castle and the title go off to your cousin, the one who lives in Canada.'

'Randolph. The bear conservator.'

'Yes. The one we've never met.'

'It's never a good time to leave the bears, apparently. Yes, he's now Sir Randolph Wakefield. Though he goes by Randy, apparently.'

'Sir Randy Wakefield?' Georgie laughed again. 'That's funny.'

'Let's hope the bears are suitably impressed. But . . .' Caspar looked unusually ill at ease. He was famously impassive and here he was, shifting awkwardly and tapping his fingers on the table, biting his lip and frowning.

'Yes? He didn't leave us a pile of debts, did he?'

She spoke light-heartedly because she didn't believe for a moment that Uncle Archie would do such a thing. He'd been very fond of Caspar. 'Sound as a pound!' he would say. 'That's our Caspar. Solid and with a good head on his shoulders.' He liked the fact that Caspar was a responsible young man who'd never gone off the rails, but had stayed sensible and sober, and focused on a career as a solicitor. 'The only sturdy oak in a family of reeds!'

That was a little unfair on the others, who were all perfectly normal but had gone in for more unstable careers in arts or tech, which Uncle Archie struggled to understand. But Caspar was one of the oldest of his great-nephews and Uncle Archie had taken less interest in each succeeding young relative. The very youngest ones barely featured in his consciousness, as they'd appeared in his early old age when his attention had been taken up with Viktoria and her two sons. No one knew anything of Viktoria's first husband except that he had also been German and no longer had anything to do with his sons.

'We do not speak of *him*!' Viktoria had said frostily when she was once asked about him, and she was as good as her word, and never did. Siegfried and Wilhelm also said nothing about their father, and everyone suspected that he was perhaps dead but didn't dare to ask.

'He did not leave us debts,' Caspar said slowly.

'Don't tell me! He discovered a Leonardo in the attic just before he died, and he's left us that.' Georgie could afford to be jokey as they had no need of anything. They lived comfortably on Caspar's income as a solicitor and hers as a cookery writer. Extra money was always welcome, but they didn't need it. So she hoped that Great-Uncle Archie had left something that would mean something to Caspar, that he could treasure – like the family standard, or the old photograph albums – but they could do without money. She was contented just as they were.

'He . . .' Caspar took a deep breath and said rapidly, 'He left us Wakefield Castle and wants us to go and live there and restore it. That's what he did.'

She didn't believe him. She laughed and said, 'Yes, but what did he really leave us?'

It was only when Caspar said solemnly, 'Viktoria is furious,' that she actually began to believe him. The smile on her face faded, her laughter stopped. And that's when she really took it in, and said what she genuinely thought about this awful development.

'This. Is. A. Living. Nightmare.'

Chapter Two

Casper had waited quite a while before he mentioned the family castle to Georgie. They met at the party of a mutual friend and Georgie had liked him on sight. He was so calm and solid-looking, as if he wouldn't turn a hair no matter what happened, but would cope in any crisis with that same unflappable air and the sharp intelligence that glinted in his grey eyes. They were complete opposites physically. He was tall and well built, with dark hair, prominent cheekbones and those poetic grey eyes, while she was short, slim, freckly and round-faced, with slightly wild strawberry-blonde hair that she twisted up and clipped into a messy bun, to keep it out of the way of her cooking. She wore glasses when she was working, and her one concession to beauty was lots of mascara to darken her light lashes.

'Your eyes are tiger-coloured,' Caspar would say. 'Orange and brown.'

'A very shy, frightened tiger,' Georgie would add with a laugh.

'No need to be frightened now, you've got me.'

She knew he was right. He was solid and dependable, and that was what appealed to her. She had a very attuned radar. Where her girlfriends went out with obvious bad boys, only to be bewildered when they turned out to be just that, Georgie never did. She found kind, serene types who liked the same quiet life that she did – rhythms and patterns and routines – and when the relationships ended, they were not in storms of tears, but friendly agreements to go separate ways.

She liked things predictable and secure, and Casper had looked safe. From that first moment, she'd had a powerful sense that she was supposed to meet him, and that if she didn't act, she might miss a vital opportunity. She'd surprised herself by acting completely out of character by going up and saying, 'Hello. I'm Georgie. What's your name?'

Once she was next to him, she realised he was really very tall. He looked down at her from his gangly height, as though surprised by the voice that seemed to be coming from somewhere around his knees, and had answered politely. Once they'd started chatting, they soon stopped noticing the disparity in their heights. Everything he said filled her with more certainty that her initial impressions were correct. He was solvent, employed, serious-minded and keen on classical music, quiet nights in and long country walks armed with binoculars to scrutinise the birds he spotted.

Safe.

They fell into step in their lives like two companionable walkers. Love didn't come like a lightning bolt, or through dislike that turned to passion, but with the gentleness of opening the door to a friend and saying, 'How wonderful to see you, come in!'

They both knew almost at once that this was going to be their future, and Georgie always suspected that Caspar was glad that there was no need to say it. No need for declarations or poems or grand romantic gestures. She knew that he preferred her to understand him without words. That when he said, 'Fancy watching a film?' he meant, 'I love you.' When he said, 'Are you in the mood?' he meant, 'You're beautiful and I desire you and want to seduce you at once.' If she'd ever asked him what he meant, he would have been confused and said, 'I don't know. I've no idea what I mean.'

But he showed her all the time what she meant to him: in the way he took her hand and held it in his own much larger one when they walked; the way she fitted perfectly into his side and under his arm while they watched television; the way he knew her moods and emotions before she did, and was already running her a bath, or cooking one of the three comfort meals he made when she was too depressed to cook herself. Every Friday night, a bunch of her favourite flowers, depending on the season, would be carefully arranged in a vase, and a bottle of good claret breathing beside it on the kitchen table.

'I love you, Caspar,' she would say and he would reply, 'I'm of a similar mind,' or 'Likewise, my darling,' or, 'The feeling is entirely mutual.'

Which made her very happy even if he struggled to say the actual words himself.

After a blissful and romantic year during which they

moved into the sunny flat near the river, Caspar made his infamous suggestion that they take advantage of the wine merchant's champagne offer and followed it up – once she'd cried and said, 'Yes, we should, yes please' – by saying casually, 'We could always have the whole thing at the castle.'

'The castle?' She'd blinked at him and wondered for a wild moment if he meant a pub that she used to cycle past on the Old Kent Road.

'My Great-Uncle Archibald has a castle. An old family place. You know the sort of thing.'

'Er . . . no!' Georgie laughed. 'What are you talking about?'

'Didn't I mention it?'

'You know you didn't!' He had introduced her to his father and mother, who lived in gentle comfort in an old red-brick house near Monmouth. It had the loveliest gardens, to which they devoted nearly all their time. Caspar said he'd barely seen them out of their gardening clothes in a decade. They dedicated themselves to the velvety lawn, the borders spilling with pink roses, lavender and silver bedding plants with spiky purple verbena at the back, the gracious trees, the arches with rambling roses and clematis, the pots of trailing geraniums, the baskets with clouds of white petunia. She had met his sister, Alyssa, who ran a homewares store in Bath with her husband Henry. She had met his little brother, Ed, who edited animation in a converted warehouse office on the Thames in the shadow of Tower Bridge. Ed had a succession of beautiful girlfriends and no money, but was funny and charming and sparky.

'But you never mentioned a castle,' she admonished. 'What

are we talking? Disney? Medieval motte-and-bailey? Ruin? Height of luxury?'

'Hmm.' Caspar had wrinkled his nose. 'Hard to say. All of the above.'

'*All?*' She blinked in astonishment. 'What?'

'It's hard to explain. You have to see it really. We'll go there for Christmas. Unless you have to be somewhere else?'

'No, nowhere.'

'Don't you ever see your parents at Christmas?'

'Adoptive parents.'

'Sorry – your adoptive parents. I know you said you're not close . . .'

Georgie shook her head. 'It didn't work out, I told you. That sometimes happens with adoptions of older children, rather than babies. So Pippa and I don't see them any more, they're not a part of our lives. We have each other.'

Caspar nodded. He wasn't the type to push for information. 'Pippa's a lovely girl. Why don't we go down and visit? We can break the news to her.'

So they took a trip down to Brighton, where Pippa lived a busy life with her husband Ryan and new baby, and had a happy evening surprising them with champagne and the first glimpse of the engagement ring.

Pippa had squealed with excitement, cried, hugged them both and then hugged them again. Ryan had congratulated Caspar and told him that he was a brave man giving up his freedom and there was still time to back out. Pippa looked a little hurt for a moment, but Ryan laughed and said, 'Only kidding. Honestly, married life is great,' and she looked reassured.

They spent the evening talking about ideas for the wedding and Caspar mentioned the castle.

'You have a *castle*?' marvelled Pippa. Caspar showed her a picture on his phone. 'That's amazing. And what a great venue for a wedding!'

'We'll have to see if Georgie likes it first,' Caspar said.

'It looks lovely in the pictures,' Georgie said, 'but I'm not really a fan of big events.'

'Take advantage of it, Caspar!' joked Ryan. 'I got fleeced for thousands for our wedding! All that cash for a party. If Georgie wants the register office and a Nando's, you should go for it. I wish I'd had that option!'

Pippa had playfully thwacked him, and they'd happily discussed weddings for the rest of the evening.

Later in the kitchen, when it was just the two sisters, Pippa said, 'I'm really so happy for the two of you. I think Caspar is perfect for you and I have done from the start.'

'Thank you. I think he is too.' Georgie hesitated and then said, 'Is everything all right with you and Ryan?'

Pippa looked surprised. 'Of course. Everything's fine. I mean . . . obviously we have some problems. He's a typical man, not very good at feelings and communication and all that.'

'Okay.' Georgie considered. 'So he finds it hard to express himself?'

'No, no.' Pippa wrinkled her nose as she thought. 'It's not exactly that. It's more like . . . he doesn't actually know what he thinks. When we have issues and I want to talk them through, he just doesn't have anything to say. So I ask him to have a think about it and tell me later. But he never does. It's odd.'

'I don't know if I understand,' Georgie said slowly. She had always looked out for her younger sister, and something was bothering her.

Pippa laughed. 'I don't know how to explain it. But most of the time, everything is fine. Just like any marriage. You have to work at it.'

On the way home, she asked Caspar if he noticed anything odd about Ryan but he said no, Ryan seemed completely normal: funny, charming and intelligent.

'You didn't think his jokes about weddings were a bit pointed?'

'What? Oh no, just ordinary banter. He's just being funny in a slightly unoriginal way. I think he and Pippa seem to have a great relationship.'

'Yes. Me too,' Georgie said, but she couldn't quite shake the feeling of discomfort when she remembered that tiny look of hurt on Pippa's face.

Georgie grew increasingly nervous as Christmas approached. The idea of a huge house full of strangers who would soon be her family made her feel sick, but she said nothing to put a damper on the visit. What she hadn't expected was the sheer beauty of Wakefield Castle. Her first view of it had been as the car turned through a pair of mossy pillars, and then glided along a winding drive that quite suddenly revealed a proper old castle, with a bridge that crossed a steely grey moat thick with waterlily pads and algae, to an old gatehouse of twin towers with an arch between them and . . . was that a portcullis? And beyond that a solid stone square house in the classic E shape, with two great wings and a central hall with a vast oak iron-studded door at the entrance.

'Caspar!' she exclaimed as they drove up.

'I know.' He smiled. 'This place is quite something. It's been in my family for years.'

'It's gorgeous!'

'Yes. It's beautiful. Come on, let's go in.'

The great front door wasn't locked, and Caspar led the way into a vast hall with a hammer-beam ceiling. Georgie gazed around, speechless. It looked as though it was about to be photographed for the Christmas issue of some heritage magazine.

'Henry and Alyssa have been at work,' Caspar remarked. 'Henry loves it here.'

'It looks amazing,' Georgie said sincerely.

The whole room was draped in greenery, with swathes of ivy looped over the enormous fireplace where a mass of logs glowed on a heap of ash. The stone chimneypiece, stained dark grey at the front from the billowing smoke of countless fires, was lined with a collection of pewter jugs, also wreathed in ivy. Two large red velvet sofas faced each other in front of the fireplace, a small acre of Turkish carpet between them. A great oil painting hung over the fireplace. Georgie stared at it. A fleet of dark-brown ships were setting sail from an elegant city over a scalloped blue sea. Caspar saw where she was looking.

'It's Charles the Second's return from exile in the Netherlands in 1660,' he said.

'Oh.'

'Not that you can see him. I don't even know which ship he's supposed to be on. And it's ironic really, as this hall hosted meetings of those in opposition to Charles the First.'

She looked around. From the ceiling hung an ancient iron chandelier holding dozens of waxy candles that emerged from a morass of holly and mistletoe. In an alcove over a Gothic doorway was the torso of a polished suit of armour, its helmet wearing a garland of ivy. There were no baubles or fairy lights. Just greenery, berries and candles. It had a wonderfully pagan feel.

Georgie looked at Caspar with something like indignation. 'You never said a word about this!'

'Well . . . I'm not sure how I feel about it. I've got mixed emotions. The castle is a love it, hate it sort of place.'

'Did you grow up here?'

'For some of my childhood. It was . . . ' – he made a face – 'noisy.'

Georgie looked around. She could imagine this place full of people, and felt a small prick of panic. 'How many of your family will be here?'

'A few. They tend to descend at this time of year.' He smiled, put down their cases, and went to wrap her in his arms. 'Don't worry, they're harmless. And I'll be with you all the time. I promise it won't be awful.'

For the first time, she wondered if he had hidden the existence of the castle and his large family because he thought that it might frighten her off to know that this was part of his life.

But it's fine, she told herself, *because this isn't actually our life. It's just a facet. It will be over soon, and I can bear it if Caspar is with me.*

A rush of anxiety hit at the sense of the space all around her. Instinctively, she used a technique she called 'blurring' where she consciously focused on something small close to her and made the emptiness retreat to the outskirts of her consciousness. The panic subsided and she breathed out. 'Is there a kitchen?'

Casper gave her a sideways look. 'Is there a kitchen? You'd better believe it. Come on. Let's go and take a look.'

Kitchens were safe places for Georgie. They were warm, nourishing spaces where recipes could be followed and the most wonderful things would result. Ever since she was small, she'd been obsessed with food.

'You ought to be the size of a house really,' Caspar would joke. 'Considering how much you love cake.'

Georgie liked cake for breakfast: big juicy slices of carrot cake, loaded with cream cheese frosting – the warmth of nutmeg and cinnamon, the plump raisins and soft crunch of walnuts, the tang of lemon in the cheese. Delicious. Or banana bread, studded with chocolate chips, rich with the hint of rum, slathered in butter. While Caspar ate muesli, she tucked into muffins: high-topped, loaded with the red blots of raspberries and crunchy with golden sugar. Despite all this, Georgie was slim, petite even.

'How do you do it?' Caspar asked.

'I don't know,' she said. 'It's just what I'm like.'

Caspar was not complaining. He loved her cooking, and was always enthusiastic about whatever it was she was trying out. 'What is it today?' he would ask, looking eager to taste whatever she was conjuring. Besides assisting a celebrity chef in recipe development and cookbook writing, she had an occasional food column in a magazine, and that meant she was often cooking out of season: making Christmas food in July, and Easter treats in November. Caspar might come home to barbecue and salads in the depths of winter and cinnamon buns in the height of summer, but he didn't mind at all. He wolfed everything down and told her she was probably the best cook in the world.

He knew that she wanted to see the kitchen at Wakefield in order to feel comforted.

'This way.' He led her confidently out of a door at the end of the hall. It was a strange feeling, to know how at home Caspar was in a place like this. It was an aspect of him that she did not know: the man to whom this extraordinary place was home.

Does he feel impossibly cramped in our flat? Georgie wondered as they walked down a corridor lined with paintings and tapestries. Did he miss cavernous fireplaces and hammer beams stretching darkly overhead, and staircases curving away into the shadows? It was strange to think of Caspar as a boy, running up and down these corridors.

40

They came to a wide stone staircase leading downwards. She followed Caspar down, around a turning and then through another Gothic stone doorway, and in they went.

'Oh!'

Caspar smiled at her. 'What do you think?'

Georgie walked slowly in, looking around. 'You're right. It's a kitchen.'

Wooden benches stretched out along the length of the room. Over the great fireplace hung a row of copper pots in ascending size, the biggest looking like a small bath. A range glowed warmly in its depths, but there was also a conventional oven squeezed in next to it. Looking about, Georgie could see that despite the antique feel to the room, there were lots of modern additions. A huge fridge gleamed at one end, and a microwave sat squat and dark on a far counter. A dresser against one wall held a large collection of blue and white china: platters, jugs, plates, tureens, bowls and dishes of all sizes.

She turned to Caspar. 'It's bigger than most restaurant kitchens.'

'I suppose it fed dozens of people back in the day.'

'How do they get the food upstairs? If that's where you all eat?'

'Yes, such a pain. There's a kind of lift thing and various warming trollies to take it all about.' Caspar rolled his eyes. 'Ridiculous really. They must have liked their food cold in the old days.'

'Or they used cloches.'

'Cloches?'

'Those metal covers you put over food – like when you order room service in smart hotels.'

'Yes, I think we do have some of those,' Caspar said thoughtfully, 'but they're silver.'

'And perhaps you use chafing dishes,' Georgie added. 'Serving dishes that are heated and keep things warm.'

Just then a door at the back of the room opened and in came a middle-aged woman with long dark hair holding a tub full of potatoes. She stopped short in surprise to see Georgie, her eyes round, then she saw Caspar and relaxed. 'Caspar!'

'Hello, Sandy.'

'They said you were coming for Christmas.' Sandy put down the tub of potatoes on the scrubbed table in the middle of the room and went over to Casper, raising up on her tip-toes to reach his cheek for a kiss. She looked at Georgie, her eyes much warmer now. 'And who's this?'

Caspar introduced them. 'Sandy cooks here, don't you, Sandy?'

'Yes, I do, and I'm doing a lot of hours over Christmas, I can tell you.'

'Viktoria isn't doing the cooking?'

Caspar and Sandy laughed, to Georgie's confusion, before Caspar put his arm around her shoulder and said, 'She hasn't yet met Viktoria, Sandy.'

'I can tell,' Sandy said.

'Georgie's a cook,' Caspar said proudly.

'Ooh.' Sandy looked wary. 'I'll have to be on my best form, then.'

'Oh, I'm just a home cook, not a chef,' Georgie said quickly.

'Don't let her fool you, she's amazing,' Caspar said.

'I'm happy to help out, if you need it? I mean, just sous chef things. Peeling, grating . . .'

Sandy smiled. 'That's very kind but I wouldn't hear of it. You're a guest. You'll be looked after. That's why Viktoria has got me in so much. Now, shall I put the kettle on? Fancy a mug of tea?'

'Yes please,' Georgie said. She was relaxing now she was in a familiar environment, even if somewhat bigger than usual.

'Lovely,' Caspar said.

'Tell me what you're up to, Caspar.' Sandy walked over to the fireplace and slid a huge copper kettle onto a hotplate.

No electric jugs here, Georgie thought, amused.

She leaned against a counter, listening as Caspar and Sandy caught up on news. Few of the names meant anything to her, but she could gather that the castle was going to be busy over the next few days. She watched with interest as Sandy started laying out sandwiches on silver trays, and loading a cake stand with scones.

They were finishing up their tea when the sound of a distant gong boomed through the house.

Caspar made a face as he put down his mug. 'We are summoned.'

'Haven't you said hello yet?' Sandy asked, whisking away the mug to the dishwasher.

'No. We were finding our feet first.'

'I'm just about ready here.' Sandy nodded at the food she'd been preparing. 'Viktoria ordered afternoon tea at four o'clock.' The kitchen door opened and two giggling teenage girls came in. 'And here are my helpers.'

'Thank you so much for the tea, Sandy,' Georgie said, wishing she could stay here in the warmth of the kitchen.

'You're welcome.' Sandy was already distracted by the girls, telling them to get changed quickly and wash their hands.

'Come on, Georgie.' Caspar took her hand. 'There's nothing to be frightened of, I promise.'

'If you say so,' she replied, a twist of apprehension tightening in her stomach, and she clutched his hand in return.

Tea was to be served in the Oak Room, named for the intricate carved panels on the walls, but really the room was dominated by a vast and ornate white stone chimneypiece, at least eight feet wide. Winter light came in through the tall, slender, diamond-paned windows, and the room was further illuminated by lamps that glowed on side tables. A Christmas tree decorated in pink and silver bows and pink fairy lights glittered in a corner. Chintz-covered armchairs faced a pink silk sofa in front of the fire, and a woman in a glamorous red wrap dress stood by a table on which sat a large vase of flowers, tweaking winter roses into position. From the back, she could be any age, her dark brown hair lustrous, but she turned at the sound of Caspar and Georgie coming in, and revealed a very well-preserved face in middle age, expertly made up. The only jarring note was her eyebrows, which seemed entirely hairless and only painted on her face in two dark brown lines.

'Ah! You're here!' she said, in accented English. 'Good. Then everyone has arrived.' She sighed. 'I've asked them all to be here for tea at four but they are late. Of course.'

'Viktoria.' Caspar strode up to her and kissed her proffered cheek. 'Happy Christmas.'

'Happy Christmas.' Her gaze flicked to Georgie with little interest.

'This is Georgie,' Caspar said quickly. 'My girlfriend. I mean, my fiancée.'

'Yes,' Viktoria said and smiled at Georgie, albeit coolly. 'So pleased you could join us.'

'Thank you,' Georgie said in a small voice. She already found the atmosphere around Viktoria difficult: it was, like her dress, red and full of spikes. Little black forks of lightning seemed to buzz around her.

'Where is Uncle Archie?' Caspar asked.

'Asleep,' Viktoria said. 'He will join us at dinner.' She sighed. 'He is very tired at this time of year.'

'This time of life,' Caspar muttered to Georgie.

He had told her something of Viktoria on the way to the castle. 'A powerful personality,' he had said.

'Nice?' Georgie had asked.

'I'm not sure nice is the right word,' Caspar had said diplomatically. 'Determined. But at least she seems to be kind to Uncle Archie.'

'How did he meet her?'

'No one is quite sure, but the story is that she wrote to Uncle Archie asking for a tour of the castle. She was a member of some historical society that gives privileged access

45

to various private houses. Alyssa thinks she was trying her luck with all sorts of elderly castle owners, writing and turning up and trying to charm them into matrimony. But it's just Alyssa's theory. There's no proof.'

'Perhaps she loves him,' Georgie had ventured.

'Perhaps she does,' Caspar had agreed in a voice that seemed to suggest it was extremely unlikely.

Now that Georgie could see Viktoria for herself, she could understand why there might be uncharitable motives ascribed to her. Viktoria was not at all a likely match for an elderly man, looking in the prime of her middle age, her hair elaborately styled into a large updo, glittering jewels at her ears and throat, and dressed as if for a cocktail party. Georgie had been expecting someone who looked more like a friendly grandmother, perhaps with greying hair, in a cardigan, kilt and sensible shoes.

But why shouldn't she make the most of what she's got? Georgie asked herself. *I'm sure living here might bring out the urge to glam up in anyone.*

She left Caspar and Viktoria talking and started wandering around the room, taking in the paintings, the family photographs in silver frames, the beautiful wooden harp that stood by a far window. The pale carpet was covered in Persian rugs, and she noticed two pugs asleep on cushions next to a radiator.

The door opened again, and in came Alyssa and Henry, each holding a small child by the hand.

'Hello, hello, we're late!' Alyssa was unmistakably Caspar's sister: tall, with flowing dark brown hair and the same high cheekbones and grey eyes. She came straight over and kissed Georgie heartily on each cheek. 'Congratulations! You two have made it official! I'm so, so delighted. I want to hear all about it just as soon as I can. Henry, shall we get Matty and Percy – say hello to Georgie, please, children – shall we get them a sandwich each? It'll keep them quiet. Viktoria, hello! Is there any tea? Well, shall I ring the bell? All right all right, you've done it, that's fine . . .' She muttered under her breath to Georgie, 'God forbid anyone should take any control from Viktoria. Horrible old bitch. Sorry! Don't listen to me, she's lovely. Oh, here's the tea, that was quick, they must have been on their way, thank goodness. Matty, do you want a sandwich?'

Georgie just smiled. She had learned long ago that in conversations with extroverts, it was often easy to say nothing and still come away with a reputation as an excellent conversationalist. She felt a small prickle of panic, sensing that Alyssa and Henry's arrival marked the beginning of the crowd, but she kept calm, glancing over at Caspar for reassurance. He was looking out for her and smiled encouragingly while listening to Viktoria. Alyssa started bustling about, sorting out the tea things and supplying her children with food, and Georgie tried to fade – this was when she gently backed away and out of the orbit of the loud and confident ones, so that she was in no danger of being their target. More people came in: Caspar's younger brother Ed and a stunning blonde girlfriend in a tweed mini dress and long boots. Caspar's parents arrived, as well as some aunts, uncles and cousins. The news of the engagement was making her a focus, and while it was nice to be congratulated, she couldn't bear too much of that all at once.

Alyssa's husband Henry found Georgie by the curtains looking out over the moat. 'Are you hiding?' he asked, munching on a ham sandwich. He looked nice, in very shabby casual clothes – jeans and a collarless granddad shirt under a yellow waistcoat – with thinning brown hair and kind eyes.

'I'm shy,' she said. 'I'm not good with crowds.'

'Fair enough,' he said. 'I'm not a great talker myself.'

'Thank you,' she replied. 'Lots of people don't seem to believe in shyness. They think you just need bringing out of yourself and start asking lots of questions. It's agonising.'

Henry nodded. 'Don't worry, you won't get asked much here. Everyone's too busy talking about themselves. It's a struggle for air time. You'll be quite popular if you don't make a play for it.'

'But that's the thing. I don't want to be popular.'

'It's your catch twenty-two then. But the good thing is, there are lots of places to hide here. Very easy to be forgotten. You'll see. If I spot you making a run for it, I'll create a diversion so you can get away.'

'Thank you,' she said, smiling. He seemed like an ally. 'I had no idea what I was letting myself in for.'

'Caspar can be quite cagey. He didn't prepare you for this then?'

Georgie shook her head. 'He didn't say a word.'

'He's terrified of women with "castle syndrome". Mention your ancestral home and they're all over you. He's had a few girlfriends like that, eying up the place and fancying a role as a chatelaine.'

'But it's not his house,' Georgie said quickly, who couldn't imagine anything worse. 'It's his uncle's.'

'Very true,' Henry said. 'And look what happened to Uncle Archie.' He gazed meaningfully at Viktoria, who was now in conversation with an elderly couple who were no doubt Caspar's parents as the man had the same tall, beaky look as Casper and Alyssa. 'I hope you'll enjoy yourself here. It can be overwhelming.'

'I'll do my best,' Georgie promised.

In the event, the stay for Christmas was fine. As Henry had observed, the fact that Georgie didn't want the spotlight played in her favour. No one seemed to mind that she sat quietly at dinner and said very little, or that she was up early and out of the door for a long walk, heading out over the bridge and into the grounds and then into the woods that surrounded the house. It was breathtakingly beautiful. When she'd climbed high enough, she'd looked down over the castle and gasped at the sight of the old house with its towers and battlements and the softly glinting moat. Henry had been right. This kind of house was big enough to get lost in, a place to find solitude and silence. She had never known a house like it, and something in it resonated with her. Her chaotic childhood, in ever-changing flats and houses, and then with Patsy and Mike, had created this longing for solitude in her, along with her chronic shyness. She had always looked for small spaces where she could be alone and quiet – compact flats, neatly arranged rooms, with order and security. The bedroom she was sharing with Caspar was large, with a view over the park, but the bed was a four-poster with curtains that Caspar pulled shut to create their own cosy hideaway, and she loved it. It had never occurred to her that a large space might provide refuge rather than panic.

Nevertheless, she preferred making her way down to the kitchen, where it was warm and busy in the way she liked. She would join Sandy, who'd make her a coffee. Once Sandy had understood that Georgie really was much happier peeling a tub of potatoes in companionable silence with only the radio playing than being upstairs with the family, she had been happy to give her tasks.

Caspar left her to her own devices but was always happy to see her when she emerged from a walk or from the kitchen. 'I'm on family duty,' he said apologetically. 'Really must talk to the rellies.'

'Should I join in?'

'Only if you want to. I'm covering for you – they all think you're a creative genius who needs time to think.'

'Well, I am, and I do.' She had brought work with her, writing up the recipes she had tested in the last month and organising them.

'Of course you are.' He hugged her. 'Don't worry, I'll protect you from them.'

But actually, it wasn't so bad. After a day, she got used to the large family mealtimes, the skittering children rushing about and getting underfoot. The older members moved at a slower pace, and spent long hours in front of the fire with books and newspapers, and no one seemed to mind that much. Viktoria didn't emerge till almost lunchtime, perfectly made up and wearing party dresses, it seemed to Georgie, but everyone else was more normal. Alyssa raced after her brood in jeans and trainers, and put them into any amount of outdoor clothing twice a day for a trip into the garden.

'They must be exercised, like dogs,' she said, shooing them out the back door and down the stone steps to the lawn. 'Stay away from the tower!' she shouted after them as they ran off, dragging the little ones after them with mittened hands.

'Tower?' Georgie asked, looking out over the frosted garden that was surrounded by the castle walls.

'Towers, really,' Alyssa said. 'I'll put my coat on and go after them. Just in case someone decides to explore the moat.' She pointed across the lawn. 'See that tower there? It's called the East Tower. It's starting to fall to pieces now. But the West Tower is off limits. Out of bounds. No one goes there now. The two towers are joined by a secret passage, apparently, not that we ever found it despite looking and looking when we were kids. Uncle Archie always forbade us from going to the West Tower as though the fence around it wouldn't stop us anyway. In fact, he never even said why there is a fence all around it. Dad – his nephew – didn't seem to know anything about it either.' Alyssa fetched her coat from a hook by the door and struggled into it, pulling it over her bulky jumper. 'Naturally I'm sure that's the place the children will be most interested in.'

'This place is full of surprises,' Georgie said.

'No end to them,' Alyssa said. 'Right, send Henry out if

you see him. No reason I should wrangle the children all on my own.'

And she disappeared off in the direction of the puffy coats and snowsuits that were vanishing in the distance.

It was Christmas Eve and there was to be a black-tie dinner.

'Viktoria's Germanic traditions,' Caspar said, coming into their room with damp hair, his shirt sticking to the places he hadn't dried himself after the shower. 'She always makes a big deal of Christmas Eve. But I must say, I rather like it. It takes the heat out of Christmas Day.'

Georgie was sitting at the dressing table, getting ready. She felt anxious. She had rarely gone to events where she had to dress up. This wasn't her familiar territory at all. She had bought a plain black dress and brought some heels out of the back of her wardrobe where they lived in a shoebox most of the time.

'You look lovely,' Caspar said, putting a comforting hand on her shoulder as he went past. 'Don't be nervous, it's the same crowd as at lunch and breakfast, just gussied up a bit.'

She breathed out slowly. 'I don't know if I'll ever get used to castle life.'

'We'll be home soon enough,' he promised. 'We can head off on Boxing Day.'

Georgie gazed at herself in the mirror. Two more days and then home. She was exhausted by all this. Had it really only been just over two days since they'd arrived? Huge families were an enormous amount to cope with. She thought of Pippa and hoped she wasn't finding Christmas too stressful, with a baby and everything to organise. Ryan helped, but he wasn't particularly proactive, so Pippa had to do all the mental work and delegate some of the physical tasks. Pippa's Christmas card had contained their special quote from A. A. Milne: *It isn't much fun for one, but two can stick together.* It had become their motto. *Two can stick together.* It often had not much been fun for two either, but they had known how much worse it would have been if either had been alone.

Caspar was pulling on his jacket. 'Ready?'

She nodded. 'Ready.'

And taking his arm, she went with him to face the crowd downstairs, thinking how much happier she'd be in the kitchen, wearing an apron and helping Sandy prepare the feast.

There was champagne in the Oak Room first, to warm them up before dinner. Then a bell summoned them all to the dining room, also lined with panelling and dominated by the long polished table now alight with candles. Great-Uncle Archie was already at the table, having been wheeled up to his position at the top where there were two places laid.

'You're over there,' Viktoria said to Georgie, pushing her lightly at the waist towards her place. 'Archie particularly asked for you.'

'Oh,' she said, feeling instantly frightened. She had barely seen Great-Uncle Archie since they'd arrived. Viktoria always announced he was resting, or being fed or walked by one of the nurses, as though he was a pet, not a person. She'd glimpsed him at lunch once and seen him in his wheelchair in the drawing room, but she'd kept her distance. Now he was in an ancient dinner jacket, a green silk bow tie, and with pearl studs down the front of his evening shirt. A few strands of white hair were combed across his pink head. He leaned rather to the side and seemed to be staring at the table.

I won't be able to hear him, she thought anxiously. *He'll talk too quietly. And he'll be deaf. I'll have to shout.*

Panic burned in her stomach and she felt her heart beating faster as she sat down next to him, watching longingly as Caspar went to his place at the far end of the table.

Great-Uncle Archie turned to face her with a smile. 'Hello, young lady,' he said in a surprisingly resonant voice, his accent from another time. It made her think of period dramas and the announcers on old news reels. 'I've been looking forward to making your acquaintance.'

'That's nice,' Georgie said faintly. Then she gathered all her courage, smiled and said loudly, 'How are you?'

'My dear girl, every day is a blessing at my age. A day in which nothing aches or breaks is a good day for me. And I must admit, I'm feeling in fine fettle.' He grinned at her, dry lips stretched over yellowing teeth.

So this is age, she thought.

It wasn't pretty. Uncle Archie's skin was simultaneously stretched and shiny, and folded and spotted. His brows were sparse except for a few long, wiry white hairs. One eye was red-rimmed and drooped half-closed, and his ears seemed so large. His neck and shoulders were bent, and his fingers knobbly and skewed with arthritis. Every movement appeared to take an effort.

Georgie felt her initial fear subside. She remembered how,

years before, when she'd cowered in front of a spider, Patsy had said to her, 'It's much more afraid of you than you are of it!' And now, so close to Uncle Archie, she saw that the dinner would probably be more of an ordeal for him than it would be for her. She felt absurdly young and fit next to him, and, to her surprise, found she admired him. He was smiling, he had got himself all dressed up to sit at this table in his wheelchair, still game for a bit of company and a chat when it was all clearly an effort.

She wasn't sure how to relate to him. She knew no one old, she had no grandparents that she was aware of. It had been years since she'd laid eyes on Patsy and Mike – they must be in their seventies now.

'We need a drink,' Uncle Archie said. He waved a finger at Caspar, who came over. 'Pour us some wine, my boy. We're rather out of it up here.'

'Of course.' Caspar poured out the wine and gave Georgie an encouraging smile. 'I hope my uncle is going to be good company.'

'I'm doing my best,' Uncle Archie said gaily, as Caspar passed him the wine glass. 'I'm an old dinosaur but I can still summon up some social skills when I need to. Happy Christmas!'

Georgie lifted her glass. 'Happy Christmas.'

'So,' Uncle Archie said to her confidingly, as Caspar returned to his place. 'What do you think of my house?'

'It's beautiful. I didn't much like it when I arrived but I do now.'

'You didn't?' He laughed, a wheezy sound that shook his

shoulders. 'How unusual. Most people go in the opposite direction. Can I ask what was wrong with it?'

'It's rather bigger than I'm used to. I found it overwhelming . . . all this space. All this room.'

'You prefer smaller houses?'

'Oh yes. Small, cosy, warm, reliable. This looks . . .' She gazed about the panelled dining room with its walnut sideboard gleaming with silver, and the oil paintings glowing in the candlelight, the fire crackling under the huge carved chimneypiece. 'It's beautiful,' she said hastily. 'But it looks like it needs a lot of upkeep. And it is rather cold.'

He laughed wheezily again. 'You are not wrong about that. I was so cold after growing up here that I went to live in St Lucia for twenty years, just to warm up my old bones.'

'Really? What did you do there?'

'I ran a bar and restaurant, called, a little boringly, Archie's.'

'Oh!' Georgie blinked at him. In a moment, the old man slumped in his wheelchair, bow tie poking into his chin, transformed in her mind into a younger version – tanned by the Caribbean sun, wearing a white shirt, standing straight and tall behind a bar and shaking up cocktails for customers. 'What kind of restaurant? What sort of food?'

'Local food,' Uncle Archie said vaguely. 'I left the cooking to my chefs. I just ran it, and spent my evenings at the bar charming the clientele into buying lots of very expensive drinks, which luckily they did. It was great fun. But in the end, I came home. Duty called. And by then I was ready.' He shook his head. 'No one chooses the circumstances into which they're born. I wouldn't have asked for it but it is a privilege to be handed a place like this to take care of. I like to think I'm a guardian of memories.'

'A guardian of memories,' she echoed, thinking of her own memories, the ones that she tried so hard to bury. Her way of guarding her memory was to put it in a box and lock it and do her best never to let it back out into the world.

'Not all good memories,' added Uncle Archie, as if reading her mind. 'No life is lived in pure happiness. Most of us endure suffering of one kind or another. We are all trying to survive as best we can.' He looked at her sharply. 'So you like my house now, do you?'

She turned her attention back to him. 'Oh yes. Particularly the outside. The walks, the park. But really . . . everything.'

'Good,' Uncle Archie said. 'That's good, I'm pleased. Now. Here comes the soup.'

When they went home, Georgie was so exhausted she had to live in complete silence for two whole days. When she had finally recovered in the familiarity and comfort of home, she said to Caspar, 'Darling, your castle is wonderful. But how do you feel about getting married very, very quietly? Perhaps just us, the siblings and a friend or two?'

Caspar had taken her in his arms and hugged her tightly. 'Of course, if that's what you want. And . . .' He hesitated and then said quickly, 'You know I love you, don't you?'

'I would hope so!' she said, laughing as he squeezed her.

'But I really do. And you're not keen on castles or big

weddings and you don't wear silly dresses and too much make-up.'

'You don't just love me because I'm not Viktoria, do you?'

'No,' he said quickly, and then gave her one of his most dazzling smiles. 'Because you're you.'

Chapter Three

August 1939

It wasn't that the West Tower was forgotten, exactly. It would be hard to forget entirely, as its twin, the East Tower, sat exactly opposite at the other end of the garden, where the wall marked its boundary. Not only that, but the square towers were set into the castle wall itself, so that it appeared as though the wall actually went through them and they were part of it. Each looked like a miniature version of the castle, small and yet ornate, with diamond-paned windows on every side, and a leaded roof that lifted up to a centre point, a decorative stone obelisk on the top. The West Tower was so integral to the structure of the castle that it could hardly be overlooked, but after Grandfather had ordered the gardeners to put up the high willow fence, it had started to fade from their collective memory. Once the fence was up, it completely hid the ground floor of the tower on every side, and the gardeners had planted rambling roses, which had flourished and insinuated themselves all through the woven fence, creating a kind of camouflage for it. In the summer and early autumn, even the fence was concealed behind a wall of leaves, thorns and palest pink nodding blooms. Where the fence met the old stone wall, a door had been put in. With jambs of solid wood, it was surprisingly sturdy, and was locked with a proper key. Why there was a fence and what the door was for, they did not know. The children never seemed to see any comings or goings, although there must have been some.

'Put to sleep, like in a fairy tale,' Miranda said. It was late, long after they were supposed to be in bed, but the twins were sitting in the window recess of their bedroom, pillows tucked underneath them to provide a barrier against the cold stone sill, looking out towards the West Tower. They sat here sometimes on nights like this, when the sky was clear, the moon was full and the garden was illuminated by its silvery light. It was only possible when it was warm. From October onwards, neither of them could bear to get out of bed once they were warm and cosy. Then, the window was obscured by a thick blanket-lined pair of curtains, holding back the gusting breeze that came through the windowpanes. The idea of sitting in the draughty recess peering out through the leaded glass was distinctly unappealing.

'Do you think it will ever wake up?' Rosalind asked, staring out at the shadowy tower just visible above its fence. 'That's how all fairy tales end. With something happening to make everything right again.'

'I don't know. Not now, I suppose. It's been too long.'

'I wonder why Grandfather put that fence up at all. It didn't seem to have any point.'

'Nothing made sense then, though, did it?' Miranda said. She sighed and laid her fair curly head on her knees. Perhaps it was making the jam from the old recipe book and seeing Mother's handwriting that had opened her mind to the past again. 'After all, that was when . . . when IT happened.'

Rosalind glanced quickly at her sister, and spoke rapidly, as though eager not to let the chance of reminiscing slip away now that Miranda had so unusually brought it up. 'Do you remember how wonderful Father was?'

'Of course.' It came out a little gruff and curt, so Miranda added, 'I think he might have been the most perfect person in the world. Along with Mother, of course.'

'They seemed to know exactly how to do everything, didn't they?' Rosalind said longingly. 'And there was all the laughing. Mother was so merry. I do miss her hugs and kisses so much. If only IT hadn't happened. Wouldn't life be wonderful? Even with the war coming?'

They only ever said IT. The misery had cut their lives in two. There was the time before, when there was the magic of Father and Mother, and the time after. All their lives, they'd known that Father was simply incredible, and that the whole world thought so too. He had been academically gifted and an athletics star at school, captain of cricket and head of house. At Cambridge, he'd won scholarships and plaudits at everything he'd tried, and afterwards he'd gone into the City as a stockbroker where he soon made his mark. He had met Mother, who had come to London from India, where she'd grown up, and met Father when she was buying chocolates in Fortnum and Mason. He had been there collecting a box of cigars for Grandfather and they'd fallen in love at once. Of course, Mother was as wonderful as Father, so it was no surprise that he persuaded her not to return to India but to stay and marry him, and they had settled down.

Father made a friend in the City who was a madly keen pilot and before too long, he had been bitten by the aviation bug as well, spending all his time on airfields training for his pilot's licence, part of a circle of gilded young men who could afford such an expensive hobby.

Grandfather had been as proud of his only son as anyone could be. Grandmother had died of the flu just after the war, and as an only child, Father had carried all his hopes. When Father wanted his own plane, Grandfather had stumped up the money for a beautiful Hawker Hart, built like a sleek silver bullet. It perched on the airfield, its nose tilted up as if eager to be off. A single pair of straight wings were directly above the pilot's cockpit and his co-pilot sat in the cockpit behind.

'A Rolls-Royce Kestrel engine,' Father said lovingly, walking around the plane, stroking its body as if it were alive. 'Much better in this than in a motorcar. You can't imagine how strong it is, and how nimble this beauty is because of it. You'll see how grand these things will be if war comes, as it's bound to. I agree with Churchill; he thinks it's inevitable. So we're getting ready. We're going to help the RAF show those gangsters in Germany what's what, you'll see.'

He showed them how the co-pilot was able to use a fuselage-mounted gun, or drop bombs from a little hatch beneath the craft, but it was hard to believe that such a pretty thing could also be so destructive when it seemed more like a lovely toy, like the tin planes and cars in Toby's toy box.

As soon as Father had his aircraft, he joined No. 601 Squadron of the Royal Auxiliary Air Force. Its rich young pilots had twin aims: to provide a backup to the RAF, and to have a great deal of fun while they did it. Father was passionate about both.

'William would live in the air if he could,' Mother would say fondly. 'As it is, he only comes down to eat and sleep.'

'You'll see, Kathryn,' he would say, eyes bright. 'These machines are going to save our bacon, I just know it. We'll be fighting in the air next time, and I'm going to be up there with the boys.'

It sounded like a magnificent adventure to be relished. War would be a game of whizzing planes sparring overhead and, of course, Father would win it.

The family lived in the tall house in Kensington, but spent weekends and holidays at the castle, so it seemed to the children as if they lived there just as much as London.

'When are you coming back to take this place on, William?' Grandfather would demand. 'It's far too big for Constance and me to rattle around in on our own. It needs a family.'

'Soon, Pops, soon,' Father would say. 'Another year or two in the City. If war comes before then, Kathryn and the children will come to you.'

'I'll go with you, William,' Mother said. 'Wherever you go, I'll go.'

Miranda had a moment of fright. Would Mother and Father disappear when war came? That sounded awful. But war might not come, and anyway, it was all a long way in the future. Now there were marvellous times of Father taking off and landing his plane in the field across from the house, on the long strip cut into it by the tenant farmer. They were never allowed up in the plane themselves but Mother went, glamorous in her flying jacket and leather helmet, the goggles perched on the top. In jodhpurs and long boots, she'd climb up behind Father and take her place in the tiny second cockpit. The plane would bounce along the rough strip, its propeller whirring and its engine revving as it gathered speed, and then it would roar past them before lifting its nose upwards and leaving the ground. The girls sat on the fence, their curls whipped by the wind. They gasped and cheered and clapped as the plane climbed, and soon their parents were small dots on top of the silver fuselage. It looked so beautiful: the glinting plane soaring across the clouds, across the sun itself.

Miranda remembered that with the exhilaration came fear. How could Mother and Father be so high, so far away, up in the air inside that silver bird? How could it stay up, made of metal and carrying two humans as well as fuel? What if the magic was to fail and they were to plummet downwards?

But no one else seemed afraid. Grandfather had been laughing and joyous, Aunt Constance smiling with enthusiasm for once, and all the staff and villagers and neighbours who'd come to watch were excited as well. And if no one else was afraid, why should she be? Nevertheless, she kept her fingers tightly crossed as the little aircraft buzzed above them, turning in circles and swooping low to show off its acrobatic skills, and only let them go when Father had landed and her parents were climbing out of their cockpits, laughing and windswept, to greet them all.

Life always seemed to be happy then. She remembered another time, later that summer, when many planes came in to land in the field and Father's friends had arrived – handsome pilots like him, in uniform tunics that were lined with red silk, wearing bright blue ties. They had spent a few days at the castle, laughing, eating and drinking and playing pranks on one another. When they weren't talking about flying, they were going up in their planes on training exercises, practising for an air pageant in which they would display their prowess as pilots. Father had just been made a flying officer, they all heard about that. How proud they'd all been of glamorous, clever Father, and beautiful Mother who supported him in every way, who was as adventurous and exciting as he was, who went up in the air with him, fearless and brave.

At the air pageant on that bright summer day, the silver Hawker Hart went up into the air and dazzled everyone with its daredevil turns and swoops. Miranda had not been there, but she had seen it in her imagination many times: the wondrous machine climbing and spinning and dancing through the air, until it had glided downwards in a graceful dive and instead of coming out of it in time to make the audience gasp and cheer, it had never pulled up but had gone headfirst into the ground, exploding into a fireball and killing the pilot and co-pilot at once.

That was when all the smiles had stopped.

Life was hideously transformed. Mother and Father were

gone. The children had become frozen things, pale and wan, locked in misery. That was when Rosalind had started sleep-walking, and the boys had begun to have night terrors and wet the bed. Miranda tried to be strong, like Imogen, who grew thinner but more determined every day to take their mother's place if she could. She decided that she would think only of now, and of what might come in the future, and the life she would make for herself.

The house in Kensington was sold, its furniture disposed of or put into storage in the castle outbuildings. They moved together to Wakefield Castle but it was no longer the place of joy and adventure they had once known. Now Grandfather was morose, occupied with his grief and his guilt. All traces of flying and planes had been removed and the children knew as if by osmosis that Grandfather blamed himself for buying that sleek, silver plane for Father.

Life had to go on, but it was like nothing they had known before. Laughter and hugs and kisses had disappeared with their parents, and it felt that childhood was over somehow. Their elderly guardians wanted quiet, well-behaved com-panions in the house, and as few reminders of their loss as possible.

A year after the disaster, men came to work on the two towers that stood at the far corners of the castle walls. They had been porters' lodges: grand outside, but very simple inside except for some decorative touches of wood panelling and plaster ceilings and fireplaces. The workmen had ham-mered and dug and put in pipes for plumbing and wires for electric light and a boiler for hot water, but there had been no explanation as to why. Then, the fence around the West Tower had been erected, leaving the East Tower exposed.

There were no explanations. By now they were used to the way that silence and mysteries seemed to swirl in the rooms and corridors of the castle.

Now Rosalind looked over at her sister, beseeching. 'Don't you ever wonder?' she asked.

'Wonder what?' Miranda's palms prickled. She didn't mean to sound gruff but somehow that was what happened whenever Rosalind approached the subject they never spoke of.

'You know what.'

'No. There's no point. They won't tell us anything anyway. So I just don't think about it, and neither should you.'

Rosalind sighed sadly. She knew Miranda's obstinacy. She stared out of the window to the garden, the moonlight illuminating the last roses of the summer around the West Tower.

The leaflets had come in July and Aunt Constance had taken them very seriously. Over breakfast, Miranda had seen that she was reading a pamphlet called *Masking Your Windows*.

'That looks fascinating,' she observed dryly, as she munched on her toast.

'How shall we manage a blackout in a house this big?' Aunt Constance said with a kind of exhaustion in her tone. But then she had brightened and said, 'We will just have to cope, that is all. The best thing to do will be to close up as much of the house as we can.'

'Do we have to cover *all* the windows?' Miranda asked, amazed.

'Close up the house?' asked Imogen, looking surprised.

'War is going to make a difference, isn't it?' Rosalind added thoughtfully.

'Well, yes, dears, I'm afraid nothing will go on as it was,' Aunt Constance said. 'We have to cover those of the rooms we'll use at night. It's going to be rather difficult, I must say. I'll have to think it all through. I need to order some things first. We must ask Mrs Graham to get out the treadle. I hope she cooperates, that's all.'

Once, when the house had been a flourishing, busy place, there had been seamstresses and laundry maids, and a room dedicated to making and mending. In it, a pair of treadle sewing machines sat unused and dusty, and the high wooden shelves still held bundles of material and linen waiting to be sewn or used for repair. It was yet another echo of how the house had once been, before the disaster.

In pursuit of her blackout mission, Aunt Constance had gone off in her pony and trap to place some orders in town. They all longed to go with her but Aunt Constance, though loving in her own way, disliked having children with her and said it was too much for Poppy, her pony, to lug enormous children. It was true that Constance was no weight herself, and so perhaps she had a point.

Bundles of black material arrived, and quantities of powdered lamp black, which was mixed with oil and water to make a very dark paint.

'It won't reflect,' Aunt Constance told them. 'I'm worried about the windows, you see. All our wonderful old windows. What if we should be bombed? They'd be lost and they're irreplaceable. And if there's any moonlight, the moat will shine light up onto the windows and they'll glimmer and be visible to an aeroplane.'

The boys' eyes were wide as they considered this.

'Shall we drain the moat?' asked Toby.

'Perhaps we should,' Aunt Constance said. 'Though I was wondering about keeping fish in it for food.'

They were astonished. There were fish in the moat but they were tiny quicksilver things that flashed through the weeds. Then Toby looked pleased. 'I'll be able to catch them with my rod.'

'So will I,' Archie said, his voice high with excitement. 'But I think I'll probably catch the most.'

The boys began to squabble over who would catch the most fish, but in whispers.

'Goodness,' Rosalind said, looking grave. 'Shan't there be any food?'

'Oh, there'll be food,' Aunt Constance said briskly. 'Perhaps not quite as much, that's all. But we're lucky. We have plenty all around us. But lights, children . . . that's what I want you to remember. If it all starts, then you can't let a scrap of light escape. We're not so likely to be gassed, which is why they've not sent us masks. Much more likely we get a bomber overhead on its way to Oxford or Bristol or somewhere like that. And one speck of light could be disastrous.'

It sounded frightening but also intriguing. There would be a game to outwit the other side and the blackout was part of it. They went to watch Alf in the workshop, cutting up beaver board and painting it inky black. Gradually he started fitting the boards to the windows throughout the castle, propping up his ladder and wedging the board he had carefully cut into the right shape for the windows. It took hours.

'I thought blackout was for nighttime,' Imogen said, as a permanent darkness descended on room after room.

But Aunt Constance was adamant. The rooms they used daily were left with their windows unboarded: the children's bedrooms, the nursery and schoolroom, the drawing room, the study, and of course the kitchen, and other rooms that would either not be used at night, or that had thick blackout blinds nailed up to be pulled down when it got dark. But the great rooms and the hallways sunk into shadow even before war was declared.

The girls were reading in the schoolroom while Imogen gave Archie a lesson, when Toby came running in to say that the gate in the fence around the West Tower was open.

'Alf's in there,' he said breathlessly. 'He took in some blackout things.'

They all looked at one another with wide eyes.

'Why would they put up a blackout in an empty tower?' asked Miranda, and her question hung, quivering in the air.

'Let's go and see. We can take a look inside,' Rosalind suggested.

The boys looked to Imogen, as they always did. She looked torn.

'Come on, Immy, you can do it,' Miranda said encouragingly. 'No one has said we can't.'

70

'Not exactly.'

'Toby's already looked,' Archie pointed out.

'I didn't go in!' Toby said quickly. 'I just saw Alf go in. But I want to go in too.'

'We all want to,' Miranda said firmly.

Imogen relented. 'Well . . . yes, let's go and look at the outside. There's no harm in that.'

They hurried downstairs, out through the back boot room and into the garden. As they dashed across the lawn, they saw that Toby was right. The gate was open. It looked quite romantic, set among the wall of late-blooming roses, in their last puffy flowering of the year, standing open after all this time.

They stopped outside.

'I don't know if we should go in after all,' Imogen said doubtfully. 'Not without permission.'

'You're eighteen years old,' Miranda said scornfully. 'Why do you need permission?'

Imogen made a face at her. 'As if you don't know! There could be a frightful row if we're not careful. You know very well this is out of bounds. It wouldn't be fenced and locked if it weren't.'

The boys hung back, waiting for their sisters to decide.

'I'm not even sure I want to go in,' Rosalind said.

'Well, we might not get this opportunity again,' Miranda declared, sounding more courageous than she felt. 'What harm can it do to look inside? I'm going in.'

She marched through the gate, and approached the door of the tower. It stood open, revealing a dim interior, and she heard the sounds of hammering from within. Inside, Alf was preparing to put up a blackout blind.

'Hello there,' she said brightly. 'You look busy.'

Alf looked around. He had two or three nails between his lips and couldn't speak, so only nodded at her as she walked in. She gazed about at the room. It had been furnished, she saw, with lamps on the side tables and some pictures on the walls. A sofa faced the grate, and a cosy armchair sat at an angle to it. A rug covered the stone floor. It looked quite cosy and certainly ready for occupancy. A door in the back wall led most likely to a kitchen, and a staircase led upwards, curling up against the tower wall to the upper storey. It was quite dim here in the front room, the fence cutting out most of the natural light from the pretty windows with leaded diamond panes, which Alf was now fitting with blinds.

The others had crept in quietly behind her and they all looked around.

'There's no one here,' Rosalind said almost sadly.

Imogen looked over at Alf, who was regarding them blankly while fishing for one of the nails between his lips. 'Why are you putting up blinds, Alf? Do you know who's expected?'

Alf shrugged, taking all the nails from his lips. 'I dunno. I was told to put these up, that's all.'

'I suppose they won't say,' Imogen said with a sigh. She saw that Archie was already fiddling with a china ashtray on one of the tables. 'Put that down, Archie! Don't touch a thing.'

He whipped his hands away and into his pockets at once. Toby nudged him with a cross look and they both stood in obedient silence.

Alf looked suddenly nervous. 'You're not supposed to be here. I was told no one was to come in!'

'You left the doors open,' Miranda pointed out.

'That was a mistake. You ought to go or I'll get a rocket. Come on now, out you go! You shouldn't be here.'

'But is someone coming to live in here?' Rosalind asked. 'It looks like it!

'I dunno, I tell you. Now clear out, you kids – pardon me, miss, and you.' He nodded at Imogen who had reached the status of adult now and couldn't be ordered about as the others were.

Imogen stood on her dignity. 'Very well. We don't want you to get into trouble, Alf. We'll go. Come on, you lot.'

She led the way out of the tower and Miranda followed slowly, taking a last look about. Once the door was closed and the gate locked, would they ever be allowed back?

Imogen came out of the nursery, having read the boys their bedtime story and turned out their lights. As she shut the door with a sigh, Miranda and Rosalind appeared from the shadows and she gave a little scream.

'You made me jump!'

'Sorry,' Rosalind said. 'Are the boys asleep?'

'Almost.' Imogen sighed again. 'I don't think Grandfather and Constance really understand what children need. I suppose there were always staff to do everything in the past.'

'Come and sit down,' Miranda said comfortingly. 'Would you like some tea or something?'

'What's all this?' Imogen said suspiciously as they went down the corridor to her sitting room. 'No tea, thanks, it's dinner soon. What are you two up to?'

'We want to know what *you're* up to,' Miranda replied.

'Me?' Imogen sounded indignant. 'I don't get up to things. That's you, Miranda. Always poking your nose into things and watching people and making up stories about what *they're* up to. Sometimes I think you don't see the difference between real life and your imagination.'

'Actually, I like facts. I like to know what's going on. And we think you might know.'

'It's the tower,' Rosalind said as they sat down in front of the unlit fire in Imogen's sitting room. 'We want to know if someone is going to live in it.'

'I have no idea, you know that,' Imogen replied. She crossed her feet primly and put her hands together. She was still painfully thin, and her big blue eyes looked enormous in her face, but stylish despite that. Imogen liked to be neat, in smart wool skirts that showed her handspan waist and jerseys of pale blue or yellow, or white twinsets, and she always wore the pearl necklace that had once been Mother's, which she'd received on her eighteenth birthday. Her dark blonde curls were coaxed into fashionable fat waves and held back with tortoiseshell combs. Miranda would never say but secretly she thought her older sister as glamorous as a film star. Imogen shrugged her slender shoulders. 'I'm as much in the dark as you are.'

'The grown-ups talk to you,' Miranda said. 'They tell you things they don't tell us.'

'They really don't say much. And I don't ask.' Imogen looked suddenly beaten. 'I don't think you know how little they want to let on. And you certainly don't know how tiring it is to look after the boys all day and every day. I know there's Lottie to help a bit, but being their teacher and their nanny is so much. I don't have time to think about much else.'

Rosalind looked abashed. 'I'm sorry, Immy, you're right. We must help you more. I can do painting lessons with them tomorrow so you can have a break.'

Imogen smiled at her gratefully. 'I'd appreciate that. I must go to town soon and do some shopping. Perhaps I could do that then.'

'But the tower,' persisted Miranda.

'I tell you, I don't know! Just be patient. It's all we can do. I'm sure it will all come out in time. Now, we'd better wash our hands and go down. You know Constance hates us being late for dinner.'

When they got to the dining room, Constance and Grandfather were squabbling about the delivery that had arrived from Fortnum and Mason that afternoon. A van had rumbled up the drive and bowler-hatted men had deposited a large order of food and wine.

'It's really very naughty, Leonard,' Constance was saying as the girls came in to take their places.

'You're the one who is talking about food all the time,

Connie, dear,' Grandfather said mildly. 'It put me in mind of the grocer.'

'Grocer!' exclaimed Aunt Constance. 'Well, really! You make it sound like a pound of flour and a tin of peaches when in fact it's a huge indulgence of extravagance and gluttony.'

'You mean quality. You can't get better than Fortnum's, you know. Don't forget, they invented the Scotch egg.'

'If you've said it once, you've said it a hundred times. And I still don't give a fig!'

Miranda said hopefully, 'Did you get candied chestnuts, Grandfather?'

She was glad that the order had arrived. Food was the only thing that made Grandfather smile these days, the only thing that seemed to take his mind off his loss.

'Crystallised fruit?' asked Rosalind. 'Do say yes!'

'Violet creams?' Imogen said, joining in. '*Chocolate?*'

'There are lots of little treats for everyone,' Grandfather said, pleased by their enthusiasm. 'I ordered it all especially. I think we need cheering up.'

Aunt Constance tutted. 'I don't believe this is even allowed. The ministry most definitely said there should be no stockpiling. Now, where is Lottie with the soup?'

'They said we could lay in dried goods and tins,' Grandfather said, his chin with a stubborn set. 'And I can't believe they care much about marrons glacés in any case. Besides, such luxuries may not be available for much longer. They'll focus on the war effort, I suppose. I asked the men if Fortnum's is opening the Officers' Department again. It made our lives worth living in '17. I said, "Don't forget, you need tins if you're going to stop the damned rats. None of your cardboard or wicker rubbish. Make sure the boys get some decent foie gras, that brought a smile to my face. But most important is the coffee. The House Blend. That's the one you need."' Grandfather shook his finger. 'The proper stuff. I told them and they wrote it down.'

Aunt Constance looked annoyed. 'I don't know how you can talk that way about war. It's not a picnic! Another generation going off to fight. After everything you experienced the first time round. All the pain and grief, not to speak of losing your eye and half your hip!'

'It'll be quite different this time, Connie. No trenches. No rats. It'll be modern warfare. We won't see much killing, not like the last time. It'll be fast and bloodless, you'll see.'

'You are ridiculous, Leonard. You're fooling yourself.' Aunt Constance tightened her lips.

Lottie came in with the soup, and the squabble ended.

In their room later, Miranda sniffed the violet cream that Grandfather had given each of them as a treat. 'Oh, what joy. I can hardly bring myself to eat it.' She looked over at Rosalind. 'I wanted to ask about the tower but I was too much of a coward.'

'Immy is right,' Rosalind said, sitting on her bed and nibbling her cream slowly to make it last. 'They won't say. They'll fob us off. And if they won't tell her, they won't tell us.'

'They can twitter all day about Fortnum's and not once talk about anything important,' Miranda said bitterly. 'I know she doesn't like Fortnum's, but can't they just agree to disagree? He's never going to give the place up, is he?'

'Fancy them falling out over Fortnum's,' Rosalind said, shaking her head. 'Of all the things. Other people fall out over communism and fascism, or socialism and capitalism. But our family are at war over Fortnum's and Selfridges.'

'Debenhams and Army and Navy,' echoed Miranda, and they both giggled but the laughter quickly faded. Miranda lay back on her bed, staring up at the ceiling. She had been feeling the dusty dread that came towards the end of August, when the land felt parched, the moat was low and the threat of school and the new term began to loom. She turned to look at her sister. 'Don't you feel as if this is the last hurrah? As though something awful is coming and no one can stop it?'

Rosalind looked down at her violet cream. 'The final meal of the condemned. All his favourite things before execution.'

They looked at one another with wide blue eyes, each seeing her own face gazing back at her. Rosalind put her half-eaten cream down on her bedside table.

'I don't fancy it now,' she said, suddenly glum.

'But then again,' Miranda said, 'nothing can be as bad as what's already happened, can it?'

Rosalind looked intense. 'But what if we lose Grandfather or Aunt Constance? Or the others? Or this house? What if it's all taken away?'

Miranda felt a rush of fear. She sat up and reached for her sister's hand. 'We won't let it happen. How can they take a place like this away? It's made to last. It's designed to be safe from marauders. And don't forget . . . we have the jam. That's the plan. If they get inside, we still have the jam.'

'Yes,' Rosalind said with evident relief. 'We still have the jam.'

Chapter Four

Present Day

Georgie cried all the way out of London and halfway up the M40. She didn't sob and wail, and she certainly didn't want to draw attention to herself, but she couldn't stop great fat tears welling up in her eyes and pouring down her cheeks. She silently wiped them away with tissues, gradually working her way through a whole packet, while Caspar glanced at her anxiously from time to time as he drove.

'Is it really that bad?'

'No, no. It's fine.' Georgie sniffed and then blew her nose. 'It's just a reaction.'

They had talked and talked and finally Caspar had persuaded her to give life at the castle a chance.

'Just one year,' he had said. 'To see if we can make it work. And if we can't, I'll think of something else. Maybe the family will agree to sell it, as no one else seems to want to take it on. And it's not so hard to get back to London when we want to.'

She'd nodded, hearing the sense of what he said. She knew

that they had lived exactly the way she liked for years and now she owed it to Caspar to give his way a chance. After all, she could work anywhere, and it was easy enough to get to London if she had to go and meet Atalanta, her boss, or any of the people involved in their work.

'I'll be so much further from Pippa when we're in Oxfordshire,' she'd said.

'That's true,' Caspar replied. 'But you really only see her once a month if that. You can still do that, easily. More, if you want. And what's even better is that she and the girls can come to us now whereas this flat is too small for them to stay.'

Pippa and Ryan had had another daughter, and Pippa's hands were even more full. She never came to London any more.

Caspar used an unfamiliar wheedling voice. 'Don't you think she'd like to have holidays at the castle? It really is a fabulous place for children. The girls will love it. There's a golf course nearby for Ryan, he's bound to be keen on that.'

Georgie considered. 'Yes, that's true.' She liked the idea that Pippa and her family might enjoy sharing the castle with them. She hadn't thought of it that way. It helped her to see some more positive aspects to balance out the dread she felt at leaving their home.

Finally, she had agreed. Caspar wanted it so much and she couldn't say no. She had put on a brave face, and smiled and said yes of course, and how fun it would be, but she knew that he understood it was a struggle for her. He couldn't guess how much.

Caspar had managed to arrange a sabbatical from his solicitors' firm, whereas it was easy for her as she could work anywhere. They had decided not to rent out the little flat but to keep it in case one or other of them needed to come back for any reason, or to allow for a break from castle life if it got too much for them. Then an American friend of Caspar's had asked if he could possibly rent it for three months while he did a placement at a London company, and it had seemed too good an opportunity to pass up.

Perhaps that was what had started the tears. It was February and still rather drab and cold and wintery, and yet that morning the sun had poured into their little kitchen, now looking rather sparse and bare with all Georgie's books and favourite implements and equipment packed up. The flat already had an empty feel, ready for its new tenant, and she suddenly missed it like a physical pain.

'Come on,' Caspar had said, picking up the last of the bags. 'The car's fit to burst. We'd better be on our way.'

Then he'd seen her face, put down the bags, and gone to hug her.

'We'll be back before too long, don't worry,' he'd said. 'It's not like we're selling it. You can always come back if you want.'

'I know,' she'd said, choked but grateful for the hug. 'I do know that.'

But somehow that started the tears, and it wasn't until they stopped for a coffee at the services on the other side of Oxford that she finally managed to stop them.

'You'll be all right, I promise,' Caspar said, holding her hand in his on top of the formica tabletop in the services.

She smiled at him and started chattering about something else, wondering why it was that she couldn't tell him what she was really afraid of.

It felt very different drawing up to Wakefield Castle knowing she was going to live there rather than be a guest. Suddenly the castle seemed to have vastly increased in size; it was much more overwhelming than she remembered. For the first time since her original visit, she noticed how much tattier it looked. Empty and without the decorations usually up when she visited, it looked distinctly down-at-heel. As Uncle Archie had aged and lost his vigour, the maintenance had been dialled down. A friendly couple who cleaned and gardened had previously lived in the gatehouse, but they had disappeared, apparently because Viktoria had been rude and difficult to work for. The garden had become messier. There was a forlorn air around the place.

'Well, here we are,' Caspar said heartily as they went into the great hall. 'Home at last.'

Georgie glanced at him quickly. That was the difference for them. This was already home to him and it was not in any way home to her. Here was a place she would never choose to live, full of furniture that she didn't pick out, and set out in ways that were unchangeable. Then she remembered: she had agreed to this and she said she would give it a chance. So she would.

'Yes,' she said equally heartily. 'It's exciting! Now. Are we in our usual room?'

'We could have the main room – you know, where Uncle Archie and Viktoria were.'

'Oh.' The idea seemed unattractive somehow. 'Well, let's take a look.'

When they got to the main suite of rooms, it was a surprise to find that it was completely empty of furniture, except for a commode chair, a wheelchair and a hoist. There were still pictures on the walls and a large gilt mirror over the fireplace but nothing else.

'That's odd,' Caspar said, frowning. 'There was a great big four-poster in here. And a rather nice walnut chest of drawers.' He went and looked in the connecting bathroom. 'All of Uncle Archie's stuff is here. All his medications and things. But nothing else.'

Georgie opened another door and saw it was a large walk-in wardrobe with empty racks and rails, except for one quarter, which held musty old tweed suits, jackets, shirts and trousers, dinner clothes and polished leather shoes. 'All his things are here as well.'

Caspar frowned. 'I suppose Viktoria couldn't be bothered to get rid of them. That will be a job for us.'

'Where is Viktoria?' Georgie said. It hadn't occurred to her to wonder where Viktoria would go, except that she supposed that she would be glad to leave the castle now that Archie was gone. Wouldn't anyone? Surely there was somewhere cosy and comfortable she would prefer to go?

Caspar was looking around, and she could tell by the set of

his shoulders that he was irritated and puzzled. 'I don't know. The will said provision has been made for her in a separate addendum. I assumed he'd got her a house somewhere – I had no doubt that she would have made sure she was looked after. I've got all the paperwork somewhere . . . I'll go back through it. Archie made a trust for her, I remember that.' He sighed. 'There was just so much to take in.'

Georgie went to hug him. It wasn't like him not to go through everything with a fine-toothed comb. 'You've had a lot to deal with.'

He hugged her back absent-mindedly. 'I don't think she could take the furniture, though. That doesn't seem right.'

Georgie looked around at the empty room, feeling a prickle of apprehension. She remembered her teacher Mrs Arthur talking to her in a classroom years before, when she was about twelve. Georgie had found school so overwhelming that when it was all too much, she had taken to escaping to an empty classroom and hiding under a desk. It was there Mrs Arthur had found her.

'You can't keep running away and hiding,' she'd said sympathetically when she'd persuaded Georgie to come out at last.

'I don't know what else to do.'

'You've got several skins less than the rest of us, Georgie, haven't you? I can see how tough life is for you. You're very sensitive, very empathetic. Do you know what that means?'

Georgie had shaken her head.

'Well, sympathy means you feel "with" someone – you can see they're suffering. But empathy means you feel things as if you are that person yourself. It's a much more intense emotion. Do you find that?'

Georgie thought at once of how she felt what Pippa felt, cried when she cried and laughed when she did. The world felt very close, life felt intense, and everything she saw seemed to take a little piece of her, from the pitiful club-footed pigeons hopping around in the road by the newsagent's to the howling baby on the train, to the television programmes she watched which seemed almost more real than her own existence. 'Yes . . .'

Mrs Arthur smiled. 'I can see that. People like you are very sensitive to their surroundings. You might find you often seem to sense things – auras and resonances – that other people are unaware of. I know that life has already been tough for you, Georgie, and I'm afraid you'll go on having a difficult time. But you'll need to develop a protective shell or it will be too much for you.'

'How do I do that?' Georgie asked, suddenly hopeful that there might be way to be more normal and to cope more easily.

'I don't know, I'm afraid. I'm sorry. If it's any comfort, you'll be more alive than most people you ever meet.'

Georgie didn't know what this meant. She only wanted an answer.

'Now, how about we come up with a way for you to have a place to retreat to when it gets too much – as long as you promise you'll stay in most of your lessons?'

This compromise helped Georgie to cope with her school years, and she learned to be more resilient as she got older.

She became more aware that Mrs Arthur was right: she did seem to sense things and read situations and understand how people were feeling without them saying it, or even really showing it. Sometimes, when she told Caspar what she thought or felt about a person or place, and then it turned out to be absolutely right, he was amazed and said she was psychic or something. She said it was intuition, but he liked to think she had some kind of power to read things.

She was feeling something now, as they stood in the huge old bedroom. The apprehension came from a sense that the space was not exactly empty. It had been vacated but not deserted. The sense of absence she had expected to feel was not there.

But in a place like this, with centuries of people having lived here, there could be any amount of energies vibrating through time. Georgie didn't consider herself a believer in ghosts, but she knew very well that empty rooms could hold traces of energy. It was the only explanation for the things she felt and experienced.

'I think we ought to find out where Viktoria is,' Georgie said softly. Then she took Caspar's hand. 'Come on, let's go and find our old room. I like that one. It's familiar.'

'Yes, you're right,' he said. 'I think I'd prefer that too.'

Caspar became very businesslike almost at once. He settled into the old study, now more like an office lined with shelves and filled with papers. Georgie made her way to the only place she could think of going: the kitchen.

She knew that most people moving into a new house

would be arranging furniture and finding homes for everything. But now that their clothes were unpacked, there was almost nothing left to do in that way. She had wondered vaguely if Caspar expected her to clean this vast place and had a picture of herself endlessly moving from to room, dusting and sweeping, hoovering, scrubbing and polishing, starting again at the beginning when she got to the end in a never-ending cycle, but Caspar had been clear: they would have help. It would be impossible otherwise. 'Sandy will be on hand, and all the cleaners. We'll have plenty of help, don't worry.'

But it turned out that Viktoria had sacked everyone.

'This is going to be a bigger job than I thought,' Caspar said grimly when Georgie came into the office with his morning coffee on the first day. 'She has got rid of everyone, including the manager, the office staff and all the support staff.'

'I didn't realise it was such a big operation,' Georgie said, perching at the edge of his desk. The study's bookshelves were crammed with files and paperwork, and there was a general air of organised chaos. It would, she knew, set Caspar on edge, but he would also relish creating order from it.

'It's not that big, really, considering that not much has gone on here for years. But it's a historic building, it needs maintenance, and of course people want to visit it. That's the way to go, I think.'

Caspar had already drawn up plans for opening up the house, running events and starting to make it pay for itself.

'Ah,' he said, as he went through an old rolodex on the desk, 'here's Sandy's number. I'll give her a call and we'll see what we can sort out in terms of getting the cleaners back at least.'

Georgie was in the kitchen, inspecting the contents of the cupboards, when Sandy came in a few hours later. She was staring at vast mixing bowls and oversized trays and pans more suitable for a hotel than a family home. This was not a scale of cooking she was used to.

'Hello again!' Sandy was grinning warmly. She was in her usual outfit of jeans, checked shirt and a fleecy gilet over the top, and she looked comforting and familiar. 'I'm so glad to see you.'

'You too.' Georgie smiled back, relieved to see someone she counted as a friend. She made some tea while Sandy filled her in on what had happened since Uncle Archie died.

'It's been bleak. We were all so fond of him and, of course, worried about what would happen next. The old fellow was not well off by the end, and we imagined this place would be sold, so it wasn't a surprise when we were all given notice – although we'd thought that Viktoria would keep us on till it went. And then we heard that you and Caspar were coming and we guessed she wanted to make life tricky for you.'

'But why?' Georgie frowned. 'She didn't have any reason to.'

Sandy shrugged. 'Some people just like being difficult. I think she thought she would get the house when her husband died. Perhaps she had plans to sell it or something.'

'She can't have expected that? Even I know that these places are in trusts and can't easily be sold, and she certainly wouldn't get control of it, I think.' Georgie shook her head. 'I don't know really. Caspar does all that for me.'

Sandy looked around the kitchen as if afraid they would be overheard. 'Viktoria might think exactly that. She's German, maybe they do things differently there. Anyway, she seemed very angry about everything and particularly cross with Caspar.'

'It's not his fault!'

'No. It makes no sense. However . . .' Sandy smiled at her. 'I can't tell you how happy I am that you're here and that you'll be wanting all the other girls back as well. I bet Caspar has some big plans for this place.'

'Yes, I think so,' Georgie said.

'And how is your work going?' Sandy asked. 'Are you still writing your magazine columns?'

Georgie nodded. 'Sometimes, it depends if I'm commissioned. Mostly I'm still assisting Atalanta Young, the television cook. Do you know her?'

'Of course I know her! I'm a big fan. Love her gorgeous red hair,' Sandy said, impressed. 'I've got some of her books. What do you do for her then?'

'I come up with recipe ideas for her, develop and test them, and work on her books and shows.'

Sandy looked shocked. 'And she passes them off as her own?'

'It's quite normal. Lots of chefs do it. They don't really have time to do research and development themselves.'

'I had no idea. It feels a bit like a con.'

Georgie laughed. 'It's the harsh reality, I'm afraid. But it's not so bad. It's a business after all, and there's no shame in getting help.'

'But you should have your name on the show and on the books! Seeing as you do all the work.'

'Oh no, I wouldn't like that. I prefer being the invisible one.'

Just then, there was the sound of footsteps on the stairs down to the kitchen. A patrician voice declaimed, 'And this is where the great banquets of the past would have been created!'

Georgie and Sandy stared as a white-haired, fine-featured woman in neat dark trousers and a ruffled blouse led a group of four other people into the room.

'Oh, hello,' she said, as she saw them. 'I'm just doing a tour.'

'Sorry?' Georgie said, blinking in surprise.

'A tour, dear,' the woman said slowly, as if to a child. 'We'll only be a moment. Are you working for Lady Wakefield?'

Georgie stared, still trying to understand what was happening.

Sandy said, 'I'm working here, Mrs Lambert, but this is Georgie Wakefield. Her husband is the new owner.'

Mrs Lambert now looked astonished. 'Really? You're the new owner's wife?' She looked Georgie up and down. 'Oh!' Behind her the other strangers were either gawping at Georgie, or gazing around the kitchen with interest. 'Well, if you don't mind, we'll just finish up in here and we'll be on our way.'

Mrs Lambert advanced further into the room and started

gesturing at the fireplace and explaining its features and how old it was, as though Georgie and Sandy weren't there at all.

'She's a battleaxe,' Sandy murmured to Georgie as the little group moved down the room.

'Who is she? Do you know her?'

'Oh yes. We know all the vollies, but she is the only one who never remembers us.'

'The vollies?'

'Volunteers. They do the tours.'

'There are tours?' Georgie asked helplessly. This was making a difficult situation much worse.

'Not usually when the family are here, and only by permission. But yes, you get used to it.'

'How many vollies are there?'

'Four or five,' Sandy said vaguely. 'They change occasionally.'

'Oh my goodness!' Georgie was about to ask where the tours went when Mrs Lambert came back past with her group.

'Thank you, Mrs Wakefield,' she said, gracious now that the shock of finding out who Georgie was had worn off. 'Very kind. I look forward to making your acquaintance better soon. I can't stop right now, I'm afraid, as I'm having tea with Lady Wakefield after this.'

'Oh. I see.' Georgie took this in. 'Tea with Lady Wakefield? But she isn't here any more.'

Mrs Lambert laughed merrily. 'Of course she is! She's in residence at this very moment!'

'She is?'

'Naturally. Where else would she be? This is her home!' And Mrs Lambert sailed majestically out of the kitchen followed by her obedient audience, leaving Georgie and Sandy staring after her in silent surprise.

Georgie found Caspar in the study, where he was working his way through vast piles of paperwork. He looked up as she came in. 'The internet is incredibly slow. I'll have to get it upgraded if we're going to get anything done. Another thing on the to-do list.' He put down his pen with a sigh and sat back in his chair. 'I might need to hire an assistant.'

'Caspar, she's still here!'

'Who?'

'Viktoria!'

'What? No she isn't.'

'She is – one of the volunteers is having tea with her right now.'

Caspar gaped at her. 'But where?'

'That bit I don't know.' Georgie shook her head. 'I had the funniest feeling about her, as though she hadn't gone.'

Caspar stood up, frowning. 'Right. Let's go and find her.'

He marched out of the study and Georgie followed, wondering if they were going to start searching at the top of the house and work their way down, looking for Viktoria in one of the many rooms. But Caspar marched out into the front quadrangle and looked about, before heading across it towards the bridge.

'Where are you going?' Georgie called.

'If she's here, she won't be in the house.' Caspar powered

on, his long strides taking him quickly across the gravelled quad. By the gatehouse he made a quick turn before the bridge, and went around the side of the great wall to where some cars were parked out of sight from the main drive and the house. He stared balefully at a bright red VW Golf. 'I thought so,' he said. 'That's her car. I have a feeling I know where she is.'

Georgie had come up, panting with the exertion of following him. 'Where?'

'She's got a nerve,' Caspar said darkly. 'This looks like deception.'

He strode back towards the gatehouse and stopped at an arched door set into the wall, with an iron ring handle and iron studs. He rapped hard with the iron ring, then turned it and walked in. Georgie followed and found they were standing in a small hallway furnished with some familiar-looking items. Caspar was already climbing the stone staircase up to the floor above the archway of the gatehouse. Georgie could smell fresh coffee as she ascended after him. She sensed a familiar presence, and almost immediately also detected a thick floral scent she recognised.

A moment later, she followed Caspar into a large drawing room set above the arched gateway. It had a double aspect, with windows that looked in one direction over the quadrangle towards the main house, and in the other over the moat and down the driveway. A fire crackled in a large fireplace, and two pretty sofas faced each other in front of it. Viktoria sat on one, and on the other Mrs Lambert, their teacups on the table between them. Both were straight-backed and astonished to see Caspar and Georgie standing there.

'What on earth is this?' said Viktoria in a tone of outrage. 'How dare you just walk in like this? I have a visitor!'

'You've got a nerve, Viktoria,' Caspar said sternly. 'What are you doing here?'

Viktoria blinked at him, but Georgie could see from a pulse in her neck that she wasn't as sure of herself as she seemed. 'What do you mean, Caspar? This is my home.'

'I don't think so,' Caspar replied. 'But even if you are living here, why haven't you let us know or said anything about it? And I take it that this is where all the missing furniture has gone.'

'It's still on the premises,' Viktoria said so quickly that Georgie guessed that she had prepared her story beforehand. 'I haven't taken anything. But Archie would have wanted me to continue to sleep in our bed, and enjoy all the familiar things we shared together.' She looked suddenly tragic. 'I don't think it's too much to ask! One miserly part of this huge place. The humble gatehouse, where the housekeeper used to live. Isn't there enough room for you and Georgie in the castle, Caspar? Do you begrudge a poor widow a tiny portion of the house to live in, or do you want me kicked out?'

Caspar sighed and shook his head. 'That's not the point, Viktoria, you're here without telling us.'

'Do I have to alert you to my whereabouts every minute of the day? That's draconian, isn't it?' Viktoria's eyes filled with tears. 'I'm sorry you wish to treat me like a prisoner on probation, with some kind of tag around my ankle. Do I need to report in to you? Are you now my controller? What have I done to deserve this? This is my home too! I suppose you want to kick me out and leave me homeless.'

Mrs Lambert stretched out a sympathetic hand. 'Oh, dear Viktoria. It's too much.' She turned to Caspar with furious eyes. 'This reflects very badly on you, Mr Wakefield. Your uncle would spin in his grave to hear you treat his poor dear widow like this! You can't possibly want to turn her out!'

Georgie felt a rush of anger. They were both misinterpreting him, purposefully, to make Viktoria look like a victim instead of a manipulative person out to get what she wanted without asking. 'That's not what he's saying,' she said as loudly as she could, but both women ignored her.

Mrs Lambert went on indignantly: 'I do think it is a little much. I can't see why you can't have Viktoria in the house itself, rather than in this cramped little place!'

The gatehouse was in fact, Georgie realised, about twice the size of their London flat.

'Roberta, you're such a support,' murmured Viktoria, looking tragic. 'I don't need much but a roof over my head is nice . . .'

Mrs Lambert cast an outraged look at Georgie and said, 'The house is far too big for just the two of you in any case. It's not as though you even have children!'

Georgie felt her face flame. Mrs Lambert had touched on the tender spot without knowing it.

Caspar clenched his fists in annoyance and spoke in the frostiest of tones. 'I have no idea who you are, and I would thank you to stay out of this. Viktoria, we will have a meeting about your residence. I don't intend to be unreasonable but I also must have full knowledge of who is living in my property, for some very obvious reasons. I appreciate the gatehouse is separate from the castle but even so – you can't simply move in and take over. What if I had promised it to staff?'

'There's plenty of space,' Viktoria said airily, but Georgie thought she could see some nervousness in the way she waved her hand as if in a show of nonchalance.

'A meeting,' Caspar said curtly, 'to get this sorted out. Please email me your immediate availability.'

'Very well,' Viktoria said, refusing to meet his eye. 'I'll check my diary.'

'Please do.'

'Can I offer you some tea? Georgie, what about you?' Her tone was sweet and conciliatory.

Why does she seem more dangerous when she's like that? Georgie wondered. 'No thank you.'

'We're leaving,' Caspar said. He headed for the stairs. 'I'll see you tomorrow, Viktoria. Whenever you're free.'

'Goodbye, Caspar, Georgie,' she said in a sing-song voice, smiling at them. She seemed to think she had won the encounter.

They went back down the stairs and were out in the quad in a moment.

'I cannot believe that woman,' Caspar said in a clenched tone. 'She's outrageous.'

'Do you want to evict her?' Georgie asked, hurrying behind him.

Caspar stopped on the gravel, almost dead centre in the quad, and faced her, his eyes questioning. 'What do you think I should do, Georgie?'

She came up to him and gazed up into his face, wishing his grey eyes were not so troubled. 'It's a tricky one. She's been clever, we must give her that. If she'd asked, you might have said no. But as it is, it's harder to throw her out without looking bad.' She shook her head. 'I don't know. I'll think about it.'

'You're right. Very hard to throw her out. But really . . . Viktoria living over at the gatehouse? It's not a very appealing idea, having her sitting there watching us.'

'Not at all.' Georgie frowned. 'I don't suppose she'll be able to stop interfering. I can't believe we've got strangers wandering around, conducting tours. I got such a shock when Mrs Lambert wandered in with her little cohort.'

'We need some firm rules.' Caspar took her hand. 'So much to do.'

'Yes. I've got to start work too. Atalanta wants a whole batch of new recipes. She wants a new angle, something to break the mould, and she wants me to come up with it.'

'You'll think of something brilliant. You always do. Come on, let's go and have tea and think about what to do with the merry widow.'

They headed back into the house.

Chapter Five

Georgie had found a little room on the ground floor to make her own, and she had set up her computer there on a table that looked out over the moat through a narrow arched window. There was a view of the rear part of the castle grounds and the crumbling towers that marked the east and west corners of the property.

Now she sat at her desk, a cup of tea cooling beside her, and put Viktoria out of her mind while she read the email that had just arrived from Atalanta.

Darling Georgie,

Thanks so much for your latest ideas, I love love love them. The problem is, they're not striking me as DIFFERENT. They don't feel DIRECTIONAL. I see what you're doing and of course it's wonderful but I just think – have we all had enough of avocado for a while? Freka feels so yesterday. I'm probably wrong! Can we have a rethink?

I hope life in the country is lots and lots of fun. So jealous!

A x

Georgie sighed. She had worked for Atalanta long enough to know that she had not liked the recipe ideas at all, and Georgie couldn't blame her. She was all out of fresh inspiration. The upset of the last few months, and the move from London, had all conspired to make her recipe well run dry. Usually she ordered out-of-print recipe books from the internet, or picked up rarities in second-hand bookshops, then scoured them for ideas she could develop, but at the moment she had no sense whatsoever of what she could use to find Atalanta's new direction. Her last idea had been American South home-style baking and entertaining, which had led to a whole television series filmed in a gorgeous house in – of course – Atlanta, and naturally they'd called the series *Atalanta in Atlanta*. In her trademark 1950s bombshell dresses with frilly aprons over the top, her vibrant red hair in an *I Love Lucy* updo with old-fashioned pin curls, Atalanta had looked gorgeous and film-star perfect as she recreated the recipes that Georgie had researched and then modified so that they became Atalanta's own.

'You'll just love my buttermilk and bacon scones,' Atalanta had purred into the camera, raising one perfectly pencilled eyebrow. 'They're moist and succulent, a complete savoury joy that will bring all kinds of excitement to your mouth.'

Georgie had caught that episode by mistake, turning the television on and finding it playing. She didn't usually watch Atalanta's shows as she was heartily sick of all the recipes once she'd created and fine-tuned them, then triple tested each one for absolute accuracy. After the book was written, checked and rechecked, it still wasn't over. Once the television show was commissioned, she worked with Atalanta and the producers on which recipes would be included in the shows, and then she had to tutor Atalanta in her Belgravia kitchen, teaching her each dish slowly and carefully. Atalanta was clever but notoriously dreamy and extremely clumsy, which made working with her a trying experience, especially for precise and cautious Georgie, who hated spilled flour, puddles of liquid and dirty utensils scattered on the surfaces, though she hid it. Atalanta usually cut herself at least once every session but at least she was cheerful and laughed at herself. Although she was charming, glamorous and charismatic, she was also highly ambitious and jealously guarded her success, aware that she'd been around for a while now and that she had to keep reinventing herself and staying relevant in order to generate her bestselling cookery books and television shows. A stint as a judge on a television cookery competition had not really worked out, nor had a trial run with her own domestic and lifestyle chat show, although her recently opened restaurant seemed to be doing well, even if it was hers in name only. She was fine when recording herself cooking. Then, she could do things over when she made a mess or swore or cut herself or had to stop for a cigarette break and a chat on her mobile phone with a friend. She knew her TV act like the back of her hand. But in other guises she was less loveable: stiffer, more awkward and much more prone to making a gaff. She usually hid her natural hauteur under her sultry cooking persona, but under pressure it came out and it was quite clear that Atalanta had very little experience of people like her viewers, and the ordinary souls who competed in cookery shows. She couldn't hide her bemusement at them and stared at their efforts with a kind of puzzled amazement. She meant well, but she was very much the aristocrat slumming it with the hoi polloi. So the books that generated the cooking programmes became ever more precious to her.

Georgie stared at the last email. She knew exactly the faint tone of exasperation that Atalanta would use despite the loving language. She also knew that Atalanta would sack her without a moment's hesitation, no matter the long years of collaboration, if she considered Georgie wasn't up to it. She felt a twinge of anxiety, thought for a moment and then quickly typed up a message.

Hello Atalanta,

Of course, I completely understand, and you're right. I had another thought this week. How about Venetian cooking? Italian is always so popular, and we could do a spin on it by invoking the beauty and romance of Venice. I can see the television programme now – gondolas, canals, beautiful palazzi. I've found some

**vintage cookbooks with wonderful recipes to plunder
and can send you some trial chapters if you're
interested? My favourite is a glorious Venetian peas
in stock.**

**Country life is taking a bit of getting used to, but I'll
manage.**

**Love,
Georgie x**

She sent the email, and wondered what Atalanta would think if she knew that Georgie was now living in a five-hundred-year-old castle in the middle of nowhere. She had a feeling it might raise her a little in Atalanta's estimation. Well, she wasn't about to tell her. She had told her friends and work colleagues that they were spending a year renovating Caspar's family home before they sold it, which had mitigated too many questions and drawn-out goodbyes.

'I bet she doesn't like the Venetian idea either,' Georgie said out loud. She stared out of the narrow window and watched as the wind ruffled the grass and shook the distant treetops. She realised how much things had changed since they'd been here for the funeral. Then, it had been steely grey skies, endlessly dripping rain and the bare bones of hedges and trees. Now she saw colour everywhere: the grass had taken on a juicy hue and was brightened by borders of daffodils nodding all along the castle walls and down the side of the moat. There were the hints of buds on trees and a sense of life returning.

'How beautiful,' she said, standing up and leaning towards the window to see better. She watched the invisible wind buffet the garden and thought suddenly, *But I can go out there if I want.*

In London, in a flat with no garden, she saw nature mostly when walking past parks or noting the blossom on the gnarled trees that lined some of the roads, but they lived in a particularly built-up, old part of town near the river and green places had to be sought out. Now she was surrounded by nature, and she remembered the pleasure of the walks she had taken on her first visit here. She'd always made a point of walking through the wood on every subsequent visit over the years. Why had she forgotten lately how much pleasure that brought her?

On impulse, Georgie went hurrying to the boot room at the rear of the castle, where she pulled on her gumboots and a quilted coat before letting herself out and down some worn stone steps to the back lawn. It was cool outside, the wind less merry and more biting than it looked from the relative warmth of the house, but it was exhilarating to feel the freshness on her face and to smell the greenery around her, the air carrying the tang of the moat. She began to march around the lawn, admiring the daffodils as they nodded their yellow trumpet heads, and inspecting the borders for signs of growth and life.

She had a sudden memory of herself as a small girl – seven? eight? – also wearing gumboots but of gleaming red rather than sensible green. She remembered the reflection of yellow daffodil heads in the shiny red rubber, and she remembered how she and Pippa had carefully picked lots and lots and taken them to give to Patsy.

The punishment had been frightful.

Suddenly unhappy, she turned away from the daffodils and headed for the far corner of the lawn, which was closed off by a fence of woven willow that was so thick with plant stems that it was hard to see the actual fence at all. She could see close up that they were rose bushes, the stems armoured by sharp thorns and with budding leaves. She suspected the fence would be invisible in a few weeks. Pushing away the memory that had shaken her, she approached the fence and saw that there was a door set into it. Going over to it, she twisted the old handle. It moved loosely but nothing bit. It had become untethered from the lock mechanism and was useless. She shook the door but it was firmly closed with the feeling of something welded into place by age. Looking up, she saw the tower emerging from the top of the fence, the twin of the one on the opposite side of the lawn.

It's like Rapunzel's tower, she thought. *Is that the right fairy tale? Or do I mean something else? Which is the one surrounded by thorns?*

Suddenly she remembered Alyssa saying something about the tower being out of bounds. And what else? Oh yes. It was connected to the other tower by a passage.

Georgie turned and walked along the wall to the other tower. This one was not protected by a fence, but the door set into it was also locked tight and even the handle did not move at all.

Oh well.

She stood in front of it, regarding it. The towers were square, with the castle wall appearing to run through them in one direction and leave in another. They were two-storied, with the roofs lifting to a point with a decorative obelisk on top. The windows were just like those of the main house: diamond-shaped leaded panes.

I wonder why they put a fence around the other one. Why not just lock the door, like this one?

She decided on impulse that she would ask Caspar for the key to the tower and take a look inside, and perhaps ask about the one that was fenced off as well. She was curious. This was her home now, why shouldn't she look around?

Just then she felt her phone buzz in her pocket and took it out to see that she'd received an email from Atalanta. She quickly opened it.

Darling,

Italian? Don't you think that's been done to death? I know you think Venetian is the selling point but I wonder if it's just too close to some other successful books. I'm really looking for something fresh. Let's think for a day or two and reconvene. Maybe have a brainstorm. We'll get there!

Oodles of love, A xxx

Oh dear, Georgie thought. *Oh dear.*
She could sense the sharp teeth beneath the smile.
I'd better find some inspiration fast.

Georgie was in the kitchen making supper when Caspar came in, tired from a long day at his desk and summoned by the delicious smells.

'How could you smell this cooking from the study?' she asked, laughing. 'All the way up the stairs and down the passage!'

'Actually, the kitchen window is just below my study,' he said. 'The aroma must have escaped. What are you cooking?'

'I'm doing a sort of duxelles of shallots and mushrooms with lots of butter and sage, and that's going to go under the skin of these chicken supremes, and then they'll roast on this bed of leeks. I'm trying out a pomme anna to go with it, and a sauce using the water that I soaked the dried mushrooms in, with a bit of brandy and cream.'

'That sounds wonderful. It must be the duxelles I can smell,' Caspar said, rubbing his hands. 'I'm starving.'

'It won't be long. Try and divert yourself for half an hour.'

'Let's have a glass of wine and chat.' He fetched a bottle and two glasses, poured some for them both. Then he leaned against the worktop, glass in hand. Caspar always liked to watch her cook when he could. He seemed to get comfort from her calm, measured movements and orderly preparation, seeing the meal forming under her hands. 'Have you thought any more about Viktoria? Have you hatched any fabulous schemes?'

She shook her head. 'Not really. I don't see what we can do.'

'I sent an email to the solicitor asking them to check the

will about what exactly pertained to Viktoria. I should have done that already. There's just so much to be going on with.'

'If she keeps herself to herself, perhaps she won't be any trouble?'

'Perhaps. I just sense she wants to put spanners in the works. Maybe I'm doing her an injustice.'

'I don't think so,' Georgie said. 'I got the distinct impression from Sandy that Viktoria thinks she's been hard done by.'

'That's hardly our fault. What did she expect?'

'Perhaps that's what we should try to find out.'

Caspar sighed. 'Are you suggesting I build some bridges?'

'Better than burning them. Now, you get the cutlery. Dinner is nearly ready.'

It was very odd, Georgie thought, to be in a house where you had to decide where to have dinner. There was the panelled dining room where they'd celebrated Christmas and other family get-togethers, but it was far too large and formal for every day. Next to it was a smaller, more casual room with a table in it, but it had the odd feeling of a place no one ever went, and a slight chill in the air that Georgie found off-putting. There was the great hall if she wanted to be surrounded by portraits and armour – and she really didn't. She preferred the room rather grandly called Lady Wakefield's morning room, decorated in soft florals with frills and fringes, and which had a lovely view of the garden, but the shiny burr table was paired with chairs so elegant and delicate they looked like they'd crumple under Caspar. Georgie decided that the best place was the room where she felt warmest and most comfortable, and so she'd colonised the end of the central kitchen table near the range, putting out some chairs, candles and a vase of daffodils, and that was where she and Caspar ate most of their meals. Caspar found it very strange.

'Well, where did you eat then when you lived here?' she'd asked.

'The nursery,' he'd said vaguely. 'Or the dining room. Naturally.'

'We're not eating there. You'll just have to get used to slumming it in the kitchen.'

'I don't mind as long as we're eating your delicious food, my love.'

In fact, it was very pleasant basking in the warmth from the range, and the stuffed chicken was excellent, they both agreed. Over dinner, Georgie told him about her problems with Atalanta.

'I'm all out of inspiration,' she said mournfully. 'I try to think of something and just see a blank page.'

'I don't know why she can't come up with her own ideas,' Caspar replied.

'She just doesn't. I can usually do that. To be fair, she does things I could never do – like appear on television.' Georgie shuddered at the thought. On the occasions that she had gone out for lunch with Atalanta to celebrate a new book or television deal, she'd disliked the sensation of them both being looked at. Obviously people were looking at Atalanta rather than her, but they were both still the focus of attention. Atalanta didn't seem to mind it. She appeared oblivious to the stares, the nudges and murmurs of people as they clocked her, and seemed to positively relish the ones who had the courage to come up and talk to her, usually to say that they were big fans and could she please give an autograph? Atalanta was always completely at ease, and had an excellent way of graciously sparing a little time and then letting it be known when they were dismissed. Georgie found it very intrusive, and she could quite see the appeal of private clubs and restaurants where celebrities could be guaranteed a kind of anonymity. When they went to those places, it was a great deal more relaxing, and she happily ignored all the other famous faces at other tables. If the horrors of fame should ever come to her – and there was no reason why they would – she would scarper to places like that in a heartbeat.

'I suppose she is good at television,' Caspar conceded, 'but she could never do it without your recipes.'

'It's symbiotic then. But I have to fulfil my part of the bargain or we'll be going nowhere. I can tell that Atalanta is chomping at the bit. There's either some pressure from her publishers or a tax bill or something – she seems desperate to get going.'

'You need something completely new,' Caspar said. He looked thoughtful. 'How about something like . . . the best things to cook in your car? You could run a little element from the cigarette lighter.'

Georgie started laughing. 'I do love it when you come up with ideas like that.'

'Meals you can make with two ingredients.'

'Brilliant. Beans on toast. As long as you don't use butter.' She giggled again.

'There you go! That's one, for starters. Boiled egg with asparagus. That's another. I have many more genius ideas like that if you should need them.' He smiled at her, then leaned over and refilled her glass. He coughed lightly in a way she recognised. It usually meant he was going to introduce an awkward subject and she tensed slightly, staring down at her plate. There was a pause and then he said, 'Wasn't that old woman horrid today? The one who was with Viktoria.'

'You mean Mrs Lambert, the volunteer.'

'That's the one. I have no idea how she thought she could be so rude. After all, I'm her employer in a way.'

'Are volunteers employees?' wondered Georgie.

'She still needs my permission to be a volunteer, and I've a good mind to take it away. Why do we need volunteers anyway?'

'Sandy said there are lots of people who want to visit the house, and as we're not open to the public, they can book these tours. It's been going on for ages, apparently.'

'Then perhaps we should think about opening properly.'

Georgie stared at him. 'You're serious about that then? I know we talked about it but that was before I knew what it's like to have people wandering around without warning!'

Caspar laughed. 'Your face! I wish you could see it. I take it you don't like the idea.'

'I . . . I . . . no.' She didn't know how to convey her sense of dread about people, unknown strangers, filling the house, tramping through at all hours of the day.

'Well, it's just a thought.' Caspar finished a mouthful of

chicken, frowning slightly. 'But it was something she said – that Mrs Lambert. It made me think.'

'Yes . . .' Georgie felt the stirring of anxiety.

'About . . . about children.'

Her stomach churned in a sickening plummet. So there it was. She'd been expecting it, she realised that now. 'What about them?'

Caspar sat back in his chair, looking unhappy. 'Georgie, don't you think it's time? Look at what's happened to us. We've got this amazing house, and I can promise you that it's a wonderful place to grow up. I'm trying something new, and I might never need to go back to London to work if that doesn't suit us. Isn't it a perfect time to start a family? I understand why it wasn't right before, with the flat so small and our careers needing our attention, and I know we wanted some years to ourselves before we had children. But time won't be on our side if we don't start soon.'

Georgie stared at him, wide-eyed. He was right. All the circumstances were just right. It was what she had been afraid of from the moment he'd suggested moving here. As night follows day, she was sure that he would suggest this. It had just come sooner than she'd thought. *I can't*, she thought, panicked.

'Georgie?' His gaze was fixed on her, his voice soft and concerned. But also firm. 'What do you think?'

'I don't know,' she said in a small voice. 'It's all been a bit overwhelming lately. Can I think about it?'

'What do you need to think about?'

She was surprised, in a way that felt clammy and

112

unpleasant. He never usually pressed her like this. 'Well . . . just to consider if I'm ready.'

'Why would you not be ready?' His tone was still gentle but there was a persistence about it she had not heard before. 'I'm serious, Georgie. I think it's right. I want us to start. What's stopping you? I want to know what you think.'

'I . . . I don't know.' She looked up into his solemn grey eyes, filled with love for him but also afraid. 'Please, Caspar, can I think about it? We can talk about it in a day or two and I promise I'll explain what I'm thinking.'

Caspar sighed softly. 'All right. I can't force you. But I do want to know where you stand, Georgie. That's only fair, isn't it?'

'Yes,' she said wretchedly, though she tried to hide it. 'Of course it is. I promise, I really will think about it.'

That was no lie. After all, she thought about it all the time.

Georgie slept late the next day, but that was partly because she'd been awake half the night, staring into the darkness while she listened to Caspar's soft breathing in the bed next to her. He seemed so untroubled. It was true that he had many stresses and strains to deal with, and the weight of the house on his shoulders, but nevertheless he seemed to cope so much more easily with things. He wasn't beset by the same fears that she was.

Of course he wanted a family. She'd always known that. Not long before they married, the vicar who was going to perform the ceremony told them that they would need to attend some marriage classes. Georgie had wondered what such classes would entail: instructions in how to conduct an argument, perhaps, or guidance for how to timetable date nights and sex? How much detail would the vicar want to go into? And how qualified was he for the role? In the end, there was only one class, a cosy hour in the vicarage with tea and shortbread, and the vicar asking things like, 'Do you both get on most of the time?'

There had been one tense moment, one that Georgie had secretly been dreading.

'Now,' the vicar had said. 'Children.'

Here it was. She'd felt herself go pale, if that was possible. She had already resolved that she wouldn't lie to Caspar. There was no way she could do that. But she feared beyond everything that when she told him the truth, he would break off their engagement and it would all be over. She couldn't bear the thought. How would she survive without him? He was her world. But she also couldn't lie.

Her hands had begun to tremble in her lap. Her tongue felt stiff in her mouth and her throat dry. She would have to speak. She would have to say something. She began to open her mouth, ready to make her admission.

'Do you want to raise them in the Protestant faith?' the vicar said, before she could say anything. 'You're both baptised, I think?'

Georgie, taken by surprise, nodded, although now she thought about it, she wasn't really sure if she had been baptised or not. Caspar said confidently, 'Oh yes.'

'Good.' The vicar raised his eyebrows. 'So I assume you'll be baptising any children into the Church of England?'

'I don't see why not,' Caspar said heartily. 'It can't do any harm.'

'No, no,' the vicar said, taken aback. 'Although we tend to think it can do a lot of good.'

'Yes, of course,' Caspar said quickly. 'Of course it can. So . . . that's a yes.' He turned to Georgie. 'Are you happy with that, darling?'

'Oh yes,' she said in a small voice. 'Very happy with that.'

'Then that's agreed.'

'Good,' said the vicar. 'Well, I really can't see any problems with your marriage. You're both very nice, very solid young people. You obviously get on well. I think you're going to be extremely happy. Just remember – never let the sun go down on an argument. Make peace, be loving, trust in God and you'll be fine.'

'Thank you, Vicar,' Caspar said.

The vicar continued: 'I don't think you need any more classes, so I'll see you for the rehearsal. Unless you'd like more tea?'

'Oh no, thank you,' Georgie said, putting her cup down. She felt as though she'd missed a step and had stumbled and then righted herself. Was the awful question not coming then? Had she escaped after all?

It seemed she had, for a moment later they were in the vicarage hallway pulling on their coats and making their farewells.

Of course I will tell him, she promised herself, suffused with relief that everything was the same: she was still engaged, they were still together, their life was continuing on as she wanted. *I will. When the time is right, I will.*

But somehow the time had never come. Caspar had easily agreed to put off a serious discussion about having children.

Well, it was here now.

She got up, her spirits low, and got dressed. Ever since they'd arrived, she wore the same things: a thermal long-sleeved T-shirt under a very warm long jumper, jeans and her fleece-lined slipper boots. This protected her from the chill of the stone floors and walls. Today, she felt cold to the bone, shivering as she hurried down to the kitchen. It was empty, a dirty dish and mug showing that Caspar had had breakfast and no doubt was in his office or off around the property to check on things. Sandy wasn't due to come in today and wouldn't be in for a while.

Georgie sighed. She needed hot coffee, maybe that would help to warm her up, and perhaps some porridge. The coffee tin was empty. Caspar must have used the last of it to make some, and he had not replaced it. Where was the coffee kept?

She went to the larder, a huge cold stone cupboard lined with wooden shelves, and one heavy marble one for keeping things cool.

'Everything here is cold,' she said bitterly. 'I just want some coffee! Where is it?'

She was surprised to find tears prickling her eyes. In a rush of irritation, she leaned up and started looking about the old jars and tins for something like coffee, although she suspected that whatever she found would be too old to use in any case. She saw some ancient jars of jam, four of them in a neat row, each with a faded hand-painted label that looked as though it had mice on it.

How old are those? she wondered. *Why weren't they ever used or thrown away? This place is full of the years-old detritus that no one can be bothered to sort out.*

She ignored the jam and continued looking. Pulling down a rusted old tea caddy, she saw that a book was propped on the shelf behind it and she reached up to it. It looked very old, with a stiff black cover, the pages browned and crinkled at the edges. Georgie pulled it down and looked at it, then opened it, her search for coffee temporarily forgotten. It was, she saw at once, a recipe book, with the recipes written in by hand. Those at the beginning were in archaic script that was hard to read, but she found that if she concentrated, and remembered that what looked like an F was actually a large italicised S, it started to make sense.

To Boil a Persian Capon with Dates & Lemons, she read. The recipe did not look at all like a modern one, with no list of ingredients and very few weighed measurements or timings. She was surprised to see a Persian recipe like this. She had assumed that old English cookery would be stodgy and plain. She read the instructions.

Take and truss a fair Capon, boil him by himself in water. Then take the broth and add vinegar, half a pint of white wine, a bundell of herbes and whole Mace. Put in marrow and dates and half a pound of sugar & rose water. Cut preserved lemons into slices, and use a larding pin to lard in ye Capon. Put ye Capon in a deep dish,

thicken the broth with ground Almond and poure upon
ye Capon.

That's interesting, she thought. *How would it work? What*
would it taste like? It sounds sweet – no salt? But the sour-
ness of vinegar, wine and lemons would perhaps make up for
that. I might give it a go. Why not?

She flipped on for a few pages and saw that there were
dozens of recipes for pies, puddings, fish and meat dishes. She
saw to her surprise that one was for sweet potato cooked in
sugar, which reminded her of a Thanksgiving dish Atalanta
had done for her American book. There was liberal use of
ingredients she used only rarely: lots of rose water, lots of
almonds, mace, flowers, all sorts of herbs. There were possets and jellies and even ice cream. There were cordials and
syrups and potions for aiding sleep or curing ulcers or colic
and headaches – dozens of home remedies with familiar
herbs and unfamiliar too: dragonwort, for example. *What's*
that? she wondered. There were recipes for marmalades and
jams; one needed *civill oranges*, and she wondered what they
could be until she suddenly realised it must mean Seville
oranges.

Her search for coffee forgotten, she took the book and
wandered back to the kitchen, reading the recipes with fas-
cination, noting as one hand changed to the next, seeing
the annotations in the margins, the additions and the notes
below.

The seed of an idea was germinating in her mind.

Chapter Six

1939

Miranda woke suddenly but didn't know why. The room was quite light and she wondered for a moment if a lamp had been left on. This was a dreadful sin, an awful waste, and she was worried in case it was she who had forgotten to turn it off. Then she saw that the curtains were pulled back and silver moonlight was pouring into the room. The great white glowing disc of the moon hung outside the window, as if it had sunk down to take a look into the twins' room.

Miranda sat up, blinking. 'Rosie?'

Her sister's bed was empty, the sheet turned back.

'Oh bother . . . not again.'

Miranda slithered out from her own warm sheets, reached for her dressing gown on the chair, and slipped her feet into her felt slippers. The bedroom door was ajar, and she went out into the cold corridor. She shivered, wondering in which direction Rosalind might have gone this time. This sleepwalking had been dreadful after the disaster, and Miranda had barely slept herself as she was so often pursuing the gliding form of Rosalind as she flitted about the house on her mysterious missions. Then it had eased off and was now only occasional, though it most often happened at a full moon. 'Your lunacy', Miranda called it. She always woke when Rosalind walked, but she was never sure how long it had been since her sister had left the bedroom, drifting out so quietly, leaving the door ajar. Perhaps it was the breeze that came through it that woke her.

Sometimes Rosalind went downstairs, usually heading for the back door that opened onto the kitchen lawn – although once Miranda found that she had somehow managed to unlock and pull open the great front door and was walking determinedly towards the bridge over the moat. Sometimes she went upstairs towards the attics.

Miranda could see no trace of her sister in the dark corridor and fumbled in her dressing gown for the little torch she kept in the pocket as she reached the stairs. The circle of yellow light from the torch showed very little but it enabled her to decide which way she would go – up or down.

Down, she thought.

That was the way Rosalind had gone on the last two occasions. She took two steps downwards and stopped.

No. Up.

She turned around and began instead to climb up the stairs. There was no attic here but a small door that opened out onto the leaded roof behind the battlements of the square tower at the east side of the castle. As Miranda climbed, there was more of a breeze and she was filled with a sense of foreboding. Sure enough, when she got to the small low landing at the top, the little door, set high into the wall and almost more like a window, was unlatched and open.

'Rosie!' she called quietly, shining her torch at the door. There was no reply.

Climbing through the open door, she emerged onto the roof leads. They were cold through the felt of her slippers and she shivered despite the warmth of the evening. She switched off the torch, as the moonlight showed everything perfectly plainly, including the figure of Rosalind, ghostly in her white nightgown. She was standing at the battlements on her tiptoes, looking over the edge.

'Rosie,' Miranda said with relief. 'You're there! Come back now, come back to bed. You're sleepwalking again.'

She had read in a book not to attempt to wake a sleep-walker, so usually she just acted as though Rosalind was already awake and tried to guide her gently into doing what she wanted. It seemed to work.

Rosalind turned to look at her, though her eyes were blank. 'They have arrived,' she said clearly.

Miranda was surprised. Rosalind rarely talked when she was asleep. 'Who has arrived?'

Rosalind gestured towards the battlements with an airy wave and turned back to look over them. Miranda walked slowly over to join her. From the top of the tower, they could look down upon the two towers set into the castle wall below, one surrounded by its flowery fence.

'Oh look,' Miranda said, forgetting her sister was asleep. 'You can see the tower very well tonight. What a moon!'

She squinted down, and saw to her surprise that someone

121

was moving behind the fence far below them. They would not be visible from a bedroom window but from here, they could just be seen: a figure bundled up in a coat and wearing a trilby hat. Whoever it was was walking up and down behind the fence, occasionally stopping as if to admire a rose, and then continuing. It seemed to take two minutes or so for the figure to walk the entire length of the fence as it curved around the tower. They watched it make two whole lengths.

'They've arrived,' Rosalind said again. 'Just like we knew would happen.'

Miranda let out a long slow breath. 'How did you guess this, Rosie? How did you know?'

Rosalind said nothing but continued to stare blankly downwards, watching the figure appearing and disappearing as it moved in and out of shadow. Without warning she opened her mouth and shouted, 'Hello!'

'Shhhh,' Miranda said quickly. 'What are you doing?'

The figure far below stopped and looked up. Miranda didn't know if the sound would travel down as loudly as it sounded next to her but evidently something had been audible.

'Hello!' shouted Rosalind again. Then, quite suddenly, she started to pull herself up onto the narrow ledge of the battlement.

'Rosie, no, stop it!' Miranda cried, horrified. 'You'll fall off!' She reached out and pulled at her sister's nightgown.

'I must go there,' Rosalind insisted, and then, with a scramble, she was kneeling on the ledge, each hand resting on the crenellation to either side of her. 'Don't try to stop me.'

'Rosie!' Miranda was frightened now. Being on the roof was one thing. They had done that since they were small, the wall of battlements providing a sort of safety barrier. But climbing onto the battlements themselves, with nothing between their dizzy height and the far-off ground, was something else. She doubted that Rosie knew at all what she was doing. She had to be stopped. Miranda flung her arms around her sister's waist and held tight. 'What are you doing? Come back at once!'

'I must go,' Rosalind said clearly, and somehow the words seemed to carry through the still night air. The figure below continued to stare up at them, a white face barely visible beneath the trilby. And then a hand stretched up and out towards them as if beckoning Rosalind down.

Miranda felt her sister's weight tip forward slightly as if she were leaning over the edge. She tightened her grip, pressed her feet into the leads and shouted, 'No, no!'

Rosalind's nightgown flapped in her face, almost obscuring her view, but she saw a door in the tower far below open and a triangle of yellow light, thrown from inside, appear on the ground. Another figure appeared and went swiftly to the first. The two were closely joined and began to move back towards the door.

Rosalind leaned further forward, as if she meant to take flight and swoop downwards before the two figures disappeared. Miranda pulled at her but Rosalind was pushing forward with her hands and now it was a battle of strength. Miranda gasped, knowing that Rosalind must surely win, with the leverage of the battlements to aid her. Her heart was racing, everything in her straining to hold on to her sister, hot tears of panic burning her eyes as she gasped for breath. 'No, Rosie, no,' she said, and it came out as a half sob and not at all convincing and powerful as she wanted it to.

And then, through her blurred and restricted vision, she saw the two figures bundle through the door of the tower, and the door shut, cutting off the cone of golden light and sending the garden below back into darkness.

Rosalind stopped leaning forward and pushing against the battlements. 'Oh!' she said in a wondering voice.

Miranda seized her chance and pulled as hard as possible. Rosalind came tumbling backwards off the ledge. Miranda stumbled back and crashed down onto the leads, with Rosalind landing on top of her. Winded for a moment, she was suffused with relief and then hit with the delayed shock. As soon as she could breathe, proper sobs came bursting out. 'What were you thinking of, you idiot? You could have been killed!'

Rosalind turned her head, blinking in confusion. 'Miranda? Where are we?'

'On the roof! You brought us up here!'

'I did?' She looked around. 'Was I sleepwalking?'

'Of course!' Miranda stopped sobbing and sniffed. 'You don't remember anything?'

'I never do.' Rosalind looked suddenly anxious. 'I didn't do anything stupid, did I?'

Miranda stared back. Rosalind remembered nothing. So only Miranda knew what they'd seen in the garden of the tower far below. 'Well . . . no . . . but you might have. That's why I grabbed you. And we fell over.'

'Is that why you're crying? Did I hurt you?'

'Yes . . . that's right.'

'I'm sorry, I didn't mean to. It must have woken me up.' Rosalind yawned. 'So it's true.'

'What's true?'

'Well, I never do remember sleepwalking, you know. So sometimes I wonder if you're playing an elaborate joke on me. But now, I suppose I can see that you don't and I must really walk around in my sleep.'

Miranda laughed despite herself. 'Yes, you do, you ninny. What kind of a joke would that be?' She pushed Rosalind away and clambered up, shaking off the chill of the lead roof. 'Let's get back. I want my bed. I've got my torch. Come on.'

Rosalind followed, meek as a lamb. Miranda tried to shake off the memory of pulling as hard as she could to stop her sister launching herself from the battlements.

The memory of that dark figure far below them played in her mind. Who had finally arrived?

I'll find out, she promised herself. *I have to.*

Miranda could still feel the unpleasantness of the night before all the next day. She was unusually muted, and did not protest at spending the sunny day inside with her sister, reading and scribbling in her exercise books. Every now and again she would have a flashback to the fear and distress of holding Rosalind back from leaping off the roof, and would shudder. Looking over at her sister, she would be half comforted and half infuriated by her placid ignorance of what had happened. Rosalind, unruffled, painted happily at her desk. Gradually, the horrible sensations from the night before began to subside and Miranda almost persuaded herself that it had been a dream. Except that occasionally she saw clearly in her mind's eye the figure that walked up and down along the perimeter of the fence, proof that after all this time, the tower had an occupant again.

She stared out of the window, gazing at the great square gatehouse with its chunky battlements, the flagpole on the top bearing the drooping flag of the family standard. Grandfather insisted it fly, although it had been at half-mast for two years after the disaster. Miranda loved her grandfather despite the way he took so little notice of his grandchildren. She had thought they might provide him with a way out of his misery and self-recrimination, but instead the distance between them seemed ever wider. The loss of his only son had stranded him in the past, with the grandchildren a generation away. Constance, his sister, was his companion there but she was a more modern creature than he was, and always had been. While he was an Edwardian, a mustachio'd officer and a staunch conservative who lived according to the patterns of his time, Constance had been a force for change. She wrote letters to newspapers and to members of parliament, and sent money to support prison reforms and better lives for poor women workers. Before the Great War, she had thrown stones at Lloyd George's car and had once walked along Piccadilly and smashed the windows of Fortnum's to draw attention to the work of WSPU and their demands for women's suffrage. She had been arrested and taken to Holloway where she had determined to go on hunger strike with the others, but when the authorities found out that she was the sister of Sir Leonard Wakefield, she'd been released, much to her irritation. Afterwards, Fortnum's had sent hampers to all the women who'd been imprisoned.

'The insult,' Aunt Constance said darkly. 'Beef tea. To keep our strength up. The patronising nature of it – too much to be borne.'

Despite escaping the horror of force feeding, she had gone on a sort of permanent hunger strike herself ever since, eating like a bird and having a horror of all sorts of rich food, especially from Fortnum's. Miranda, though, respected her prickly aunt. Women had the vote now, thanks to the work of people like her. She might be eccentric, in her britches and riding her pony and trap, but she still supported the improvement of women's lives, and had protected her own rights by never marrying – at least, that was Miranda's theory.

And she was certain of her aunt's integrity. Which made the appearance of their visitor all the more puzzling.

Why are they keeping all this so secret? Why can't we know the truth?

She had an idea that they were trying to be kind, in their restrained, tight-lipped way. Perhaps they thought that the children's hearts – already broken by loss – could not sustain any more.

We need the truth. Everyone does. I will find it. I will bring it to light. I will make everyone see it and say it!

Her pencil lead broke suddenly. She had been pressing so hard into the page of her exercise book that it had snapped beneath her and left a jagged scrawl over the paper.

The next morning was Sunday.

Miranda woke early, a riot of birdsong penetrating the castle walls, as though the birds were singing an elegy to the summer that was nearly over. Eventually, unable to sleep or read, she got up quietly and dressed, and went downstairs to wait for the coast to be clear. There was already activity in the kitchen, but she didn't want any breakfast. Instead, she loitered in the passages and in the morning room until she heard her aunt come down, disappear to the kitchen for a cup of tea with Mrs Graham, and then leave for church, her hat tied firmly under her chin with a green ribbon to keep it in place as she cycled.

Once her aunt had gone, Miranda slipped out of the French windows in the morning room, the ones that gave out towards the back of the house. Rosalind was still dozing upstairs, Imogen was in her sitting room, and the boys were playing trains in the nursery, and so the coast was clear. Miranda had not been able to sleep easily since Rosalind's sleepwalking, waking up several times in a rush of panic and checking that her sister was still in her bed. So far, she had been, apparently unaware of what she had seen on the roof that night. But the sense of vigilance would not go away. Perhaps it was the general feeling of menace in the air. Miranda had noticed conferences in the study, Aunt Constance suddenly emerging from talking to Grandfather and looking grave.

In the garden, the air was fresh and tangy with the breeze from the moat and the first hint of autumn. She made her way across the lawn, following the perimeter of the wall and the flower border, until she reached the fence around the West Tower. She had not imagined or dreamed those figures far below when she had looked down from the roof, she knew that.

Miranda walked along the fence. There was no way to see over it. The dense foliage prevented her from seeing through it. Even without the roses, the fence was well woven and only glimpses could be seen through the sturdy willow. Beyond the fence was more foliage, the greenery on the other side. She reached the door and stared at it for a moment before, with a racing heart, she took hold of the knob and tried to turn it. It moved slightly but came to the kind of stop that meant it was locked. The keyhole could not be seen through – there was an escutcheon on the other side to prevent peeping.

She stood and listened again, her heartbeat calming to normal. Silence but for the birds.

Then, unexpectedly clear in the still of the morning, she heard a door open and footsteps on paving stones, and then a splash as something was emptied of water. A kettle? A bucket? She held her breath even though she was invisible to anyone within the perimeter of the fence.

Footsteps again and then a voice. 'Of course, if you want some air.'

How odd, Miranda thought. *I think I know that voice. From ages and ages ago. But who is it?*

A lighter, softer voice replied, whose words could not be discerned.

Miranda froze for an instant, and then leaned closer to the climbing roses. She felt the pull of a thorn in her hair, and ignored it, listening as hard as she could.

'It is a beautiful day,' said the first voice, its tone kindly. 'Come out and see the sun.'

The lighter voice replied but, like a strain of music, it was sound without words.

'Of course. Of course you will. If you wish it. But you're not well enough, not quite yet. Now sit here, and I'll fetch you some tea.'

Shoes on the paving stone again and then silence. Miranda leaned even closer to the bushes, desperate to see something, but there was nothing to be seen but stems and leaves and petals. Frustrated, she pulled away and found her curls had become somehow tangled with more than one thorn. Another scraped her scalp hard as she moved, and she yelped loudly with the pain.

There was a moment of silence and then the soft voice spoke more loudly.

'Hello? Who's there?'

Miranda was quiet, though tears had sprung to her eyes with the stinging on her head. Her fingers were trying to untangle her hair, being pricked and stung all the time by thorns.

Footsteps again, first on the stone and then the soft thud of shoes on grass. Quite suddenly, Miranda sensed a presence on the other side of the fence, directly opposite her. She stopped moving, overcome by the sensation of the other's nearness.

'Hello?' the voice said again.

A vast longing swept over Miranda, a yearning that she had been working ceaselessly to quell for as long as she could properly remember. *Oh,* said a voice in her mind, *it's you.* It was so clear she wondered if she had spoken out loud.

'Are you there?' asked the other voice, and the longing in it seemed to match her own.

She desperately wanted to reply. But what would she say? What if she said the wrong things? Wrong things had been said before now. No one ever knew quite what to say that was right. No words came to her now, just tears, hot and full in her eyes.

Blast these thorns, she thought, scrabbling harder to untangle her hair. She began to pull free, feeling hair rip from her head.

There were more footsteps on the path and then the first voice. 'Now, Mrs Black, what are you doing there? I have your tea. Would you like to drink it outside?'

'No. I'm going back in. I don't want to stay out here any longer.'

'Very well, Mrs Black. Perhaps that's for the best.'

Miranda walked back stiffly across the lawn. She had waited until the two sets of footsteps had retreated and then she had finally got herself free of the thorns. Her hands were covered in scratches and there were blobs of blood under her nails. She felt dazed.

Mrs Black? Who on earth is that? What can be going on? It doesn't make any sense!

'Miranda! There you are!'

Rosalind was running across the lawn towards her. Miranda waved at her. 'Yes, she said, 'I'm here.' She decided in that instant not to tell her sister what she had heard. She couldn't risk those night walks, not if they were going to lead to the roof again. To keep secrets from Rosalind was awful. She never had. But she had to now, she was sure of it.

'We have to go inside,' Rosalind said breathlessly. Her blue eyes were wide and anxious. 'Grandfather has said we all have to go to the study at once.'

They hurried together back through the morning room and down the passage. Grandfather was in the study, warming up the large wireless on the table near the fireplace. It came crackling into life, whining and squealing as he searched for the home service.

'Sit down, girls,' he said gruffly. Imogen came in, herding the boys. 'You too, boys, sit on the rug. Ah. Here we are, here we have it.'

They sat down, solemn and silent. Aunt Constance came in, breathless. She had been cycling quickly back from church, from the red of her cheeks and the messiness of her hair.

'Is it time?' she asked as she flung her hat onto a chair.

Grandfather nodded. His one good eye was grave. 'It's time.' He sank into an armchair. They listened as the announcer introduced the prime minister and he confirmed at last what they had known must come. His voice filled the room. It was war. It had begun.

'War,' Aunt Constance said unhappily. 'Some will celebrate. I cannot.'

Grandfather said nothing but rested his head on his hand and glared at the floor.

It is like a wave, Miranda thought, as they sat cross-legged on the hearth rug. Everyone was solemn but not surprised. The wave had been coming for a while now: a huge, dark, curling wall of water that could be seen a mile off, racing into shore to engulf everything in its path. You could run but not far enough and not fast enough. That was how this war had felt. Inexorable. And now it was here, curling over their heads, about to crash over them. It would whirl them up inside it and they would be destroyed and lost, or flung somewhere new and different. Who knew how it would end?

'A humiliation for Chamberlain,' Grandfather said at last.

Constance said, 'The Carters have already given notice.'

'Even Alf?' asked Imogen.

'Yes. They all want to do their bit.'

'Fast and bloodless,' Grandfather said, but without the conviction of before.

Miranda thought of them all: the elderly couple who cared for them, the five children – though Imogen was practically grown-up – and the various servants who were left. The strong young men would go, Mrs Graham would go. They would be alone.

And now the mysterious Mrs Black. She's here too.

That thought made her shiver with a kind of horrified excitement, an almost sickening mixture of fear and delight.

But what if the Germans come? How will we fight them?

She remembered the jam that she and Rosalind had made, and pictured those jars with their poisoned innards tucked safely out of sight in the storeroom. The thought gave her comfort. While the house was full of weapons – from the old pikes and halberds and swords on the wall of the great hall to the guns in Grandfather's gun cupboard – she doubted they would ever be able to be put to use. Their weapons would have to be much craftier than that: the deadly strychnine hidden inside the soft sweet blackness of jam. The gentle persuasion to make the enemy take his own life with a mouthful of it.

Aunt Constance stood up, her eyes slightly reddened. 'The blackout starts tonight, children, do you understand? It all starts from now. We had better just get on with it.'

It was desperation that gave her courage. She knew she would not be able to stand the thoughts racing around her head for much longer without them bursting out. Or else she would run back to the tower and force her way through the gate somehow, to find out if what she suspected was true.

Outside her aunt's study door, she barely hesitated, and then rapped hard on it.

There was a pause from behind it and then a voice, sounding thickened. 'Yes? Who is it?'

'Miranda.'

Another pause. 'Come in, my dear.'

She opened the door. Her aunt was standing by the window, looking out towards the castle walls. When she turned, Constance's eyes were damp and red, and the end of her nose was shiny.

'Are you all right, Aunt Constance?' Miranda asked.

'Yes, yes. It's all so dreadful and grave. Come in and sit down.' She beckoned to a chair and sat down herself. 'I can't help thinking of the loss and death to come. I lost my own fiancé in the Great War, and so many friends and relations. I can hardly bear to think that it is all going to happen again. But what can we do? Let us hope it is over quickly.' She tucked her handkerchief in her pocket. 'What is it, dear? What do you want?'

Miranda's heart fluttered. Her courage began to melt away but it was too late to back out. She remembered the sound of that light, musical voice and then she knew she had to speak.

'There's someone in the West Tower,' she said quickly.

Aunt Constance went still and then said in a sombre voice, 'Ah. You know that, do you? That's rather quicker than we were expecting.'

'She said her name is Mrs Black.'

'You spoke to her?' Aunt Constance said sharply.

'I just heard her say it. There's someone else in there with her, isn't there?'

'Yes. A servant who cares for her.'

'Why is she here?'

There was a long pause and Aunt Constance dropped her gaze to the rug as she considered. 'She had to leave the place where she was living,' she said at last. 'And we offered her a home for a while.'

'I don't understand,' Miranda said intensely. A kind of

fury was building up in her and she wondered what might happen if it continued. Perhaps she would go mad and start throwing things around. That was no good. She had to say it, even though the words were like great stones in her mouth that she couldn't spit out. 'I don't understand why we're not allowed to say it.'

'Say what, my dear?'

'That our mother isn't dead. That you sent her away for all this time. Father is dead, we know that. But why can't we know that Mother isn't dead? I heard her voice! I know it was her.'

Aunt Constance stared at her and then sighed sadly. 'You're right, of course. We are trying to protect you and the others, and to protect her. It is so hard to know what to do. Your mother isn't dead. But I'm very sorry to say that she isn't your mother either.'

'What do you mean?' demanded Miranda, her face burning as blood rushed into it. 'How can you actually put our mother – who we haven't seen in years – into the tower and not tell us? How can she not be our mother any more?'

Aunt Constance shook her head. 'I am no doctor. I cannot explain it. She doesn't know she's your mother. She doesn't know who she is. She believes she is Mrs Black and she has thought so from the time she learned of your father's death. She doesn't know she has children. And we have been told that to tell her otherwise would risk her sanity completely. It might condemn her to a life of sedation and restraints. It seemed kinder all round to let her live in an institution where she could be helped to recover in the time she needed. And

we are protecting her from the scandal of such a condition.
People can be very cruel.'

'But what about us?'

'We are protecting you as well. Perhaps it is better for the
boys to think they have no mother than that she is mad and
doesn't know them.'

'They would never forgive you if they grew up believ-
ing their mother was dead when she wasn't, mad or not!'
Miranda felt her eyes sting with indignant tears. 'And I want
to see her.'

Aunt Constance looked at her with pity. 'I can see that. I
can see your confusion, Miranda, and I understand it. But we
are still deciding what is best. Until then, Mrs Black remains
in the tower and I would ask that you tell no one that she
is there.'

'Mrs Black! You mean my mother.'

'I honestly believe that if you want your mother to come
back to you, then you must accept that she is, for now, the
person that she says. I fear that if we rip that away, we may
kill her. It is all that's keeping her alive.'

Miranda buried her head in her arms and sobbed, suddenly overcome with the awfulness of it. She felt her aunt
stand up and come over, then lay her hand softly on Miranda's shaking shoulders.

'There, there, dear. Cry. It's good for you. There are many
tears today. There is much to endure. We will think about
what is best. But you must be brave and strong, for your
mother's sake. You are the bravest and strongest of all the
children, I've always seen that. Sometimes you make me

wring my hands about you, you're so spirited and determined. But that means I think you can do it. Can you? Can you keep this secret for now?'

'Yes.' It came out wetly, muffled by her jumper. 'Yes. I can.'

'Good girl. And I will tell you what I know in due course. Now dry those tears and let's join the others for lunch.'

Chapter Seven

Present Day

Caspar came into Lady Wakefield's morning room with two steaming mugs and put one down in front of Georgie. 'Coffee,' he said somewhat unnecessarily.

'Thank you,' Georgie said, looking up from the recipe book that she'd been poring over.

Caspar looked over her shoulder. 'What is that book? You've been lost in it all day.'

'It's a recipe book I found in the larder. It's fascinating.' She looked up at him with bright eyes. 'I don't know when it starts but it's quite early – it could be Jacobean or perhaps a bit later. I'll need to do some proper research. Then it goes on from there, with new recipes added in different handwriting, and some of them annotated by later hands. Fewer recipes are added as it goes along. I suppose that's perhaps because the ladies of later centuries trusted to their cooks. But there are some towards the end in more modern hands. I think those are twentieth century – the language and style is almost from today although the recipes are a bit dated – lots of things that are potted or in aspic. Isn't that interesting?'

'Yes, very. Can I take a look?'

'Of course.' She passed him the book. 'Careful, it's a bit brittle. But it's survived remarkably well, especially if it was properly used. Did you know about it?'

Casper shook his head. 'Not at all. I've never seen it before.' He scanned some of the early pages. 'This really is old-fashioned.' He peered closer at the handwriting, trying to make it out. 'It's not easy to decipher, is it? What's metheglin?'

'A drink. Spiced mead, apparently. There are quite a few drinks and cordials at the beginning, and lots of remedies later on.'

'Hydromel,' Caspar read aloud. He frowned. 'Honey water?'

'Yes, another form of mead, I think.'

'Tea with eggs sounds horrid.'

'I think pap sounds nasty.' Georgie laughed. 'But it's really just porridge, I think. Look at this: boil your milk in a pipkin. Doesn't that sound lovely? I wonder what a pipkin looks like. There are so many drinks and remedies. Of course, people must have done a lot of home brewing and a lot of making of medicines without a local pharmacy to call on.'

Caspar regarded her with interest. 'You look brighter than you have for a long time.'

'I feel as though this has fallen into my hands for a reason. I've been looking for inspiration and this arrives – a gift from the universe.'

'Do you think you can use it for Atalanta?'

'That's what I've got in mind. I'm trying to think how I

can adapt it for her in some way that will update some of what is in here.'

'Does it need updating?'

'Oh yes, if it's going to be something she can author herself. I'm working on some ideas. Obviously people don't need to have their home remedies any more and not that many are going to be interested in making their own mead, but I'm sure there is a lot that I can draw on. I've thought about homemade liqueurs based on some of the recipes here. I love the sound of a rosemary aqua vitae.' She picked up the book and flicked through again. 'And that's before we get to some of the brilliant recipes for fish and meat and vegetables.'

'What a find.' Caspar smiled at her and leaned in to kiss her cheek. 'I'm so pleased.' His mobile shrilled in his trouser pocket and he took it out and looked at it. 'Oh, it's the solicitor. I called him about Viktoria. I'll take this outside and leave you in peace.'

She heard him greeting the lawyer as he strode out of the room. As soon as the door was closed he was no longer audible. One of the benefits of this large place was the peace and quiet. She had never known such soft silence, certainly not in London. She lost herself again in the recipe book, stopping only to make notes on her computer, until Caspar came back in, looking cross.

'What is it?' she asked, apprehensive suddenly.

Caspar threw himself onto one of the flowery sofas and growled. He was usually so calm but lately Georgie had noticed he was showing a lot more emotion. Perhaps it was some sort of liberating effect of being back in his childhood home. 'Viktoria,' he said darkly.

'Oh no. What now?'

'There was an addendum to Uncle Archie's will. He very lately granted her the use of the gatehouse for her lifetime. They didn't tell me this originally because we got so bogged down in the main body of the will and the trusts and all the rest of it.'

'Can he do that?'

'Well, apparently so, because otherwise we have to liberate enough money to give Viktoria the cost of a flat in London.'

Georgie stared at him. 'But that's not possible!'

'No. Otherwise I would, obviously – to get rid of her. I certainly don't want her hanging around and I'm sure she'd rather be in London, swanning about as Lady Wakefield, than stuck in our gatehouse.'

'Then why is she here?'

'I think it's to force our hand. She will assume we want to pay her off. Perhaps she thinks we've got more money than we actually have. But it's all locked up, as you know, and I'm going to need a hell of a lot to cope with the repairs. The conservation team are coming next week to take a thorough look at everything and let me know what the damage is.'

Georgie's face fell. 'So we've got Viktoria here for the fore-seeable.' She shrunk down a little into herself. 'That's what I don't like about this place. It's not our own. It's far too big for us. I feel like I'm rattling around.'

Casper beckoned her over, and she went to him, lying down on the sofa next to him and snuggling close. She inhaled his warm smell and found comfort in the strength of his body. 'This is nice,' she said gently.

'We won't be so alone once a baby comes along,' Caspar murmured against her ear. 'I really think it's the right thing for us, Georgie. For you as well as for me. For both of us. I want to start a family with you. Have you had a chance to get your head together?'

'Well . . .' She felt the familiar chill of fear. 'You see, it's this cookbook. It's driven everything else out of my head. Just give me a chance to get my ideas to Atalanta, and then I really will think seriously about it. I promise.'

'We could start now,' Caspar said teasingly, hugging her tightly and dropping a soft kiss on her cheek.

She laughed. 'I'm working! Or at least, I should be.' She pulled away and stood up. 'And you need to start thinking about how we're going to get Viktoria sorted out.'

'All right, good point.' Caspar got up too. 'Back to the grindstone. See you later, sweet cheeks.'

She was relieved that he had allowed her to escape the subject so easily. She turned back to the book, and pushed it out of her mind, along with the anxiety it always raised in her. She itched to cook, as she always did when she needed safety.

I'll cook a meal from here tonight, she decided. *But which one?*

Once Georgie had decided on her dish, she also made some other choices. So far, she had sourced her ingredients from the local high street and supermarket, driving over to shop. Now she determined she would get as much as possible from the castle and its immediate surroundings. She would have to learn more about the place before she knew entirely what was available, but for now, she was going to use herbs from the garden. That would be a start. Behind the kitchen door was a long strip of garden set between two red-brick walls that she suspected had been a kitchen garden, or a remedy garden. Was that what they were called? Perhaps it was called a physic garden, like the one in Chelsea that had been started as a source of medicinal herbs and plants for the apothecaries of London. There were certainly plenty of herbs in the beds around the kitchen door and in the little knots of garden with higgledy paths between and around them. She spotted rosemary, mint, oregano and at least three types of thyme. There was sage and parsley and dill. The recipe book called for ingredients like sugar, cinnamon, dates, raisins, pistachios, almonds, nutmeg, mace and ambergris (if that's what ambergreece was), imported from abroad, of course. The plants and herbs required must have been available in the castle garden but she had no idea what they were, despite their poetic names – names like sorrel, celandine, pimpernel, wild-dragons, agrimony, featherfew, avance and tormentil. She would learn to identify them, with the help of a plant recognition app and the internet, and she would test their flavours and medicinal properties.

For now, she started on something easy: a capon boiled in broth. At least, it had sounded easy, but now she was working on it, it was not so straightforward. The recipe didn't proceed like a modern one, telling her what she needed in terms of ingredients, and what to do step by step. Instead, she had to read it several times to understand what was required. The recipe only mentioned at the end that she should have used salt at the start. And while there was some lovely description – the 'plumpsome raisins of the sun' sounded particularly nice – what was fair water and what was sack? The instructions were vague: what did 'let it boil then mingle, then boil on' even mean? On top of that, quite a few ingredients were only needed 'if you will'.

Trial and error, she thought, as she beat together blanched ground almonds, rose water and cream. Ground almonds featured in many recipes and she guessed that this was a natural thickener. She liked the 'snippets of tost' which the capon would lie on, once he'd been boiled in his broth. There were no potatoes anywhere in this early part of the book so she guessed that they had not yet arrived from the new world. The tost was certainly toasted bread, to act as the necessary absorbent carbohydrate for the chicken stew.

It ended up taking a very long time, and she had no idea if she had it right, but the finished result looked promising – an enticing fowl that had been roasted and boiled and now sat in its creamy stew of dates and raisins, flavoured with rose.

'Well? What do you think?' she asked as she and Caspar took their first exploratory mouthfuls.

Casper looked thoughtful as he ate slowly, savouring it carefully. 'It's not what I expected,' he said at last.

'Oh dear. What did you expect?'

'I don't mean it in a bad way. I suppose I thought it would be tasteless. Stodgy. Meat and turnips sort of thing. But this has quite an exotic flavour. Almost Moroccan. Quite flowery. And actually the capon is delicious, very well cooked.'

'Yes, it's not at all dull and plodding.' Georgie took another mouthful. 'That's what surprised me. Several of these recipes have flavours that we in this country would have considered quite exotic in the late twentieth century.'

'Quite,' Caspar replied. 'I'm surprised that this book was here all along, because I don't remember eating chicken with almonds, dates and raisins when I was growing up.'

'Nor do I,' Georgie said feelingly.

Caspar ate a bit more. 'It's quite sweet.'

'Lots of the recipes are sweet-savoury. There's sugar and rose water and cream in this. I want to try another recipe of beef with marigolds. Doesn't that sound lovely? So pretty.'

Caspar laughed. 'I do really like this! Slightly odd but very nice.'

'It might need to be tweaked for a modern audience but I'm really inspired by this idea.'

'Have you run it past Atalanta yet?'

Georgie shook her head. 'I want to get it just right before I pitch it properly. But I've told her that I've had some inspiration so I hope that will have calmed her down a bit.'

'I'm very glad the house has delivered for you.'

'It has,' she answered, smiling. 'It really has.'

Georgie was awake again in the night, certain she'd heard something. A flash through the thick curtain made her get up and she went to the window to look out. It was black outside but the sky was alive with lightning, as though up in the heavens someone was switching a giant light bulb on and off. There was no thunder to go with it, and no rain, which gave the whole thing an eerie but quite beautiful effect. Each bolt lit up the world in a flickering flash so that she could see the woods and the two towers at the far corner of the castle grounds.

It is spooky here, she thought. And yet, she wasn't afraid. Perhaps it was because Caspar was sleeping deeply in the bed, his large, solid frame providing the security she needed to cling to.

Or, she thought, *perhaps it's because I know that fairy tale castles and towers and thunderstorms are not as scary as real life.*

The terror was behind her, she told herself that all the time. The effects were still with her, she knew that. But she had learned coping mechanisms. She had spent her twenties coming to terms with everything that had happened, seeing a series of therapists until she'd found one who understood and was able, at last, to help.

She was not afraid of thunder and lightning, places or things. She was afraid of people: unpredictable people, the ones who were supposed to care for you the most and who, instead, were the ones who hurt you the worst. As a child, she would have run through any number of thunderstorms to be free of the flat she had called home, and the people she called her parents. If she'd ever had that chance.

Georgie stood and watched the light display for a while longer. There were jagged forks of lightning as well as the sheets. *What caused it all*, she wondered? She knew vaguely about static and electricity but not really how it all worked.

How beautiful it is, she thought. A sudden long series of lightning sheets – so rapid as to be almost constant – lit up the towers, one fully visible and one shielded by the old fence. The uncovered one was so pretty with its trefoil shape, the diamond-paned windows and decorative battlements, like a miniature castle itself.

Georgie was struck by a sudden urgent desire to take a look inside. She wondered why on earth she hadn't done so already. They were locked, but there must be keys. The towers had seemed simply decorative things, hardly real. Now, in the flashes of lightning, she saw them for what they were – tiny houses, complete in themselves.

But why did they shield one? That's the real mystery.

She closed the curtain against the light show outside, and went back to the warmth of their bed and the solidness of Caspar's presence.

Georgie approached the East Tower over the wet grass. It must have rained heavily after the lightning show as the world was sodden, but she had been asleep by then and not noticed the downpour. When she had woken, she had not remembered her desire to visit the tower until she'd seen the wetness of the world and remembered the midnight storm.

Now she made her way towards the fenceless tower, clutching a ring of ancient keys in her hand.

'I have no idea where the keys to the towers are,' Caspar had said with surprise when she'd asked for them. They were having breakfast before he started on his day in the study. 'I went in one when I was a boy and the gardener opened it up – he'd been keeping his tools in there. Spades, scythes, hoes and ladders and the rest.'

'What was it like?'

Caspar had shrugged. 'I don't remember. Dark? Dusty? I was shooed out pretty quickly. I think he was told to take his tools out in the end. For some reason, the towers have never been much used and not really liked.'

'But why? They're so pretty. I've never seen anything like them, set into the wall like that. They're like playhouses, almost.'

Caspar shook his head. 'No. We never got that vibe. Quite the opposite. We were distinctly told to stay away.'

'Do you mind if I take a look?'

'Of course not.' He smiled. 'You might discover some family secrets in there.'

'Are there any?'

'I don't think so,' he said vaguely.

'But you have got family secrets?'

'You know, just the usual.'

'What are the usual?'

'The kind everyone has – fallings-out, ill-advised marriages, annoying step-great-aunts who won't leave the property.' He laughed. 'What are yours?'

'Mine? Oh, none. I don't have any,' she said lightly.

'How unusual. Now, if you want the keys for that tower, I know that there's an old bunch hanging in the cold room. Maybe they'll be on that. Worth a try.'

Now Georgie stood at the door of the East Tower. Close up, it was even prettier than she remembered, though somewhat dilapidated. The stone was in various hues of yellow – from dark honey to light beige – and spotted with green, grey and gold lichen. The thick glass in the leaded diamond panes was impossible to see through as it was rimed with dust.

Well then, let's try this . . .

She inspected the bunch of keys. There was a variety of size and age of key, but it was obvious that only four of the dozen on the ring were likely candidates for the large old lock set into the door.

With fingers numb from clutching the cold iron ring, she clumsily picked one of the four at random and inserted it into the old lock. It didn't budge when she tried to turn it, so she pulled it out and tried another. That didn't work either. Soon she had tried all the keys, and none had turned.

'Oh, that's disappointing,' she said out loud. She had been expecting that one would slide easily into place and the door would open. Ridiculous. Nothing worked like that. She examined the bunch of keys again. A strong feeling rolled over her: *I should try again.* So she worked her way back through them, taking her time and trying to sense whether the key was genuinely not a fit for the lock or whether age and time was the factor. The third key she tried slid into the lock more easily than the others, and while it refused to turn, there was the slightest give as she pushed against it that made her sure it was a real possibility.

'I need some oil,' she said to herself. 'I should have thought of that at the start.'

She turned and was about to head back to the cold room to see if she could find any oil lurking about, when her eye was caught by the old fence around the West Tower, and she changed direction and started walking towards it. The door set into it was much newer than the tower itself and it suddenly occurred to her that one of the keys might fit that lock.

The lock was indeed more modern, and she selected a likely looking key from the bunch. It slid right in and, to her surprise, turned quite easily. The knob of the gate didn't turn but that didn't matter as it simply opened under a push from her shoulder.

'Oh,' she said with surprise. 'I'm in.'

It was the strangest sensation: she felt a thrill of the forbidden as she stepped beyond the gateway, and the sense of being an explorer of a place forgotten by time, like the first to open the tomb of an Egyptian king after centuries. Beyond the gate, the tower was surrounded by brambles that had grown up high against the walls and windows. The place looked in much worse condition than the other tower, the stone stained by the vegetation pressing against it, the windows partly obscured by the climbing tendrils of ivy suckered to it. Georgie realised that she wouldn't be able to get near the door without some secateurs to make inroads. The roses that had been planted into the wicker fence had spread and now made a thorny barrier to the door.

Sleeping Beauty, she thought. *That's the fairy tale with the tower and the thorns. Sleeping Beauty is inside, and the prince hacks his way through with his sword.*

She felt a clammy sensation of fear. Was there someone

inside who needed to be rescued? And was she the prince? Had she inadvertently given herself the task of rescuing someone, or something?

I don't want that, she thought firmly, and she turned at once on her heel and made her way back through the gate, which she shut behind her, though she didn't lock it.

I can't even rescue myself. I'm hardly in a position to rescue other people.

Then she scolded herself. How could she be so silly? There was no one in the tower. It was deserted and had been for years.

I'll forget this tower, she decided. *It's the other one I'm interested in. I'll get some oil and see what I can do.*

Once she got back to the house, Georgie realised she didn't have more time to mess about with oil and keys. Her phone showed her that a raft of messages had arrived and she had a lot to deal with, so she went to the morning room and settled down in front of her computer.

There was a message from Atalanta.

'Oh dear,' Georgie murmured as she hovered over it, hesitating before she opened it. 'I really wish I'd had just another day or two to get my thoughts in order.'

But of course, Atalanta was in a ferment of eagerness and she wanted things sorted out as quickly as possible. If they didn't come up with their idea soon, then the broadcast and publication schedules meant that any new book or television series would be put back a whole year, with the resulting drop in income as well.

Georgie clicked on the message and it popped up in the adjacent window.

Hello darling,

I know you said you've got a big idea and want to finesse it but I really have to see you! We need to talk. It's urgent, darling! I'm coming down at once. Send me your address.

Love and kisses
Atalanta xxxx

Georgie stared at the screen. This was not what she had wanted at all. But perhaps this was actually the best outcome. If Atalanta saw the castle and the old cookery book, it might talk to her sense of theatre and the dramatic. Any excuse to dress up in some kind of costume was meat and drink to her. She practically had it written into her contracts.

She wrote back saying she would love Atalanta to visit, gave her address, thinking again how strange it was to put 'Wakefield Castle' as her home, and asked her to write with the dates she had in mind. That would, she hoped, buy her a little breathing space to consider how she would pitch the idea when Atalanta got here.

She was working on her pitch document when Caspar came in a little later. She looked up and saw that he looked tense and white-faced.

'Is everything okay?' she asked.

'Not really.' He came and sat down on the sofa near her desk, looking beaten.

'What is it?'

'There was a tremendous storm in the night.'

'I know, I saw the lightning. Though it wasn't raining when I went back to sleep.'

'Well, the rain came later. Gallons and gallons of it.'

'I noticed the moat was looking full.'

'And unfortunately it came in through the attics over the great hall. The roof is completely shot and it's flooded up there. We've got some water through onto the hammer-beam and plaster ceiling.'

Georgie gasped. 'What? That's awful!'

'Yup. I've been sweeping water out all morning along with the gardeners.' Casper sighed. 'I knew this place was going to be a burden when they read out Uncle Archie's will. But this . . . this is a bit more than I hoped to handle. The roof over the great hall was looking dodgy, but I thought it would hold out another year or two while we got our financing in place. I've got a list of organisations that might supply a grant for us. But now it's urgent.'

Georgie jumped up and went over to him, sitting beside him. 'I'm so sorry. How on earth did I miss this?'

'You were out when it all kicked off. Thank goodness Sandy noticed on her way in earlier and was able to make some calls to get people in.'

'I'll go and look at the damage.'

'It's depressing but I think we can salvage it. We've

patched the hole with some tarp in the meantime. I hope that will hold if we get another storm.'

'After all this time!'

'Yes, centuries of storms. It only takes one to wreak such havoc.' Caspar shrugged. 'That's how it goes.'

She hugged him. 'I'm sorry, darling.'

He hugged her back and sighed. 'Well, we've done all we can this morning.' After a moment, he said, 'Did you manage to open that tower door?'

'No. It was stuck. I plan to go back with some oil.'

Caspar thought and then said, 'Come on, let's do it now. I'll help you. I can provide a bit of brawn. If you really want to take a look inside.'

'I do!'

'Good. Then we will.'

Armed with a can of WD40, they went back together across the lawn to the East Tower. The sun had come out and the sky was blue and dotted with innocent-looking fluffs of cloud, as though they were claiming ignorance of the damage they had caused in the night when they dumped tons of water on top of the castle and set the moat foaming and swirling.

Georgie watched while Caspar anointed the lock liberally and then tried the keys one by one. She couldn't remember which was the one that had moved so very slightly; they all looked the same. But with the second key, Caspar made an interested sound, and then grunted as he pushed it round.

'I think we have it,' he said slowly as he pressed hard. 'Ah, yes. Here we go.'

With a scraping noise, the key inched around and they heard the old mechanism grind and move.

'That's it,' Caspar said, and he pushed at the door. It scraped over the stone floor and opened.

'Oh my goodness,' breathed Georgie. She stepped into the gloom. The floor was covered in dust and dirt and rubbish, including old garden tools and an ancient wheelbarrow, and the ceiling was festooned with cobwebs. She could see a fireplace set into one wall, and that there was wood panelling on the walls. There was no furniture but a pile of broken chairs and a blanket box of black stained wood. It felt much larger inside than she expected, and a wooden door showed that there was probably another room beyond. A boxed-in wooden staircase disappeared up towards the upper floor.

'It's so dark in here,' she said, looking towards the windows. They were just as exquisite on the inside, with their enchanting diamond panes set into the golden stone, but so thick with grime that barely any light could get through.

Caspar was looking around. 'What a mess,' he said.

'It's not that bad,' Georgie replied. 'It's dirt, really. A good clean would transform it.' She sniffed the air. 'It feels dry. Ventilated. It must have been well built, as it's been able to breathe.'

'That's true.' Caspar walked over and knocked at the wooden panelling. 'It feels sound. No hollow noises, no thud of wetness. And . . . ' – he peered at the floor – 'no mounds of sawdust on the floor, so it doesn't seem to have woodworm or deathwatch beetle. Not that I'm an expert. We'd need to get it checked out.'

Georgie noticed a dusty light bulb hanging from the plaster ceiling, and spotted a switch by the door. She clicked it but nothing happened. 'So there's electricity but it's not working.'

'Turned off, I expect,' Caspar said. He went over to the door in the far wall and opened it. 'Well, well.'

'What?'

He stepped aside and let Georgie take a look. Beyond was another room, lighter than the other, with two trefoil windows that were less filthy than the others, though still dusty. The light they let in was grey through the filter of dust, but the panes glowed pale green, grey and pink with the illumination that came from the sun and from the reflections of the moat below.

'How pretty!' exclaimed Georgie, enchanted. She clapped her hands. 'A kitchen!'

It was a very basic kitchen, with a short range of cupboards, an old steel sink with high-mounted taps, and a rusty electric stove with elements of coiled iron under a rackety grill. The electrics were wall-mounted; thick cream cords climbing up the walls, which had been covered with thick white tiles, and extending along the ceiling till they disappeared out to connect to the main supply. Copper pipework did the same. The floor was covered in detritus and old newspapers.

Caspar laughed. 'I might have known you'd like this room.' He walked over to another door and found himself in a tiny scullery. Another door led into a very basic bathroom. 'Best not look at that,' he said quickly, closing the door. 'But there's an ancient boiler in there so it had hot water.'

Georgie was still gazing around the kitchen. 'We're so used to everything being hidden,' she said. 'Our cables are hidden in the walls, our pipes tucked away where they can't be seen. I rather like seeing it all on the outside – the workings visible. It's charming.'

'I don't think they had a choice,' Caspar said, rubbing dirt from his hands as he came back into the kitchen. 'Imagine trying to chase your electrics into these walls! The tower would laugh in your face as it blunted all your tools.'

Georgie laughed. 'Yes. It wouldn't take any nonsense.' She looked up at Caspar, her eyes bright. 'Let's go upstairs.'

The stairs felt secretive tucked into their wooden casing, and they creaked as Georgie and Caspar climbed them.

'They seem sound,' Caspar said, as they made their way up.

'It's all in very good condition,' Georgie said. 'Oh! I love it!' Higher up and free of the shadow of the wall, the double-aspect diamond windows let in streams of light. The floorboards were dusty but still fine. The walls were panelled, like the lower floor, and the fine carving could be seen much better, along with the graceful squares of the plastered ceiling.

'This was for the porters?' Georgie said.

'No expense spared at Wakefield,' joked Caspar.

As below, the upper floor was divided in half, and beyond was a set of smaller rooms that mirrored the kitchen, scullery and bathroom below, except that they were simple rooms, meant as bedrooms. Each had a fireplace, the grandest in the large room and the others neat and recessed. The staircase continued up to a dusty attic that was head height only in the centre, where it lifted upwards beneath what outside looked like a decorative obelisk on the roof.

'It's charm itself,' Georgie said, releasing a breath that she hadn't realised she had been holding. She was inexplicably excited. The tower had set something alight inside her.

'I can see why it appeals to you,' Caspar said.

'Really? That's odd, as I don't even know myself!'

'It's so miniature. So cosy. So complete. Like our flat.'

She laughed. 'Perhaps that's right,' she said. She took his hand and squeezed it. 'I love it, in any case. I might give it a clean and see how it comes up.'

Caspar gave one of the quizzical looks she loved so much. His eyebrows turned up at the inner edges, his brow wrinkled, and he twisted his mouth into a comical expression. 'Yes. You've got time for that. I can see how, with the huge castle to deal with and a cookbook to plan, you'd like to add this to your to-do list.'

'The castle is *your* to-do list,' she said tartly. 'And this can be mine. Do you have any other plans for it?'

'Oh no,' he said, and smiled to show he didn't really mean that the castle was her responsibility. 'In fact, consider it yours.'

'I will, thanks,' she said lightly, but inside she thrilled just a little. She couldn't help responding very seriously to what he said.

Mine. The tower is mine. How wonderful.

Chapter Eight

The cherry-red sports car came flying up the driveway, whizzed beneath the gatehouse at reckless speed and came to a halt in front of the great door of the castle, sending up a spray of gravel in its wake.

'Atalanta's here!' Georgie shouted as she hurried past Caspar's study, having seen the car's dramatic arrival from the window of the main passage. Atalanta had been relatively understated and reserved until her divorce, from a communications billionaire who had famously never touched any of the delicious food she prepared but preferred a simple diet of sardines on toast. Her divorce payout should have been huge, but Atalanta, proud and independent, had walked away with very little, comparatively. Instead, she'd given her red hair a fierce new bolt of colour and her style a glamorous sex-kitten makeover. She'd spent some of what she'd received on her car, and the billionaire had bought her a mews house in Belgravia, modest by Belgravia standards.

'She's not exactly on her uppers,' Caspar would say when

Georgie talked about how much Atalanta needed money from her books and TV shows.

'No, but she ought to be very comfortable indeed after her marriage, but really she accepted far less than she should have, considering the way she lives,' Georgie replied. 'She's a bit chaotic. Always being surprised by tax bills.'

'Poor Atalanta,' Caspar said dryly. 'Do fetch me a plaster for my bleeding heart.' As a very organised person, he had little comprehension of or tolerance for chaotic people who, he felt, just needed to pull themselves together and try harder. 'Doesn't she have an accountant?'

'Several, I think. That's part of the problem. Anyway, the billionaire was horrible,' Georgie said stoutly. 'She put up with him for far longer than she should have because she's so lovely.'

'You're her champion. But you don't have to fix Atalanta's problems, you know. She's a grown-up and responsible for herself.'

'Of course,' Georgie would say, but secretly she would feel very responsible for Atalanta's problems. Even though Atalanta was famous and successful and endowed with talent and beauty, she often gave the impression of being needy and helpless, and of being in awe of Georgie's abilities. It wasn't just Georgie's, either. She had seen Atalanta charm dozens of people, from juniors and TV show runners, to media moguls and high-powered agents. Before long, they would be eating from her hand and offering to get her whatever she wanted or needed. Georgie felt huge pressure to provide all of the answers that Atalanta required, smooth out her problems and guarantee her the next project that would keep the coffers filled. She knew logically that it would not be a disaster if Atalanta could not holiday on Mustique, but there was something about the way Atalanta's green eyes would fill with tears as she explained in a shaking voice that she desperately, desperately needed this little break; it was the only thing holding her together and keeping her sane in a world of trouble and pain. Georgie's tender heart could not help being touched. She was moved. And she would do all she could to help.

Georgie opened the huge front door to see Atalanta climbing out of her sports car, pushing her sunglasses back into her long red hair to get a better look at the house. She was wearing black-and-white checked cigarette pants, a tight turquoise sweater and red ballet pumps, and looked as though she had just stepped out of a production of *Grease*. Getting out of the car on the other side was her assistant, anxious and white-faced.

'Oh my god!' shouted Atalanta, staring up at the castle, her hands on her hips. 'What the hell? What the absolute hell?'

Her cut-glass accent undercut her comic-book hair and fifties clothes, and gave her gravitas. *Why should that be?* Georgie wondered. Somehow Atalanta, in her retro fancy dress, was taken far more seriously by people than Georgie was, despite her understated yet stylish jeans, white shirt and navy cashmere, all of which made her look like common sense itself.

'You made it,' Georgie said brightly, coming quickly down

the steps. She embraced Atalanta, getting the full waft of Chanel No. 5 and the thick, powdery scent of cosmetics. She felt the soft, slippery waxiness of Atalanta's bright red lipstick touch her cheeks. 'How was the journey?'

'Fine,' Atalanta said carelessly. 'Though Jane found it a bit hairy, didn't you, Jane?'

Her assistant nodded, still looking pale. 'I didn't like that bit where you drove on the wrong side of the road for a while.'

'Just a bit of queue jumping,' Atalanta said airily. 'You know how I hate queues.'

'I think that traffic queues are not the kind you're allowed to jump,' Georgie said, and Jane looked grateful.

'What on earth have you been doing, hiding this from me?' demanded Atalanta, gazing back at the castle. 'When did you turn into Lady Muck, you dark horse?'

Georgie laughed. 'It's silly, isn't it? Caspar inherited it from his uncle.'

'You're not Lady Something now, are you?' enquired Atalanta, and Georgie thought she discerned the faintest anxiety in the question and guessed that Atalanta might be worried that Georgie had been promoted in such a way that she, Atalanta, might find it harder to boss Georgie around.

'No. Just Mrs Wakefield, same as always.'

'Oh.' Atalanta sounded relieved and then said quickly, 'What a shame, you should be a duchess to swan around here! Never mind. Do give us the tour!'

'Let's get a cup of tea or something first, then I'll show you around.' Georgie smiled at Jane, who was already tapping away on one of her two mobile phones. 'Do you need the Wi-Fi?'

'Yes, please,' Jane said gratefully.

'Come on. Let's go inside and get sorted.'

Caspar popped out to say hello but didn't linger. Georgie took Atalanta and Jane to freshen up and then made them mugs of tea that they could easily carry on the tour. In the kitchen, Atalanta went into a rapture.

'Oh, Georgie, just look at this place! It's like something from the National Trust! It's amazing. Oh, I love it. What a place to cook.'

'It is wonderful,' Georgie said, seeing the old place afresh and realising she had already grown used to its beauty and proportions. She no longer even noticed the vast size of the fireplace or the age of the kitchen range when she put the kettle on in the mornings. 'It's just a touch on the large side. I don't find it all that easy for rustling things up, in a funny way. It's all so spread out.'

Atalanta burst into a peal of laughter. 'You are funny! This is the kitchen of *dreams*, Georgie! The kitchen of dreams. So much space.' She ran a hand along the countertop. 'So Downton. Love it.'

Georgie remembered how rarely Atalanta cleared up after herself and realised that she probably envisaged herself simply making mess after mess, moving to a fresh spot without ever worrying about filling up the surface. No wonder that was part of Atalanta's kitchen of dreams. A cohort of cleaners and washer-uppers no doubt also featured.

Atalanta wandered to the range from where Georgie had just taken the kettle to make the tea. 'How on earth do you cook on this?'

'Trial and error, really. Instinct.'

Atalanta inspected it. 'No temperature gauges. I don't think I could do without my gorgeous appliances. So straightforward and easy. These days I can run them all from my phone, easy as pie.'

Atalanta had a range of amazing ovens, including sous vide and steam, as well as induction hobs and gas rings, all controllable to the last degree.

'I would have thought the same once,' Georgie said. 'And yet, it's strangely freeing without all the dials. The oven is always hot. You just put in your roasting tin and cook. Or move your pan around the hotplate to slow it down or speed it up.'

She was almost surprised to hear herself say this, as she had mourned the lack of modern cooking equipment at first, and had considered the range distinctly second best, if not third best. And yet now, she realised, helped along by the recipes in her book that never mentioned temperature or even cared much about quantities or even the ingredients themselves, she could see that there was another way to cook that wasn't about exact amounts and slavishly followed temperatures. There was something that was just . . . cooking.

She had a sudden flash of memory. She was seven years old and her sister Pippa, only five, was crying with hunger, her nose running and her mouth turned down.

'Don't worry, Pippa, I'll make you some tea.'

She'd used a chair to climb on the countertop and open a cupboard and from there she had taken a tin of beans. She had opened the freezer beneath the fridge and found a squashed packet of fish fingers. How had she opened the beans? How had she known how to turn on the oven? Somehow the beans had heated in a saucepan, the fish fingers had crisped up on the tray she'd put them on. They had fallen ravenously on the simple meal, slopped messily by Georgie onto their plastic plates. Pippa had stopped crying. Georgie had felt so proud even though she knew there would be trouble when Patsy got home. But they'd at least been full, and the dreadful hunger had gone away.

Cooking. An instinct. Driven by need.

Atalanta was wandering away from the range and looking at the rest of the kitchen. 'Don't get too used to freestyling it,' she said over her shoulder to Georgie. 'The punters need their info. We can't just say "cook till it's done". Very unprofessional.'

Georgie thought of her recipe book, which said exactly that, and decided she would wait until the right moment before she brought it up.

Jane wanted to skip the tour so that she could concentrate on her emails, so Georgie showed her to Lady Wakefield's morning room, which Atalanta trilled over, loving the frills and florals.

'Is this where you work now?' she asked as Georgie gave Jane the password. 'With this marvellous view?'

'Yes. I know I'm lucky,' Georgie said, and felt it suddenly very strongly. She had hated the whole idea of the castle so violently and for so long that she had forgotten how very special it was to live in a place like this. Atalanta seemed to be looking at her with a new respect, as though Georgie had somehow and outrageously trumped the mews house in Belgravia. 'If you're settled, Jane, we'll leave you to it. Come on, Atalanta, I'll show you the rest.'

She took Atalanta first to the great hall, leading her into the huge space, with its ornate fireplace and the torso of armour gleaming in the alcove and the great oil painting of Charles II's return. The water damage on the plaster ceiling wasn't too noticeable in the gloom.

Atalanta stopped just inside, gasped and then gaped. 'Oh my . . . *Crumbs*, Georgie. Just crumbs. Honestly. You could hold a huge party here, it would be magnificent.' She whirled into the large space, dancing over the great flagstones in her red ballet pumps. 'In fact . . . perhaps we can launch the new show from here! What a room! I love it!' She turned and twirled and finally threw herself onto one of the red velvet sofas. 'Is this really all yours?'

'It's Caspar's. And you know what these places are like – they don't belong to anyone. They seem to belong to the future, more than anything else. Everyone seems to feel a massive obligation to pass them on, like a sort of dreadful pass-the-parcel that no one wants to be landed with when it all goes pear-shaped.'

Atalanta laughed. 'Then you must make the most of it while the parcel is in your lap and it hasn't disintegrated.'

'It is rather disintegrating, to be honest.'

Just then, the door that opened to the courtyard clanged

as the iron bolt was lifted up, then creaked as it opened, and a figure was silhouetted against the light outside.

'What is the meaning of this?' it demanded in a German accent.

'Viktoria! Hello.' Georgie was flustered. She had entirely forgotten about Viktoria as a real person rather than just an unpleasant idea, not having seen anything of her for days.

Viktoria marched into the room, looking majestic in a red silk kaftan embroidered with black roses and black high heels. Her dark brown hair was whisked up into a beehive, and her face was fully made up, her lips post-box red. 'I was in the bath,' she declared, 'when the most awful noise went off below me.'

Atalanta snorted. 'That does sound funny!'

Viktoria sent an icy glance in her direction. 'Who are you? I am talking about the explosion that went off under me!'

Atalanta laughed harder and tried to stifle it. 'Sorry, sorry . . . ignore me.'

'I'm sorry, Viktoria, I have no idea what you mean,' Georgie said helplessly.

Viktoria stiffened and said coldly, 'I'm obviously being very comical. However, it was no laughing matter to me. I was in the bath – it is directly over the gate. And I hear something approaching at a great speed, very loudly, like a jet plane. But it doesn't go over me – it goes under! I heard it explode through the gate, and it was completely terrifying. I screamed. I thought the gatehouse would be destroyed. It was not at all funny. And when I was finally able, I looked out of the window and saw that red thing parked by the house.' She sniffed. 'This would not have been allowed when Archie and I were in residence. It's completely disrespectful.'

Georgie didn't know what to say or how Viktoria expected her to make amends.

Atalanta stood up, her laughter conquered and a contrite look on her face. 'It was my fault entirely. That's my very silly little car. I must apologise to you . . . er . . .'

'Lady Wakefield,' Viktoria said, still stiff.

Georgie could see that Atalanta was turning her charm on full. 'Lady Wakefield. My humble apologies. I drove recklessly. I had no idea that the gate was so narrow and certainly not that there was someone in the bath overhead! How horrid for you to have me make that racket. No wonder you were startled. I am so, so sorry.'

Viktoria looked a little mollified. 'Well. Thank you. And you are?'

'Atalanta Young.' Atalanta stepped forward, one hand out, her smile dazzling, projecting her full star persona.

Viktoria stared at her and frowned. 'I think I have heard of you.'

'Atalanta's a famous television chef,' offered Georgie. She hadn't told most of the family of her connection with Atalanta, preferring to keep it fairly quiet for the sake of Atalanta's reputation. 'She's visiting us.'

'Oh. Oh yes. I knew I had heard your name.' Viktoria unbent a little and managed a smile. She took Atalanta's hand and shook it. 'Pleased to meet you.'

Atalanta focused her full attention on Viktoria and purred, 'The pleasure is all mine!'

Viktoria stood a moment longer, a touch of uncertainty about her of a kind Georgie had never seen. 'Well. As long it doesn't happen again.'

'It won't. I will be quiet as a mouse next time. You won't hear me at all. I promise. And I do apologise again. Really.'

'Thank you.' Viktoria turned to Georgie and said with a touch of her usual imperiousness, 'Please try to keep any other visitors under control, Georgie. You are supposed to be the chatelaine now, not the circus master!' Then she turned on her heel with a billow of red silk and went back out through the door, which clanged shut behind her.

'Oh, how hilarious,' Atalanta said. 'Is she a vampire or something? She's straight out of Transylvania!'

'No . . . she's Caspar's step-great-aunt.'

'Brilliant, like something from *The Munsters*. I'm surprised she could hear the car through her coffin.'

'That's a bit mean.'

'Well, really. What a fuss. I thought I'd die laughing when she was talking about her explosions down below.'

'She's less amusing to Caspar, I'm afraid. She's moved into the gatehouse and won't leave.'

'Just whizz back and forth underneath in a car a few times a day, and she'll soon be off,' Atalanta said with a laugh. 'Now show me the rest of your castle, Mrs Chatelaine, and then we can have a chat about work.'

Georgie showed Atalanta over more of the house, but once they had seen the grandest rooms, Atalanta lost interest. She wasn't bothered about the upstairs, or the garden beyond

170

looking out at the moat. Georgie had been planning to show her the East Tower, hoping to convey some of her excitement at its beauty and potential, but now she saw that Atalanta would probably only see a dirty old wreck, so she decided to keep it to herself. Instead, she took them back to the panelled drawing room, tasteful and comfortable as decorated by Viktoria, and they sat down on the pink silk sofa with fresh tea.

'Now, darling Georgie,' Atalanta said solemnly. She had draped herself in a cashmere throw from the back of the sofa as it was cold, and its pastel pink looked striking against her red hair. 'We need to thrash out this new idea. It's urgent. I need some cash. If we don't come up with something soon, we'll have to wait another year to pitch ideas, and you know how fickle the public is. The latest bakery show winner will get their own series and there won't be anything left for poor little me. I know you're all comfortable now, living in your glamorous and luxurious castle, but I don't want to starve!' Atalanta smiled sweetly while Georgie damped down her indignation at this completely false picture of their circumstances. 'So what is your big idea?'

Georgie took the recipe book from the table next to the sofa where she had put it in readiness and handed it to Atalanta. 'This. This is my idea.'

Atalanta frowned, looking distinctly unimpressed as she looked at the battered old book, and Georgie started talking. She talked about the way that the recipe book created a vivid picture of domestic life in the house, a way to touch and taste the past. She talked about the way that, in these uncertain modern times, gripped by financial strife and health emergencies, the past was a safer, happier place. She talked of the joy of household economy in a cost-of-living crisis – not wartime rationing or deprivation and misery, but using what was available, fresh and local, and of connecting to a past that loved the flavours of almond, rose and honey.

'Here is my idea,' Georgie said. 'Your next cookbook is inspired by the cooking of the past, based on the real recipes in my book. We could even film it here. An episode for each era, perhaps. You could wear the appropriate costume and we could set the kitchen for each period. Continuity and change in the kitchen. *Atalanta in the Castle*. Something like that.'

Atalanta looked thoughtful. She turned the book over. 'Is there anything decent we can make in here?'

Georgie felt slightly exasperated. 'Did you see any recipes?'

'I can't read them, darling, such strange writing. But I suppose that even if the book is useless, we can always fake it.'

'The book is not useless. It's fascinating. I've seen programmes about historical cooking, and documentaries about Mrs Beaton and all the rest – but I've never seen a programme that shows you how to cook old recipes in a modern way.'

Atalanta made a face. 'Is it sexy enough? That's my worry. We have to convince television executives, you know. They worry about advertising and viewing figures. It has to strike a chord. Italy is sexy. Greece is sexy.'

'You don't want to do those places!'

'Because they're already done to death, I said.'

'Look, let me write the pitch for you. I'll draft some recipes and we can try them out. If you like them, we can cook a dinner party for all the major players and let them try the food themselves. I wouldn't suggest this if I didn't think we could make it work. I haven't been wrong so far, have I?'

Atalanta put the book down and picked up her cup to sip at her Darjeeling. After she had thought for a moment, she said, 'All right, darling. I like it. It's different. I love the castle. There's plenty of room for filming. Write the pitch and we'll go from there.'

Georgie was exhausted after Atalanta had left. She felt deeply sorry for Jane, who had climbed with obvious reluctance into the red sports car, clutching her mobile phones and a spiralbound pad covered in notes.

'Drive carefully,' Georgie called, hoping that it might stop any reckless overtaking but knowing it was probably futile.

Atalanta had waved from the window and then naughtily roared twice at top speed around the front quad, sending up waves of gravel, before crawling at a snail's pace under the gatehouse, and then accelerating away down the drive, beeping wildly on the horn.

Georgie waved her off, laughing despite herself. Atalanta was annoying but she was always amusing, and no one could stay cross with her for long. Besides, the way she had charmed Viktoria showed that perhaps the older woman was not immune to persuasion one way or another.

Caspar came out of his study with a cartoonish expression of exaggerated fear on his face. 'Is the coast clear? Is she gone?'

'It was fine. But gosh . . . she's draining.'

'That's why I've come out. To make you a gin and tonic and hear all about it.'

'It's a bit early for that . . . but all right, you've talked me into it.'

They sat in the last of the afternoon sunshine in the drawing room, and Georgie told him about their discussion. 'I couldn't persuade her straight out, but she is open to it. I'll need to come up with my pitch. And it will have to be brilliant.'

'You can do it,' Caspar said encouragingly. 'I have complete faith.'

'And how was your day?'

He sighed. 'Depressing. The roof. I've been discussing the kind of figures you hear about when people win the lottery. But going out, not coming in.'

'That's worrying,' Georgie said.

'It certainly is.' Caspar took a sip of his drink and stretched out his long legs, crossing them in front of him and suddenly perking up. 'Hey, did you say Atalanta thinks it would be a good idea to film here?'

Georgie nodded. 'We mentioned it. There's plenty of room for all the lights and cameras and so on. Plus, all the genuine antique atmosphere.' She smiled ironically. 'Although we could always fake that.'

'But . . . the television company . . . they'd pay us, wouldn't they? To use the kitchen? To film here?'

'I suppose they would.'

Caspar looked delighted. 'But that's marvellous! It could

be the answer to the roof problem! Or part of it. Can't you see?' He sat up straight, and gazed directly at Georgie. 'You clever, clever thing, Georgie. You might have stumbled on the answer to Atalanta's problem and my problem at the same time!'

'Well, that's good. No pressure,' she joked weakly. 'As long as I can conjure up the perfect programme.'

'Oh, you will,' Caspar said confidently, looking happy and more relaxed. 'I have complete faith in you.'

Georgie sat back on the sofa, feeling suddenly overwhelmed. This morning, Caspar had said she shouldn't feel obliged to fix Atalanta's problems. Now she was fixing those, and his as well. She felt as though she might buckle under all this.

This is exactly what I didn't want to happen, she thought anxiously. *I knew the castle would be too much for us. I knew it would fall on me. Oh dear. What will I do?*

Georgie couldn't sleep that night. Her sleep was always the first thing to go when she was worried, her anxiety sparking her awake at exactly 3 a.m., as usual. How did worry know what time it was? It was a mystery. Her anxious brain decreed that the hours between three and five would be a roller coaster ride of adrenalin and exhaustion as her thoughts raced in ceaseless panic; it was some kind of rule.

And how is that going to help matters? she wondered.

Caspar slumbered deeply as usual, perhaps even with a little more ease than lately, now that Georgie had supposedly found a way out of the financial mess.

Georgie lay there, worried about the idea she'd had and the responsibility of pulling it off, and then worried about not sleeping. Restless and getting hot, she slid out of bed and went downstairs. The house was more than eerie in the darkness and she disliked the sensation of padding through it in the silent blackness, flicking on lights as she went to banish shadows to the corners. It was like being in a vast and deserted hotel. The stuff of nightmares and horror stories.

'It's ridiculous!' she said out loud. 'Utterly ridiculous that two people should be living here quite alone. Except for Viktoria, of course.' That made her laugh, as she thought of the absurdity of the situation: two people in this enormous house wanted a third person – currently holed up over the gate – gone, because she made them feel uncomfortable.

At least laughing at this situation took her mind off wandering in the castle alone at night. She made her way down to the drawing room where she'd left the recipe book after her talk with Atalanta. She flicked on the overhead light and the room was illuminated, seeming somehow more ordinary than it was when the lamps were lit. It felt like a stage set in a theatre when the actors and audience are long gone, the spotlights and filters are turned off, and just the dull house lights are left.

Georgie went to the side table where the recipe book sat, old and brittle, and sat down on the sofa next to it. She picked up the book and riffled through it again, wondering exactly how she would face the challenge of distilling it into both a modern cookery book that people would actually want to cook from, and a successful television series. And yet, it was such a good idea. She was fascinated by every page. At the very end of the book were some recipes that were obviously wartime ones, such as carrot soufflé, which seemed to be mostly grated carrot with a hint of fat and one egg to bind it together. Georgie hoped it was nicer than it sounded. The recipe for mock fish cutlets made her sad: ground rice and mashed potato, flavoured with anchovy sauce and simmered in milk.

Who wrote all these recipes? she wondered. *The handwriting at the end is another one entirely.*

Opening the book again at the front cover, she noticed for the first time that there was a list of names. The earliest said *Scribed by Wm Bailey for Elizabeth, Lady Wakefield.*

So the first lady of the house didn't write it out herself. Perhaps that explained the very neat, if archaic writing, and the regularity of the script and recipes. Georgie scanned the rest of the names: all Wakefields. The house had been in the same family all that time. But who knew how they were related? Each one had a life and a story and a connection.

She looked at the names at the end of the list:

Kathryn Wakefield

Constance Wakefield

M & R Wakefield

That was odd. A pair of Wakefields this time.

And then the last name on the list, quite unexpected and quite different from the others. Not a Wakefield this time, and not written in a flowing hand but pressed deeply into the page in capital letters.

ETTI BOULE

Georgie stared at it, frowning. That was a surprise. Who was Etti and why was her name written in that way? Why was she not a Wakefield?

She felt an unpleasant shiver down her spine. Closing the book, she put it back on the side table and, suddenly tired, thought she would go back to bed.

As soon as she had decided, she wanted nothing more than to be warm and safe with Caspar. She hurried out of the room, switching off the lights as she went upstairs, speeding up until she was scampering into their bedroom and closing the door behind her, glad to be back.

It's nothing, she told herself as she climbed back into bed. *My overactive imagination.*

She remembered her teacher Mrs Arthur telling her that she had an unusually vivid imagination.

'It's part of what makes you so sensitive. You can imagine everything very clearly. But you have to be careful. You can feel the pain in the world as intensely as the pleasure, and you can think your way into other people's lives with very little trouble at all. At least, from what I see. And you need to be careful that you know the difference between imagination and real life.'

Georgie had not really understood at the time. She assumed everyone felt and saw as she did. But now she knew that was not the case.

Why do I feel uneasy? she asked herself as she pressed against the smooth warmth of Caspar's back. She thought of the recipe book and how she had seen it as a golden gift from the universe.

But, she reminded herself, *nothing is wholly good. There is always a dark side.*

Etti Boule.

Something about that name gave her an unpleasant sensation, reminding her of things she didn't want to remember. Why should that be?

She pushed it from her mind by trying to recall the exact recipe for her capon in broth, and as she remembered beating cream into ground almonds, her mind drifted and she fell asleep.

Chapter Nine

1939

The announcement of war seemed like an anticlimax at first in terms of any actual fighting. The boys stayed up late looking for Germans for three nights, but there was nothing.

There was so much to know, though. The wireless was a constant stream of announcements telling everyone what they could and couldn't do. But at least there was a crackle in the air at last, a sense that people were keen to get on with doing something. The blackouts were something. Joining the army was another. There was a rush to organise, and step up, and start helping in small ways. Aunt Constance had taken on the kitchen garden and was scanning seed catalogues to order all manner of vegetables. Imogen had been to town on the bus to inquire about what she could do.

'Why can't we stand in crowds?' Rosalind asked. She was knitting, making minesweeper gloves out of knotted string, which she had taken to with gusto. 'I don't see how that affects anything.'

Miranda was working much more slowly on a balaclava. Everyone was knitting, it seemed. The vicar's wife had collected boxes and boxes of gloves and scarves and socks and it was only a week since war had been declared. 'I suppose more people are easier to spot, and more will be wounded if they get bombed.'

'I can't think when I did last stand in a crowd,' Rosalind remarked.

'That's because we're country mice. The town mice are in crowds all the time.'

Rosalind glanced over at her with a frown. 'Are you all right?'

'Of course. Why do you ask?'

'You just seem . . . preoccupied.'

'There's a war on. It's a lot to think about.'

'Well . . . all right, if you say so. But you seem rather different at the moment. You will tell me . . . if there's something wrong?'

'Of course.' Miranda sounded firm but she felt dreadful. She had been labouring under the weight of the secret of the tower and its occupant. Usually she would tell Rosalind just about everything but now she could not tell her the biggest secret of all. Sometimes she felt she would burst with it. Aunt Constance had asked her to be brave and strong and wait until she said anything, but it was getting more and more difficult. She felt magnetically attracted to the tower and yet would not permit herself to go near it. Now it was Rosie who slept soundly and Miranda who lay awake, staring into the utter darkness of the blackout and wondering what to do.

It had been a welcome distraction when Grandfather made his announcement that morning at breakfast.

'We are going to have a visitor,' he said at the breakfast table.

'Who?' the young ones demanded, excited.

Miranda said nothing, but felt a swell of excited nausea in her stomach as she suddenly wondered if they were going to reveal the presence of the mysterious Mrs Black.

Grandfather consulted the telegram he was holding. 'It's a Mr Humphries and it's all rather thrilling.'

No one made a sound but there was a sense of anticlimax. Mr Humphries didn't sound very thrilling.

'He is from the Natural History Museum in London. Mr Humphries is going to accompany a collection of the museum's exhibits that will be sent here for safekeeping. They wrote to me about this years ago; I'd forgotten all about it. The whole blessed lot will be arriving on Friday.' He looked thoughtful, squinting through his good eye at the telegram. 'They don't say what it is. Just that there will be some dozens of cases.'

'Could it be a dinosaur?' Toby piped up, his face red. Mr Humphries might be dull, but a dinosaur was not.

'I suppose it might be, they don't say what's coming.'

'A dinosaur!' Toby breathed. 'Will they put it up in the hall?'

Miranda burst out laughing. 'Bless your heart, they won't be putting it on display! How silly!'

Rosalind gave her brother a kind look at his hurt expression. 'I imagine whatever they send will be in crates and parcelled up very safely so it stays protected until the war is over.'

Grandfather said, 'And he's going to stay. He's going to carry on working here, apparently. He'll keep doing his research.' He smiled suddenly. 'Fancy that. Another chap. It might be fun.'

Imogen sighed. 'What a pain. That's the last thing we need. Why isn't he going off to join the army like everyone else?'

Aunt Constance said, 'Quite. It's ridiculous. As though we can't be trusted to guard a few crates. I suppose it's a protected profession.' She sighed. 'And on top of everything else, that's another mouth to feed. I suppose we ought to be grateful that there is so much from Fortnum's. I'm sure he'll appreciate tinned quail no end.' She opened a letter beside her plate, read it quickly and tsked with irritation. 'What an annoyance!'

'What is?' asked Grandfather.

'St Margaret's has been requisitioned for the war and is closing until further notice. I was about to look out your uniforms, girls, and now there's no school to go to.'

'Oh, what a shame,' Rosalind said, though she looked far from unhappy. 'I suppose we'll just have to stay right here. All together. Nice and safe.'

'Stay here indefinitely?' Miranda said with an edge of panic to her voice. 'I was going to take up typing this year. Mrs Brooke promised I could learn shorthand as well, so that I can start training to be a journalist.'

'Well, St Margaret's is closed for the duration. The nearest suitable school you could go to is in Brampton. That's twelve miles away,' Aunt Constance said thoughtfully. 'How on earth will you get there now that Carter's gone off to sign up? Perhaps Leonard can take you.'

The girls had previously been driven to school every day by Carter, the driver and butler, but he had left, along with all but the most ancient gardeners. His son Alf had returned to the village, having been rejected for active service, but he couldn't drive.

'I'm not using my petrol to drive you chits to school,' Grandfather said. 'I only got my ration books from the post office yesterday. They've been damned fast about limiting the petrol and I got only one unit of motor spirit. That's a gallon of petrol in normal lingo. My old motor is thirsty and I'm not burning up all that precious fuel like that ferrying you about.'

'We have to go to school, Aunt Constance,' Miranda said quickly. 'Otherwise, it's a victory for the enemy. Disrupting women's education is exactly the kind of thing that would please Hitler the most.'

'That is a very good point, Miranda. The boys can still be taught here or in the village. But you big girls must study.'

Imogen looked up. 'Actually, even the village school is going to have difficulties. Most of the teaching staff are going off to join up. Mr Clayesmore has talked to me about becoming a teacher to help the war effort. Perhaps Miranda and Rosalind could help as well.'

'It's a possibility.' Aunt Constance folded up her letter. 'Something will have to be done. You twins can't simply sit out the war in the schoolroom doing nothing at all. I will consider.'

'Talking of school,' Imogen said, getting up, 'we're late to start. Come on, Toby, come on, Archie. Upstairs. We've got spelling and French this morning.'

The boys groaned but got up obediently to follow their sister. Once they'd gone, Miranda said, 'Lucky Imogen. She's eighteen. There's going to be plenty for her to do. She went into town and got lots of leaflets. So many exciting things. We're going to be stuck here with children and dinosaurs. Not you, of course, Grandfather. Actual dinosaurs.'

Grandfather wasn't listening but Aunt Constance raised an eyebrow.

'There'll be plenty for you to do, Miranda, don't worry about that.'

Miranda went quiet, suddenly remembering the secret she carried and wondering if Aunt Constance was somehow referring to it.

'Perhaps you could teach yourself to cook. That might be something you could contribute to the household.'

'Yes, perhaps I could,' Miranda said meekly, and Rosalind looked over at her in surprise, not used to Miranda being so pliable.

Aunt Constance stood up. 'And I'll look into a correspondence course for you in typing and shorthand. How would that be?'

'Yes please,' Miranda said. She felt suddenly grateful to her aunt, who had heard what she'd said and was going to help if she could.

'Don't worry on my account,' Rosalind said quickly, evidently not keen on the idea of learning at home. 'I'm going to help Imogen with teaching if she starts at the village school.'

'Good idea. I'm sure there are many ways you can be useful. Now. I must get on. I'll be in my study if you need me.'

It was only the next day that the lorry from the Natural History Museum came roaring up the drive and stopped in front of the great hall. Men in overalls and very heavy boots got out and pulled open the doors, while one of them, a slender, gentle-looking man in round owlish glasses, neat in a tweed suit and woollen tie, got out with a clipboard and wandered up to meet Grandfather, who was standing in front of the huge doors, watching the goings-on.

The clipboard man had fair hair cut like a schoolboy's, and behind his glasses his eyes were brown, the same colour as his chestnut-brown moustache. He looked very young, although he must be close to thirty. He went over to Grandfather. 'Hello, sir. Arthur Humphries. We're from the Natural History Museum.'

'You do surprise me,' Grandfather said dryly.

'I'm glad you're expecting us,' Humphries said quickly. 'We're very pleased you've agreed to house our specimens for the duration.'

Grandfather fixed him with a steely look through his one good eye. 'It's lucky your director approached me first, Humphries. After you lot came along, I had all sorts. The V&A wanted to put most of their sculptures in my hall. I had to turn down the British Museum, the National Gallery – well, I did offer them the attics as paintings are a deal lighter than what you want to store. But they said no, they had some more suitable places. They're worried about roofs leaking, and mice and bats. That's no surprise, I suppose. My floor is the thing and I promised it to you. The V&A were most disappointed.'

'We're so grateful, Sir Leonard,' Humphries said politely, keeping his nerve in front of Grandfather's brusqueness. 'And your floor is perfect.'

'No cellars. No foundations either, come to that. Just good solid lias floors sunk into the dirt. Nothing is going to fall through those, Mr Humphries.'

'That's the idea. Now . . .' Mr Humphries consulted his clipboard. 'We'll bring in the heaviest crates first. Can I please see the hall? I need to plan the disposition.'

Grandfather led Mr Humphries into the hall, from where all the furniture had been moved by Alf and a village man the previous afternoon, to leave the vast space quite empty. They all filed in after them, to watch the mysterious planning.

'I'd forgotten how large it is,' Mr Humphries said, looking around. 'It's longer than a cricket pitch. But rather darker than I remembered?' He looked up at the huge windows, now covered in black boards.

'My sister rightly feels we need to protect our precious windows in case of aerial attack. We've all heard that there are serious concerns around a German invasion in the very near future. No doubt we expect an amphibious attack but there will be attacks from the air as well, that's quite certain. Tell me, Humphries, have you heard any more of the civil defence league? I'm very interested in that, very interested indeed.'

'Well, no, I haven't, I'm afraid, it's not my area of expertise . . .'

'It should be everyone's area of expertise,' Grandfather said sternly. 'Every able-bodied man has a duty to protect his country.'

Mr Humphries flushed. 'Of course. I just mean, I've been devoting myself to the conservation of the museum's treasures – the *nation's* treasures.'

Grandfather looked less fierce. 'Ah. Yes. I understand. No doubt we will learn more while you're staying here. Do you have any luggage?'

'I'm going back to London today with the lorries, then I'll return on the train with my suitcases.'

'Very well. Let's get started then.'

The boys seemed very excited by the arrival of dinosaurs even though they were boxed up, and raced about getting underfoot. Miranda had not seen her brothers so energetic and cheerful for many years, and she enjoyed the sound of their laughter and chatter in the hall as they engaged the museum men in conversation.

Miranda and Rosalind took out tea to the movers, who were startled by the frequent reappearances of Miranda and Rosalind until they realised they were identical twins.

'Uncanny,' one said, taking his cup from Rosalind. 'There's no telling you apart.'

'You can when you get used to us,' Miranda said, as she came up with another tray.

'It's very odd,' the man said again, shaking his head. 'Like seeing double. And I'm not going to have time to get used to you, miss. But thanks for the tea.'

The workmen were soon sweating in the heat of the day as they heaved the great crates into the hall. The crates were in some cases ten feet by ten feet, and clearly holding things of great weight. Other cases were slender and evidently lighter.

'What's in them?' Toby asked, when a pair of men went by carrying a large crate between them. 'Can you tell us? Is there a Tyrannosaurus Rex? Not a whole one, but pieces?'

'We don't know,' one replied. 'Could be anything. Could be a complete lion or tiger or something.'

'Gosh,' breathed Toby, wide-eyed and clearly longing to be allowed to look inside. But there was no chance of that, the crates were firmly nailed shut.

'May we keep one?' Archie asked hopefully. 'After the war, just for our very own?'

'That's not for me to say. But I doubt it.'

Crates were stacked against the walls, their labels impenetrable to the children. More and more came in, under the careful instruction of Mr Humphries.

Eventually when the lorries were almost empty, Mr Humphries looked about and frowned. 'All that's left are my personal research crates. It's going to be far too dark for me in here. Is there anywhere lighter where I can work?'

It was decided that the small dining room, hardly ever used and without much character, would be the place for Mr Humphries's work. Several crates marked with his name were placed against the wall once a bookcase had been moved out of the way, and the table was shifted to provide a desk for him, illuminated with a lamp from the sideboard.

'Perfect,' he said with satisfaction. 'This will be just the ticket.'

The lorries, empty now, except for the workforce and Mr Humphries, trundled off down the drive back to London. Imogen had chivvied the boys upstairs to get washed before their tea. Miranda and Rosalind were in the great hall, staring at the mountains of crates and boxes that glimmered faintly in the gloom. Lanterns had been lit around the room, but only one or two were still alight.

'It looks like a warehouse,' Rosalind remarked. 'Somehow I thought it would look a little more interesting.'

'Like a crypt.'

'Yes, or a strange collection of headstones. What do you think is in there?'

'Lots and lots of dead animals, birds and insects,' Miranda said crisply. 'Bones, skulls, skeletons, preserved bodies, stuffed bodies, fossilised bodies. Eggs, nests, teeth . . . I don't know. That kind of thing. What else would we get from the Natural History Museum?'

Rosalind looked even paler in the twilight of the hall. 'Oh dear. How horrible. I don't like to think of that at all! All that death!'

Miranda walked over to the nearest crate and touched it. 'Or we could think about it another way. It's preserved life. These things would have vanished if they weren't being kept like this. And perhaps all this past has got something to offer

190

us all for the future. The research and work they do must have some point, mustn't it?'

Rosalind shuddered. 'But skeletons, bones . . .'

'I wonder why we find them so frightening. The dead can't hurt us. It's the living that we ought to fear.'

They were quiet for a moment. Miranda thought about the fear that they all shared – invasions, bombers, cruelty, violence and death. It might come. Things were normal at the moment, but the very presence of these crates and boxes showed that the adult world was taking the possibility of those awful things very seriously. And somewhere in Europe, they were already happening.

'Perhaps you're right,' Rosalind said softly. 'I'm sure there's nothing to fear. It is eerie, though.'

'We'll get used to it,' Miranda said briskly. 'And we're going to have Mr Humphries here.' She wanted to change the subject, suddenly afraid that dwelling on morbid things might make Rosalind more prone to sleepwalking. She hadn't done it for a while and now that the house was so dark at night, without even moonlight to light the corridors, Miranda was afraid it would be more dangerous. 'Let's go upstairs.'

They turned and wandered out of the hall.

'Do you think he's going to live in the tower?' Rosalind asked as they went. 'And that's why Alf was getting it ready?'

'I don't know,' Miranda said stiffly. 'Perhaps.'

It was horrible to hide something from Rosie. But she didn't dare tell her what she knew – at least not yet.

'It's the obvious answer,' said her sister.

Rather than say anything about it, Miranda took her sister's hand. 'At least we'll have the excitement of a young man living here. Just fancy – a man who falls between the ages of eight and seventy-four. Perhaps one of us will fall in love with him.'

Rosalind laughed. 'He didn't look very romantic.'

'I expect our desperation will make him look like a hero to us. But perhaps we ought to let Imogen fall in love, as she's the eldest.'

'She wants to marry someone grand. I can't imagine she'll be interested in the man from the museum.'

'She might not be able to fight it.' Miranda put the back of her hand to her forehead and sighed dramatically. 'Oh, Mr Humphries! It's the way you hold your clipboard! I simply can't resist!'

'Miss Wakefield,' said Rosalind in as deep a voice as she could manage. 'The way you teach your brothers geography is divine. I am madly in love with you.'

They both giggled.

'Well, he's not coming back till Monday,' Miranda said, as they reached the stairs. 'So we'll have to wait until then to find out, won't we?'

The next morning, Alf Carter hitched Harris instead of Poppy to Aunt Constance's cart. Harris, a great Shire horse, was strong enough to pull a cartload as well as luggage.

'Why are we going there?' Miranda asked, after their aunt had told the twins to get ready to accompany her to the station.

'War work,' she said. 'And if you're not going to school, you can make yourselves useful.'

Although they complained, the journey was actually very enjoyable as they rolled along the lanes under the canopy of trees in the warm sunshine. There were fewer motor cars now, with petrol rationed, and it felt calm and restful as Harris clopped away.

The station was a different matter. It was bustling with women in coats and hats, looking forceful and determined as they organised their tables all along the platform. Among them were men with armbands that announced them to be reception officers.

The tables were covered variously in clothes and shoes, undergarments and pyjamas and dressing gowns of all types, caps and hats, coats, mittens and scarves. Others were covered in towels and face cloths; another set with tooth-brushes, toothpaste and bars of soap. Another table was more ominously devoted to combs and potions and a large hos-pital screen. Some nurses were stationed at that table, big red crosses on their white aprons. Other tables were attended by gentlemen and ladies with piles of paper and clipboards and a sign that announced *Billeting*. As well as the many women, there were station attendants, policemen and a contingent of nuns.

'What an enormous fuss!' Miranda said, her eyes round.

'This is the tail end. The evacuees started arriving last week,' Aunt Constance said. 'Just imagine all the organis-ing.' She seemed quite invigorated by it all and was as jolly as she'd been for a long time. 'Now come along, the train is due very shortly.'

'I thought they said don't stand about in crowds!' Rosalind said. 'This is a huge crowd.' Standing in front of a sign that announced that public train services were much reduced, she looked anxiously about.

'Don't worry,' Miranda said soothingly. 'This kind is fine.' She had noticed that Rosalind was becoming more nervous lately, obsessing over the new rules and worrying endlessly about where everyone was. She turned to look down the far end where there were tea urns steaming and burbling, and piles of rock cakes.

Rosalind's eyes were filled with tears. 'Oh, it's too bad. Are they really sending all these children away from their parents?'

Miranda went and took her hand. 'To keep them safe, Rosie.'

Rosalind's eyes overflowed and fat tears flowed down her face. 'But without their parents . . . I can't bear it.'

'I know. It's awful. But it won't be for long, just till the war's over. Look, here comes the train now!'

They could hear it before they saw it, the clanging wheels and the chunter of the steam, and then it rounded the curve of the track and the great black engine came into sight, a plume of white smoke flying back behind it. The bustle on the platform grew greater.

'Stand back, girls, you'll only be in the way,' shouted Aunt Constance, craning her neck to see the train over the crowd.

They stood obediently near the railings, grateful to be far

from the melee, and watched instead as the train slowed to a halt. Pale faces were pushed up against the windows, staring out. The guards went up and down opening doors, and more grown-ups emerged onto the already crowded platform, now accompanied by what seemed like a vast stream of children, of all ages, from tiny to tall and gangly. Each held a small case or a bag, or had a knapsack, each had a label tied to their coat or jacket, and each had a small box slung over one shoulder.

The girls watched as the train emptied and the task of allocation and organisation began. Aunt Constance disappeared into the crowd and made her way to the billeting table. The children were being made to stand in long queues, waiting to be processed by the ladies and their various tables. Miranda expected noise from that many youngsters but they were muted. There was some talking, and some crying, but most were solemn-faced or curious. So many different types of children.

'Are all the children in London here?' wondered Rosalind.

Miranda was observing them: small girls with ribbons in their hair, older girls in berets and buckle shoes, skinny boys in stout boots; freckled faces, pale ones, hungry ones. Many looked very poor, Miranda realised. They had so little with them.

Aunt Constance came back towards them, looking flustered. 'I'm in trouble,' she said. 'I wasn't supposed to come to the station. Billeting families for our village are supposed to be waiting at the village hall. All the children are going by bus. But I've found a nice pair of brothers and they're just doing their paperwork now. I thought a few boys would even things up a bit.'

Miranda had somehow not really believed that Aunt Constance, with her dislike of children, was truly going to offer a home to evacuees, but a few moments later, a lady in a green coat and a brown hat was shepherding two boys towards them.

'Here we are,' said the woman. 'This is Tom and Robbie Foster. Tom is nine and Robbie is seven.'

The boys were holding hands. They wore knitted shirts buttoned up to the collar under rough wool jackets and grey shorts above skinny legs. Both wore the same strong brown boots with laces, but they were patched, and the older boy's sole was flapping loose. They each had a knapsack and Miranda could see that the label on the older boy read: *LCC Evac III/367 Thomas Foster, 24 Clapham Road SW9.*

The woman continued. 'Now, boys, you'll be good for Miss Wakefield, won't you? She has a very special house for you to live in, I'm sure you'll enjoy it. Thank you, Miss Wakefield, we have all your details, you can go whenever you like.'

'Good. Now. Hello, young men,' Aunt Constance said briskly. The boys were staring at her and Miranda could see at once that her aunt's white hair and the customary britches and jacket over a shirt and scarf at her neck made her look unusual, perhaps even frightening. Both boys had the same brown eyes, scatter of freckles over their cheeks and soft brown hair neatly cut. They looked poor but they were clean. 'These are my nieces, Miranda and Rosalind. They are twins – you'll learn which is which in time. Now, let's get home and have some tea.'

The boys said nothing but continued to stare about them, their hands still tightly clutched together. Their fingers were white with gripping.

'Poor little things!' Rosalind said. 'Just imagine how their mother must be feeling.' Her blue eyes filled with tears.

'She is probably relieved they won't be killed by bombs,' Miranda said to cheer her up, but it didn't seem to work and Rosalind sniffed hard.

'Follow me!' said their aunt, and the boys obediently walked behind her as she strode out of the station. The girls followed. Aunt Constance walked briskly to the cart. As soon as the boys saw where she was headed, they stopped dead, and the girls nearly went into the back of them.

Aunt Constance reached the cart and turned, surprised that she was alone. She beckoned. 'Come along! Come on now.'

The boys didn't move. 'We're not going over there,' said the older one firmly. He had a tight, twangy London accent quite different from theirs.

'What nonsense, of course you are. Come along.' Aunt Constance went to swing herself up into the driver's seat but still no one moved.

'What's wrong?' Rosalind asked softly, crouching by the younger one.

'I ain't going near that thing,' he said in a high voice, pointing at Harris the Shire horse.

'I'm sure he looks fierce to you, but he's actually very gentle. He'll just pull the trap along for us.'

The youngest boy shook his head. His brother looked determined. 'We ain't getting on that cart,' he said.

'Don't they have horses in London?' asked Miranda. 'They must have!'

'Yes. But not that big and not all shaggy and furry like that one. He's a beast.'

No matter how they tried to shift the boys, they would not budge. There was a bus being loaded with all the other children that was going to take them to the village hall. The boys agreed to go on that, so the girls went with them and Aunt Constance, annoyed but seeing there was no other way, drove Harris back with the suitcases.

The bus rumbled back much quicker than the cart could make the journey. As they went, the girls observed the children, some excited, others blank-faced and evidently shocked to find themselves far from home, and some weeping tears of homesickness.

'You're right. I'm glad we've got some evacuees,' Rosalind said suddenly. 'We have so much room, it's perfect for boys. I think it will be very good for Toby and Archie.'

'Weren't they sweet yesterday with the museum men?'

'I haven't seen them that happy for ages. Now they'll have two friends as well.'

'More work for Imogen.'

'We must help her. She can't be a mother to four of them. It's not fair. That can be our war work for now, along with the knitting.'

Miranda looked out of the bus window. This war was going to dominate everything. It might mean the end of her own dreams. She'd hoped to be away from home in a year or so, living in London and finding some proper work, learning to be a journalist and starting to make something of her life. Now she would be stuck here in limbo for as long as it all took. She could guess that Rosie's tender heart was moved by all these poor scamps so far from home, and she'd be happy to join Imogen in mothering them all.

But she had wanted something more than that. Was it selfish to be upset?

There has to be a way, she thought, *to make more of my life even with a war on and being stuck at home. I just have to find it.*

Chapter Ten

Present Day

'Where do you want this, Georgie?' Sandy shouted across the kitchen. She had just finished plating up a huge flank of beef, which had been decorated in a riot of edible flowers; mostly marigolds in hues of orange and yellow, but also a border of dark purple, velvety pansies. Sandy had put the beef on one of the castle's great pewter platters, and surrounded it with curls of lamb's lettuce.

'Oh, Sandy, that looks magnificent!' Georgie said, with a look of gratitude. 'Put it in the alcove by the range to keep warm. Funny to think that is what they would have done the very first time they cooked it here, most likely.'

The kitchen was bustling with people helping to prepare the feast according to Georgie's careful instructions. Upstairs, the great hall was set for banqueting, with a long trestle table laid with more of the pewter ware – plates, dishes and goblets – as well as modern cutlery and glassware. On the great sideboard were glass decanters and jugs, holding wines and liqueurs of all types and flavours. That was all being tended to by another team of helpers, dressed in period costumes that Atalanta had insisted be ordered from Angels, the top costumier in London. Her own costume, which had come from the archives of the National Theatre, was a secret.

Georgie was still in jeans and a T-shirt as she oversaw the final preparations for the meal. The first guests would arrive in just over half an hour but there was still so much to be done. She had been working incredibly hard since Atalanta's visit, making a pitch for the book and programme, choosing and adapting and trialling recipes, and coming up with this evening's menu. Now at last it was close. The kitchen was full of delicious aromas. In the still room, jellies and junkets and syllabubs and possets were chilling. Bowls of fruits with more flowers and candied nuts were waiting their turn.

'Go up and get ready,' Sandy urged as she went past with the great flank of flowery beef. 'You've done all you can and I've got everything in hand.'

'You've been the perfect sous chef,' Georgie said with a smile.

'Thank you. Now go up and relax. Our work is nearly over but you've got another whole job to do with that lot arriving.'

'You're right, Sandy. I will.' Grateful for Sandy's chivvying, she put down her apron and headed for the kitchen stairs.

Caspar had been very impressed when she explained her plan to launch the new pitch for Atalanta. 'This is quite out of character for you, Georgie,' he said. 'A party on a grand scale. I always thought that was your idea of hell.'

'Oh, it's still my idea of hell,' she'd said, laughing, looking at him over the top of her tablet where she was typing more ideas over breakfast. 'But some hells are inevitable and this definitely is. We need to win over the TV executives and publishers if we want to get this programme made. And right now, it's all we have. So I'm putting everything into planning this dinner.'

'I'm still very proud of you,' he said. 'I know you hate having people in your home, hate crowds. And here you are, planning exactly that.'

Georgie was thoughtful as she took off her glasses. He was right. Once, this whole venture would have filled her with fear and trembling panic. Why had she felt able not just to handle it, but actually to suggest it? Dozens of people, a feast to prepare, even a costume to wear, Atalanta to impress. And yet, where was all the fear? Of course she was apprehensive. Pulling off an impressive meal for twenty was never easy, let alone one that was entirely of her own devising, even with the inspiration of the recipe book. But something had altered in her outlook.

'It's strange, isn't it?' she said slowly. 'I feel as though things have changed a bit since we came to the castle. For both of us. It's not what I expected at all. You're less calm, and I'm calmer. You're more restless and frazzled and I seem to be braver, in some silly way. Perhaps it's the very fact that the castle isn't mine. I don't know.' She shrugged. 'It's very odd.'

'It is odd,' Caspar agreed. He rubbed a hand through his hair, leaving it standing upright in patches. 'And I think you're right. You're the one who dreaded coming here, and

I was all for it. And yet, I'm finding that life is much harder than I expected and you seem to be flourishing.' He smiled at her. 'I'm very pleased for you, of course. But I'm not particularly enjoying feeling so hassled.'

'It's probably just a phase,' Georgie comforted him. 'We'll go back to our old selves, like memory foam.'

'Sooner the better,' Caspar said darkly, and then added quickly, 'Speaking for myself, of course. I'm all in favour of your feeling in fine fettle.'

She smiled at him. 'Thank you. I want the same for you.'

Later, on her own in the East Tower, carefully cleaning the diamond-paned windows with soapy water, washing away the grime of years, she'd wondered if it was partly the discovery of this funny place that was helping her feel stronger. She went once a day to the tower to clean, in silence. Sometimes she was there for no more than twenty minutes and other times she spent an hour or two, or longer. The time passed in a flash no matter how long it was. There was something so meditative about the utter quiet and the instant results she saw, as she brushed away cobwebs, swept up rubbish, and cleaned away dirt and dust.

And, of course, I'm good at cleaning and keeping things neat.

Each time she went back, the tower looked just a little brighter. She began to love going there, emerging refreshed despite the fact that her hands were filthy and her nails rimed with black.

Once she left the sitting room area and started on the kitchen at the back, she began to find herself fantasising about how she would arrange it if she could to make the perfect little kitchen, exactly suited to how she wanted it. She had often thought of how she would improve Atalanta's Belgravia kitchen, where many of her programmes were filmed, and what she would have done with the flat if they'd had the time and money. Now she plotted exactly where she would place everything, and how she would create a tiny utility and larder in the scullery area. She already knew just where a small table and chairs would go in the kitchen, close against the windows so that there was lots of light, a view of the moat and the parkland beyond. And she also knew how she would make a little bathroom on the second floor, to be shared by two bedrooms, and how the top floor would become a study.

Sometimes, as she cleaned and dreamed, she looked across at the castle where she actually lived, and laughed at herself. That was her home, and here she was, dreaming of this tiny place and how cosy it could be. Most people wanted to go the other way, to a larger place. She had all the room anyone could want and yet longed to find cunning ways with storage in a house that was no more than a corner of her actual home.

When she wasn't in the tower she was also dealing with an onslaught of emails from Atalanta, either from her or from Jane, as Atalanta grappled with the new project and the myriad questions it engendered. No wonder the peace and quiet of the tower – far from the range of the Wi-Fi – was such a refuge.

It was Atalanta who had suggested the costumes.

To bring it all to life and really knock their socks off! she had written. **I've got a great idea already. Can't wait!**

Georgie knew that there was no question of Atalanta doing any of the actual cooking. She tended to only do the practical stuff when the cameras were rolling. But Georgie was used to that, and it was probably a good thing that she and Sandy were overseeing the catering at this important stage of the project.

And you must wear something appropriate too. I'm sure the castle has lots of old clothes you can sort through. I bet you find something wonderful!

Georgie had blinked at that. A flicker of her accustomed shyness and panic raced through her at the thought of dressing up and showing off, calling attention to herself. But then she had rebuked herself. She wouldn't be the only one. Perhaps it was a good idea.

'Are there any clothes stored here?' she asked Caspar, after she'd read and absorbed Atalanta's latest message.

'I have no idea,' he said, looking blank. 'Clothes? I don't know. You could try the attics, I suppose. There's tons of old stuff up there. Boxes and boxes of it.'

'The attics,' she echoed. More house. More space. More things. She found it so very odd, the way people who lived in places like this seemed to think that they needed to preserve the evidence of their existence. She had done all she could to dispose of her own past, and to shed it like a skin she no longer needed. The sight of anything left over from her childhood was repellent. But here, nothing was thrown away. Everyone in the family seemed to matter – hence the endless family photographs and portraits. There was no escape from the past and the people in it.

Perhaps they don't need to escape, she thought. It was a strange notion. She had always assumed that everyone was fleeing something. The idea that home was a place of safety and memory was quite alien to her. Perhaps it was a good thing. What would be in museums if no one ever kept anything?

I am the guardian of memories.

Who had said that? Georgie racked her brain. Someone had. Not that long ago.

I am the guardian of memories.

In that case, she thought, *perhaps I am the guardian of forgetting.*

A day or two later, she climbed the staircase to the attics at the top of the castle. As she went higher, the staircase became increasingly less grand. By the time she was at the attic floor, it was a narrow and plain staircase: uncarpeted, unvarnished and dusty. There seemed to be an endless series of attics, a later addition to the original castle which was built before people were so intent on keeping things, perhaps. They had been added to the top of the house and concealed behind the battlements, with tiny dormer windows to let in light. They were a different beast to the servants' bedrooms on the floor below: small rooms but each with decent windows and a fireplace. There were no comforts here and the walls were unplastered, square brick extrusions showing clearly where the chimneys were.

Georgie opened the first door and saw that the attics were linked across the entire top of the house, room after room, and as far as she could see, every one was piled high with boxes, crates and baskets. There were piles of furniture in various states of decay, paintings leaning against one another in stacks. Near her, a dusty rocking horse stared into space, his mane and tail moth-eaten and his wooden legs stretched out on his rockers in a stride that hadn't been taken in decades. Old tricycles and dolls' houses, bookshelves with dozens of abandoned volumes. Rolls of carpet and old rugs, piles of curtains and heaps of linen of all kinds. Everywhere she looked there was more detritus of lives lived.

Georgie stared around, overcome.

She had travelled light through life, making as little mark as she could. She had felt as though there was some virtue in drawing as little attention to herself as possible. She had assumed that she deserved so little, and that there was some kind of virtue in renunciation, like a nun in centuries past. But here, the mood was different. It demanded notice and claimed ownership, of time and space and things. There was an exuberance about the amount of stuff here, as though this family, the Wakefields, were shamelessly declaring that they needed and deserved all this to live life well. How were they so confident? What was it that made some people so fearless about what they intended to take from the world during their tenure here, and others so miserably deprived, or so unsure of their dues?

Life can be lived so many ways, she thought. *How do we know what is the right way?*

She felt overcome suddenly, as though the ghosts of years past had all descended on her in a great company and were shouting in her ears. 'Look at this!' they were demanding. 'This is my toy car. This is my favourite book! These are the curtains that hung in my bedroom. This is my carpet. This is the suitcase I took to school!'

Without thinking, she shut her eyes and pressed her hands over her ears. 'Oh, do stop!' She said it out loud and as she spoke, the voices of the past became quiet.

Your imagination is so vivid, Mrs Arthur had said kindly. *You're so sensitive, Georgie. Be careful.*

Georgie opened her eyes. The attic was silent, dusty, crammed. She took a deep breath and then coughed, as the dust of years entered her lungs.

She ventured forward, deciding to stay in this first attic for now, and began to look around. Against one wall, she saw mountains of wicker hampers and, going over to them, she saw that they were all stencilled F&M on the lids in black paint.

F&M. Fortnum and Mason.

She had known nothing of such a place growing up. It was only as an adult that she had learned of these hallowed names and renowned labels, spoken of with a kind of breathless reverence: Harrods, Paxton and Whitfield, Foreman and Field. Luxury foods of the highest quality whose tins were treasured as much as what they contained. Fortnum's, she knew, was a venerable shop on Piccadilly in London that specialised in luxury food but as far as she understood, it sold fripperies like crystallised violets, marzipan fruits and fancy biscuits. It was a tourist mecca for teas with royal names. She had never been in, and never been interested in visiting.

Nevertheless, these hampers were enchanting: caramel-coloured woven wicker, fastened by straps of leather and buckles. Someone in the house must have spent a great deal of money at Fortnum's. She opened the top one. Its straps were worn and almost fell apart as she pulled at the buckle. Inside was a mass of ancient sawdust and coiled nests of dark, brittle straw. She brushed them aside but there was nothing inside at all. She lifted that hamper down from the pile and opened another that was just the same.

Why keep all these hampers if you're not going to put anything in them? she wondered. *Pretty though they undoubtedly are.*

Then she opened another and found it empty of the straw nests but full of exercise books. She lifted one out. *Toby Wakefield, History* was written on the front, and she flicked it open to see printed lesson after printed lesson, each one carefully titled and underlined. *The Victory of Henry VII in 1485* and underneath neatly written points:

Henry VII had a claim to the throne through his mother, Margaret Beaufort. She married Edmund Tudor. She was of the House of Lancaster.

Henry defeated Richard III at the Battle of Bosworth. He was of the House of York.

*The victory of Henry VII marked the end of the Wars
of the Roses when he married Elizabeth of York and the
two dynasties became one.*

Georgie blinked in silent surprise. She knew nothing of the
past, other than the names of a few kings and queens.
She was not interested in looking back but only forward.
She remembered very little of her schooling beyond a sense
of tension and difficulty and a desperate need to cling on to
information long enough to write it down in an exam and
then be free of it for ever.

Toby Wakefield. Who was he?

At the bottom of the page were tiny sketches of dinosaurs.

She skimmed a few more pages of the laborious handwritten script, and picked up another. More lessons learned
by Toby Wakefield. Geography this time. Maps and solemn
bullet points of facts. All the books in the hamper were his.
She closed it and moved it aside. The next was full of books
inscribed by Archie Wakefield.

Great-Uncle Archie!

It was quite heartbreakingly sweet to see his childish
handwriting with all the mistakes and scrubbing out, the
letters going up and down over the lines. Evidently younger
than Toby when writing in this book, he had spent a lot
of time forming his alphabet and learning to join letters
together. She thought of the old man in his wheelchair, his
skin taut and shiny where it wasn't deeply pitted and wrinkled, his hair sparse, his eyes dim. Once he'd been a child;
peachy, soft skinned, bright and beautiful. She could see him

now, bent over his book, his tongue sticking out with effort as he made his pen form the letters: *the quick brown fox jumped over the lazy dogs.*

Oh. It was so sad. And yet . . . was it sad? To be born, live, grow old and die? Was it?

If it isn't sadness, then what am I feeling?

Georgie closed that hamper and moved to the next. The one beneath had fewer books in it, with names in spiky script scrawled on the covers: *Rob Foster* or *Tom Foster.* The books were sparse, heavy with pencil and lacking the neatness and precision of the others. They weren't Wakefields. Why had their books been preserved? Among the books, she saw a small cloth pouch. Pulling it out, she felt that it had something of weight inside that chinked as she lifted it. Marbles? Coins? She opened the neck of the pouch and shook it into her palm. A stream of small stones fell out into her hand, tiny and shaped like stars. She stared at them. How pretty they were, small, grey-white and with a fern-like pattern on their surface that made them look like snowflakes.

What are they? They look like fossils. But I've never seen star-shaped ones like this before. They remind me of Swedish Christmas cookie stamps.

After a moment, Georgie put the stones back into the pouch, hesitated and then tucked the pouch into the back pocket of her jeans.

Time was getting on and she hadn't found even a single bit of clothing. Was it worth continuing to look in the hampers? She closed the lid and put the hamper on the pile of the ones she had looked in, deciding to turn her attention to the large blanket boxes on the opposite wall where she thought she might find clothes. After an hour of wrestling with the heavy-lidded boxes, she had found vast amounts of thick curtains, ancient sheets, eiderdowns and blankets. She had also found clothes, but only old children's things – shorts, shirts, jumpers, dresses and skirts, along with school uniforms from many years ago.

Eventually, she gave up. She could search for days. This one attic seemed mostly to be concerned with children – at least she'd only found toys and school books and junior clothing. Even if she worked her way through the other attics, there was no guarantee she would find something suitable.

'I don't want to dress up,' she said out loud, feeling suddenly quite certain. 'I don't want to, and I won't. I'll tell Atalanta that she can do the dressing up and I'll concentrate on the food.'

This decision felt good and right. She was not at all used to telling Atalanta no, but this time she would and she would stand firm. Having made up her mind, Georgie turned to go. Her eye was caught by the pile of hampers near the door and she hesitated. The one on top seemed to be almost vibrating as though it was trying to get her attention.

She walked over to it. The buckles were fastened and the straps on this hamper were strong and in good condition. She undid them easily and opened the lid. Beneath was a jumble of exercise books, just as before. The names were clear: Miranda Wakefield and Rosalind Wakefield.

M & R Wakefield. The initials that are in the recipe book. Her interest was piqued at once. She picked one up. It

212

held French exercises in a bold hand that wrote with a flourish. This was Miranda's book. She chose another that had Rosalind's name on it: geography, in handwriting that was similar but a little less exuberant.

Sisters, then.

This hamper was no more interesting than the others, she decided, and went to close the lid. Then she saw another book, with a dusty pink cover, and on it in capital letters: ETTI BOULE.

The name below M & R. How strange.

She felt the same unpleasant sensation she had when she first saw that name.

Georgie picked up the book and stared at it.

Just then she heard footsteps on the stairs outside and Caspar shouted, 'Georgie! You're needed. Can you come down?'

'Yes, just coming!' she called back. She went to replace the book and then, on impulse, closed the hamper lid and headed for the attic door, the book still in her hand.

Since then, Georgie hadn't had a chance to think about the book but had tucked it into her bedside table along with the pouch of stone stars to look at another time. She had been working flat out at all hours, trying to form a modern cookery book from the castle recipes, testing and planning. She had also had to write a pitch for Atalanta's agent and publishers, which was then sent on to the television production company.

Now the castle was bright with lights, the front quad full

of smart cars, the outdoor lanterns lit, and the great hall thronging with people. Sandy had got helpers in from the village to serve drinks and canapés, and Caspar had asked Henry and Alyssa to come and decorate the great hall in the style of the court of Charles II. It looked magnificent: they had created great garlands of greenery and fruit, full of red and black satin ribbons and with very realistic birds and woodland creatures within them. Iron candelabra, six feet tall and wreathed in ivy and gold braid, blazed with rings of candles. Great tureens and platters spilled with displays of fruit and flowers. The central table was also alight with candles, and dominated by an extraordinary copy of the ship in the painting over the fireplace, but made in pastry. Henry had baked it at home in sections that he packed into sturdy boxes, transported to Wakefield and assembled on the table. Then he had painstakingly painted the whole thing with food dyes and edible gold, and hung it with red satin sails.

'Henry!' Georgie had gasped when she'd seen the finished result that afternoon. 'How amazing!'

'I enjoyed doing it,' he said modestly. 'Kept me busy. Once it would have had blackbirds or something inside, but I haven't gone that far.'

'I'm glad to hear it.' She gave him a hug. 'Thank you. What an achievement!'

'It should keep for quite a while,' he said. 'And how are you, Georgie? Are you adapting to castle life?'

'Yes, oddly I am. I didn't expect to. But I'm getting used to it.'

'Good. We must catch up properly tomorrow and you can tell me all about it.'

Henry wasn't attending the dinner but would stay the night, while Alyssa, having helped to decorate the hall, had gone back to Bath to look after the children.

Georgie changed into a plain black dress, grateful that she didn't have to don a costume. Atalanta hadn't minded in the least, which had surprised Georgie and made her wonder if perhaps she had given in too easily to her demands in the past. Something to remember. Now she came down the stairs with Caspar, nervously eyeing the throng below. They seemed happy enough, sipping on champagne and eating the canapés: tiny tarts filled with quail's egg and cheese, morsels of chicken breast stuffed with herby mousses, paper-thin cured beef rolled around oysters grilled in vinegar and tarragon.

'The hall looks incredible,' declared Caspar, clearly impressed.

'Thanks to Henry and Alyssa.'

'They're very talented. But who are all these people?'

Georgie looked over the throng, seeing some familiar faces from her work with Atalanta. 'That's Atalanta's agent, Bryony, and some others from the agency. Over there is the editor and the MD of her publishing company, along with the heads of sales, marketing and publicity. Then there's the television lot – they're mostly together by the fireplace.'

'What a lot of people to keep the enterprise going.'

'Atalanta makes them a lot of money. It's a big deal.'

Caspar took her hand and squeezed it. 'You're a big deal, too. She couldn't do it without you.'

Georgie smiled back at him. 'Thanks, darling. And I couldn't do it without you.'

Just as they reached the bottom of the stairs, the great door of the hall opened to reveal Atalanta standing in the doorway, spot lit against the darkness outside. She looked like a magnificent Van Dyck painting, in a lavish dark green, low-cut velvet gown, its bodice studded with pearls and criss-crossed with gold thread. Standing proud behind her head was a great collar of stiff lace. Her red hair was glossy and smooth on top, and then curled into ringlets that hung about her ears, where extravagant pearl drops glowed. She looked breathtaking. The room broke into spontaneous applause and appreciative whistles.

'Hello, darlings!' she announced flirtatiously, when the clapping had subsided. 'How wonderful to welcome you to Wakefield Castle for my seventeenth-century feast! You are in for a treat. And just in case you're wondering, I'm here as Lady Castlemaine, the oldest but cleverest of all of Charles the Second's mistresses!'

The assembly burst into fresh applause as Atalanta sash-ayed in.

'She is brilliant at this,' Caspar murmured to Georgie, who was smiling at the display.

Georgie was laughing. 'I do love her! She is shameless but fun.'

'She's very clever at keeping her brand going.'

'Exactly. She can win anyone round.'

Just then, a small band of musicians who had quietly

settled against one side of the hall, struck up with their lute, cellos and flute.

'I just hope the food goes down as well as Atalanta has,' Georgie said, casting a wistful look towards the kitchen.

'It will be as fabulous as always, and I know because I've been lucky enough to be your guinea pig.' Caspar gave her an encouraging smile. 'Relax, if you can, and enjoy it. The hall looks amazing. I had no idea it could look so magnificent. They're all in for an incredible experience.'

'I'll just be glad when it's over. I don't think I'm cut out to be a chatelaine.'

Just then, Caspar's face changed. 'Oh dear. Oh no.'

'What?' Georgie asked anxiously.

'Over there.'

She followed Caspar's gaze to see that the doorway was occupied once again, not by Atalanta but by another woman in a striking evening gown of bright blue silk.

'Viktoria.' He looked annoyed. 'What is she doing here? I'll get rid of her. It's too much.'

Georgie put a hand on his arm before he could march over. 'Wait, don't cause a scene. It'll be much worse than having her here.' She thought quickly. 'How about we set another two places – there's plenty of room and more than enough food. And get Henry down to join us, and he can manage her.'

'Really?' He looked doubtful.

'Really. You go and fetch him. I'll talk to her.'

'All right. It's more than she deserves. But all right.'

Caspar went back upstairs. Georgie picked up two glasses

of champagne from a tray, took a deep breath and went over to Viktoria who had walked into the room and was gazing about haughtily.

'Hello, Georgie,' she said as Georgie approached. She took one of the glasses. 'Thank you. The hall looks somewhat overdone – are you putting on some kind of play?'

'It's a work event, Viktoria, and rather naughty of you to come.'

'Naughty?' Viktoria raised her brown painted eyebrows. 'What can you mean?'

'Well, you weren't invited.'

'What are you talking about? Of course I'm invited.'

'I don't think so . . . I didn't invite you.'

'You didn't, no. But . . .' Viktoria looked around the room and her gaze stopped on the flamboyant figure of Atalanta whose low-cut gown was getting a lot of attention. 'She did. Atalanta Young. She invited me. And here I am.'

'Atalanta?' echoed Georgie, astonished. 'Did she?'

'Yes,' Viktoria said coldly. 'Someone around here has some manners, at least. No doubt she wished to make it up to me – after she frightened me out of my wits.'

Georgie gaped at her, too surprised to speak. She was still searching for something to say when Caspar and Henry came up, to divert Viktoria and release Georgie so that she could oversee the feast.

As long as Viktoria doesn't ruin it, she thought as she hurried out towards the kitchen. *I don't know how she would, but she might.*

Had Atalanta really invited her? And if so, why, knowing how Georgie felt about her? What could she hope to gain?

I'll think about that later, she decided. There was beef and capon and all the rest to think about now. And after all, the future of the castle itself rested on the outcome of tonight.

Chapter Eleven

Georgie looked out of the window to see yet another party of sightseers walking across the quad, crunching over the gravel, and following in the wake of Mrs Lambert, who marched at the front holding a small red flag on a stick for the crowd to follow. She sighed.

'I really can't cope with this,' she murmured to herself.

Ever since the night of the banquet, the stream of visitors had been increasing. Atalanta had released a series of photographs of herself in her splendid costume. They were very good, as she had made sure to hire a professional photographer who had taken many shots of her looking fabulous, as well as of the great hall and the magnificent pastry ship. These had adorned her social media and then been picked up by the press. They'd been delighted by Atalanta's latest incarnation as a sexy royal mistress, her buxom chest daringly displayed in the low-cut dress.

'It's all good stuff,' Atalanta had said happily when she spoke to Georgie. 'It's whetting the appetites for the new show. And putting pressure on the telly execs to commission it.'

The banquet had been a great success, as far as Georgie could tell. The meal had gone off without a hitch and everything had tasted marvellous. Even she had to admit that the food had been a triumph and she had received many compliments for it, all along the same lines: that her guests had not been looking forward to a historical feast, but that they had been pleasantly surprised by how delicious and unusual the food had been. Her rosemary liqueur had been a particular success, as had the lavender ice cream, made in the traditional way by churning in a tub chilled by ice and rock salt.

She had not been able to enjoy the feast quite as much as she would have liked, owing to Viktoria's presence. 'Did you actually invite her?' she asked Atalanta, when she got the chance.

'You know what they say,' Atalanta had said, her eyes sparkling with mischief. 'Keep your friends close and your enemies closer. It can't hurt to soften her up. She would have hated to be left out. So I thought, let's have her along.'

'You could have said.'

'You would have said no.' Atalanta grinned. 'Don't worry, she's loving it. And the head of Bright Eye TV is all over her. She's being a lamb. Trust me, it was a good idea.'

The banquet had resulted in the cookbook being commissioned, so now Georgie was working hard on that. But the publicity was bringing more people to the castle, keen to see where Atalanta had frolicked and to witness the marvel of the pastry ship, still on display in the great hall.

She went to find Caspar, who was in the study, making all the arrangements for the roof restoration. 'Darling, I'm not going to be able to write if people keep traipsing around the house while I'm trying to work. They always visit the kitchen and Lady Wakefield's morning room – the two places where I spend most time.'

Caspar looked up. 'Yes. I see that.' He sighed. 'It seems ridiculous that you can't find somewhere to work privately in this huge place.'

'Well, I've got a plan.' She sat down on a chair opposite his, put her hands together and smiled winsomely.

'You have?'

She nodded. 'I've been thinking about it for a while. I want to renovate the East Tower.'

Caspar frowned, taken by surprise. 'You do?'

'Yes. Hear me out, before you say no. I've got some money saved and I would like to use it to renovate the ground floor and put in a proper little kitchen. I can use it for work. It will be much, much better than using that great place, with visitors coming and going all day. I know that visitors are good. I get that you want to start having proper opening hours and charging for visits, and all the rest. Sandy and I are thinking about putting out tables and chairs and doing some teas and things. But I also have to have some peace and quiet to work, if I'm going to get this book done, and do the recipe testing.'

'Well.' Caspar smiled back. 'I think it's a wonderful idea.'

She was surprised he was so positive so quickly. 'You do?'

'Yes. I could see how much you liked the tower from the start. But how fast can you sort out the renovation?'

Georgie felt a rush of excitement. Caspar really seemed to mean it when he'd said the tower was hers. 'I've already done some research and I found a local builder who has just had a project moved and wants something to fill the gap. He can start really soon. And I know exactly what I want and how I want it.'

'There is one thing . . .' Caspar frowned. 'Permissions. We're grade one listed.'

'But we're not changing anything,' she said. 'It's already got the water and electricity installed. We're just modernising what's already there. There won't be any changes.'

'And that's in the rules?'

'According to what I read.'

'I trust you. There will be inspectors checking on our roof repairs, I expect. I'm sure they'll let us know if we're doing anything they don't like.'

Georgie beamed. 'Thank you, Caspar. I think it will make all the difference. I'll call the builder now.' She jumped up and went to go.

'Any news from the telly?' Caspar asked, his voice hopeful.

'Not yet. But I'm sure we'll know soon. I'll let you know as soon as I do.'

When Georgie saw the text from Pippa, she felt a surge of guilt. She usually made sure to keep in touch with her sister. Pippa was so busy with the children that it was Georgie who made the overtures, asking if she was free for a chat and if she was okay, chasing up if one of the girls was sick or if Pippa had something notable going on. But over the last few weeks, she had been so distracted by her work and castle life that she hadn't reached out as she usually did.

That's another way this place is affecting me, she thought. *All my usual patterns are disrupted, even my relationships.*

Pippa's text read:

Hi! Long time so speak. Are you around for a catch-up? I could do with a vent! xxxx

Georgie wrote back:

Darling Pippa, I'm so sorry I've not been in touch. It's been manic. Of course I'm around. Let me know a good time and I'll call you. I hope everything is okay. xxx

She looked back at Pippa's text. It sounded fairly normal but the need to vent worried her. There was always lots for Pippa to cope with, and she had all the usual stresses and frustrations and demands of parenthood, but this sounded like something else.

Ryan. It has to be Ryan.

She realised that for some time she had been aware that Pippa was increasingly unhappy. It had all started so well. After a few dodgy characters when she was younger, Pippa had been blissful when she'd met Ryan. She'd gushed over him so effusively that Georgie had been very keen to meet him. According to Pippa, he was handsome, funny, intelligent and wonderful company. So it was a surprise to find that Ryan was quiet and mild-mannered, and self-effacing to the point of saying very little at all, although he was good-humoured and cracked a few jokes when he did speak up. He was nice-looking but nothing special, a little weak-chinned and pallid if anything. But in his company, Pippa sparkled. Ryan nodded along with everything she said, and they seemed to be in tune with just about everything. Ryan liked the same music, the same food, the same television programmes and the same holiday destinations, and he was gainfully employed in a tech company as a computer pro-grammer. He was a sports nut, which Pippa wasn't but she discovered a newfound interest in golf, cricket and football, talking excitedly about the Masters, the Ashes and the FA Cup as if she had always adored them. Georgie was amused. It was love, that was clear. And there must be more to Ryan than she or Caspar could see, because if Pippa loved him this much, then in private he must be a lot more interesting than he was in company.

Nevertheless, when Pippa and Ryan got engaged after only six months, Georgie was a bit dubious.

'Do you need to get married so fast?' she'd asked Pippa, while admiring the ring that glinted on her engagement finger. 'What's the hurry?'

'There isn't a hurry, it's just that if you know it's right, then it's right. Besides, it makes sense to move in and make it permanent – Ryan's lease on his flat just came to an end. So why not get on with it? We want to start a family while we're still young as well . . .' Pippa had looked suddenly worried. 'You do like Ryan, don't you?'

'Of course I do. He's very nice. I just wonder . . . is he too easy-going? He never seems to have an opinion on anything, except sport. He lets you run around after him as well.'

Pippa looked defensive. 'He's a bit shy and vulnerable. And maybe a bit immature. But he'll grow up, that's what marriage does for people. He really is so lovely.'

'All right,' Georgie said, thinking that she was glad that Caspar had grown up before she married him and so she hadn't had to wait for him to do that. 'As long as you're sure, that's all that matters. And as long as he's kind to you.'

'He is,' Pippa said fervently. 'He's really kind.'

And yet, when Georgie saw them together, she was struck sometimes by how little Ryan did for Pippa and how much she did for him, fussing over him and making sure he was all right while he occasionally made her a cup of tea, if he was making one for himself.

Perhaps I was too motherly towards her when she was growing up, Georgie thought, *and Pippa wants to take the maternal role for a bit. Well, if she enjoys looking after Ryan, and he likes to let her, fine. It obviously works. And it will probably change when children come along.*

On Pippa's wedding day, Georgie had taken the role of her father and mother rolled into one. She had helped Pippa get ready in her beautiful lace wedding dress, and had proudly walked her down the aisle. She was also making the traditional father of the bride speech, but before she did, Ryan got to his feet and the longer he spoke, the more uneasy she felt.

This speech is a weird take-down of Pippa, she thought with surprise. *It sounds affectionate but really, it's not. Am I the only one who thinks so?*

She looked around to gauge others' reactions as Ryan talked on. He hardly used Pippa's name, instead calling her 'my bride' or 'the woman who is now my wife' in a slightly silly voice, getting a laugh every time. Apparently Pippa had been desperate to marry him from day one, and he had wanted to run for the hills. Everyone laughed, even Pippa. A little later, he implied that she was bossy and overbearing, and made a joke about her bad housekeeping, which Pippa laughed at though she looked a little mortified. 'Whoops, I'm in the dog house now!' joked Ryan. 'I'd better get the lawyers on the line! Needed a bit sooner than expected, perhaps!'

Georgie was confused. Everyone was laughing away and applauding as Ryan teased. Then he said that Pippa was a great girl and he was the happiest man alive. More cheering and applause.

But he had not really said anything warm about Pippa at all. He had not mentioned love. He had not said she was beautiful on this, her wedding day, or thanked her for marrying him. He had not even said anything nice about her at all until the last throwaway remark.

Georgie got up to speak. She'd made some notes but now she spoke without them and said everything in her heart about Pippa, as if to rebalance Ryan's slightly snide tone. She said how much everyone valued and loved Pippa, what wonderful qualities of sweetness and kindness she had, what a marvellous teacher she was and how good she was with small children, and how radiant she looked in her wedding dress. How she was the best sister in the world and how much their relationship meant to Georgie.

'I'll always be here for you, Pippa, just as you are for me. And now you have Ryan to help and support you through your life as well. I know that with the love you both share, anything is possible. We wish you so much happiness and joy on your wedding day and always.'

Pippa had sobbed and they had hugged, and then everyone raised a glass to the bride and groom. No one else mentioned Ryan's speech, except to say how funny he had been, and so Georgie did not think about it again.

After the wedding, Pippa had seemed happy enough with married life. Obviously the fizz of new romance had worn off and she and Ryan were less starry-eyed. There had been the decision to move to Brighton, which meant an end to spon-taneous meet-ups, to Sunday afternoons in the park after a lovely lunch cooked by Georgie, and all the various ways in which the sisters had seen each other. Gradually they'd got used to not being in touch as much as they once were, especially after Pippa had their daughter Izzy and, two years after that, their second daughter Sofia. When her maternity leaves were over, Pippa continued to work as a primary school teacher. Life was busy for her and she seemed happy and fulfilled.

But something had subtly been changing. Pippa laughed less. She sounded more harried and stressed and was having difficulty coping with everything. All marriages had rough patches. She would have said if anything was seriously wrong, wouldn't she?

A text pinged up on her phone.

Today has turned crazy. Can we talk tomorrow? I'll call you after bedtime? x

Georgie texted back that she'd be waiting and tried to put the anxiety about Pippa out of her mind.

Sam Locke, the builder, came over the next day to inspect the tower and give Georgie a timescale for the renovation. He was a large man, tall and well built from years of working on building sites, and with startling blue eyes that seemed to see everything. His dark hair was kept razored short, but it suited him, as did the scattering of grey stubble over his jaw. In his well-worn jeans and a loose checked shirt, he looked casual and relaxed but his approach was direct and to the point.

'This place is in good nick,' he said, after they'd walked around the East Tower once. 'From what you said, I thought it was a wreck.'

'It is a wreck, isn't it?' Georgie asked, looking around.

Sam shook his head, and took out his phone. He swiped the screen and then started talking into it: 'Structurally sound, possibly weak joists but no signs of infestation. Roof to be fully inspected. Possibility for relining and further insulation. Chimneys to be inspected. Full rewiring and plumbing, new consumer unit. Some woodwork to be removed, some plasterwork blown. Installation of kitchen and bathroom.' He stopped talking and looked at Georgie. 'I find it easier to do this. I'm dyslexic, so it's easier than writing.'

'Of course,' Georgie said. 'It sounds like quite a big job.'

Sam shrugged. 'It can be done quite fast if the structure is sound and we have all the units on site. You'll need to order your gear pretty swiftly and you might find you're restricted to what's in stock. But I know some people and can pull strings if necessary.'

'This sounds exciting,' Georgie said. 'And you can start right away?'

'It's your lucky month. The businesswoman who was renovating her new house is suddenly and unexpectedly getting divorced and the grand design is off. We can start on the bones if you get on with ordering your kit.' Sam grinned and his previously serious face looked quite boyish. 'I've got a rather excellent electronic tape measure, so I'm just going to do some measuring, then I can send you a plan of the tower and you can start making your design.'

Georgie said quickly, 'I was wondering about putting a bathroom upstairs, in the little bedroom over the downstairs bathroom, and using the current bathroom as the downstairs loo and utility, perhaps with a shower in there.'

'Oh, really?' Sam laughed. 'So you do want to shake it up then? Just a little?'

'Just a little,' she echoed brightly, 'if it's possible. As there is already plumbing in place on the ground floor.'

'That does help,' he said, giving her a knowing look. 'You've obviously done your homework. Right, I'll get on with the measuring and we can get that plan drawn up.'

Georgie was elated by the fact that her scheme to get the tower into shape was going to become reality. She could envisage herself there, in a cosy and well-equipped kitchen, cooking and testing, with her laptop on the kitchen table so she could write things up easily as she went along. It would be a perfect place to hide away in peace and quiet. When Sam sent through the plan of the tower along with his quote for the work, her elation faded somewhat. The cost was much larger than she'd expected and that was without the fixtures and fittings for the kitchen and bathroom.

She pushed her anxiety about cost to one side. She had some savings. She had fixed her heart on making the tower into her own place and she was determined to do it, no matter what.

Georgie made her call to her sister that afternoon.

'Hi, Pippa, how are you?'

'Oh, you know – just about coping!' Pippa sounded tired and talked for a while about all the issues she was facing with the children and going back to work. Georgie listened sympathetically, standing in the morning room and staring out of the French windows as she did, but it didn't sound quite enough to justify how low her sister sounded.

'Is Ryan helping you?' she asked. 'You sound at the end of your tether.'

'Not really,' Pippa said, sounding glummer than ever. 'He does what I ask him, but he just doesn't take any initiative. He doesn't seem interested in helping me. If I ask him to do the girls' supper, he puts pizza in the oven. Ten minutes' work. And that means I can't do the same – they have to have some decent meals. We don't have a cleaner, so I do all that.

When he's looking after the children, he watches movies with them and nothing gets done.'

'Have you tried talking to him? Maybe he doesn't realise how stressed you are.' Georgie said this despite feeling dubious about Ryan ever stepping up. It had been a running joke between her and Caspar that Ryan never lifted a finger, but it had stopped being funny after a while. Both of them had begun to feel that Ryan was not as harmless and amiable as he had first appeared.

'I have talked to him, over and over. I've tried to explain that I just can't cope on my own.' Pippa sounded close to tears. 'But it doesn't do any good. It's like he can't hear me. He just hears me complaining and thinks I'm endlessly nagging him for no reason. It's as though he honestly thinks he does his fair share. In fact, the reason I wanted to talk to you was that a couple of nights ago, he did this huge martyr act, told me he does loads of childcare and half of the housework. I couldn't believe it. I feel devastated. If he can believe something so untrue, then all my work and effort is invisible, like it never happens.'

Georgie heard a quiver in her voice and knew she was crying.

'When I was upset that he could claim such a thing, he told me that my childhood had made me a very damaged person. That I was angry and selfish and spoiled and I was making his life a misery. He said I was a tyrant and I acted like he was never good enough, but that actually I was to blame for all the problems and if I would just stop complaining all the time, my life would be happier and so would his.'

Georgie gasped. 'But that's so unfair, Pippa!'

'I know.' She sobbed properly. 'I still can't believe he could say something so cruel and untrue.'

'And ungrateful! After all you've done for him!' Georgie felt her indignation turning to white-hot rage. 'How dare he? It's because you were so badly treated that you became such a good, caring and generous person yourself! You're a marvellous mother and you work yourself to the bone for your children and the children at school.' She felt choked by anger. 'I want to call him and tell him exactly what I think.'

'Don't do that,' Pippa said, her sobs subsiding. 'It won't help. He won't listen.'

'But what are you going to do, Pippa? This sounds extremely unhealthy.'

'I don't know. I'll be okay. I just needed to get it off my chest, I suppose.'

'Can you get some marriage counselling? It sounds like you need a professional to help Ryan understand your point of view. You need someone who can see what he's doing and make him stop.'

'You're right. I'm going to look into it.'

'Oh, sweetheart. I hope this is just a bad patch. Surely some therapy will help? That's what it's for. To help couples when their communication breaks down.'

'Yes, of course. It's the obvious answer.' Pippa still sounded hopeless and sunk in gloom.

'I'm so busy here right now, but as soon as I can, I'll come and see you, all right? And you must call me whenever you want. And Pippa . . .'

'Yes?'

'Are you keeping a diary?'

'Oh . . . well, sometimes. Off and on.'

'I think you should keep a diary of what's happening and what Ryan says. If he is able to make these claims, and it's your word against his, it might help if you've actually got evidence of what happened – a record of what you've done and how little he does.'

'That's a good point,' Pippa said. 'If I can find the time, I will.'

'A few words, that's all you need. Keep it on your tablet or something so he can't find it. And promise you will look into counselling?'

'I promise. Thank you, Georgie. It helps knowing you're there.'

'I'm always with you, Pippa, you know that. Just like I always have been.'

Georgie went for a long walk after her talk with her sister. Throughout her life, she had looked after Pippa with a fierce protectiveness, like a tiny lioness and her cub. Protecting her sister had given her life meaning, and given her the strength to carry on when things seemed too awful.

What role could she play in Pippa's life now? She was an adult, she had been married for years and was a mother. It wasn't for Georgie to go storming in and try to solve her problems. Besides, those problems were not so easy to solve now. Adult life was more complicated and nuanced than the simplicities of childhood. All they had wanted then was safety, kindness, love and security.

Perhaps not so different after all.

But what I can do?

As she walked, she thought about the last thing she had said to Pippa: *I'm always with you.*

That's all I can do for now. Be there for her, listen to her and let her find out for herself what is best to do. I hope that counselling will help them.

A small voice of doubt told her that Ryan would be impervious to therapy because he had already shown that he couldn't listen. If he didn't care enough to listen to Pippa, why would he care about anyone else?

But she mustn't judge him beforehand. They would have to wait and see.

Chapter Twelve

1939

Mr Humphries had been put to lodge in the East Tower, and he ambled over the lawn to the house in the morning to have breakfast and start work in the chill little room that had been chosen as his study. He was neatly turned out, his short fair hair well combed and his moustache neat. He gazed out from behind his owlish glasses, somehow remote as though they were an effective barrier between him and the rest of the world.

'What is your area of expertise, Humphries?' demanded Grandfather a few days after his arrival. He had come in late, as usual, when the rest of them were nearly finished.

The twins and Aunt Constance were there, but not the younger ones. It was not just that the arrival of the Foster brothers had prompted a small revolution in the nursery, which was now in a ferment of noise and rough play that was often actual fighting, but the evacuees were terrified of Grandfather and his eyepatch. They refused to go near him, so all meals were now had upstairs.

Miranda had wanted to question him herself, but Humphries always brought a journal with him that he read intently from the moment he sat down, even while buttering his toast and slathering it with Fortnum's Seville marmalade, drinking his tea while supposedly lost in it, and no one liked to interrupt him. Grandfather had no such scruples.

Humphries looked up from his reading. 'I'm a palaeontologist,' he said mildly. 'Animal and avian fossils, mega fauna especially.' Every sentence he spoke had an air of finality as though he expected no further questions.

'Dinosaurs?'

'I prefer birds. May I trouble you to pass the marmalade again, please? How kind.' Arthur Humphries blinked almost sleepily behind his owlish glasses as Miranda passed him the marmalade, wondering how he could get more onto that one triangle of toast. He dropped another spoonful on top of the soft mountain already there, and instantly lost himself in the journal while Grandfather was still coming up with another line of questioning.

'And what are you doing in that study all day?'

Mr Humphries looked up and took his time to reply. 'Oh, this and that. Research. Writing papers. Reporting to my superiors.'

'Do you have family?'

'No one who's going to miss me while I'm here. Right. Now, I must start work. Good day to you.' With a final sip of tea, Mr Humphries got up and put on his jacket, and headed out of the dining room.

Miranda was impressed by his failure to be cowed by their

grandfather or to oil up to him, as many others might have. Mr Humphries had a sense of himself and seemed content to gently fend off the older man's curiosity. As a result, they still had very little idea of what he was up to.

The twins were getting up to go when Aunt Constance said to Rosalind, 'My dear, can you ask Imogen to come down to my study? I've told Lottie to go up and mind the boys. I would like to talk to all three of you there.'

Rosalind looked surprised but said, 'Yes, Aunt,' and ran off.

Miranda and her aunt walked down the corridor towards her study.

'Is this about Mother?' Miranda asked. Her stomach curled over with apprehension.

'It is. Your grandfather and I have agreed that the time is right to bring her presence into the open.' Aunt Constance smiled at her. 'I know what it must have cost you to keep this secret from Rosalind. I suppose you did keep it?'

Miranda nodded, flushing. It had caused her a great effort but she had done it. The memory of Rosalind nearly throwing herself from the battlements had been enough to keep her firm when she'd felt like wavering. She couldn't risk that again, and if her sister knew that her mother was in the tower below, who knew what her subconscious might impel her to do.

'Well done.' Aunt Constance put a hand on her shoulder. 'I'm proud of you, Miranda.'

A swell of pride rushed through her. Praise was rare from Aunt Constance. It was sweet when it came. 'Are you going to tell us all now?'

'You have a right to know. And it cannot be concealed

much longer in any case.' They stopped outside the study door, and Aunt Constance opened it to lead Miranda in. It was a cluttered room, but not messy, despite being full of books and papers and pictures. The desk was covered with neat piles of pamphlets and letters. Aunt Constance had many charitable and political interests to which she had devoted her life. Miranda remembered the fiancé killed in the Great War. Perhaps this work had been the only way for her aunt to carry on. She had never thought of her prickly stand-offish aunt as anything other than an old woman with no need for a husband or family, but once she had been young and in love with everything before her, as Miranda was now.

And just like her, my life is going to be dominated by war.

She felt suddenly glad she had no fiancé to watch march away and never come back. Not yet, at least. Though how she would get a fiancé stuck here, she couldn't think.

Aunt Constance went to sit at the desk. She turned to face her niece, her grey eyes piercing. 'And have you been back to the tower?'

Miranda opened her mouth to deny it and then remembered that, despite her own imprecation not to go, she had been there the day before. Ever since she'd heard her mother's voice, she had been tinglingly aware of her presence in the tower but had forced herself to stay away. Then, out in the garden, she had found herself standing by the fence, thinking of the tower and its occupants.

Perhaps she's come back because of the war, Miranda thought. Wherever they took her might no longer be available, like the way that St Margaret's had been requisitioned.

She wondered what would happen to people who now needed places of refuge – the ill and disabled and lost. It made sense that places like Wakefield could be purposed to hold them. It was large enough and safe enough.

That thought comforted her. *They have sent her home. She'll be protected here. But what will it mean for us? What will we do?*

She'd had the urge to shout and scream, to tear at the roses, to pummel on the door, and to demand that they be let in or Mother be brought out. *Let's have an end to it!* she wanted to yell. *Why are you all doing this to us? To her? What is so very bad about her knowing us?*

She felt helpless against the decisions of her elders. They had simply to trust that there were reasons for everything, just as they were now told of all the mysterious wartime rules and protocols that must be observed. Grandfather had said that the weather reports were no longer to be published in case they helped the enemy. The news would be censored, letters would be read, schools would be shut, theatres closed. Children would be taken from their homes and parents. All for a greater purpose, all for everyone's good. It was a matter of trust.

She knew it and she understood it and she was not going to complain. But that didn't change the hurt and confusion.

There was silence behind the fence, although the solid tower walls and the dense foliage would absorb most noise.

What does Mother do in there? How is she passing her time? Will this be her life for ever?

Miranda felt her eyes sting.

I'm not going to cry like a baby, she told herself firmly. *Much worse is happening to other people, just remember that, Miranda Wakefield!*

She said to her aunt now, 'I only looked. I didn't say anything. She wouldn't have known I was there.'

'It's understandable,' Aunt Constance said. 'Ah, here are the others.'

Rosalind came in first, panting. She flung herself on a chair as Imogen came in more sedately, looking apprehensive.

'Sit down, Imogen. How are our little guests getting on? Are they calming down?'

Imogen sighed as she sat. 'Not really. It's like the Romans and the Vandals up there. I've never known Toby and Archie like it. They're full of aggression. And the Fosters leap on them and start fighting at the least word. I hardly know what sets them off. One minute it's calm, the next a flurry of arms and legs and flailing fists and shouting. The big one, Tom, bites when he isn't snarling, and the little one, Robbie, pinches.'

Miranda realised her sister looked exhausted.

'There's two cups broken this week, and a vase,' Imogen went on. 'A dent in the fender. Half the train set has gone missing. I'm not sure how long we can go on like this.'

'Oh dear,' said Aunt Constance, frowning. 'I do find it odd that they should be finding it quite so difficult here. Mrs Guthrie told me that her evacuees seem to be having the most wonderful time, they don't miss home at all as far as she can tell. And this is a little boys' paradise after all. They should be scampering about and having fun. How are lessons?'

'Dreadful!' Imogen groaned. 'The Fosters are woefully badly educated, except for insults – they've got buckets of those to throw at our boys. I'm sure they can't read half as well as Toby, or even Archie. I don't know if they're troubled or naughty or both, but they're both as bad as each other, and whatever it is seems to be catching.'

'Perhaps we would be better off sending them to the village school,' said Aunt Constance. 'It sounds too much for you to cope with. Looking after your brothers was one thing. But four naughty boys . . .'

'Lottie says she's giving notice,' said Imogen unhappily. 'Goodness knows what I'll do then.'

Miranda and Rosalind swapped looks, Miranda fearful in case she was asked to help, and Rosalind enquiring, as though she thought they should offer.

This is where we are not so twin-like, Miranda thought. *Rosalind is more like Imogen – loving and giving and womanly – and I am not.* She felt lonely suddenly, removed from anyone like her and with no chance to meet a kindred spirit either.

'I could give them art lessons on the lawn,' Rosalind suggested. 'If it helps.'

'It might,' Imogen said dryly, 'but good luck getting the paint on the paper. Better wear a raincoat as they're bound to start chucking it about. I am ready to join the forces – it can't be as hostile as the nursery.'

Aunt Constance picked up a stamped envelope from her desk. 'I've written a letter to Mrs Foster, the boys' mother. I'm sure she wants her mind set at rest as to how they are.

I've told her they're doing very well and are settling in. I haven't mentioned the fighting, the crying, the breakages or the refusal to be in the same room as your grandfather. It will only worry her. I have told her that they are both eating heartily, which is true. And let us hope all this aggression gets worked out of them before too long. Rosalind or Miranda, can you please cycle down to the village later to post it?'

'I will,' volunteered Miranda, hoping it might get her out of the painting class. She jumped up and took the letter from her aunt.

'Thank you.' Aunt Constance put the lid on her fountain pen. 'Now. You're probably wondering what I want to speak to you about.'

Miranda felt nervous; the other two looked mildly curious, clearly not expecting what was about to come.

'Now, girls. There is no easy way to say this, so I will simply state the facts. I'm going to speak of something very painful for all of us.' Aunt Constance took a breath, looking uncomfortable but determined. 'You both know that after your dear father died in such awful circumstances, your mother was terribly ill. She was taken to a place where she could be helped and where she was looked after.'

The atmosphere was immediately tense. Rosalind's eyes became very round and open, as they did when she was nervous or apprehensive. Imogen went quite still, except for her fingers plucking nervously at the cover on her armrest. She spoke first. 'Of course.'

'Yes,' Rosalind said in a small voice. 'We knew she had gone away because she was ill.'

She and Miranda exchanged quick glances. This alone was almost more than had ever been said before. They had not gone to their father's funeral because they had been considered too young for such a miserable and solemn occasion, but they knew at least that he was dead. It was many weeks later before they were told that the reason they hadn't seen their mother was that she was not well. She had had a nervous shock, they were told, and was recovering somewhere. They would see her when she was better. But she had never got better and after a while, they had learned not to ask when she would be coming home. It caused Grandfather pain that set him shaking and sniffing, then furious, and made Aunt Constance's face crease with anguish.

'Don't ask, children, please don't ask,' she would say, her voice pained.

After a while, the boys seemed to forget they'd ever had a mother, although they were not the same as before: quiet and muffled and stiller than they had been. The girls remembered but their memories were fading and too painful to recall in any case.

Miranda's stomach swirled with nervousness as she waited for whatever her aunt would say next. Would she really tell them everything now?

Usually so confident and unflappable, Aunt Constance was uncomfortable and stared above their heads as she continued. 'We kept all this very quiet, to protect your mother from the scandal. A hint of nervous breakdown can ruin a woman's prospects for life. She can never be properly accepted into polite society; her chances to marry again are slim. And we couldn't tell everyone what had happened to poor, dear Kathryn. It was much worse than a nervous breakdown for her.'

'Where you go, I'll go,' whispered Miranda, suddenly remembering.

Aunt Constance glanced at her. 'What's that?'

'That's what Mother said when Father said he would go to war and we would all live here. She was going to go with him, wherever he went. And I suppose she did. They both went away.'

Rosalind looked at her, amazed, and Miranda knew that she guessed instantly that Miranda knew something she did not. Her blue eyes were hurt. Miranda looked away, abashed.

'Well put,' Aunt Constance said. 'Imogen knows a little of this, don't you, dear?'

Imogen nodded slowly. She looked suddenly older than her eighteen years. 'You said that Mother went into a fugue state – isn't that what they call it? Yes. When she recovered from the initial shock, she created a new personality for herself and she has lived as that person ever since.'

Aunt Constance nodded. 'It's hard to understand, but that's true. She calls herself Mrs Rebecca Black and says she is from South Africa, the wife of a diamond exporter who is living in Cape Town to manage the mine. She has no children.'

Rosalind gasped. She looked again at her sister, her eyes questioning and furious as if to say *did you know?* Miranda tried to show by her face that she didn't know all of it, but she was sure she looked guilty and she glanced away.

Rosalind turned to her aunt and said angrily, 'That's why we've not been allowed to see our mother?'

Aunt Constance stood up and walked to the windows, staring out towards the West Tower. 'We did what we thought was right. That is all I can say. We don't understand this other identity but we believe it is a way for her to survive her grief. That's what the doctors are telling us. There is no physical reason why she cannot be herself. There is no external injury. But her internal injury, her mental wound, is very great. They don't believe that she can face life as her old self. And so she has created this new one. At first, we believed it would be temporary and she would return to you children as your mother. Until then, we believed it was dangerous for you to see her, for all your sakes.'

'Why are you telling us now, Aunt?' Imogen said clearly. 'There must be a reason. Is there anything wrong with Mother?'

Rosalind still looked angry, but now she was not looking over at her sister at all, which made Miranda more uncomfortable.

Aunt Constance said, 'She's physically well but the mental fugue remains as great as ever. I don't know if she'll ever recover her mind. I'm so sorry.'

Miranda found tears instantly streaming down her face and saw that Rosalind was crying too. Imogen was white-faced, her expression set and her mouth tight with repressed emotion.

'She is there but not there. You have a mother – but one who doesn't know you. I wish it were otherwise. There,

there, dear children, don't cry so hard. Do you have a handkerchief, Rosalind? Here, have mine, it's clean.' Aunt Constance's unaccustomed tenderness was almost as hard to bear as the news about their mother.

Miranda knew that now she must tell them the next part. Aunt Constance said, 'There is something else to know. Dear Kathryn's hospital is going to be a military hospital now, reserved for soldiers. They wanted to send her far away to Scotland and we said no, that we would take her. The condition was that we would respect her fugue state and continue to address her as Mrs Black. This we promised.'

Rosalind had wiped her tears and now she sat up straight, gasping as she clutched the handkerchief. 'You mean she's coming here?'

'She's already here,' Aunt Constance said simply. 'In the West Tower with her nurse companion. Whittaker, her lady's maid, has come to care for her. She's as loyal as a hound and won't hear of anyone else looking after her.'

Rosalind stared, speechless.

Imogen, astonished, instinctively looked towards the tower at the end of the garden. 'Mother's here?' she said wonderingly. 'Can we see her?'

'I'm sorry, my dear, but not yet. That may change. We hope she will grow mentally stronger but at the moment, isolation is best for her.'

'Should we tell the others? Everyone else in the house?' asked Imogen.

'Not yet. We will in time. It will be impossible to keep her presence a secret for much longer. And besides, she may improve to the point where she can walk upon the lawn and so on. Then we will explain that we have a guest, a convalescent who needs her privacy and a home on account of the war. The boys will probably not know her in any case. You girls would, naturally.'

Rosalind said, 'If she comes out, or if we go in . . . must we still call her Mrs Black?'

'Yes, for now, as she wishes it. The doctors tell us that is best. Attempting to break her illusion may trigger a relapse to the worst of her psychosis.'

'It's awful,' Miranda said in a broken voice. 'It seems so unfair that we should lose Father and Mother, when Mother was not in the crash. She didn't die but it's almost worse – because she's here and yet not here.'

'It's very cruel,' Aunt Constance said sadly. 'I'm more sorry than I can say. It is a great worry for your grandfather and me. We are anxious about what will happen to her if we should die – how you would cope with it. But we are well enough at the moment, I'm glad to say.'

Miranda bowed her head and stared at the floor.

'Now. We had better get on. Have a little time to yourselves and then get back to your tasks for the day.' Aunt Constance smiled at them, and then turned back to her desk.

Outside, Imogen flitted away, drawn upstairs by the sound of a rumpus above. Rosalind faced Miranda at the bottom of the stairs, angrier than Miranda had ever seen her.

'You knew!'

'I knew there was someone in the tower. I found out by accident,' Miranda said, almost frightened. 'I didn't mean to.'

'You knew it was Mother!'

'Aunt Constance told me when I asked, but made me promise not to say—'

'You lied to me!' Rosie clenched her fists, standing stiffly, clearly furious.

'I didn't lie!' protested Miranda, her face scarlet. 'I didn't say anything!'

'That's lying. Keeping a secret like that is the same as lying – letting me believe what isn't true.'

'I had to do it!'

'Why?'

'I had to promise and . . . I was trying to protect you.'

'Trying to protect yourself, you mean.' Rosie's face was crimson too, and she looked close to tears again. 'I just can't believe it. I can't believe you would do it.' She turned and ran up the stairs two steps at a time.

'Rosie, come back!' Miranda called after her, but her sister had raced away and didn't reply.

After a miserable morning with her sister refusing to see or talk to her, Miranda cycled down to the village to post Aunt Constance's letter. She tore down there at top speed but took her time coming back, savouring the cooler breezes of autumn and the colour that was showing in the leaves. She felt a little better.

At least the secret is out, she thought. *At least I don't have to hide it from Rosie any more. I'll make it up with her later, when she's had time to calm down.*

As she turned in through the gates, she saw a figure

striding up the drive in sturdy boots, walking trousers and a thick green jumper.

'Hello, Mr Humphries,' she said, as her bicycle came up level with him. 'Are you taking some time off from the dinosaurs?'

He glanced at her and smiled, his brown moustache bristling over his top lip as he brushed a lick of fair hair away from his eyes. 'Hello there. Now. Which one are you?'

'Miranda,' she said politely.

'Of course. I'm sure one of these days I'll get the hang of telling you apart.'

'I shouldn't think so,' she said, but nicely. 'You have to spend a bit of time with us for that. How is life in the tower?'

'Fairly comfortable. The views are splendid, the quiet is quite something after London. I live in Earl's Court, near the station, and the trains rumble past all the time. It's quite deathly here by comparison. I fear it's going to get somewhat cold, though,' he went on. 'The chimney isn't drawing, there's lots of smoke when I tried lighting the fire. But we shall see. It's probably just cold.'

'How long have you worked at the museum?'

'Ages and ages. I'm practically an exhibit myself. Gerontasaurus.'

'What?' She played with her feet on the pedals so that her bicycle remained level with his slower walking pace. She wobbled slightly but stayed up.

'Geron is "old man" in Greek. It's a hard G in Greek but soft in English, so we get "geriatric", meaning elderly. So a gerontasaurus is an elderly dinosaur. That's me.'

'How old are you?' asked Miranda, curious.

'Twenty-six.'

'Oh yes, that's quite old. Still, not as old as Grandfather.'

'No. He is the gerontasaurus rex. So, tell me, what do you do with yourself all day? Shouldn't you be in school?'

'I wish!' Miranda said emphatically. 'We can't go. It's been requisitioned and we can't get to Brampton every day, even on the bus because the timings don't work. So we're stuck here. Rosalind doesn't mind, but I do, very much.'

'Oh dear, that's no good.' Mr Humphries frowned. 'You'll atrophy here, if you're not careful. You need to keep your mind moving. What do you want to do anyway?'

'Be a journalist,' Miranda said quickly. 'It's what I've always wanted.'

'That sounds like a good career – assuming you don't get married.'

'I won't for ages and ages, until I'm thirty.'

'Oh, a late bloomer in romance. And why not? We might still be at war by then. Only joking,' he added hastily when he saw Miranda's horrified expression. 'I think a career is an excellent idea for women. We have several in the museum, as secretaries. Are you interested in science?'

'Not really.'

'Well, don't dismiss it. It's not just test tubes in labs. There's ever so much to know about the world, reaching back into the past, and looking forward into the future. Although admittedly, I am more of a looking-into-the-past man.' He gave her a sideways look. They were approaching the bridge over the moat now. 'Are you the one I see palely loitering in the garden?'

'Sometimes,' she said vaguely.

'What's so interesting about that other tower? I've seen you standing outside staring at it.'

'Oh . . . nothing.'

'Really? Because I've got the distinct impression there's at least one person in there.'

Miranda thought fast. 'Well, now you say, there is a guest in there. She's a convalescent. A friend of the family. She needs peace and quiet so she's living in there in strict privacy.'

Mr Humphries looked pleased. 'So I was right. Strange state of affairs but I suppose if one needs the privacy, one would have it in there. Well, I was going to explore and knock and say hello, but I won't now.'

'Probably for the best.' She changed the subject quickly. 'So, what's your work all about then?'

Mr Humphries gave her a sideways glance, almost mischievous. 'It's rather exciting. Look, we're almost back at the house. Why don't I show you?'

The desk in Mr Humphries's study was covered with textbooks, scientific journals and open notebooks with pages of inky black scrawl, along with an ashtray full of cigarette butts, pencil shavings and a large sharpener. He gestured to it all proudly. 'There! My research on Dinornithidae.'

'On what?'

Mr Humphries perched on the desk and lit a cigarette, puffing out a cloud of smoke while he fixed Miranda with a bright gaze. 'Have you ever heard of the giant moa? No? It's an extinct bird that existed in the islands of New Zealand during the late Pleistocene–Holocene era. Think of it like a giant ostrich – long-necked and flightless, without even vestigial wing bones. Here are some pictures.' Mr Humphries put down his cigarette, shuffled about some papers and brought out a photograph of three bird skeletons with their eggs. One was very small with a round body, little round head and long curved bill. Mr Humphries pointed at it. 'The kiwi. The only nocturnal ratite.'

'Very sweet,' Miranda said. 'I've never seen one.'

'They're native to New Zealand but we have one in our collection.' Mr Humphries frowned. 'Have you never been to the Natural History Museum?'

'To see the dinosaurs,' Miranda said politely. 'I wasn't much interested in the birds.'

'How strange. Anyway. As you can see, the ostrich skeleton in the middle is really included just to show the scale, as there are plenty of live ostriches about, if you know where to look. The real beauty is this.' With a slow smile, he touched the image of the moa skeleton. The same shape as the ostrich but a third as high again, it towered over the other two birds.

'It is huge,' Miranda said with interest. 'Was it taller than a man?'

'Oh yes. The largest ostrich can be eight feet tall. The giant moa of the South Island was twice as tall as a human at over twelve feet. Imagine a great bird that large! Imagine it walking past the window – you'd only see its legs. It would stretch up to the second floor of my tower. Imagine! And people did see them. Some species survived the great Oligocene drowning event – when the North Island of New Zealand was submerged – until humans arrived there from Polynesia. We know this because they are represented in Māori cave art. But the last surviving species were hunted to extinction or had their habitats destroyed.' He pulled out another print, a line drawing of the great moa with its long curving neck, beady eyes and short beak.

'That's got the most enormous feet!' Miranda said with a laugh.

'The heavy-footed moa. Not elegant and probably not very fast.' He showed her another print of a great eagle attacking a moa. 'This was their only predator until humans arrived. The Haast's eagle. A massive bird. Imagine it in this room, nearly touching the ceiling, its wingspan as wide as the room, its feet bigger than my desk.'

Miranda shuddered. 'Like something from a nightmare.'

'It died out when the moa did,' said Mr Humphries, looking at the print. 'No moa left to eat, you see.' He picked up his cigarette, inhaled and frowned again as he released a cloud of smoke. 'Of course, the mystery is how the moa got to New Zealand in the first place, considering it was flightless. Perhaps one day we'll find out.' He looked suddenly excited. 'And do you know what is really wonderful?'

'No,' Miranda said, touched by his enthusiasm.

'The existence of the moa was posited by Richard Owens, the founder of the Natural History Museum himself. He was shown a simple piece of femur and from that he deduced the existence of a giant bird like an ostrich, and called it

the Dinornis. He was laughed at and mocked until gradually enough bone was recovered for us to assemble whole
skeletons and he was proved quite right. Not just one species, either, but several!' Mr Humphries looked delighted
at the memory of this triumph. 'That's my work. To continue the study of the species of moa, to further knowledge
and learning about them. For example, some species we
consider different may be the same but affected by sexual
dimorphism – that is to say, that the female and male are different sizes and shapes. It's all fascinating. I must say that this
war is going to rather disrupt all that.' He smoked again with
a disgruntled air. 'Leaving the museum and all its resources is
hardly ideal. But that's how it is.'

'And you have some moa here?' Miranda asked, looking
at the boxes and crates on the floor. She noticed that on the
desk, under sheaves of paper, was a microscope.

He stubbed out his cigarette, leaving the white butt
crushed in a pile of ash. 'Oh yes. There are whole skeletons in
some of the crates in the great hall. Meanwhile, I'm studying
bone fragments. And egg fragments. Obviously eggs are not
very good at surviving long periods of time. They tend to get
smashed. Still, we have a lot of fossilised egg pieces and the
remains of embryos. But look.' He beckoned her over to a
wooden crate on a table by the opposite wall. 'Look at this.
It's my greatest treasure.' She followed him over, intrigued,
and watched as he carefully unlatched the lid of the crate.
Inside was a lot of wool and straw, which he pulled back
to reveal a large, smooth putty-coloured stone object. 'A

complete moa's egg. There are only a few in existence and this is one. Isn't it a joy?'

'Well . . . yes, very nice,' she said, thinking it looked just like a huge stone pebble.

'There is probably a fossilised embryo in there, likely complete. One day perhaps we will have ways to study the egg without breaking it. But for now, it's intact. Very precious. Very. It is one of the reasons I'm here. To make sure it is kept safe during the war.'

'That is interesting,' she said, thinking of the giant baby bird inside the stone egg, imagining it curled up, fast asleep in there. 'It is huge. I don't think Toby could get his arms around it. Fancy laying that! And this is what you are doing all day.'

Mr Humphries sighed. 'There are barely enough hours.'

'Thank you so much for showing me,' Miranda said sincerely.

'You're most welcome,' he said, turning back to his desk. 'Any questions you have about the moa, I'd be happy to answer.' He looked up. 'And if you want something to do, I'm sure I could find something for you. I want some articles typed up. Would you be interested?'

'I can't type.'

'It's a way to learn. I've got a typewriter with me but I'm dreadfully slow.'

'Oh!' She blinked at him. He had just offered her exactly the thing she had most wanted. It had been her reason for going to back to St Margaret's, to learn the skill that would take her to London and get her a job on a newspaper. 'Could I? Really?'

'Of course, if you want to. It would help me as well.'

'Then yes please. I'd like that very much!' She looked doubtful. 'I'll be slow at first, though, does that matter?'

'Not a scrap. We'll start tomorrow.'

She smiled at him, elated. 'Thank you so much! I'll come after breakfast.'

Mr Humphries was reaching for another cigarette, already absorbed in something else. 'Good. Do.'

Then she ran away up the stairs to find Rosie.

Chapter Thirteen

Present Day

Atalanta called later that week, jubilant and excited. 'Guess what? Bright Eye have sold the project. We've been commissioned!'

'That's wonderful news,' Georgie said, delighted. 'Do they want to film it here?'

'I wasn't sure at first. They were looking for somewhere nearer to London to cut down on transport costs. They've even mentioned Hampton Court.'

'What?' Georgie said, dismayed. 'But here is perfect!'

'I know! I said that. And they gave it some thought and decided I was right! So we are going to film at Wakefield. Won't that be glorious?'

Georgie laughed. 'You strung me along there, Atalanta. It will be glorious. Caspar will be delighted.'

'The producer will be in touch, to sort out the contracts and discuss episode ideas. But congrats, darling, really. You've come up with a cracking idea. We're both going to be paid for another year. That's all good, isn't it?'

'Yes, very good. To be honest, it's a huge relief.'

She only realised how relieved she was when she was able to give Caspar the news. He was jubilant about the large location fee that would be paid to them. It would cover not just the hiring of the castle but payments towards disruption and loss of visitor income.

'The roof is taken care of!' he exclaimed. 'Not completely, but enough to get started and cover a big portion. That's a huge weight off my mind.' He saw Georgie's expression. 'But I can see you're a bit anxious.'

Georgie nodded. 'I'm pleased because of the money, of course. But all those people. All the noise and the coming and going. At least when they film in London or in other places I can get away if I need to. But they'll be in our home for weeks on end.'

'How bad can it be?' Caspar wondered.

'You've never seen it all. The lights, the cables, the cameras, the people, the endless takes, the set-ups . . .'

'You're right, I haven't seen it. But the upside is that all those people are going to stay here and we can charge for board and lodging!'

Georgie winced. 'It's just awful.'

Caspar put a sympathetic arm around her shoulders. 'Listen, we will press on with your tower as soon as we can. There'll be more money for that too. And then you'll have your hideaway to disappear to when you need peace and quiet. Does that make you feel better?'

'Yes. Actually, it really does.'

'Good. Then call the builder and say we want to start as soon as possible.'

After her call with Sam Locke, Georgie sat at her desk in Lady Wakefield's morning room staring into space, feeling worried again. Despite the excitement of Sam starting almost at once on the tower, the reality of the work involved and the anxiety about Pippa conspired to bring her spirits down.

As she sat staring into space, Georgie heard the familiar tones of Mrs Lambert's voice echoing down the passage as she led another parcel of visitors around. She seemed to do most of the tours; the other volunteers scarcely seemed to get a look in. Usually, Georgie put on her headphones at the first hint that a tour was coming by, and pretended not to notice when a gang of people crowded into the morning room to hear Mrs Lambert declaim about the pictures and the history of the room. She was just reaching for the noise-cancelling headset when she heard the word 'fossil' which made her stop, one hand reaching for the headphones.

Fossil? She hadn't heard that before. She thought suddenly of the pouch that she'd put in the cupboard by her bed and forgotten about. All those lovely star-shaped stones with their snowflake patterns. On impulse, she got up and went to the door, opened it and heard Mrs Lambert's regal tones echoing in the great hall. She hardly ever listened, and only seemed to pick up the same words when she did happen to tune in. Now she heard something new.

'And in 1939, at the outbreak of war, the Natural History Museum sent some of its collection here. This hall was full of packing cases, carefully stored to protect them from the Blitz. Before you ask, no, the packages were not opened! We don't even know what was in them! They all went safely back to London at the end of the war.'

Georgie was intrigued. This was a new fact about the house. How interesting. Fossils in the house! And in war-time too.

She remembered the wartime recipes at the back of the recipe book, and the last names. The hamper full of old exercise books, the uniforms and children's clothes that looked like wartime ones. And Etti Boule, the last author mentioned in the list of cooks.

It all felt somehow connected.

Mrs Lambert was now talking about her favourite topic: the painting over the fireplace. Georgie slipped out of the morning room and headed upstairs to her bedroom. Taking the exercise book out of the cupboard, she sat back against the side of the bed to read it. She stared at the letters pressed into the cover; solid capitals instead of the joined-up old-fashioned script in the girls' other books.

Inside, there was a strange jumble of text, some of it apparently in code, and sketches and diagrams. The book was in at least one hand, although it was a mixture of writing and printing that could be the same hand in different guises.

Towards the end, there was a long story entitled *The Crimes of Etti Boule* scribbled in a rapid, young hand. Georgie cast her eyes over it: it seemed to be a dramatic tale of a wicked woman.

They don't seem to like this Etti very much, Georgie

thought. *Perhaps she was a cook or a servant or a nanny or something, and they hated her.*

She suddenly thought of Great-Uncle Archie as a boy. The Wakefields – Toby, Miranda and Rosalind – were his brother and sisters. Perhaps the other children, the Fosters, were friends or cousins.

Her eye was caught by a sentence at the end of the book. *Where is the egg? The egg is the thing that matters! We must find the egg.*

She stared at it for a while, wondering why this resonated with her. An egg? Why did they care about a lost egg?

Rationing. Perhaps eggs were in short supply.

But, she reasoned, they were in a large house with big grounds and all the bounty of the countryside. No doubt there were chickens and ducks; there must have been eggs everywhere. Perhaps it was a treasure that they had lost. A rare bird's egg, perhaps. Or, more likely, an ornament. Georgie saw in her mind's eye something like a Fabergé egg, made of rock crystal or marble, hollowed out and decorated with jewels and gold.

She stared into space, imagining such a valuable object. How strange it would be if there was a hidden treasure like that somewhere in the house.

Georgie closed the book, smiling to herself. The likelihood of finding some lost precious artefact was extremely small. It was the stuff of fairy stories and not of real life. Whatever the egg was, it had no doubt been found many years ago, or else no longer mattered.

She was feeling an odd kinship, though, with the Wakefield

children of eighty years ago. It was hard not to when their voices came echoing across the decades through this funny book. She couldn't help wondering what lay behind all this fantastical gibberish.

I will take another look at the recipe book, she decided. *Perhaps Etti herself wrote one of the recipes. I can try one or two of those wartime ones out, perhaps. It could be interesting.*

With the help of Sam Locke's measurements and a handy design app that allowed her to play with layouts, Georgie pressed on with her plans for the tower. There seemed to be hundreds of decisions to make, but she knew what she liked, and thanks to her online scrapbook, she already had the details for many of the things she wanted, from drawer handles to light fittings and tiles. Then it was a question of ordering what she wanted and arranging delivery. It wasn't long before vans started arriving with the orders.

'It's lucky there's so much room here,' Caspar said, as they directed another truck around to the garages.

'That is an upside,' Georgie said with a smile. 'I do not deny the benefits of storage space.'

They were returning across the quad from waving off the delivery men, when Viktoria came out of the gatehouse door. She had been away for a while, they thought, in London, but her bright red VW had appeared in its parking space a day or so ago, announcing her return.

'What is all this?' she asked loudly, waving an arm in the direction of the garages behind the house.

'We're doing some work on the East Tower,' Caspar said. 'Some sprucing.'

Viktoria raised her thin brown brows. 'Oh really? I always thought those funny little places could be improved. Are you doing the West Tower?'

'Not yet,' Georgie said, slightly anxious in case Viktoria was going to have an opinion or decide to thwart her in some way. 'Maybe one day.'

'I wanted to take down that horrid fence in front of it. But Archie wouldn't hear of it. He wouldn't even let me go inside it.'

'That doesn't sound like Uncle Archie,' Caspar said mildly. 'He was usually very amenable.'

Viktoria shrugged. 'I know. But it was something he was very firm on. We had to the leave the West Tower completely alone. But he would never say why. I always told him that time would only make it worse. That didn't seem to matter to him.'

'He must have had his reasons,' Georgie said. She turned to Caspar. 'Perhaps we should take a look. I tried a key in the gate lock but it didn't turn. At least, not much.'

Caspar shook his head. 'I've got far too much on,' he said. 'I really can't take on that tower as well as all the rest. We should let sleeping dogs lie as far as I'm concerned.'

'You will have more trouble when it falls over,' Viktoria said with a shrug. Then she smiled an unusually charming smile. 'But that will be your problem, Caspar, not mine! So there is a positive side to all this.'

'Thank you for reminding me,' Caspar said dryly.

'Would you like to come in for some tea, Viktoria?' asked Georgie, suddenly remembering Atalanta's advice that it was better to get Viktoria onside than alienate her.

'Thank you, but no,' Viktoria said with a gracious incline of her head. 'I have to get ready for a cocktail party at the Manor.' And she turned back towards the gatehouse. 'By the way, you can thank me later.'

'What for?' Caspar asked.

'You'll see,' she said over her shoulder. 'In time.'

They watched her go.

'How does she do it?' Caspar said. 'That curious mix of annoyance and confusion I always feel around her.'

'I think they call it passive aggression,' Georgie said with a laugh. 'She's very good at it!'

Sam Locke was as keen as Georgie to get the tower complete, hoping to fit the whole job in between two much bigger ones, and he sent over a large workforce to get the grunt work done of stripping out the old fixtures and fittings. A skip on the lawn rather spoiled the look of the back garden but it wasn't there for long, before being hauled away full of the rubbish of years.

Georgie went to take a look around when it had been stripped bare and was enchanted by the clean lines and sense of space and renewal. 'Oh, it's great.'

Sam looked about, nodding under his hard yellow hat. 'It really is. They weren't as good at maximising space as in our modern designs. That kitchen was put in any old how. You'll be able to keep this feeling of space if you're clever.'

'That's what I've been working on,' Georgie said excitedly. 'Did you see the plans I sent over?'

'Yes, they're very good. Better than I expected.'

She flushed with pleasure. 'Thanks. I'm pleased with it.'

'You should be. And it's all clear as day. I'm getting the cabinets handmade locally. I know it all looks very good but the truth is that there's barely one straight line in an old place like this and the shape means that off-the-shelf just isn't going to work. It'll be quicker to get them made up exactly as we want them.'

'Fabulous. And what's the timescale?'

'As long as the rest of your kit gets here, then we're on course for the four weeks. With some late nights and weekends.'

'I'll do anything I can to help,' she said. 'Sanding, painting . . .'

'My boys will see to that,' Sam said with a smile. 'No disrespect but they're good at it. What is it you do?'

'Write cookbooks,' she said, almost apologetically.

'Well, none of them are any good at that, so why don't you carry on and leave them to it?' His sharp blue eyes twinkled at her. 'You can trust us.'

'Good point,' she said with a laugh, 'and very well made. Thanks, Sam. I'll do that.'

It was a strange feeling, Georgie found. She was busy all the time, getting up early to start work on the new book and sketch out episode ideas for the programme, emails flying back and forth between her, Atalanta and the producers.

When she had time she went out to the tower to see how things were progressing, taking pleasure in each new change no matter how small. The rewiring made her happy, and even the installation of a new circuit board made her clap her hands with pleasure. The tower was dusty and full of tools and piles of planks and plastic bags of rubbish, but she could see every day how it was emerging.

The strange feeling felt like what she imagined as contentment. Once she had only thought of it as something she could achieve through silence and solitude, with only Caspar for company. But now, people and work and noise and activity were doing the same job, and perhaps even doing it better.

Even the troops of visitors coming through, with a volunteer at the head, didn't make her feel so oppressed. She almost enjoyed seeing another group appear at the kitchen door while she was cooking up a new recipe from the old book. Mrs Lambert had taken an interest in Georgie's activity and turned out to be something of an expert on old cookery herself, and also a huge fan of Atalanta Young. Now she brought groups into the kitchen with an air of respect, and told them proudly that the kitchen was where the old cookery was being resurrected and that Atalanta herself was going to film here in due course.

'We mustn't disturb Mrs Wakefield's work!' she would say reverently. 'She's doing some extremely important research – unless she would be kind enough to share a little of it with us?'

And before long, Georgie would find herself extolling the green pistachio sauce she was making, or talking about the different variety of herbs she was using for her roasted veal.

It was a surprise, as she had always hated and feared the idea of public speaking. She had become a cookery writer precisely so she could stay hidden away in the kitchen and only have to communicate via her cookery columns and books. But now she found she forgot her painful shyness when she was here in the castle kitchen, talking about the things she was passionate about to a small group of eager listeners.

'The thing is,' she said to Sandy, who was helping her almost every day, 'I just don't know how Mrs Lambert found out about my work. Perhaps I told her.'

'You must have,' Sandy said. 'Or Caspar did?'

'Or perhaps one of the girls who was waitressing that night of the big feast. That's most likely.'

'You'll find it hard to keep a secret,' Sandy said. 'You'd think you'd be safe enough in a place like this, but no man is an island, as they say. Things come out quicker than you'd imagine, and it's hard to keep a celebrity visitor under wraps.'

'You're right,' Georgie said. 'That must be it. Now, we'd better get on with this infusion, it must be nearly ready to be heated again.'

Georgie popped the last pill of her blister pack and swallowed it. She felt a sudden rush of panic. Was this her last pack? Surely not. One of the first things she had done when they moved to the castle was to register with a local surgery so that she could continue ordering her contraception on repeat prescription. She was always careful to make sure that there was at least a month's worth left. There should be one more blister pack in the box.

She got down on the carpet in front of her bedside cupboard and opened it, looking for the box. Pulling out a few things, she saw the soft pouch she'd brought down from the attic, took it out and shook some of the stones inside into her palm. As she gazed at the tiny stone stars with their fern patterns on them, she remembered what Mrs Lambert had said to her tour about the fossils kept here in the house during the war. Was it just a coincidence that she had found some tiny fossils in the attic, in one of those old hampers? The books and clothes all looked like wartime issue.

But these can't be anything from the Natural History Museum, she said to herself. *They look like something you might find on a beach, not precious enough to merit being carefully stored in wartime. But perhaps I'm wrong. I wonder what was kept here, though?*

Georgie had never been to the Natural History Museum. She had not had a childhood where trips to museums had featured. Nor had holidays or playgrounds or trips to the beach. That had been for other children, the ones with happy homes. She would see their mothers arrive at school at the end of the day and long for one of them to be hers. They seemed so beautiful, so cosy and warm and loving, taking ownership of their offspring in order to whisk them home for their tea and story and bath and bedtime. At least, that was what Georgie supposed must be happening in those wonderful places: the safe homes with loving parents. It wasn't like that for her. So often the school office had to call Patsy or Mike to ask why she and Pippa had not been collected again. So many afternoons were spent sitting in a classroom with a cross teacher doing her marking and keeping one eye on them. So many hours were spent waiting in the playground by the gate, hoping to see Patsy or Mike coming around the corner. Although in a way, it was worse when they did turn up, annoyed that once again the girls were putting them out.

'You two are nothing but trouble,' Patsy would say crossly. 'You'll catch it later, you'll see.'

But when the head teacher came out to ask wearily why they were late again, they were all smiles. They called the girls 'sweetheart' and smiled mistily at them, promised them treats and talked about their favourite television shows. They were so convincing that even Georgie sometimes believed that a hot meal in front of the telly was waiting for them when they got home. Of course, there never was anything of the sort.

What was it about primary school that seemed to accept their situation so easily? The girls looked neat but were clearly hungry and tired. And yet, no one seemed to mind all that much. One of the dinner ladies gave Georgie extra helpings if she could but there wasn't much available. By the time the last children came to get their meals, the dinner ladies were scraping out the big metal tins to get enough food for them onto the plastic plates. Seconds were almost unheard of. The food was nasty, but Georgie still watched wistfully as the scraps were chucked in the bin. Some children barely touched theirs, but they had snacks in their school bags and a proper dinner to look forward to.

Georgie put the stones back in the pouch and put it down. The vividness of her flashbacks had crashed her mood. She felt enveloped by a blackness that hadn't been part of her life for a long time now. Not since they had arrived at the castle.

She saw her box of pills and checked that there was another blister pack inside. There was. She would order a repeat prescription tomorrow. She sat back against the side of the bed, staring at the carpet. She was still there, gazing bleakly into space, when Caspar came in.

'Hello,' he said, surprised. 'What are you doing there? Are you all right?'

She looked up, shocked out of her reverie, and managed to smile at him. 'Yes, I'm fine.'

He came over and sat down on the floor next to her, taking her hand and gazing at her with earnest, worried eyes. 'Are you sure? You look very sad.'

She said, 'I was just thinking about how I never went to the Natural History Museum.'

'You didn't?' He stroked his thumb over the top of her hand and she was comforted by his soft touch. 'Now that's awful. We must make that right as soon as possible.' Caspar was quiet for a moment. He knew that remarks like this meant that something had pulled her back into the past – a past he didn't quite understand or know about but one he knew had been difficult. 'I've been wondering if you need a break. You've been working so hard and there is so much going on. Perhaps we should take a trip away. London might be nice. I miss it myself, in fact. Do you realise we haven't left the castle beyond trips for shopping since we got here?'

'It does take over.' She felt better. Then considered. Did she want to leave? Or was she becoming more agoraphobic than

271

before, just in a much larger place? That would be ironic after her great reluctance to come here in the first instance. 'A trip to town would be very nice.'

'Good. I fancy it too. I'll start arranging it. Maybe you could see Pippa.'

'I'd like that.'

Caspar hugged her and dropped a gentle kiss on her lips. She returned it, but with a quick movement of her hand, she pushed the box of contraceptive pills just slightly under the bed so that it could not be seen.

There was no point in reminding him of that, when things were going so well between them. The roof had completely taken his mind off the fact that Georgie was meant to be considering babies, and she had no intention of bringing the idea back into his mind.

Chapter Fourteen

Caspar was as good as his word and organised a trip for the next week. 'While the iron is hot,' he said, 'we must strike.'

Georgie had mentioned the idea for a trip to Atalanta, who had promptly arranged a very luxurious boutique hotel in Kensington.

'My thank you gift,' she said. 'For coming up with the idea for the new book. And I can guess how hard you're working on the prep for me. I'm about to have a fortnight at a very nice clinic in Austria where I will be made lovely and thin again, so it's only fair if you get a treat as well.'

They arrived in their suite on the Friday evening, popped open their welcome champagne and drank it by the picture window of their drawing room.

'That's the Natural History Museum, right there,' Casper said, pointing at the pale stone of the museum's intricate Gothic facade. 'What a coincidence. Did Atalanta know you wanted to visit?'

'No,' she said. 'I didn't mention it.'

'Another Georgie moment.' He smiled at her. He said she was followed around by odd coincidences and that she almost made him believe in portents and signs, astrology, tarot and dream reading. Georgie said it probably happened to everyone. 'Now, I've booked that incredibly expensive Japanese place you wanted to eat at. So why don't I run you a bubble bath and you can get ready with another glass of this very good champagne?'

The Saturday morning of their weekend started very well. The meal the night before had been delicious and a great treat. They had walked back to the hotel hand in hand in the warm evening, enjoying the sights and sounds of London after so long. Back in their suite, they'd gone to bed and had delicious sex, and in the morning, Caspar had woken her, insistent that they do it all again.

The morning was lazy, with breakfast in a nearby cafe and then a walk in a park. After lunch it was time for the trip to the museum. They queued with everyone else and then made their way in. Inside the great entrance hall, Georgie was overwhelmed by the sight of the huge blue whale skeleton that dominated it, and the beauty of the tiles and the great staircase.

'This is amazing!' she said.

'Isn't it?' Caspar looked around appreciatively. 'I took it for granted as a child. Now I'm spellbound.'

They wandered hand in hand through the collections, looking at butterflies, moths, flies and mosquitos; birds of all shapes and sizes, from emperor penguins and emus to tiny hummingbirds. Primates, great cats, wolves and bears. Whales, sharks and all manner of fish and sea life.

When they found themselves back in the entrance hall, Georgie was bright-eyed. 'That was fabulous. I could go back round it all again, no problem.'

Caspar laughed. 'Not today. Maybe another time. But I'm glad you enjoyed it.'

'I really did.' She saw the information desk and nudged him. 'Do you mind if we go over there? I want to ask something.'

'Of course.'

They went over and waited their turn. Then Georgie explained that she had a letter for the archivist.

'You could have sent an email,' the man behind the desk said.

'I know. But emails can vanish into the ether. You never know if they've been read or not. It's easier to ignore them. So I wrote this letter. Can you pass it on to Natalie Spiller, please?'

He took the envelope from her as though it was something that ought to be an exhibit itself. 'Okay. I'll send it up to her office.'

'Thank you so much.'

Caspar took her hand as they walked out into the sunshine. 'I didn't know you'd planned to do that. What's the letter about?'

'It was something Mrs Lambert said – about there being fossils in the house during the Second World War. I've written to ask the archivist for more information.'

'Fossils.' Caspar looked thoughtful. 'Yes, perhaps I knew

that. I heard Uncle Archie say something about it. But I can't remember what exactly. Why are you interested?'

'I don't know. Just a few things that have made me think about what was in the house during the war.'

'I'm sure Mrs Lambert will be delighted to have some fresh information for her visitors.' He squeezed her hand lightly. 'Let's get some coffee, and I could do with some cake.'

That evening, Georgie had a long soak in the hotel bath, using lots of the delicious oil on offer, and got dressed in a blue silk dress that set off her fair hair. It was a little tighter, she noticed. She was putting on weight, something that usually happened at recipe-testing time. Caspar always told her it suited her, but she didn't think about it much. It usually dropped away when her eating went back to normal.

Looking at herself in the mirror, though, she noticed that she did look different from how she had a few months ago. It was not just that her face was rounder but her eyes seemed to have a different look in them.

Perhaps it was her imagination but maybe she looked slightly less haunted.

'I've got a little surprise for this evening,' Caspar said, as he put in his cufflinks and got out his jacket. 'I wasn't going to say anything but maybe you'd appreciate knowing beforehand.'

'How exciting.' Georgie put on her mascara. 'What is it?'

'I've invited Pippa to join us for dinner.'

Georgie looked up at him, touched. She had told him that Pippa and Ryan were having problems, and that Pippa had found a counsellor that she thought might be able to help them. Ryan had agreed to go, and they were waiting for their first session. 'Caspar! That's so kind – on our romantic weekend too.'

'I had you all to myself last night,' he said, coming up to kiss her. 'So I don't mind sharing you tonight. I know how much it would mean to you to see her.'

'Thank you, sweetheart. That's so thoughtful.' She smiled up at him, her heart full of gratitude. She knew suddenly and clearly that Ryan would never do such a thing for Pippa. It made her appreciate Caspar all over again.

'You're welcome. Are you ready? We should get on our way.'

They walked to an Italian trattoria a few streets away; not as glamorous as the smart Japanese the night before, but a place that they had always liked for the warm atmosphere and hearty food. The houses in Kensington were elegant: tall, white and well kept, with iron railings in front, shiny black doors and clean steps. This part of the city was monied, an enclave for the rich – financiers, lawyers, media executives, businessmen and women. The cars in the road were smart, the shops, delis and boutiques tasteful and clearly expensive.

Georgie had not known this kind of lavish world existed when she was growing up. To her, London was the deprived area around Lewisham where Patsy and Mike had their flat on the tenth floor of a high-rise block of apartments, one of several built around an estate. It had no doubt been conceived of as a beacon of civilised and modern living when it was constructed in the early seventies, but it hadn't worked out that way. There was concrete everywhere, just a few straggly trees here and there, and some bushes that were usually full of rubbish. The playgrounds had worn out over the years through use and vandalism and were never replaced, so the swings were broken, the roundabout didn't move and the climbing frame was chipped and covered in graffiti. The slide still worked but that was all. Not that it mattered, as the playgrounds were where big kids hung out, smoked, took drugs, fought and indulged in taking stuff from younger kids. All around the estate, spray paint covered every surface, and skateboarders and cyclists used it as a giant skate park. The bins were always overflowing, the lifts never worked and the staircases always stank of urine.

It always seemed like a long walk to the bus stop or to the park.

Despite this, Patsy and Mike kept their flat looking nice. Many of the families did. The Patels on the floor above them were very proud of their home, which was colourful and welcoming and smelled of delicious spices. How they managed to keep so cheerful and organised with grandparents, parents and five children all living in there, Georgie couldn't guess.

As Patsy and Mike's flat was clean and neat, the social workers who came around always complimented Patsy on how well she kept her house. They didn't seem to notice that there were few signs that children even lived there. There were no photographs of the girls, no toys in the sitting room, no drawings on the fridge, no school books or tins of crayons on the table. In the sitting room was a vast television but no DVDs of cartoons or films for children. There were no picture books, sticker albums or comics on the one bookshelf.

The girls' room was extremely tidy as well, their beds tightly made and tucked in. The beds had a small chest of drawers between them, a plain lamp on it. There was one painting, a religious one of angels around a table. Each bed had a soft toy on it but there was no other sign of toys, books, possessions or the general mess of childhood.

This, thought the observers of the girls' lives, was a sign of how well they were looked after.

Patsy made tea, Mike turned on the charm, the girls sat quietly and obediently and nodded yes or no when they were asked anything, as the social workers – usually a different one each time as they seemed to move on at dizzying speed – filled in their forms and went on their way, always in a hurry and with far too much to do.

In some way, Georgie and Pippa had understood that these harried women – it was almost always women – were the only way that they were going to get out of the flat. But where would they go? Everyone seemed to think it was so right that they were with Patsy and Mike. Who would listen to them if they dared to say that they didn't like it?

When Georgie saw the Patel children with their mother in her beautiful bright sari, skipping and chattering, badgering her for sweets or hanging off a hand while the other pushed the buggy, she was in awe of their freedom to simply be themselves. They seemed to have no fear of their mother, not in the way Georgie was afraid. They were polite to their parents and grandparents but they were also cheeky and funny, and showed how they felt without any worry for the consequences.

What must it be like? wondered Georgie. *To feel like that?*

There was not a day when she and Pippa did not live in fear. In her mind, quite suddenly, she was walking back from school, climbing the stairs with the tinny, musty odour of urine all around her, the feeling of dread climbing within her, increasing with every step. The sound of her shoes echoed through the stairwell, *slap*, *slap*, *slap*, taking her closer to the tenth floor.

'Here we are,' Caspar said, pulling her back to the present. 'Right on time. You're always punctual to the minute. I don't know how you do it, you never seem to be checking your watch.'

'Instinct,' Georgie said lightly, grateful to leave the stairwell in her mind. She could feel her heart racing and she took a deep breath. She hadn't gone back there in her imagination, to the flat, for some time. But the effect on her was always the same.

Caspar pushed open the door to the restaurant and she felt comforted by the familiar surroundings, the warm greeting of Marcella, the owner, and the scent of food that filled the air. Here there was laughter, acceptance and lots to eat. That was what she needed right now.

There was no sign of Pippa. They settled at their table, Caspar ordered the wine and they munched on salted breadsticks wrapped with prosciutto while they waited for her. After a while, Georgie checked her phone to see a text from her sister.

I'm so sorry. I can't come. Everything is fine but I can't make it after all. I'm sorry, Georgie. I will call you very soon. Give my love to Caspar xxx

'What's wrong?' Caspar asked, seeing her expression.

'Pippa's not coming.' She read out the text.

'That's a shame. I'm so sorry, Georgie. You were really looking forward to seeing her.' Caspar clicked his tongue with annoyance. 'She should have made the effort.'

'We don't know why she isn't coming,' Georgie said. 'One of the children is probably sick.'

'Why can't Ryan look after them? For once?'

'You know what he's like – quite spectacularly lazy around the children, though he can always find time to play football, cricket, golf and watch every major sporting fixture. Anyway, it might not be that, we don't know.'

Casper filled her glass. 'I'm sorry for you, darling, I know you wanted to see her. I did too.'

'It's all right,' Georgie said, wishing she didn't feel so uneasy. It was more than disappointment. It was a kind of dread. 'I just hope she's all right.'

'You can call her later and check. She says she's fine,' Caspar said. 'I think we should order.'

'Yes,' she said, relieved to put her mind to the menu, where life was easier and safer.

The plan had been to go back to the castle by train on the Sunday after making the most of their luxurious suite until checkout time. Caspar ordered breakfast to their room and they ate it propped up by mountains of pillows.

'Why is it that hotel beds are so nice?' Georgie asked, taking a mouthful of croissant. 'I mean, we live in a castle and sleep in a four-poster bed. That ought to be luxurious. But it's nothing like this. It's so comfortable. I could stay here all day.'

'I should think that it's partly because the beds get changed every day – by someone else.' Caspar was making great inroads into smoked salmon and poached eggs, as if he had not devoured a huge plate of pasta the night before. 'I must check the time of our train.'

'Actually,' Georgie said slowly, 'I was going to talk to you about that. Would you mind very much going back alone to Wakefield?'

Caspar looked surprised. 'That's an unexpected end to our romantic weekend! Are you leaving me?'

'Of course not. I'd like to go down and see Pippa, while I'm so close.'

'That's a very good idea. Of course you must.'

'Thanks, darling. I'll text her now.'

A couple of hours later, Georgie was on the train to Brighton. Before she left the hotel, she had written a text to Pippa.

I'm so sorry to have missed you. I've got a feeling that something is wrong. I should have come to see you ages ago but as I'm so close, I'm coming down from London today. I'll fit around your plans but I really want

to see you, however briefly. Please let me know how we can do this xx

Ten minutes later, her phone chimed to show that a message had arrived and she opened it.

I'm so sorry about last night. I want to see you but please don't come to the house. I can meet you at a cafe by the front at 3 p.m. It's called Florian. I will see you there.

Georgie felt both relieved and more worried. Pippa was all right, but there must be a reason why she didn't want Georgie at the house.

She stared out of the window and worried until the train drew into the station.

In the cafe, Georgie settled into a window seat, then changed her mind and took a seat at a table at the back instead. She ordered a coffee and waited. It was a quarter past three when the door opened and Pippa came in, looking anxiously for Georgie. Her face brightened when she saw her, and she waved as she came over.

Georgie stood up to hug and kiss her. 'Pippa,' she said urgently, staring into her sister's face. 'Are you all right? What's happened?'

Pippa looked surprised. 'What do you mean?'

'Look at you.' Georgie scanned her sister. Pippa had always been well turned out, as Georgie was. They both had understated styles but liked to be elegant and presentable. Pippa, Georgie thought, was the prettier, and always looked good, with shiny fair hair and discreet make-up. But now her hair was dirty and unbrushed, her face bare. She was wearing a well-worn sweatshirt, jeans and trainers. She didn't look all that clean either. 'You don't look yourself.'

Pippa looked down at herself as if confused. 'Perhaps I could have made more of an effort . . .'

'When did you last have a shower or wash your hair?'

Pippa shook her head. 'Well, I don't know . . . a couple of days ago?' She touched her hair self-consciously and flushed. 'I didn't realise it was that bad. Sorry.'

They sat down and Georgie signalled for another coffee, then she took her sister's hand. 'I'm not criticising you, darling Pippa. But you don't look right. How long have you been wearing those clothes?'

'I don't know. I just put them on.' She laughed bitterly. 'Sometimes I don't take them off.'

'What do you mean?'

Pippa shrugged. 'Sometimes I can't be bothered to get changed for bed. I just sleep in my clothes.'

Georgie's eyes filled with tears. 'What? Oh, Pippa, what's happening? What's going on?'

Pippa bit her lip and stared at the table. Then she looked up, sighed and said, 'Ryan. It's Ryan, of course.'

They talked for an hour, Pippa rushing to say as much as she could before she had to go back. 'The kids are playing next door with my neighbour Debs and she's going to feed them. But I'll have to get them before too long.'

Georgie listened while Pippa told her the truth about how Ryan was treating her. She said that it had been wrong from the start but she had just never really noticed. 'I rushed about doing everything, as though that was normal, and I didn't notice that he let me. And I mean, he *let* me – as though he was doing me this huge favour by permitting me to do his laundry and clean his house and have his children. And with Ryan, his way is just ordinary life. When he watches telly all evening, and I sit through more golf or whatever, that's just normal married life. But if we watch half an hour of what I want, I'm getting this huge treat and I should be grateful. It was subtle at first, because I didn't really notice. But once we had the kids and the real hard graft started . . . then he got more and more resentful if I complained. If I said nothing but did what he wanted, he was fine. If I complained, he just acted as though there was nothing he had done and I was the one with the problem.'

'He sounds passive aggressive,' Georgie said. 'And that's the best possible take on it.'

'I think it's more than that.' Pippa told her story after story of tiny aggressions that Ryan had inflicted on her, from the constantly sabotaged birthdays and Mother's Days, to the forgetting of important work commitments, to booking the car for its MOT on the day she'd said she definitely needed it. One by one, these incidents didn't sound much, but it was horribly familiar to Georgie. She knew that this kind of constant undermining made a pattern.

'You told me to write it down and so I did. And I've started to see that he always acts in the same way. If I point out what he's doing, it makes no difference. Nothing changes. In fact, it gets worse. It's like the more I see it, the less he bothers to hide it.'

Georgie pushed her empty cappuccino mug to one side. 'Would it help if I talk to him?'

Pippa grabbed her hand. 'No,' she said urgently. 'Don't do that.'

'Why not? What's he doing?'

Pippa looked away. 'Nothing exactly. It sounds like nothing. He throws these fits, and runs out of the house. He kind of . . . loses it. I can't really explain it.'

Georgie felt that Pippa was hiding something but she didn't want to push her. It was clear that there was a serious rift. 'Have you been to counselling?'

Pippa nodded. 'We've had two sessions. But I don't think it's going to work. He just doesn't really seem to be listening. He stares at the floor or else looks agonised, or tells things in a way that just isn't true. But if I say it's not true, the counsellor tells me that it's Ryan's truth and that he's entitled to that.'

Georgie said, 'But do you love him?'

Pippa thought for a while, her expression pained. 'I don't know. He's not always awful. When he's my lovely Ryan again, I really love him. And sometimes when he's throwing these petulant tantrums I feel sorry for him because he really appears to be in a state of confusion and upset. I want to comfort him and help him. When he says he loves me and wants to make it better, I want the same. And then . . . it just all goes back to the same place, as though we can never get off the merry-go-round. And then I don't love him. I just feel desperate.'

'He needs help,' Georgie said firmly.

'He doesn't think so. He thinks I'm the problem, not him. He says if I just leave him alone, we'll both be happier.'

'So he wants a quiet life, in which you submit and ask for nothing while doing all the work?'

Pippa looked very tired suddenly. 'I suppose so. And maybe he's right. I just don't know if I've got the stomach for this fight. He knows I'll keep a happy facade for the kids, for our neighbours and friends. He knows it'll probably be easier for me to give in than to leave.'

Georgie said, 'We both know what that sounds like.'

Their eyes met across the cafe table. Georgie read in Pippa's face that she knew what Georgie was saying.

She said quietly, 'It's all very well to put on a good show. But that doesn't mean that life behind the scenes isn't unbearable.'

Pippa looked away, frightened. 'It isn't like that,' she whispered. 'It isn't like before.'

'Isn't it?'

Pippa looked agonised suddenly. 'Please don't say that, Georgie! We've spent our lives getting away from that. I can't bear the idea that I've put myself back where I started. I had so much faith! I believed in him. I can't give up unless I know for sure that it's hopeless.'

Georgie took her hand and said, 'You're not back where you started. We both survived. We both learned to get through. You can get through this too. I can help you and you are strong enough.'

But Pippa had slumped again. 'I feel like such a failure.' She looked up at her sister. 'Perhaps he's right and it is all my fault.'

'This is not your fault, Pippa! You are not responsible for his behaviour. He won't accept responsibility for yours, will he? Well, you have the same right. He doesn't have to act like a spoiled child and throw a tantrum when he's held to account. He could choose to talk problems through and own his actions.' She thought back to that wedding speech. Ryan had been criticising beautiful, kind Pippa on her wedding day. He had quietly but firmly told the room that she was a difficult woman and she was lucky to have him. It came back to her with a flash of complete insight. Pippa had never had a chance.

'You need to see where the marriage counselling takes you,' Georgie said. 'You need someone who can see what he's doing and make him stop. Because we both know what it's like to live that way. It's unendurable. If he can't change, you'll have to leave him.'

'I can't do that,' Pippa said, starting to cry. 'I know it's mad, but after his tantrums, he's so sweet to me, he makes love to me and says he loves me. I just feel that if I can make him understand that I need some help and support, that I can't cope on my own, then he might see that he's being unreasonable. And anyway . . .' – she wiped away her tears – 'I can't leave him. He's already told me that he'll fight for custody of the children. I can't do that to them. And

I can't face it for myself either. I've got to stick it out, for their sakes.'

'You have to do what's right for you,' Georgie said. 'But if the counselling fails, then you can't go on like this, Pippa. You really can't.'

Pippa nodded miserably. 'I must get back now. Debs is waiting. I'm already late.'

They said goodbye outside the cafe.

'Ring me if you ever need me,' Georgie said. 'I mean it.'

'Thank you, Georgie. Thank you so much. I'm so glad you know. You can't think how glad.'

'I hear you, Pippa. I believe you.'

Pippa's eyes filled with tears again. She whispered, 'Thank you. I needed to hear that.'

They hugged tightly and parted. Georgie stood watching her sister walk slowly away, and felt a burning rage that she hadn't experienced for a long time.

Georgie went home on the train, more worried and preoccupied than before. The change in her sister was so marked. Pippa had once been bright and confident. It had taken time for her to recover from their childhood experience, but once it was behind them she had bounced back more easily than Georgie. She had been positive and optimistic about the future, excited about her life.

Now she looked haunted and broken, as though she was existing in a state of constant anxiety. Her confidence was clearly shot.

What is going on? wondered Georgie. *How could Ryan change like this?*

But he hadn't changed at all, that was the reality. He had always expected Pippa to look after him with nothing in return. She recalled Ryan's parents and their obvious and gooey admiration for their son. Georgie had wondered what amazing qualities they were seeing, as they remained so much a mystery to everyone else. Were his parents the problem? They had clearly never breathed a word of criticism or held to him to account in his life.

Perhaps it didn't matter how he had ended up this way. It was now a question of whether he could change his behaviour.

But his attitude towards Pippa was worrying Georgie the most. He didn't seem to care how she felt, not even a little bit. It was all about the facade.

It made panic churn deep in her stomach and the memories come rolling back. She felt a great drive of guilt coursing through her. She, Georgie, had let this happen. She had taken her eyes off Pippa and allowed her to be vulnerable. She had let violence and wickedness come near Pippa again when she had promised, had *sworn*, that she would never let anything happen to her again.

It's all so horribly familiar, she thought. *I feel like I've been here before, but now I'm powerless to help her. Once I could protect her, but now I can't. Her only hope is that he will change. Does Pippa have that time to gamble on something so unlikely?*

Somehow she did not think so.

*

Georgie was surprised by how happy she was to see Wakefield as Caspar drove her up to the front door after collecting her from the station. She used to dread this place and now she was delighted to be back even after so little time away. She had started to feel safe here. It was a world within a world.

Caspar was grim-faced. His smile had faded as soon as he'd seen Georgie's weary and worried expression. 'How was she?' he asked.

'Not good. Much worse than I feared.'

'Things have got worse with Ryan?'

Georgie had nodded.

'An affair?'

'No. Not that. At least, she didn't say anything about it. Much stranger and more complicated.'

'Oh dear.'

He had asked no more on the journey home and she had not wanted to speak about it. But much later, after a simple supper and a rest, she told him the whole story. To her surprise, Caspar did not seem to grasp the seriousness of what she was saying. When she mentioned the wedding speech, he said, 'Oh, surely he was just joking! I remember that speech from the wedding video – everyone thought it was hilarious. He obviously adored Pippa on their wedding day.'

She felt annoyed. 'That's the whole point. You think it was hilarious but you didn't hear what he was actually saying. You thought he was joking when he was telling us all a very important truth.'

Caspar shook his head. 'I think you're overthinking that one.'

Georgie said, 'But it's precisely this that he relies on – that people will always think the best of him, take what he is doing in a positive light! Can't you see that?'

'You can't really mean that Ryan made a conscious decision, on his wedding day, to tear Pippa to shreds. I don't see that at all.'

'You're right, not a conscious one. I don't think he thought, *Ha ha, I'll show that cow what for and tell everyone how awful she is.* He thought he was being sweet and funny and I've no doubt that he thought he loved her. But he showed us the truth! He can't help it.'

'I suppose so.' Caspar shook his head. 'I still can't see it of Ryan, though.'

Georgie sighed. 'I know, it's hard. But that benign, mild-mannered exterior is not the full story.'

Caspar looked grave. 'He might have some mental health issues – depression, perhaps. And possibly Pippa does need to back off and give him some time to recover. It might be that Ryan needs understanding.'

She stared at him. A light seemed suddenly to illuminate her mind, and she could see everything very clearly.

So this is what Pippa is afraid of, she realised. *Ryan is making himself the victim. He is putting the blame onto her. I can see that now.*

She suddenly saw a situation in the future where Ryan played the martyr and told everyone that Pippa had driven him to leave her. Good people would take him at face value. They would not think that he was capable of being

292

manipulative in this way. And he might use that in some way to punish her, to take her children even.

No wonder she is afraid. I am too. He is cleverly trapping her exactly where he wants her.

Oh, Pippa. How are we going to get you out of this?

Chapter Fifteen

1939

Miranda came running out of her room at the sound of violent shouting. She had been lost in the *Teach Yourself Shorthand* book that had arrived for her that morning when the rumpus on the landing broke into her concentration.

Out on the landing she could see Imogen attempting to part Toby and Tom Foster as they fought and kicked and struggled with one another, now rolling on the landing rug and chasing each other around like whirling dervishes.

'Stop it, you little wretches!' cried Imogen, grasping for them while trying to keep clear of kicking boots and punching fists.

Archie was jumping up and down, shouting, 'Let him have it, Toby, let him have it!' while Robbie watched with huge glittering eyes. It wasn't clear if he was relishing the struggle or was appalled by it.

Just as Miranda was wondering if she should intervene, Mr Humphries came bounding up the stairs, shouting, 'Now then, boys, what's the trouble, eh?'

They barely seemed to hear him.

Imogen stood back, flustered, her fair hair askew and cheeks flushed. She called out over the racket. 'Oh, Mr Humphries, did they disturb you? I'm sorry! I don't even know what set them off! Toby, Tom! Do stop, won't you?'

'Here, you boys!' Mr Humphries shouted, and suddenly the four of them froze. The panting strugglers, now on the floor, turned to look at him and the two smaller spectators stared. All four looked as though they hadn't seen a creature like him in their lives.

Perhaps they haven't, Miranda thought. *Toby and Archie haven't seen a grown man – aside from Grandfather – in the house for years. Who knows about the Fosters?*

A couple of postcards had arrived from Clapham written in careful script, assuring the boys that they were keeping well at home and that Dad sent his love – not that the boys had responded in any way when Aunt Constance read them out, just listened blank-faced before scampering away. But there was a father somewhere, even if the love being sent was making its way from some training camp.

'That's enough scrummage,' Mr Humphries said firmly, pulling the older boys to their feet. 'You're going to wear Miss Wakefield out.' He looked over at Imogen and gave her a charming smile, his brown eyes crinkling behind his glasses.

He is rather handsome, Miranda thought with surprise. *The glasses aren't so bad after all. I wonder if he wears them for protection as much as for seeing?*

Imogen was still flushed with embarrassment. 'I can't think why I can't keep order.' She looked at the boys, still breathless but now peaceful. 'You should listen to me and behave!'

'A good prep school would put them right – no offence, Miss Wakefield. These boys are too old to be in the school-room. They need some proper lessons and decent sport to burn up all that youthful enthusiasm.' Mr Humphries regarded them thoughtfully. 'You little scamps. I think we'll have a nature lesson and give Miss Wakefield a morning off.'

'You can't do that, Mr Humphries, I can't take you away from your work!' Imogen protested.

'You're not. These boys are. But don't worry, I can do some field work if I need to. I can't sit at a desk all day.' Humphries looked back at the boys. 'I have a feeling that you lads are rather enjoying this violent feud of yours. Which is all very well. But I think a new rule is needed. Your battles can only take place outside when you're not in lessons.' He gestured around. 'You've got a castle here, after all. What better place for it?'

The boys looked at one another, narrowing their eyes and curling their lips.

Oh, Miranda thought, amused. *It's a game. It's all a game for them.*

She felt suddenly buoyed up. Her little brothers had barely been children for years – not carefree, happy and curious like they ought to be. And now, suddenly, through the medium of fighting, they seemed to be rediscovering their joy in life.

Mr Humphries clapped his hands. 'Jackets and caps on. We're going out. Meet me by the back door in ten minutes.' The boys scampered away to obey in a way they had not for Imogen. He glanced over at Miranda. 'Are you coming with us?'

She opened her mouth to say no, and then said, 'Well, why not?'

'Excellent.'

Imogen stepped forward, her hands clasped. 'This is too good of you, Mr Humphries—'

'Why don't you come too, Miss Wakefield?' he said. 'If you can stand being around these terrors? I promise to knock their heads together if you command it.'

Imogen went pinker and then said, 'I would like that – I mean, not the heads. The field trip.'

'Excellent. We'll all go.'

Miranda turned to return her book to her room and saw Rosalind disappearing down the passage in the other direction. She had barely spoken to her since the interview with Aunt Constance and showed no interest in warming their relations. Instead, when she wasn't painting, Rosalind was spending most of her time in the kitchen, teaching herself to cook now that Mrs Graham was going to Bournemouth to live with her sister for the duration.

Surely she'll soften in time, Miranda thought. *But I wish she'd come with us.*

Mr Humphries took them on a field trip around the castle grounds, pointing out the flowers and foliage, examining rocks and pebbles and identifying birds.

'They're off for the winter!' he exclaimed, pointing out a flock of migrants. 'Off to sunny Egypt.'

The boys looked up. They had been a little in awe of Mr Humphries at first, but had soon warmed up. Their hostility to one another had abated and now they were chattering and asking questions, knocking stones about with sticks and grubbing in the grass and flower beds for whatever they could find. They followed him obediently as he led them out of the castle grounds and into the fields at the side of the house.

Like chicks following a mother hen, Miranda thought.

The boys were more like cubs following a bear, prone to rolling around and bounding off, always veering back to the parent after a while. Imogen walked along with Mr Humphries and they chatted easily, looking very similar with their fair hair and tweed jackets. Mr Humphries smoked as he pointed out the mysteries of the brook at the far end of the field, and the boys took off their boots, despite the cold, and began wading in the shallow water and exploring the mud with sticks.

Archie found an old glass bottle, which he displayed with pride. 'Look! What is it?'

'Ginger beer, I think,' said Humphries, inspecting it. 'Victorian. Well done, young chap, you'll be a mudlark yet.'

Toby and Tom found lots of shards of pottery, some glazed, some terracotta.

'People always do like throwing things in brooks,' Mr Humphries said thoughtfully. 'I think we can understand that, can't we?' And he picked up a stone and threw it down the brook, where it landed with a satisfying splash. That started a competition to throw stones down the brook, which kept Toby, Tom and Archie occupied while Robbie continued to grub in the mud of the shallows.

'He's very nice, really, isn't he?' Miranda said, stuffing her hands in her pockets. 'I thought he'd be a bore at first, but he's not really.'

'He is nice,' Imogen agreed. 'It's rather shaming how easily he's making the boys behave.'

'They're doing the things boys like, I suppose. Perhaps they've been shut up too much. More freedom. They say boys are like dogs, but perhaps they're like cats: you give them freedom and trust they'll come back rather than keeping them on tight leads.'

Imogen laughed. 'You're quite the philosopher! Well, I can't pretend this isn't a blessed relief. I was getting rather tense about the whole business.' They stood for a moment, watching the stone tossing, and then Imogen said, 'I can see you and Rosie aren't getting along.'

'She's cross because I found out about Mother and didn't tell her. But it was only a few days before.'

'You kept a secret from Rosalind?' Imogen gave her sister a quizzical look. 'And you're telling me? I thought I was excluded permanently from your private club. Things really have changed.'

'I do want her to forgive me,' Miranda said soberly. 'I hated hiding something from her. But I was on a promise to Aunt Constance. And . . . I was worried about her sleepwalking again.'

Imogen nodded. They all knew about Rosalind's tendency to express her fears through nighttime wandering.

'I'm sure she'll forgive you,' Imogen said kindly. 'Give her time.'

Miranda nodded. She looked up at her older sister. 'We

didn't mean to exclude you, you know. I suppose that, as twins, we can't help it.'

'I suppose you can't.' Imogen smiled at her. 'And I'd rather you were close than not. Honestly. Now, I'd better get those boys back home, their feet are turning blue.'

Imogen took the cold, wet boys back to the house to get ready for lunch, finding them docile after the exertion of their morning outing, and happy to return clutching their treasures. The morning also seemed to have resolved the simmering aggression between the boys and they chattered all the way back, with Toby and Archie promising the Fosters that they would take them to the stables and show them the horses.

'You'll like Harris when you get to know him,' Toby told them confidently. 'He looks frightening but he's really a lamb.'

'A lamb?' Robbie said wonderingly. 'What?'

'Not a real lamb,' Toby said kindly.

Miranda laughed when she heard their conversation as they followed Imogen away.

'What's so funny?' Mr Humphries said, coming up to her, rolling down his sleeves from where he'd been dipping his arms in the water.

'Just the boys. You've really worked a miracle today.'

Humphries shrugged. 'I should have done it before now. I knew that they were finding it tricky to get on. I know boys, you see, having been one. And I've got an older brother whom I adore, but would happily have murdered from age five to about fifteen.'

Miranda nodded. They fell into step as they strolled back towards the house, watching the little party in front hurry on ahead.

After a while, Mr Humphries said, 'I've been meaning to talk to you. Your aunt had a long discussion with me last night.'

'Yes?'

'I told her that I'd noticed I had a neighbour. I've seen a rather beaky lady come and go from the tower, very early in the mornings before you lot are awake, laden with baskets and what have you. Your mother's maid, I'm told. Your aunt explained the situation so obviously I wanted to know if I could help in any way. I'm terribly sorry that you're all in this dreadful predicament. It must be truly awful. If it's any comfort to you and your sisters, I'll be keeping an eye on the tower. Your aunt says they are doing well so far, and that the patient is calm most of the time at the moment, though they are keeping her heavily sedated. The move back to the familiar surroundings has to be handled carefully, apparently. I thought you'd like to know that, in case no one has said.'

Miranda felt a mixture of relief and prickling embarrassment. But it was better that he knew and it made sense that the only able-bodied man around, apart from Alf, was able to contribute to Mother's welfare.

'Thank you,' she said, staring at the ground as they walked. 'It's very odd, to have a mother who doesn't know who she is.'

'I've heard of a case a bit like it. They call it a fugue state. The brain has to protect itself from some awful knowledge and so it simply blanks it out. And other things can go along with it, so that there is a kind of amnesia. That seems to be what your mother is suffering. Your aunt told me that when she comes closer to being herself, she starts to suffer from great fear and dread, and uncontrollable fits. That's why they keep her calm with medicine.'

'So the doctors can help?' she asked hopefully. After all, Mr Humphries was a scientist and might know about these things.

'Perhaps. I'm sure there is research into it. But at this moment, I suspect that doctors are focusing on other things.'

'Yes, of course.' Her spirits swooped. The war – that great, doom-laden thing going on so far away – would even affect Mother's potential to get better. It seemed so unjust.

He gave her a sideways look. 'How about you take your mind off it by doing a little more typing for me? You made a good start but I'm sure some practice would help.'

'Yes please, I'd like that,' she said after a moment. 'I really would.'

'Excellent training for a journalist, after all. Come and see me tomorrow and we'll get started on my latest article.' Mr Humphries shivered suddenly. 'That turn in the water was a little chilly, you know. I'm rather looking forward to getting back. Miss Wakefield promised cocoa when we return, and I'm looking forward to it.'

Miranda found her twin in the kitchen, where Rosalind was sorting out eggs in the basket she had collected them in. Mrs Graham had handed over care of the flock of chickens to

Rosalind, who had taken to looking after them with much enthusiasm and was keeping the family well supplied.

'Oh, hello,' Rosalind said coolly, as Miranda came in. 'How was your field trip?'

'We missed you.'

'I had lots to do.'

Miranda came up to her and tried to look into her eyes, but Rosalind wouldn't look back, instead concentrating on brushing muck and straw from the shells of the eggs. 'Please, Rosie, can't we be friends again? I'm really ever so sorry about not telling you. It wasn't for all that long and I was on a promise.'

Rosalind's expression stayed cold. 'Of course we're friends.'

'But we're not, are we? Why are you so cross?'

Rosalind said nothing for a while but her mouth had tightened and Miranda thought she detected a wobble in her chin. When she finally spoke, although she was concentrating very hard on her eggs, her voice was high and strained. 'I can't bear to be left out. Mother matters just as much to me as she does to you.'

'She probably matters more,' Miranda said softly. 'That's the thing. I was worried about you. You know you sleepwalk when you're anxious and I didn't want to risk you walking in the blackout.'

She still didn't want to tell her sister about the battlements. It would surely scare her. It still scared Miranda to think about it and she preferred not to.

There was a pause as Rosalind absorbed what Miranda had said. 'I see,' she said, her voice slightly less strained.

Miranda continued. 'I couldn't bear for you to be hurt, and I know you can't help it when you walk. That's the only reason I didn't tell you, I promise.'

'I haven't walked since they told us,' Rosalind said. 'Well, since Aunt Constance did.'

Grandfather had not yet breathed a word on the subject, although he knew that they were now aware of their mother's presence at the castle. It all seemed to be still overwhelming for him and a lifetime of repression was not about to stop now.

'No. But perhaps that's because, at last, there's been some honesty on the subject.'

Rosalind turned her blue gaze to her sister, looking her full in the face for the first time since they'd fallen out. 'What do you think about Mother being here? Why can't we see her? It's just more cruelty!'

Miranda told her quickly what Humphries had said. 'They're keeping her sedated. She wouldn't know us or talk to us.'

'It's still so hard to understand why Mother would not want to be with us.'

'It's an illness,' Miranda said gravely. 'Not a question of wanting. And we must all be very brave about it.'

'I'd still like to see her. Sedated or not.' There was a longing in Rosalind's voice that Miranda knew well. 'Wouldn't you?'

'Of course.' She put an arm around her sister. 'I'm desperate to see her too. I'm sure we will, soon. And when we do, won't that be something?'

Rosalind managed a wan smile. 'Oh yes.'

Miranda hugged her. 'Are we friends again? Am I forgiven?'

'Yes . . . I suppose so.'

'Good. Then let me tell you about Mr Humphries and the miracle of the brook.'

'If you must . . .' Rosie handed her an egg. 'And you can get the muck off this while you're doing it.'

She knew they were friends again.

Peace had been restored in the nursery, but the four boys played their battle games around the castle. They could be found engaging in mock fights all over the place, using the great house as their battlefield. It kept all their free hours occupied, and no one knew when they might come across a tiny regiment of two, armed with toy guns and bows and arrows, crawling on their stomachs along a passage to avoid the enemy, or planning strategy behind a sofa in the Oak Room, or setting up camp in the cellar.

'Boys being boys,' Mr Humphries said mildly. 'And quite right too.'

Despite the new and unaccustomed obedience in the castle schoolroom, Imogen gave up on lessons and started working as a teacher at the village school, where the absence of the younger schoolmasters and the influx of evacuee children had created a need for more staff. Aunt Constance was persuaded to give up her pony and trap, and each morning Imogen drove the four boys to school, picking up some others from outlying cottages on her way. At the school, she put Harris to spend the day grazing on the playing field, before bringing them all back in the afternoon when school was over.

The war did not seem as frightening as they had all anticipated. In fact, very little was happening as far as they could tell. There was not much about the war on the wireless, the newspapers gave hardly anything away and life seemed to be settling into a strangely static routine as the autumn led on. The bustle of things had subsided – the making of plans for the future seemed an odd thing to do with everything so uncertain. Nevertheless, they became accustomed to change without even realising it. The girls did the cooking now that Mrs Graham had gone, though Lottie had mercifully rescinded her notice and was still helping. Alf had gone off to work on the roads, as he'd been rejected for service, so Mr Humphries commenced each day with an hour or two of splitting logs and topping up the log baskets in the house – one by the range in the kitchen and another in the Oak Room, where they were starting to spend their evenings altogether. As the rest of the house grew colder and they needed to conserve electricity as well as obey the blackout, it made sense to keep one fire and one set of lights going. This had the effect of bringing them together in a way that hadn't happened before now. Grandfather read papers and books, Aunt Constance wrote letters and the rest of them played games. Sometimes they listened to the wireless, or there was music on the gramophone, or Imogen played the harp that stood in the corner of the room, on which, although she'd learned for four years, she only knew three pieces. Rosalind occasionally played the piano, which she did beautifully although she did not believe it. Mr Humphries, who had moved into the house for the sake of economy, usually started up the whist and gin rummy.

He had been kind to Miranda too, setting her up with his typewriter and letting her bash away on it, making endless mistakes as she copied out articles for him which she had the distinct feeling that he didn't need. But already she was learning her way around the typewriter keyboard and could type 'the' and 'and' without even looking.

These cosy evenings would be great fun usually, Miranda thought, as they sat around on the rug by the fire, dealing another hand. But there was the constant worry of what was happening in the West Tower. It was getting colder. She had seen Mr Humphries delivering wood to the door but what if that were not enough?

When she'd asked Aunt Constance about it, she looked grave. 'Try not to worry,' she said. 'I'm taking care of the situation, but if it gets much colder, we will have to think again.'

It was late on a Sunday evening and they had just had their supper of eggs on toast. As they all sat around the fire in the drawing room, Miranda noticed Robbie Foster was playing with little grey counters on the rug. Just as she wondered what they were, Mr Humphries also noticed.

'I say, young man, what are those you've got there?'

Robbie looked up. Since their field trip, Mr Humphries had taken the boys on several exploring tours of the castle, and Robbie in particular seemed fascinated by the house and the grounds. They were always coming across him in odd places, emerging from rooms or staircases, or finding him prowling around. Now, Robbie picked up one of the stones and got up to take it over to Mr Humphries. 'I found them in the brook when I went digging there,' he said, showing it on his palm. 'There are lots in the mud.'

'Let me see.' Mr Humphries peered through his round glasses, took the stone and held it up to the light. 'Ah. How lovely. Yes. This is a crinoid fossil. *Pentacrinites fossilis*. The five points make them look like little stars, don't they? They are found in certain parts of the country – Wiltshire, Dorset and around here, as well as other places. They're a hundred and eighty million years old, just fancy that!'

'Are they plants?' Robbie asked, squinting at the stone. 'These patterns look like little leaves.'

'No, they're actually creatures related to sea urchins and starfish. They're sometimes called sea lilies, though, as their stems have these tiny tentacles and those are what makes the pattern.'

'They're very pretty,' Robbie said.

'Very. How clever of you to find them. Perhaps you'll study fossils just like me, one of these days.'

Robbie looked delighted, and the boys crowded round to see the special fossil stones that Robbie had discovered.

Imogen came over, curious. 'May I see?'

'Of course.' Mr Humphries stood up and showed it to her.

'Like a snowflake,' Imogen said, wonderingly. 'A tiny stone snowflake.'

'That's just it,' Mr Humphries said, smiling.

Aunt Constance looked up suddenly. 'The star stones? We used to find them in the streams and rivers all the time when we were children. My grandmother said that if you wear one of them, it means you'll have victory over your enemies.' She laughed dryly. 'I doubt that victory is ever that easy.'

'What harm can it do? You must have this, Miss Wakefield,' Mr Humphries said gallantly, putting the stone into her hand. 'I'm sure Robbie can spare one from his collection.'

'Thank you,' Imogen said shyly. 'It's terribly sweet. I'll treasure it. Thank you, Robbie.'

'Well,' Mr Humphries said, 'whatever might help to protect you.'

They looked at one another and then looked awkwardly away.

'Boys, it's time for bed,' Imogen said quickly.

The four of them, now thick as thieves, scrambled up.

'We have to go to the stables first,' Toby said importantly.

'To feed the 'oss,' said Tom Foster.

The evacuees, with the help of Toby and Archie, had overcome their initial fear of Harris, and he was now their favourite thing in the world. They called him 'the 'oss' and were always off to visit him. When he pulled the trap to school, they were enormously proud and showed off to the other children like anything, particularly their fellow evacuees.

'Now, don't be afraid of the 'oss. Like Archie says, he's a lamb,' Tom would say grandly, stroking Harris's flank. 'Aintcha, 'Arris?'

Miranda particularly loved the way Tom said Harris with a rolling r. Robbie loved him too, but was just as keen on the dogs, the chickens and every animal they met. They even seemed less terrified of Grandfather and his eyepatch, now that they had spent so many evenings playing cards as he read the paper. And Robbie appeared to have adored Mr Humphries since the day of their first field trip.

'All right,' Imogen said, glancing quickly at Mr Humphries and then away. 'Feed the 'oss. I mean, the horses. And then bed, double-quick time!'

As the days shortened, and darkened and the blackout felt as though it lasted all the time, the weather changed. December brought chill and frosts, and as Christmas approached, the temperature suddenly plummeted.

Miranda knew that there were urgent discussions going on between the four adults: Grandfather, Aunt Constance, Mr Humphries and Imogen. She and Rosalind loitered outside the study and listened to the voices behind the door.

'You can't risk it!' she heard Mr Humphries say. 'It is the lesser of two evils!'

Later, the twins bearded Imogen in her room, one lone lamp burning behind tightly closed blackout blinds.

'What's going on?' Miranda demanded as she scrambled into bed next to her sister. 'Brrr. Why is your hot water bottle so cold?'

'You've got to tell us,' Rosalind said firmly, getting in the other side. 'It's all about Mother, isn't it?'

They had been hoping for weeks that they would be

permitted to visit their mother, but they were told whenever they asked that she wasn't in a fit state. When they asked what was meant, there were awkward silences. If it weren't for what Mr Humphries had said, and what Imogen hinted at, they wouldn't know that Mother was in an ongoing state of high anxiety that meant she was being kept sedated most of the time.

Imogen had told them that when Mother found out that the war had started, it had caused a severe relapse into what Aunt Constance called 'a state of grief'. Father had been going to fight in this war, and they had all been sure he would be a hero. But now Mother was remembering all over again what she had lost.

'We're in a pickle now,' Imogen said to her sisters, as she pulled her eiderdown quilt over the three of them. Despite wearing nightgowns, dressing gowns, slippers and having the quilt, they all still felt cold. 'Whittaker went away for leave and they hired another nurse. Now she's going. She can't take any more. She says she's the one going doolally in the tower with no one to see or talk to. And she says they'll freeze to death if they stay there. So she's going and there's no one till Whittaker gets back.'

'Let her go. We can take care of Mother until then,' Miranda said stoutly.

'Of course we can,' said Rosalind.

'That's what Mr Humphries thinks,' Imogen said, 'and I agree with him. But Aunt Constance and Grandfather think we must find a hospital to put her in. They think she might go off the rails completely if she's brought into the house.'

'How can she if she's sedated?' Miranda asked.

'Well, quite. Besides, it's our duty in wartime to take care of our own if we can. Hospitals and doctors and nurses are going to be needed for soldiers. That's what Mr Humphries says.'

'I don't know why the others want to send her away!' declared Miranda crossly.

Imogen gave her a look. 'Come on, now. You know they care for her. They want to do what's best.'

'I think Mr Humphries is right and it's a risk we have to take,' Rosalind said. 'Even if Mother goes to a hospital later, she can't stay there in the cold with no nurse. We don't have a choice.'

'That's what I think they've realised. Aunt Constance is writing letters to doctors and hospitals, trying to find somewhere. But it's already so cold. Whittaker isn't back till Christmas and the covering nurse leaves on Friday. Mother will have to come in then and that's that.'

By Friday, it was already too cold for school and certainly to ride in the trap, and so the holidays had been started early.

Grandfather managed to get the Buick running, turning over its engine until it was thoroughly warm, and then he drove the departing nurse to the station. Miranda caught a glimpse of her hurrying to the car, wrapped up in a coat and scarf, her hat low over her face, clutching a suitcase. The afternoon was already darkening, a thick fog dropping over the park and frost icing everything. Although she could not see the nurse's face, Miranda was glad she was leaving. She did not seem kind enough for Mother. The Buick made its way slowly through the fog and gloom, heading off for the station.

So Mother is alone, she thought, wondering what would happen next. She had an idea what it might be. She had seen Imogen and Lottie preparing a bedroom on the first floor, dusting it out and making up the bed with fresh linen. This room had a little dressing room attached as well as a bathroom, and a single bed had been made up in there.

Now she went downstairs and found Imogen, Mr Humphries and Aunt Constance bundled up in coats, and obviously preparing for a mission.

'Let me come too,' she said at once, guessing what it was. 'I'll get my things on.'

'No, Miranda,' Aunt Constance said strictly. 'Go to the schoolroom and help Rosalind with the boys. She's making paperchains with them. Go along now.'

'I won't,' Miranda said, sounding braver than she felt. 'I want to help you. You need me.'

'Another pair of hands would be useful,' Mr Humphries said mildly. 'Can't Miranda help us?'

Aunt Constance looked torn.

'Please,' Miranda said. 'Let me.'

'All right. Get your coat and boots on. Quickly, though. While the children are occupied.'

She raced to put on her outdoor things, and joined them as they headed out towards the tower. The lawn was crunchy with frost and the air sharp in her nostrils, but there was still enough daylight to see by, although only just. The fog was cutting off visibility and once it was dark, with all torches forbidden, it would be impossible to see.

For the first time in a long while, the gate in the fence around the tower was open. They went through in silence, Aunt Constance leading the way, then Imogen and Mr Humphries, with Miranda bringing up the rear. Aunt Constance opened the tower door. Inside, there was a muted golden light. The grate was full of glowing coals and an oil lantern burned on the side table. The room was not warm but not freezing either. In an armchair by the fire sat a figure apparently asleep, covered by a thick plaid blanket, its face turned to the wing of the armchair so that Miranda could not see it.

She was holding her breath, she realised, and her heart was racing. So there was Mother. After all this time.

She tiptoed forward to look at her.

Mother's hair was still golden, she could see that, but threaded through with grey at the temples. Her face, in repose, looked so young except for a hollowness to her cheeks and a sunken quality around her eyes. Her nose and mouth were still very fine, and her skin hardly lined. Miranda was overcome with a wave of love and longing. She wanted to run over, shake her awake and say, *Mother, Mother, I'm here! You're home, we're taking you home, isn't that marvellous?* She wanted to cover her face in kisses and hold her hands, and watch her eyes open and fill with the joy of recognition. 'Oh, Miranda, my darling,' she would say. 'How are you, sweet girl? And where's my Rosie, and the others? Why on earth have I been away so long?'

But Miranda didn't move. She just remembered to breathe in, and tried to stay calm.

'Now, where's that wheelchair?' Mr Humphries asked. 'Did you say there was a wheelchair?'

'There, by the stairs.' Imogen pointed at it. 'The nurse has left Mother's suitcases there too.'

'Then let's get started.' Mr Humphries wheeled the chair to where Mother was sitting and then said softly yet firmly, 'Now, Mrs Wakefield, I'm just going to lift you into this chair, if that's all right . . .'

'Mrs Black,' Aunt Constance said hastily. She took the blanket off Mother; underneath she was wearing a woollen two-piece suit and stout shoes, dressed as if to go out. 'Please call her Mrs Black.'

'I'm sorry, Mrs Black.' Mr Humphries carefully put his arms around her so that he could lift her up.

Mother moaned and her eyes opened. Miranda gasped to see them, blue, like her own, and so familiar and dear. But they were blank, the life within them fuzzy and confused.

Mother looked at Mr Humphries. 'Are you my doctor?'

'I'm a friend, here to help you,' he said. 'We're taking you somewhere nice and warm where you can rest.'

He lifted her up very easily and she did not resist as he moved her lightly to the wheelchair and sat her down in it. Aunt Constance moved forward to tuck the blanket around her. Imogen picked up a coat, hat and several bags, including one that must surely contain Mother's medication. Miranda, directed by her aunt, picked up a smaller suitcase and bag, while Aunt Constance took the larger ones. Mr Humphries wheeled Mother carefully to the front door and out, over the doorstep and into the garden, where the air was turning freezing and the fog was denser than ever.

The others followed behind him. Then Imogen said, 'I'll just be a moment.'

She put down the things she was carrying, and went to the fire where a jug of water sat on the hearth. She threw the water over the hot coals, where it sizzled and spluttered and hissed as the coals flared and went out. Then she went to the table, picked up the lamp and lowered the wick. It went out, and the room sank into darkness. Once their eyes adjusted, Imogen picked up the things she had put down and they all went out, Imogen shutting the door behind them, and they hurried after Mr Humphries who was making slow progress across the lawn with the wheelchair.

It seemed to take forever in the icy evening to get the chair over the grass to the house. Mr Humphries got the chair up the steps as gently as he could. Then, at last, they were inside, the door closed against the bitter cold. They took Mother at once to the drawing room to warm up in front of the fire. She had fallen asleep again and did not wake, even when the logs crackled and snapped. They sat about and watched her for a while, all muted following their strange mission. After a while, Mr Humphries said, 'I can carry her upstairs. I think that's best.'

'Yes, that's a good idea.' Aunt Constance stood up. 'Let's take her up now before the children come down. Imogen, you come with me. Miranda, stay here.'

'But—'

'No.' Aunt Constance held up her hand. 'You've done enough. No more. Come, Mr Humphries, we will take her now.'

Mr Humphries obediently lifted Mother up again, and carried her, gently and almost reverently, out of the drawing room. Miranda followed the little procession until they reached the bottom of the stairs and then stayed where she was, watching them slowly ascend, Mr Humphries carrying Mother and the women bringing up her things.

Like a royal procession, Miranda thought. *Or a procession in a temple. Mother is a queen, or a priestess.*

She watched in a kind of awe, seeing her mother in her home for the first time since the disaster.

Mother has come home, she thought, almost overcome. *She's come home to us at last. And I know we can make her better. I just know we can.*

Chapter Sixteen

Present Day

Sam Locke was as good as his word. The work on the East Tower continued at a great pace. The slowest part was the start of the process as they worked on the bones of the building and the utilities. Once that was done, the exciting things began – the installation of new radiators, the lighting and the putting in of the new bathroom and boiler. To Georgie's excitement, it seemed to change almost by the hour as the tradesmen went swiftly about their work.

'The main issue you're going to have is cold,' Sam said to her as they looked around at the progress on the ground floor. 'There's lots of bare stone in here, and not a lot we can do in the way of insulation. We can't touch the original features, of course. We can't lay underfloor heating or anything like that. You might find a cast-iron range is a good option – it will heat this kitchen – and there are some good economical electric options which could work well.'

'I need a standard oven for recipe testing,' Georgie said doubtfully, although she could see the sense of a heat source.

'You can actually fit both in if you want, if we swap

318

things around here.' He pointed to the plans to show what he meant.

'You're right. I'll think about it. Good idea.'

'You're better off in the sitting room where there's the panelling to provide a layer between you and the stone, and you've got the big fireplace, and you can fit carpet and heavy curtains over the windows and doors to shut out the drafts. You'll be quite cosy in there, I should think.'

'Yes.' Georgie smiled. 'Cosy is just how I like it.'

The tower was going to be ready before too long, and she started to think about furnishings. She went around the castle looking for the odd bit of furniture that wouldn't be missed, and went back to the attics to search through boxes for old curtains. She found plenty to choose from and spent a happy few hours measuring and considering and choosing, making sure there wasn't too much damage from age and moths in the ones she selected. She found some old berry-coloured velvet curtains that would be just right for the sitting room, and a shiny floral chintz for the bedroom upstairs. For the kitchen she was having some roman blinds made by a seamstress in the town.

'It's like you've got a playhouse for grown-ups,' Caspar said fondly as she showed him all her finds and checked with him that he was happy for her to take things out of the castle. 'You can take whatever you like, I don't mind. If Viktoria can take things to the gatehouse, I think you can take things to the tower.' He laughed. 'I feel like we're starting up a little commune of the Wakefield wives.'

She laughed too, but not as cheerily. It wasn't so pleasant being likened to Viktoria. She didn't appreciate the implication that she was behaving just like her.

'Anyway,' Caspar said, 'I don't mind if you need a place of your own to escape to. Everyone needs a bolthole. Now, I'm off to meet the environmental specialist to discuss what we do with the park. I'll see you later.'

'Have fun.' Georgie watched him, her mood a little deflated. The mention of a bolthole made her think of Pippa. She had been thinking of ways that she could help her sister, beyond keeping in touch as often as possible, and she had suggested to Pippa that she and the girls come to stay, to give her a break from Ryan. It was going to be beautiful here in high summer, she told her. **Perfect for a holiday for you all, even Ryan if you can bear having him too.**

It's a good idea, Pippa wrote back. **But Ryan knows that I'll talk to you – you're the only one in the world I would tell what he's really like, so he's not keen to see you. On the other hand, if I portray it as a break for him where he can just please himself all day, that might work. Or he might let us come on our own, which is the best solution. I'll keep you posted.**

In the meantime, Georgie kept in touch, sending a message every day. Back would come Pippa's messages, sometimes brief and sometimes pouring out a torrent of distress and confusion at Ryan's behaviour. They were often difficult for Georgie to read, not just because of descriptions of what

Ryan said and did, but because the force of Pippa's pain hit her like a truck. The sensitivity she had suffered from all her life was particularly heightened when it came to her sister. In the past, she had felt Pippa's emotions almost more keenly than her own, and she had never lost that burden of responsibility. As a small girl she had felt a need to care for her younger sister that was almost like a compulsion, a duty that she had no choice but to obey. Even now, she worked to protect her sister, not just from the pain of her own life but from any pain in Georgie's. She had kept so much of her own suffering from Pippa. It was her role to care for her sister, not the other way around.

Now, with Pippa in pain, her need to do something and fix everything was kicking in hard, but she felt helpless being so far away. She had a powerful urge to get her sister to Wakefield, a place where she had begun to feel better herself. But that didn't seem likely.

Something would have to happen, though. It was becoming quite clear to Georgie from Pippa's messages that Ryan had a deep-rooted behaviour pattern. From a distance it was easy to see how it worked in action, and she found that she could almost predict exactly how he would speak or act in any situation. And yet Pippa, who lived with the repeating pattern hour by hour and day by day, seemed endlessly shocked and surprised by Ryan.

He actually looked me in the eye and told me that I never asked him how he felt about things! I couldn't believe it, I ask him all the time! The problem is that he won't

respond. Can't he see that a married couple needs to communicate? That I'm trying to reach out to him?

Oh, Pippa, she thought sadly. *Of course he can't. That must be obvious. I think you need to stop trying to achieve the impossible. He isn't going to listen to you.*

Pippa reported that counselling was not helping at all. Ryan's line was that she was a perfectionist and if she could just accept him as a normal, imperfect human, she would be happier. The counsellor seemed to agree with him, which left Pippa speechless at the injustice.

He's not normal, whatever he might think, Georgie thought to herself when she heard this. *He doesn't listen. He doesn't give an inch. And yet on the surface he seems reasonable.*

Like an outwardly solid structure that was actually badly built, Ryan's weaknesses and fatal flaws were only evident when he came under stress. He had looked dependable but the reality of being a husband and father had revealed the truth. How long could Pippa go on shoring up the collapsing building? And at what cost to herself?

Georgie felt agitated by Pippa's distress. It would invade her and take over completely if she wasn't careful, so she went to the tower to be calmed by the kitchen units being installed. Sam Locke was there.

'Ah, I was hoping to see you,' he said as she came in. 'I really want you and Caspar to take a look at the West Tower. I had a look from the top floor of this place and from what I can see over that fence, it could do with a survey and perhaps some repairs.'

'All right,' Georgie said. 'That's probably a good idea.'

'Why is that weird fence all around it?' he asked, taking out his phone.

'I don't know. No one does.'

'You should think about taking it down then. It spoils the symmetry of the lawn.'

Georgie was mildly surprised. 'I suppose it does. I hadn't thought of that before. It's just there. You stop questioning once you get used to things.'

'Not me,' Sam said with a smile. 'Get Caspar along and we'll take a look.'

'Of course. And how much longer till the tower is ready?'

'I think we're on course for the end of next week. Which is lucky as I have to be at the Manor to start on their party barn at the beginning of the week after.'

Stirring her sauce frantically with one hand, Georgie reached for the recipe book which she had propped up on a chair by the range.

This is why I need my little testing kitchen, she thought crossly. *This place is impossible to work in!*

The writing in the recipe book could not be read from a distance, and she was always forgetting the exact wording of the next step in the recipe she was following. There was nowhere near the range to put the book so that she could see while she cooked. And she had put the chair just too far away for her to reach the book as she cooked. Stretching as far as she could, she only managed to knock it off the chair and onto the hard stone floor.

Immediately anxious in case she had damaged it, she dropped her spoon, which fell completely into the pot of sauce, and bent down to pick up the book. It was fine, as far as she could see, but when it had fallen, a small folded scrap of white paper had become dislodged from inside and was now lying on the floor. Georgie picked it up and unfolded it.

At the top of the paper was handwriting that she now recognised. It was Miranda's. What was below was a recipe.

Etti Boule's Secret Blackberry Trifle, it read.

Etti Boule again, Georgie thought, surprised. *And why is this in Miranda's handwriting if it's Etti's recipe?*

She read it.

Take a dozen sponge fingers and soak in sherry.

Make custard with the powder and milk. Follow instructions, or make fresh if you know how.

Spread the blackberry jam on the rusks very VERY thickly.

Pour over the custard and leave to set.

Whip cream and cover the custard with it.

Decorate with blackberries.

DELICIOUS. You'll never forget it.

Good rats eat the good berries.

Bad rats eat the bad berries.

Bad berries kill bad rats.

What a strange recipe, she thought. *No quantities except the sponge fingers or even much care about what goes in – make custard if you know how. It's quite funny really. But what's the point of it? And what is so unforgettable about it? It doesn't seem awfully secret either.*

What's this funny doggerel about rats too? Next to it was a little sketch of a dead rat, lying on its back with its mouth open and its stiff paws curled over.

She noticed that underneath the recipe were some diagrams, like those she'd seen in the exercise book upstairs: little circles, a larger circle, arrows pointing here and there. At the bottom, in another hasty scrawl: *Don't Forget.*

Georgie stared at it all for a few moments, but it made no sense so she folded it up again and, after a hesitation, put it in her pocket.

As she continued cooking, she thought about the occupants of the house in wartime. The hampers upstairs had revealed that there had been children there in those years, during their mid to late childhood. Their voices kept coming to her one way or another. Every time she went up there to look for furniture for the tower, she felt their presence strongly, through their toys and possessions and clothes, and through the voices that came echoing over the years inside the books, not that she had looked in them again.

Like the recipe book, she thought. *That has voices as well.* Voices telling you about what they liked to eat and how they made it and why. The book was a way to preserve wisdom and knowledge and joy. A way to pass life on somehow and to protect memory.

That little phrase echoed in her mind again: *I am the guardian of memories.* Who had said that? It had resonated with her, as she had spent so much time stopping Pippa from remembering by storing up and holding the memories of their childhood all by herself, keeping them away from her sister as much as she could. It had been a hard burden, she realised. She had locked it away so completely that she had told no one, not even Caspar.

Georgie had taken up the spoon and was stirring her sauce again, but she was hardly seeing it. Her mind was suddenly moving around an idea she'd had fermenting for a while.

Pippa's new pain was causing her anxiety. She had felt it coming back to her in the old ways. Panic. Agitation. Racing thoughts. Sudden waking in fear. A need to be alone, to be silent. Her sensitivity to life had sharpened and she was feeling the buzzing in the air, the vibrations, that were heightened when she was in this state.

The voices in the recipe book were getting louder too. And in the attic and in the exercise books. She was starting to become more receptive to them than she wanted.

Georgie put down the spoon, removed the sauce from the hotplate and put it on the table. She sank into a chair there, and put her head in her hands.

Life at the castle had unexpectedly been calming. She had begun to understand what it might mean to live more normally, the way she thought other people must – at least, the ones who had not been tormented as she had. Was that coming to an end? How could she cling on to that precious calm?

She took a deep breath and looked up.

'So,' she said out loud. 'Do I ignore the voices? Or do I listen to them?'

She had spent her life trying to close out the past. But perhaps it was time to listen instead. The recipe book had fallen into her lap and the voices inside it had given her the means to work and learn new things. Perhaps Etti Boule, whoever she was, wanted to tell her something as well.

I will listen, she decided. *I'll listen and I'll try to understand.*

The first voice to listen to was unexpected. It was in the form of an email from Natalie Spiller, the archivist at the Natural History Museum.

Dear Georgie,

Thank you for your letter asking about fossils stored at your family home in the Second World War. It came at a fortunate time as we are just in the process of organising our archive for use in a documentary on this very subject. I can confirm that a large selection of palaeontology from our collections was sent to Wakefield Castle for the duration. The curator, Mr Arthur Humphries, went with them to continue his research on extinct birds and their fossils and he stayed at the castle for some time. We have a few of his letters in our archive, as curators reported in during their time spent overseeing the storage of the collections and continuing their research. For example, the curator studying

Diptera did important work on mosquitos and malaria during the war, contributing to necessary medical advances.

If you would like to access our archive, you are welcome to make a request for what you would like to view and make an appointment to visit. For obvious reasons, we don't send out originals, and copies are only granted for bona fide research.

I hope that has answered your question, but do get in touch if you have any further queries.

Best regards,
Natalie Spiller

Georgie read it through twice, with interest. Fossils in the castle. That was interesting. She wondered if they'd been able to look at the specimens, but then supposed probably not. They'd hardly let a load of children start playing around with their precious exhibits after all the effort of getting them out of London for safekeeping.

She thought of the little stone stars. They looked like fossils.

Oh dear. Did those naughty children steal the little stones from Mr Humphries? But they look very common, the kind of thing you might find on the beach. Not worth sending out of London.

On a whim, she searched online for star-shaped fossils and, sure enough, dozens of images appeared of stones just like the ones she had in the pouch. Crinoids. She read with interest that they were the remains of tiny sea creatures. According to a witchcraft site, they also had magical powers of conferring victory over enemies. Perhaps that was why the children had treasured them so much during wartime.

She smiled at the thought. It was magical thinking, but what did it matter if it offered hope?

These fossils were very common and not worth anything. They were unlikely to have been selected for special preservation. Georgie wondered how they had come into the house. She left the morning room and went upstairs to where the pouch still sat in her bedside cupboard.

Sitting down on the floor, she picked up the pouch and emptied the little stones into her palm, then ran them from hand to hand, listening to them chink against each other, feeling their weight and the sensation of them against her skin.

Had they brought the children good luck?

She put the little pile on the floor and took out the exercise book again.

The Crimes of Etti Boule, she read.

The writing was not a coherent story but a sort of collection of details about the mysterious Etti. It seemed to have been written at all sorts of different times, with repetitions and contradictions: *she is very thin . . . she has red hair . . . her eyes are evil . . . she lives in the tower . . . she lives in the cellar . . . she lives in the attic . . . she kills people.* There were a few florid sentences that seemed like the start of a story but they always tailed off. And the last one finished with: *Don't Forget! Don't Forget! But WHERE IS THE EGG?*

I can't make sense of this. I can't work out whether Etti is a real person or not, she thought. She felt that her theory, that she was a real person that the children had disliked and therefore fictionalised for revenge, was probably closest to the mark. But they must have hated her.

And there was the interest in a lost egg. She'd forgotten about it. An egg. She saw the image of a brown hen's egg in her mind and felt that vibration she sometimes had when her brain was trying to tell her that she already knew the answer to this.

Then she saw that, after a lot of blank pages, there was one last bit of writing, a short poem. She read it.

Etti Boule
Is kind and cruel
She took a fool
And keeps him still

She keeps him deep
She keeps him cool
Etti Boule
Is kind and cruel.

What is that? Georgie thought, startled. *It's like a creepy nursery rhyme.* She read it again and shivered.

Her phone buzzed in her pocket, and she put down the book and took out the phone. It was a message from Caspar.

Can you come down? Sam has got ten minutes to look at the tower with us.

She texted back: **Of course.**

After putting the pouch and book back in the cupboard, she got up and went to leave. At the doorway, she stopped and looked back at the cupboard.

Don't forget to listen, she told herself. *Just listen.*

Sam was waiting for them in the garden by the West Tower, dictating into his phone. He stopped when he saw Georgie and Caspar coming across the grass towards him.

'Morning! Have you got those keys?' he asked as they approached.

Caspar held up the bunch from the storeroom. 'Here they are.'

'Great. I've got the lubricant if they fancy a bit of that. Often very useful in tight situations.' Sam grinned at his mildly risqué joke, and took the keys from Caspar when they reached him. After a few moments and an application of the oil, the key in the fence gate turned and the door opened, slow and stiff on its rusted hinges. Sam gave them a squirt of the lubricant and the door began to move more easily, though it was also hindered by the mass of foliage that had grown up behind it. It tore away as Sam pushed the door open.

'Just like a fairy tale,' Georgie said with a laugh.

'That's what I was thinking,' Caspar remarked. 'Let's hope we don't find a princess who's been sleeping for a hundred years back here.'

'I don't know, that sounds interesting,' Sam said, holding back thorny stems easily with his thick gloves and letting them pass through the overgrowth.

The tower behind looked in much worse condition than the other. It was covered in ivy, which had grown over the diamond-paned windows. Some panes had broken, the rest were filthy. Some stone had crumbled under the onslaught of the ivy's tentacles, and the door looked as though it had rotted at the base, letting in dirt and plant detritus.

'Poor tower,' Georgie breathed. 'It's a mess.'

Sam was looking for the key on the iron ring. 'This looks about right,' he said, selecting one and putting it in the door lock. It took some effort but turned eventually. He pushed open the door over piles of leaves and dirt and it opened to reveal a room exactly like the East Tower but furnished simply, in the style of eighty years before. Everything was faded and rotting, but it was still possible to make out the burgundy wool of the armchair and the floral linen of the sofa, now with springs and wool exploding from its innards.

'This is so strange!' Georgie said, looking about in astonishment. 'It's as though someone only just left! But what a mess.'

Lamps were broken on the floor, along with the remains of wine glasses and a jug. A teapot lay in two neat halves in the grate. Chairs lay on their sides and the armchair was hard against the wall, the remains of a rotting rug twisted up underneath it.

'And left in a hurry,' Sam said grimly. 'And turned over the room on the way out.'

Caspar was also gazing about, frowning. 'So you don't think all this has just fallen or collapsed over time?'

Sam shook his head. 'No. Things decay but they don't throw themselves around the room. It looks like there was a bit of a melee in here. But why didn't they tidy it before they locked it up?' He kicked at a pile of leaves and uncovered a broken teacup. 'Here's something else. Very peculiar.'

Georgie went to the door that led through to the kitchen and opened it. 'Oh my goodness, it's like a time machine in here. Perfect wartime kitchen.' She walked in, gazing about. 'It's still got tins and packets on the shelves. And look at this old stove! A bit like the one in the other tower, but much earlier.' She peered into the sink. 'There are still pans in here, and cutlery. Along with a dead mouse and a lot of mess.'

Sam came into the room behind her. 'There you are,' he said. 'They didn't even wash up. Whoever left here did it in a hurry, that's all.'

Caspar followed him in. 'That's interesting, but the main thing is how urgently we need to repair this old place, and how much it will cost. To be honest, Sam, right now I'd just like to do the minimum to keep it together until we've done the restoration of the main house. Can we take a look around so you can give me an estimate?'

'Of course,' Sam said, taking out his phone. 'Let's start at the top and work down. I always like to inspect a roof. Assuming the stairs are safe enough to climb, of course.'

They headed out of the kitchen together, leaving Georgie on her own, looking around. She could feel the dust and dirt in her nostrils as she breathed in. Great stringy clouds of cobweb, weighted down by dust, filled every corner of the ceiling and hung from shelves and cupboards.

Eighty years of filth, she thought. It made her itchy, as though she needed a shower right away.

She examined her feelings in this tower. It felt different from the other one.

Sadder, she thought. *I wonder why. And yet, it doesn't feel bad here. Just sorrowful, as though it's in mourning for something.* She pulled herself up with an inner laugh. *Perhaps it's just because it's such a time warp and I'm projecting like mad.*

Picking up a cloth, she rubbed at one of the windows and cleaned away a patch of dirt. Light came in at once, illuminating a small patch on the counter.

You can always bring the light back, she thought, *if you try.*

Then she went upstairs to find Caspar and Sam.

Chapter Seventeen

Sunlight flooded through the French windows of Lady Wakefield's morning room. Georgie had to pull the curtain over them a little so that she could still see her screen. She had written a thank you email to Natalie Spiller, saying how much she appreciated the information and that she might well make a request to see the archive relating to Wakefield at some point in the future.

> **Just one quick question, if I may. Did the collection at Wakefield contain any dinosaur eggs? And did any of them go missing? I know it's a strange question but I read something in the house that made me wonder.**
>
> **Thank you so much for your help.**
>
> **Best wishes,**
> **Georgie**

She sent it off, hoping that Natalie Spiller didn't think she was a bit loopy, or that she had some sort of knowledge of missing artefacts.

Outside, the weather had turned balmy, with pure blue skies and lucid sunlight that made the fresh new greenery on the trees and hedgerows look almost neon. Blossom was everywhere, in great pink and white puffs on the branches of hawthorns and cherry trees, and the air was filling with the feathery dust of pollen and leaf fluff.

Georgie longed to go out. She returned her screen to her book and looked at how much she had accomplished. The recipes were nearly complete, the end was in sight. This was just the beginning of the process, but the legwork was nearly done. And after that, she would be able to take a breather while other eyes appraised and considered what she had done. There would be another draft after this, and Atalanta was famous for her sudden changes of mind and late-night demands for rewriting or new material. But she was usually right, and the whole thing was infinitely better for the collaboration.

I think I can spare an hour for a walk, Georgie decided.

In the hall, she looked out of the window and saw that over the gatehouse the family flag was fluttering hard in the breeze. It might be cooler than she thought. She went to get a hoodie and bumped into Caspar as he came up from the kitchen.

'Going for a walk?' he asked with a smile. 'Would you like some company?'

'Of course. I'd love it.'

They went out together, making their way out to the park, crossing the moat by the little bridge. Underneath it floated saucers of water lilies with pinky white buds shaped like fat candle flames, some on the point of bursting open.

'It's so beautiful, isn't it?' Caspar said, looking around. 'We're very lucky, aren't we?'

'Very,' Georgie said fervently. 'I had no idea it would be like this.'

'You didn't want to come.'

'I did not!' She laughed. 'But I'm glad we did.'

As they went out into the parkland and towards the woods, Caspar talked about the West Tower. 'Sam thinks we should get that fence down and clear the roses. All that undergrowth is hurting the stonework, and we'll need to do that before he starts work as they'll require the access.'

'When can he start?'

'Not for a while. After the Manor's party barn is finished, I should think. But there's no hurry for more building bills, I must say. How is the East Tower?'

'Nearly, nearly done. They're grouting the bathroom and painting the kitchen today. The panelling is being stained and the chimneys swept – then I can put the rugs down. All the furniture is in the stable, waiting to be moved in. The white goods are arriving tomorrow, and they'll go in as soon as the counters are fitted. It's all good.'

Caspar gave her a sideways look. 'It's great – but you don't seem as excited about it as you were.'

'I am,' she said sturdily.

'Georgie . . . I know you. You're not.'

'Okay.' She slipped her hand into his large, warm one. 'Maybe I'm not quite as upbeat as I was.'

Caspar tucked both their hands into the pocket of his jacket. 'Is it Pippa? How is she?'

'She's in a bad way. She told Ryan she was thinking about him moving out in a temporary separation.'

Caspar looked grave. 'Was he angry?'

Georgie sighed unhappily. 'She said that he doesn't get angry when she talks about that sort of thing. He's almost strangely blank and emotionless as if he doesn't really care if they stay married or not.'

'But surely he responds to what she's saying?'

'No.' She glanced at him, almost pleadingly. 'That's what I'm trying to say. His reactions are sort of backwards. If Pippa tries to have a calm, rational discussion in which she explains how she feels and asks how he feels, he can't take it, gets upset, says she's criticising him and runs away. If she gets upset and says she doesn't think he loves her, and she might want to leave him, he's just blank. Cold and blank.'

Caspar looked confused. 'It doesn't make sense. But at least they're going to counselling. Surely that will help.'

'I'm afraid it doesn't seem to be helping much at all. They can't get anywhere. Pippa thinks he's just playing for time, to keep the status quo going, to keep her with him.'

'Why would he do that if he doesn't love her? Why not just have a respectful and constructive break-up and save both of them from all this stress? If he doesn't respond when she says she wants out, then he clearly isn't really bothered.'

Georgie shrugged. 'Well, he doesn't respond when she says it. But later he'll suddenly be very loving and make her a cup of tea, or get some flowers or something, and say he doesn't want them to split.'

'Ah. Okay. So he does love her.'

Georgie felt exasperated. Why take Ryan at face value when his behaviour showed him to be something else? 'Caspar, he's pretending. Putting on an act. After he has time to think it over, and consider, he seems to decide that his life with Pippa and the girls is probably better and easier than his life without them. Can't you see that? So he tries a little bit of romantic business to calm her down and make her happy. But he never addresses the things she is actually trying to talk to him about, so it's just a sticking plaster. He shows no concern for how she feels, not even to ask if she loves him.'

Caspar looked bewildered. 'He's a puzzle, isn't he? He seems very low on normal human feelings.'

'For Pippa. But not for himself,' Georgie said briefly. 'I'm worried. Pippa is getting more and more stressed and upset. I can't see a good outcome.'

'I know that you're feeling it very hard. I'm sorry.'

They had reached the woods, and turned to sit down on a large fallen trunk and survey the park. Some clouds had sprung up to dot the sky but the sun still shone brightly. The castle looked stately and secure surrounded by its cushion of green parkland, the drive curving away into the distance.

Caspar put his arm around Georgie and said softly, 'It's a shame, really, sweetheart, because I wanted to talk to you.

I know you've had a lot on your mind but I've also been thinking very hard about what we were discussing before all this.'

'Yes?' she said slowly, her apprehension building.

'I've waited a good while now. You must have had a chance to think about it. I know you've been so busy, but you said yourself that it was easing off a bit. The tower is nearly finished. And I really want to plan for the future. Are we going to be here for much longer? Should we think about selling the flat?'

'We could talk about the flat,' she said quickly. 'What do you think about it?'

'That isn't what I want to discuss, you know that, Georgie.'

He turned to face her full on, his grey eyes serious. She thought about how much she loved him: his kindness, integrity, and endless support. His quirks and habits. His laughter and warmth, the taste of his kisses and the feeling of his arms around her.

I love him. I don't want to lose him.

Caspar said, 'You've been talking about how Ryan won't discuss the things that are important to Pippa and how that hurts and frustrates her. Please don't do the same thing to me. I've been patient. I've given you time. But I deserve to know what you're thinking about having children.'

She gazed at him miserably. She wanted to throw her arms around him and smother him with kisses and beg him not to say any more about it. *Don't spoil it*, she wanted to cry. *Don't spoil what we have.*

'Georgie?' His expression was anxious. 'Please?'

She looked away, unable to take the beseeching look in his eyes. The moment that she had dreaded so much was finally here. And he was right, she owed it to him to tell the truth. She had owed it to him for years. When she spoke, her voice was uncertain and quivering. 'Caspar, I'm so sorry. I can't do it. I can't have children.'

'What?' He looked stricken. 'You can't? You never said! Why not? Have you seen any specialists?'

'No – I don't mean that. I mean, I *can't*. I might be able to, physically. As far as I know, everything is normal.' She finally looked at him, knowing that her eyes were pleading. 'I'm so sorry. It's so complicated to explain. I've tried to change how I feel about this, but it just hasn't been something I can do. I wanted so desperately to get through it and feel that I could have children. But I can't.'

He was quiet, absorbing this, and she waited nervously. Then he said, 'You mean you won't.'

She gasped. His voice was harder than she expected. 'Well . . . no, it's not like that—'

'That's what it amounts to, isn't it? You don't intend to try. Is that it?'

'No . . . no! That makes it sound much worse than it is.'

Caspar looked hard and bitter. 'You don't want children and you never told me. You've strung me along all this time, letting me believe you did, when you knew how much I wanted a family.'

'It's not that I don't want them . . . it's that I don't dare . . . It's so complicated!' Hurriedly, she put out her hand to him. 'Please, Caspar, let me explain. Please try to understand—'

'Georgie, I have given you all the understanding I possibly can! But I can't understand what you don't even have the guts to tell me!' His face was distorted and he pulled his hand away.

She stared in sudden fear. She had never seen Caspar look like this. The way he was talking was new to her. 'Please, just listen—'

'No. You've had more than enough chances to talk to me.' He stood up and glared at her, thrusting his hands into his jacket pockets. 'I can't believe that you have the nerve to criticise Ryan when you've been behaving in exactly the same way. You could have told me years ago that this is how you feel. You've deceived me. It wasn't fair! How could you? I . . . I can't believe it. I just can't. I've got to think about this.' He turned and began to march away.

Georgie stood up, her legs weak beneath her, and realised she was shaking violently from head to toe. 'Caspar,' she called. 'Please. Please come back! Please let me explain!'

But he was striding off across the park towards the house, his shoulders stiff, and he did not turn back.

When Georgie got back to the house an hour later, she went to the study but Caspar wasn't there. She felt cold even though it was still warm outside.

After he had left her, she had burst into violent tears. She had handled it so badly. She had shocked him instead of preparing him. It was obvious now that she should have explained first why she felt so unprepared to be a mother.

Not just unprepared but incapable. Perhaps then he might have some sympathy for her plight.

But he was right. She had done a terrible thing by hiding this from him for all this time. It was selfish. She had told a lie through omission and she had told it to protect herself, so that Caspar would love her and marry her and build a life with her. She had been deeply afraid that he would not if she told him anything like the truth of her feelings.

It was wrong. She had hurt him.

More than that, what had she done to his love for her? Had she killed it? Was it all over in the space of ten minutes?

The shock was almost too much to handle.

She had wept and cried until all the horror was exhausted. Then, after sitting mute and stunned on the log for some time, she realised that she must get back and try to talk to Caspar. They'd both had some time to absorb what had just happened, and now she had to try and repair it.

The walk back was nothing like the happy companionable stroll from earlier. She plodded miserably, her eyes on the ground, every footstep hard. She couldn't find any pace even though she was desperate to get back and see him.

Now, looking at the empty study, she felt a stirring of anxiety. She hurried down to the kitchen but he wasn't there. Calling his name, she sprinted up to the hall and then up the stairs to their bedroom.

On the bed lay a note. Her stomach swooped in a bitter, frightened somersault. Was this the moment when he told her it was over? Trembling, she picked it up and read the few handwritten lines.

Georgie,

I'm sorry I walked away but I had to take in what you told me. I'm still struggling to understand it. I need a bit of time to think it over so I've gone away for a few days. I'm fine, don't worry about me, but I need some space to think. I'll be in touch very soon but I'd appreciate some time to myself, so don't contact me for the moment.

Thanks,

Caspar

She read it over several times, trying to take it in. It wasn't the end she had feared but it was still awful. He had gone. She didn't have a chance to explain and make it right before he went away to think, so how could he bring her side of it all into his considerations? He couldn't possibly understand.

She cursed herself again for the stupid way she had told him the most important thing she had to say.

And I can't even write to him. He's asked me not to.

Georgie lay down on the bed, clutching the note, possessed by a misery so profound it was like being squashed flat by a great weight. Tears flowed down her face as she stared into space, and finally, almost as a reaction to her despair, she fell asleep.

When she woke, it was a few hours later. She felt groggy and confused. Then the memory of what had happened hit her and she groaned. Scrabbling for her phone, she found it on the bed beside her and picked it up to see if Caspar had messaged her. There was nothing from him but there was a voice message from Sam to say they were nearly finished for the day.

'We're ready to start moving things in upstairs, so come tomorrow if you can and let us know where you want it all put. See you then! Bye.'

Georgie listened to it, the dead weight of sadness still on her. This morning she would have been thrilled to hear this, eager to get the furniture in and the tower complete. Now she couldn't care less if she never saw the tower again.

If her life with Caspar was over – and it might be – then nothing mattered. Not cooking, not the new book, or the television show or Atalanta or the castle and certainly not the tower.

Nothing mattered, and nor did she.

She rolled over and closed her eyes again, wanting only to sink to a place of oblivion where she did not have to think or feel or mind.

The next morning, after a fitful night, she made her way to the East Tower. She heard Sam in the tower kitchen and went in to find him. He smiled as she entered but it faded to concern when he saw her properly.

'Georgie, are you all right?'

'I'm fine,' Georgie said, her voice sounding bleak even to her ears.

'You don't look it.' He went over and put a hand on her shoulder. 'Honestly, mate, what's up? You look like you've just had some really bad news. Is Caspar around?'

'No,' she said. 'He's had to go off for a while.'

'Oh. Okay.' He looked hard into her face and evidently saw that there was no way she was going to talk about it. He probably assumed they'd had a row, she thought, which was not wrong. He changed the subject.

'Let's get this tower kitted out then? Just as you'd like it? Come on, come up with me and we can start planning. The boys are getting the furniture from the stables right now.'

She went upstairs with him without enthusiasm but before long, Sam had managed to lift her mood a little. He was gentle but persistent, pushing her to make decisions instead of allowing him to take control, and gradually she began to feel a bit better.

'Want to talk about it?' Sam asked lightly, when they'd finished plotting the furniture layout.

Georgie shook her head.

'Look, everyone has a bust-up from time to time. If that's what's happened. I don't want to presume, but it looks like that. I'm just saying that Caspar is a brilliant guy, he adores you, it's obvious, and you two are just great together. Everyone thinks it. I'm sure whatever has happened will get sorted out. Hey – don't cry like that, mate! Come here.' He pulled her up against his great frame and wrapped his arms around her, rocking her slightly as if she was a child. 'It's going to be all right, you'll see. Let's go down and I'll make you a cup of tea.'

Feeling heartsick but slightly comforted by the sturdy warmth of Sam's hug and his words of reassurance, she managed a smile and followed him back down the stairs. Her telephone buzzed on the way down, and she quickly grabbed it from her pocket, hoping for a message from Caspar. It was one from Pippa.

I can't take much more of this. He's just run out of the house again in a complete state.

Georgie stared at it. Pippa was the one person that she could care about in the face of all this – her sister and her children. But she also felt exhausted at the sight of more drama and angst. She typed back:

Oh no. I'm sorry. What caused it?

Pippa's reply flew back.

I don't even want to write it down. Can I call you?

Georgie hesitated, feeling torn. Then she wrote:

Sorry, love, I'm busy right now. Can we talk later? Write to me if you want to. Sending you lots of love, take care. xxx

Sam put the kettle on to boil in the kitchen, where the countertops were now on and the last of the painting was nearly finished. A box of kitchen things sat on the floor, and he got some clean mugs out.

'Everything okay?' he said lightly, looking at Georgie absorbed in her phone.

'My sister,' Georgie said, putting the phone back in her pocket. 'Her marriage is on the verge of collapse.'

'Sorry to hear that,' Sam said. 'I've been through that myself. It's awful. More than awful.'

'Oh? When was that?'

'Four years ago.' He shook his head. 'Worst time of my life bar none. It'll never be that bad again. I moved out, she kept the house and the kids.'

'Was it amicable?'

Sam laughed. 'I've heard of these amicable divorces but I've never seen one. If it's that amicable, then why the hell are you getting divorced, if you've got kids? You ought to bloody well fix it. My missus had an affair and then decided to be with him and threw me out. Completely out of the blue as far as I was concerned, though she said she'd been unhappy for ages and I should have seen the signs. I hadn't noticed a thing. By the time I knew about it, it was all too late. Bolt from the blue. Devastated.'

'I'm sorry,' Georgie said softly.

Sam shrugged. 'We all have crap to deal with. She's probably got a different version, to be honest. Maybe I wasn't working at it as hard as I should have. Too late now. Sounds like your sister is going through the mill.'

Georgie nodded. 'I suppose it won't be over for some time.'

'The shit is just beginning unless they can pull it back. But it sounds like they might be past that.'

'I'm afraid they are.'

'Kids come first, that was my motto. As long as people can be adults about how they treat the kids, then everything else can be dealt with. But those children didn't ask for their worlds to be turned upside down.' He nodded firmly, and she thought how kind and sensible and forthright he was. 'The children's welfare comes first.'

Georgie nodded back, staring. At last she said quietly, 'Yes. Children's welfare comes first. Sam, I'm going home now, is that okay?'

'Of course. Sure you're okay?'

'Yes. I just need to think. I'll be back later.'

She lay on her bed, eyes closed.

Children's welfare comes first.

That's what people said, what they pretended they believed. But it had never really been like that at all, not for her.

Her earliest memories were mixtures of dark and light, misery and happiness, with no understanding of why it should be one and not the other. There was chaos, she remembered something of that. Later she was told – by Patsy – that her real parents had been drug addicts, young people who should never have had babies, and who existed in squalor, totally unable to look after children. They'd been found one day, wandering around the local park, unable to find to their way out, pushing the girls in their pushchairs around and around. 'It was only a small park,' Patsy had said, laughing. 'They must have been off their nuts!'

After that, there had been serious interventions. The girls had been monitored by social workers since birth but their parents had been good at hiding the extent of their drug use.

'They said it was a loving home,' Patsy said scornfully. 'But how can you love your kids if you take drugs all day long and can't keep the house tidy?'

By then Georgie had felt that she could understand that a tidy house didn't equal love. In fact, it could equal the opposite.

By the time Georgie was four and Pippa two, the sisters were fostered out. No placement ever seemed to last long. They would be found new carers and told this would be their home for the foreseeable future. It would all start again: a new house to learn, new routines, new foster parents who had their own outlooks, habits and foibles. Bedtime changed, bathtime changed, their clothes changed, even their toys could change. Meals would be different; there was a different school, a new uniform, new parts of town, new bus routes.

Some homes were wonderful: warm and loving and nourishing. Those often had children already, and were spilling over so much love that they had extra to give to those who needed it. Others were colder and more like institutions. But mostly people were kind and met the needs of Georgie and Pippa as best they could. No matter where they lived, they would be taken every month to a building with a large room full of beanbags and brightly coloured chairs and tables, with soft toys and games, jugs of squash and plates of biscuits. Then Mum and sometimes also Dad would be there, and they would all play together for a few hours and then Mum would start crying, and Dad too sometimes, and then it all turned awful with the social workers taking the girls away, and their parents shouting and screaming.

After a while the visits with their parents stopped and no one ever explained why.

The last home they went to was with Patsy and Mike.

For years, Georgie wondered why people like them wanted to offer a home to children when they seemed to loathe the trouble and nuisance that they brought with them. She thought it must have been the money they received for fostering. But how could that have been worth the trouble, when the girls seemed like such a burden?

Right from the start, life with Patsy and Mike had been awful. Their tidy home was a place of misery and stress. Even now, Georgie hated to think of it: the atmosphere of disapproval and meanness, the lack of heat, the lack of decent clothes, the lack of anything that might make a child happy. But worst was the lack of food. Patsy, skin and bone herself, controlled it tightly. No one could touch the food but her. She cooked small meals and gave out small portions. If she was angry or upset, the portions got smaller until sometimes the children got what looked like doll-sized platefuls. The cupboards and fridge were perfectly arranged and ordered and monitored so that nothing could be taken without it being noticed.

It was agony to open the fridge, as Georgie did sometimes, and see the food within that she dare not touch. She tried slicing miniscule bits of cheese from the block, or ripping a tiny shred of ham from a packet. She would take one cherry tomato from the punnet or one biscuit from the tin. But it was no good. Patsy saw it.

Georgie wondered if Patsy had purposefully put so many enticing things so close at hand in order to trap the children. She seemed to thrive on the daily drama of feeding or not feeding the children, monitoring them, and when they failed in some way, administering punishment.

Smacksies was bad enough: Patsy's hard palm, sharp, on the bottom. She made them lift their skirts so she could hit them harder.

Beltsies was worse. Mike wrapped his belt around his hand so that the buckle was on his palm and then smacked them with it, wherever would not be seen at school – on their bottoms and the tops of their thighs. It was hard not to scream and cry when beltsies happened.

Basket was a different type of horror. Less painful but more drawn out. In Mike and Patsy's room was a large wicker laundry basket. Going into the basket was horrible, not just because it was cramped and uncomfortable but because of the ghastly smell of worn clothes. Patsy and Mike were clean people, but the reek of their clothes was something Georgie hated. She abhorred being close to Patsy, with her bony body. Her sharply sweet odour had something bitter and repellent in it. Mike smelled of aftershave, lots of it. The thick scent of that musky male perfume was choking.

After an hour in the basket, the smell receded a little but it was still so choking and airless and awful in there.

Why did they want us? Georgie would think.

Now, with the wisdom of years and distance, she knew

it was more than that. Patsy loved the control she had over the girls, and their relative powerlessness. The control she wielded over them was total, and she seemed to enjoy depriving them. *No. You can't. That's not for you.* Those were her favourite phrases. She liked to keep her home free from the clutter of children. 'Your mess,' she would say, throwing away their pictures from school, their favourite things, anything she could find. 'This isn't your home, you know! It's ours.'

She implied all the time that the girls were naughty mavericks, out to get their own way and destroy Patsy's carefully managed environment, to take advantage of her, to steal from her. And so they must be watched at all times, punished pre-emptively as well as after the event, taught where they came in the scheme of things and made to understand, through harsh rules and strict enforcement, that Patsy was the mistress here.

Patsy wielded control over Mike too. He was her creature, an acolyte, brainwashed into accepting her view of the world. But his attitude was a little different. He said that this was happening for the benefit of the girls. 'For your own good,' he would say, misty-eyed, as he got ready for beltsies. 'So you grow up to be decent adults. It hurts me more than it hurts you.'

Even at eight, Georgie knew that this was a lie.

She devoted her life to protecting Pippa from as much punishment as she could, taking the blame for everything and so getting more in the way of the worst punishments, for she seemed irredeemably naughty. That meant Pippa was saved some of the worst. But Patsy and Mike had no favourites.

They liked to play the girls off against one another whenever they could, praising one while criticising the other with no real grounding in reality. They seemed to want to drive a wedge between them, but they never succeeded. Perhaps that frustrated them.

It was a huge shock when Patsy and Mike adopted them.

At a ghastly celebration meal in a local restaurant with Patsy's parents there too, Patsy and Mike told the sisters that they were now their permanent family. It was one of the worst moments of Georgie's life. Pippa didn't seem to understand but was very happy to get a bowl of ice cream as a treat. Georgie did understand. She had been holding out for another placement, a new home where there were warm, kind parents and plenty to eat. Now it would never happen. Tears had dripped into her plate, and she was terrified that they would be seen and punishment would follow. She had urged herself to stop and, to her relief, they had dried before anyone noticed.

'Now you're a lovely little family!' Patsy's mother had cooed. 'Two pretty girls all your own!'

And Patsy said, 'It's all I ever wanted, to be a mother.'

Georgie had understood, dimly then but more clearly now, that Patsy had wanted to create the idea of a perfect family and that she and Pippa fitted the bill: pretty, fair girls, like storybook sisters. Patsy was fair too. The sisters looked like they could be her daughters. It was obvious that the children helped create the perfect facade for Patsy and Mike and that seemed to be all they cared about. They should look like a family but not be one. The home should look perfect but, like

354

the props in some kitchen showroom, the fridge was filled with food that could not be eaten and bottles that could not be drunk from.

It was all for show and underneath was awful suffering.

It had taken years to escape from them.

And all that time, Georgie had known one thing for sure: never, never could she have children and risk anything like those childhood horrors of hers happening to them.

Chapter Eighteen

1939

Later on in the day that Mother was smuggled up the stairs and into her own bedroom, Grandfather came back from delivering the nurse to the station. The Buick, its headlights shaded so that it was hard to see through the fog, came rumbling up the drive, over the bridge, under the gatehouse and pulled to a stop in front of the house.

Grandfather got out and opened the passenger door. A woman in a coat and hat climbed out with a small child in her arms. Grandfather took two suitcases from the car and led her up the front steps. Inside, he shouted, 'Hallooo! Everyone, come here! We have a visitor!'

Miranda came hurrying from the morning room where she had been typing, and was first to arrive in the hall. The visitor was a youngish woman with neat dark hair, the child – a girl of about two – sitting on her hip. The girl was clearly overwhelmed at the sight of the house, her eyes round and her mouth open.

Grandfather spotted Miranda. 'Ah! Are those boys about? Tom and Robbie? Call them, will you?'

Miranda ran up to the nursery where Imogen was making high tea for the boys in the little kitchen there but there was no sign of the gang.

'Where are they?' asked Miranda. 'There's someone to see the Fosters. It must be their mother.'

Imogen, startled, took her saucepan off the stove. 'They're with the horses. I told them to be back in five minutes for tea.'

Miranda hurried down the back stairs into the kitchen where Rosalind was starting on the grown-ups' supper. 'I think the boys' mother is here,' she said excitedly as she ran through on the way to the stables. 'She's in the hall with Grandfather!'

Just as Miranda was about to head outside, she ran into the boys on their way back from tending to Harris and Poppy, smelling of horses, straw and hot mash.

'We're just coming!' Toby said indignantly when he saw his sister. 'We're not late!'

'We even left time to wash our 'ands,' Tom announced proudly. The Fosters had not seen the point at first but had condescended to join in with Toby and Archie in washing up after being in the stables.

'It's not that!' Miranda said breathlessly. 'There's a surprise for you in the hall, that's all, so you'd better be quick!'

After a second's pause, the boys ran for the hall, the twins following.

It took a moment for Tom to grasp who was standing in the hall.

'Mum!' he shouted. 'It's Mum, Robbie, can't you see?'

Robbie gasped and they almost fell over themselves in

their rush to get to her. They threw themselves at her all at once, sobbing. She was laughing and crying as she stooped to hug them both as best she could with the child in her arms, who looked sleepy and surprised at the energetic welcome from the boys. 'Oh now!' she said laughing in a choked way. 'You're setting me off! How are you, my lovely boys? Pleased to see us, are you? Mind Sylvia, she's just woke up!'

Toby and Archie stood wide-eyed, watching the reunion, not moved at all but slightly curious. Imogen had come down and was wiping away a surreptitious tear.

Maybe it's a relief, Miranda thought, seeing it. *After all, if their real mother is here, Imogen will get a breather. But it must be odd for Toby and Archie. Perhaps they're wondering why they don't have a mother. Perhaps it will drive them all apart again.* Having no mother was something they shared.

Rosalind was cooing at the baby, clearly delighted at the turn of events.

Aunt Constance came along the passage into the hall. 'What is all this rumpus?' she asked and stopped short at the sight of Mrs Foster. 'And who is this?'

'Connie, meet Mrs Dolly Foster,' Grandfather said. 'She's come to visit us. I found her on the station platform, asking the guard how to get to Wakefield Castle.'

Aunt Constance looked surprised but only for a moment before her manners took over. 'Well, how charming. How marvellous to meet you, Mrs Foster. We have written, of course, but never spoken.' She advanced with her hand held out. Mrs Foster managed to extract one hand from the clinging boys and took Aunt Constance's hand, shaking it as she bobbed a curtsey.

'Very pleased to meet you, ma'am,' she said shyly.

'We're very happy to see you, of course, but perhaps a card before you arrived . . . ?' Aunt Constance raised her brows.

Mrs Foster flushed and started talking quickly, while making her boys let her go and stand politely beside her. 'I do apologise, but I made the decision so quick, there wasn't the time. I missed my boys something awful and there's Christmas coming and I just couldn't stand not to see them. I heard a rumour, see, that there's bad snow coming and I thought, well, what if I'm cut off from them? I've always known there's the train, you understand, and that I could get to them if I needed. But if there wasn't that . . . when it's already going to be a sad Christmas what with all the nice things not happening, no lights or candles or anything like that. And I've been making their presents, and what if I couldn't get them sent and they had nothing from me on Christmas Day?' Mrs Foster took a breath. 'Well, I couldn't bear it, that's all, and a telegram would cost a bit too much what with the train fare, so I thought that as you live in a castle you'd like as not have room for me and I had to bring the baby. I know it's a terrible liberty, ma'am, I hope you'll forgive me.'

There was a long pause. The rest of the family watched as the little family clung together with Aunt Constance and Grandfather looking on.

'It's unexpected,' Aunt Constance said. 'But you're right, we have plenty of room. How long do you intend to stay?'

'Well, ma'am, I know it's a lot to ask, but I thought that over Christmas perhaps . . .'

'Oh! That long!' Christmas was still some time off.

'I'll earn my keep,' Mrs Foster said earnestly. 'I don't intend to sit about, if that's what you're worried about. I've got the baby to mind but I can still work and would be happy to. Little Sylvia is no trouble and eats hardly anything. Being with my boys is all I want.'

'Sylvia is very welcome, and I can't pretend that an extra pair of hands won't be useful,' Aunt Constance said thoughtfully. She smiled. 'You seem a very decent woman, Mrs Foster. Of course you're welcome to stay as long as you like. I don't suppose you cook, do you?'

'Cooking was my work before the kiddies,' Mrs Foster replied, smiling broadly. 'I worked in a big house in St James's for a while.'

'Well, that's marvellous news!' exclaimed Grandfather, looking more animated than he had for a long time. 'We've been struggling rather since our cook left. The girls try their best but it's testing. For all of us. That settles it, doesn't it, Connie?'

'Mrs Foster would be welcome even if she couldn't cook,' Aunt Constance said diplomatically. 'But if she can, so much the better. However, let's get you settled in. Can I take your coat, Mrs Foster?'

'Oh, thank you.'

The boys had stopped crying and were bright-eyed and

grinning as they realised that their mother was going to stay with them. They started begging her to come and see their room.

'Go on,' Aunt Constance said, as she took the other woman's coat and hat. 'Go and look around and I'll see about your room. Miranda, Rosalind! I need your help, please. Imogen, perhaps you can show Mrs Foster up with the boys. Leonard, hang these up, will you? I need to get some linen.'

Miranda knew that Aunt Constance had told Mrs Foster about the presence of Mother in the bedroom on the first floor. There was no other way, as meals had to be prepared for Mother. Food that could be easily eaten by someone in a state of sedation was required, that could be put on a spoon and held to their lips. Porridge, soups and stews, nourishing and simple to swallow.

Not only that, but she needed care and that meant that everyone was stretched thin. Aunt Constance managed Mother while Imogen was teaching. Mrs Foster helped with the boys when they were home from school.

'It is providence,' Aunt Constance said solemnly, 'that brought Mrs Foster to us exactly when we needed her.'

When the holidays came, Mrs Foster fell into the role of caring for Mother, taking turns with Imogen and Aunt Constance, while Miranda and Rosalind looked after the boys. Rosalind had taken to little Sylvia very strongly, almost as though she was enjoying having a charge all of her own, and a very sweet one at that. Sylvia had huge dark eyes and thick black hair, and was unusually quiet and docile for a two-year-old. She fell in love with Rosalind, and when she wasn't with her mother, she followed her around like a faithful puppy.

Grandfather and Mr Humphries maintained a discreet distance from the quiet drama going on beneath the surface of things and pretended that, apart from Mrs Foster's sudden appearance, nothing out of the ordinary was happening. There was no sedated woman living in one of the upstairs rooms, tended to at all hours. Grandfather patrolled the house and grounds, doing what jobs he could with the help of the last remaining elderly gardeners, or preparing his guns and old service revolver for the coming invasion. Mr Humphries had stopped his field trips now that the weather was so cold and the boys were at school, but in the holidays they could not resist going to see him for at least an hour a day to talk about fossils and extinct creatures and their skeletons. Robbie in particular was fascinated. His curiosity had been piqued by the crinoids he'd collected and now he had lots of questions about sea creatures and how their fossilised remains could be found in rivers in the middle of the countryside. He and Mr Humphries were often deep in discussion for an hour at a time.

With the appearance of their mother, the transformation of the evacuees from angry, frightened exiles to happy, energetic boys was complete.

It's not fair, Miranda thought, seeing her own brothers ignorant of their mother's presence. *It's not fair at all*.

It made her angry herself, even if Rosie couldn't see it in

the same way. She was just happy Mother was here and safe. What good would it do the boys to see her sedated and not knowing them?

'I don't know,' Miranda said obstinately. 'It just isn't fair and that's all.'

'Why can't we see Mother?' Miranda begged her aunt. 'Please, Aunt Constance! It's agony having her here, and only getting that glimpse when she came in. Rosalind hasn't seen her at all! It's not fair. In fact, it's cruel.'

'Let me think about it,' Aunt Constance said gravely. 'I promise I will consider carefully.'

Imogen told them when they asked nightly what was happening.

'We were so worried at first that she might recognise her surroundings and become agitated,' she told Miranda and Rosalind. 'But if anything, she seems a little happier. Perhaps it's because she feels more at home in the new room.'

'Not the one she shared with Father?' asked Rosalind.

'No. Not that one.'

Grandfather had kept the room as a shrine to the young couple, untouched since Father was killed. No one had ever been allowed back in.

'Do you think she might be getting better?' Miranda asked, longingly.

'Perhaps. Mrs Foster is very good with her, so gentle. And the food she is making is lovely. Mother seems to positively enjoy the soups. I'm sure they're helping her.'

The girls looked at one another, hardly daring to hope.

'Perhaps they should give Mother less sedative and see what happens?' suggested Miranda.

'We mustn't hurry it,' cautioned Imogen. 'But wouldn't that be wonderful?'

'To have Mother back,' Rosalind said longingly. 'It would be more than wonderful.'

Christmas was nearly upon them. The weather was getting colder and worse was predicted. Even though there was a news blackout on the weather, the newspapers were talking of the bitter conditions.

'You're getting rather good,' Mr Humphries said to Miranda, examining her latest attempt at typing up some of his notes. 'This has hardly any errors. All the spacing is just right.'

She smiled at him, pleased by his praise. 'I'm learning quite a bit about avian extinction as well. It's interesting. But more importantly, I can type almost without looking at all. My *Teach Yourself Typing* book has helped as well; there are lots of exercises in it. I just wish my fingers would do exactly what I want.'

Mr Humphries smoked on his cigarette, frowning over her text again. 'Well, if by chance you don't become a journalist, you've got yourself the beginnings of secretarial skills and they could take you far.'

'Secretary?' Miranda was unimpressed.

'Don't be too quick to dismiss it. It's an excellent career and can leads to lots of other opportunities. I know you see yourself as a reporter with a notebook chasing exciting stories, but most reporting is rather dull. You might find that getting yourself a position on a woman's magazine, like *The Lady*, might be better.'

Miranda wrinkled her nose. 'I've seen those in the post office. How to make a lovely home. How to cook delicious dinners. I don't want all that.'

'Then think about study. You could go to one of the women's colleges at a university.'

Miranda tried to think and gave up. 'The war is going to ruin everything,' she declared. 'All my plans up in smoke.'

'We're all in the same boat,' Humphries replied, smoking again. 'And many won't come back from it. So think about that.'

Miranda was abashed. 'I suppose you're right. I will think about it – study, I mean. And proper jobs. And I know you've helped me get a useful skill. I'm grateful.'

'You're welcome.' He stubbed out his cigarette. 'Now tell me, how is your mother?'

'Imogen says much the same. Aunt Constance speaks to the doctor once a week and he thinks we must keep her medication at the same level for longer, to give her the best chance of a slow and sure recovery.'

'He is no doubt correct. But it must be hard for you children. Do the boys know?'

'No. And they don't seem to notice much.'

'They might notice more than you think.' Mr Humphries took a sip from the teacup on his desk. 'Your sister is a wonderful nurse, isn't she?'

'Rosalind?' Miranda said innocently.

He flushed very lightly. 'No. Miss Wakefield. Your older sister.'

Miranda smiled. 'Oh yes, she's wonderful. She's with the boys right now, painting strips of old newspaper to make Christmas decorations.' She looked at Mr Humphries, who was staring at the floor through his owl glasses, his expression unreadable. 'Will you be with us for Christmas?' she asked.

He seemed pleased that the subject had been changed. 'I'm not sure, Miranda, it depends on the weather. I do have a family and they would like me to get to them for a few days at least. As long as the snow holds off, I might be able to get away. And I've had a letter from the head of the museum. There's a chance I might be called back to London quite soon.'

'What?' Miranda exclaimed. 'But why?'

'Reasons,' Mr Humphries said vaguely. 'It's all rather confidential. I can't go into it with you, I'm afraid.'

'But the moas! The egg! You need to stay with them, don't you?'

'The moas are safe enough in their boxes. It will be a bore to pack up my research, I can't deny that.' He gestured at all his paperwork, the microscope and the fragments he was working on in their box. 'But it won't take that long. I could even leave my research here, as I'm fairly confident that they'll send me back at some point. But I'll probably take the egg.' He glanced at its cask. 'I don't like to leave it anywhere, really. I never feel happy when it's out of my sight.'

'Please don't leave us!' Miranda was surprised at how upset she felt at the idea. Perhaps it was because Mr Humphries had been so tender and strong with Mother, but she felt that he had become a trusted member of the family. He had opened new worlds for all of them, but particularly for her, and for the boys.

'You'll be fine without me,' he said sturdily. 'Lots of women are coping without their menfolk, you know. And we're not even related.'

Miranda said sadly, 'I know you're right. We'll miss you, though.'

'We must be brave. It's wartime. I don't need to tell you that.'

'No. I understand.' Miranda got up and smiled. 'Let's hope it doesn't snow so you can get home for Christmas.'

They all worked together to get the house ready for Christmas. Mr Humphries put aside his work and went out to find a good tree to be their Christmas tree, and to cut down lots of mistletoe, ivy and holly with the best berries that he could find. They would be frugal. The wireless was full of admonitions to spend as little as possible, and posters up in the post office and shop reminded them all over again. But in many ways, it didn't feel all that different from last year. They had the old decorations for their tree, and there were still the stores of Fortnum's goodies that Grandfather had laid in. They would provide plenty of delicious things for the Christmas feast, and some treats for the children's stockings too. The tricky thing was presents, but Imogen felt that they could reuse some of the toys in the attic for the young ones, and be imaginative with what they had.

'I could help you, if you like, Miss Wakefield?' suggested Humphries. 'I'm quite good with my hands and can do a bit of repair or repurposing if that's any use.'

'I'm sure it would be helpful, thank you,' Imogen said, going slightly pink, and they went up to the attic to search for likely objects, coming down animated and smiling in one another's company.

'Who knows what we'll get,' Rosalind said. 'But it doesn't matter. Christmas is for children really, isn't it?'

The twins worked together to make a gift for Mother instead, embroidering six white handkerchiefs with flowers. For the other women, they made lavender sachets and Rosalind painted little landscapes of the park for them, which they framed in cardboard. She also made colouring books for the children's stockings, drawing the outlines of snowmen, angels and merry Father Christmases for them to shade in with pencils.

'What do we give to Grandfather and Mr Humphries?'

'We knit for our lives!' Rosalind said, and they unravelled some old worn jumpers to use the wool for nice mufflers and scarves. Old copies of the *London Illustrated News* were cut up to make wrapping paper.

Once the tree was up in the drawing room, and everywhere festooned with ivy and homemade paperchains, there was a proper Christmas feel to the house and everyone's spirits lifted. There was a slight dip when Mr Humphries announced he'd be leaving on Christmas Eve, but he promised that he would return a few days after that. They had grown so used to having him about that he would be missed.

Grandfather took him to the station, a Christmas present of a box of Fortnum's chocolates tucked into his suitcase.

'Goodbye!' they all shouted, waving from the front door as the car rolled away, but no one lingered in the cold for long, running back into the relative warmth of the house, shivering.

'We have to do it,' Miranda said in a low voice to Rosalind as Aunt Constance shut the great front door against the bitter chill. 'I tell you, it's our only chance. We won't get another.'

'But it's so risky!' Rosalind whispered back. 'He must guess it's us.'

'It doesn't matter. It isn't about him not knowing it was us. As long as we refuse to admit it, then he can't do anything without proof. Don't you see?'

'I'm not sure,' her sister said unhappily. 'I need to think about it. It's such a huge thing to do and it might not work.'

Christmas Day came sharp with icy frost.

'Is it a white Christmas?' Toby asked, staring out of the dining room window at the glistening park beyond.

'No,' Grandfather said. 'It just looks like one. But that's not snow, it's thick, thick frost. Come on, boys, have you finished your breakfast? You can all help me light the yule log.'

Once toast and porridge had been eaten, and tea drunk, they all trooped into the great hall. In the fireplace, the log had been prepared and on the mantel, tethered by pewter goblets, were four fat stockings – Grandfather's old green army socks – one for each of the boys. They whooped and skipped with excitement when they saw them. Dolly Foster watched with shining eyes as her boys fell on the stockings when Grandfather handed them over, eager to see what was inside.

'I suppose we're not children any more,' Miranda murmured to Rosalind, a little sad that this year they would not have the excitement of that wonderful bulging repository of pleasure and surprise.

'Isn't it strange? But I'm enjoying giving as much as I used to enjoy getting.' Rosalind looked over at Imogen, who seemed rather sad as she watched their little brothers and the two evacuees shouting and exclaiming over their small gifts and sweets. 'Are you all right, Imogen?'

'I'm just a little sad . . . a little sad Mr Humphries isn't here. I'm going to church with Grandfather and Aunt Constance. It would be nice if he were here too – to come with us. For numbers, you know. Four is more friendly.'

'Oh yes, for numbers,' echoed Miranda with a smile. 'Look at how happy Mrs Foster is! She's laughing like anything to see Robbie's joy at that little wooden spinner Mr Humphries made.'

Dolly Foster looked much happier now she had been at the castle more than a week. She had been tense when she arrived, something they'd all put down to her fears about how she would be received, but it had stayed with her for some time, showing up in a nervousness whenever there were unexpected knocks and bumps or a stranger at the door. Now that had faded and she had taken to life in the castle with relish, finding great pleasure in being reunited with her sons. Everyone had grown instantly fond of baby Sylvia with her plump face and angelic eyes and good behaviour. When Dolly was thanked for her work, she said, 'Oh, I don't think of it as work. We're all mucking in, aren't we?'

'Some more than others, my dear,' Aunt Constance said warmly. 'I don't know how we coped without you.'

Now Dolly came over with little Sylvia who'd been having her breakfast in the kitchen where it was warm. 'Merry Christmas, my dears!'

'Merry Christmas, Dolly. How was Mother when you went up?' Imogen asked, quietly so the boys wouldn't hear.

'Very well. She had just woken. I left her with a cup of tea and wished her a very happy Christmas.'

Miranda looked at her aunt and decided to go for the thing she most wanted. 'Aunt Constance, mayn't we see her today?' she whispered. 'Please? As it's Christmas?'

Aunt Constance looked in two minds, which meant she was not going to say no at once. Miranda felt a spark of hope. 'I'll think about it. But Kathryn has made some progress over the last few days. We've decreased her sedation. It is quite something that she can sit up in bed and drink her tea by herself. Perhaps she is strong enough to see you, and perhaps it might even benefit her. I will think about it while we're in church. Now, I must get my coat and hat if we're to be in time for the service. Come on, Leonard, Imogen. We'll leave the young ones to their breakfasts.'

Huddled at their corner of the breakfast table while Mrs Foster was overseeing toast and porridge for the boys, Miranda whispered to Rosalind, 'I think we should see Mother.'

'What?' Rosalind looked scared. 'Without permission?'

Miranda was impatient. Now that she knew Mother was upstairs drinking tea and perfectly rational, there was all the reason in the world to go and see her. In fact, it was taking all her strength not to run there right now. 'Don't you want to see her?'

Rosalind's eyes filled at once with outraged tears. 'Of course I do! It's only because I thought she was asleep that I haven't gone in already. How can you say that?'

'Now, now, it's all right, I know you want to see her. We could wait ages for Aunt Constance to make up her mind. But we've got a chance right now. Imogen says she's calm. She still believes she's Mrs Black, but we won't say anything to upset her, will we? Come on, Rosie, what a chance. Let's take it.'

She gazed beseechingly at her sister. This was something she longed to do, but not alone. They ought to be together for such a moment.

Rosalind hesitated, then said firmly, 'All right. We'll do it now when we're not going to be missed.'

Miranda squeezed her hand. 'Thank you.'

They slipped out of the dining room and hurried up the main stairs, their hearts beating faster at their audacity. They collected their present first, and then, outside Mother's first-floor bedroom, they stopped, Miranda ready to knock. Their mirror-image blue eyes stared into one another's, reflecting back their twin apprehension and excitement.

'Ready?'

Rosalind nodded. 'Ready.'

Miranda knocked, and they held their breath to listen.

There was a rustle behind the door and then Mother's low musical voice said, 'Yes? Who is it?'

It was too late to back out now.

Miranda pushed open the door and there was Mother sitting up in the large bed with the Chinese red silk headboard, propped up on her pillows. She was drinking her tea, with a book open, propped on a stand on the table by her bedside. She wore a plain white nightgown and looked, Miranda thought, very beautiful as usual: pale and fine boned, her fair hair tied back.

'Hello?' she said, but with the mildest curiosity. 'Please come in.'

'Good morning . . . Mrs Black,' Miranda said, finding the name odd in her mouth.

Rosalind followed. She had not seen Mother the night she was taken from the tower and she gazed at her with round eyes and an expression of hesitant surprise. 'Good morning,' she said in an odd, high voice. 'Merry Christmas.'

'Good morning to you both. Oh, you're twins, aren't you? Have we met before? You look familiar. Do you also live in this house? Merry Christmas to you too. The woman with the tea, Dolly . . . she said it's Christmas Day. I can't think why I didn't know before. I would usually go to church, I believe, though I must say, it's a long time since I last remember going.' Mother sipped her tea again.

The twins stole a glance at one another. This was more than they expected. She seemed to remember them and something of her own past. Apart from looking frail and tired, she appeared outwardly normal.

'We live here,' Miranda said, her voice shaking. 'And I think we met a while ago.'

'And we . . . we brought you a present,' Rosalind said tentatively. 'If you don't mind.'

'Mind? Why should I mind?' Mother smiled, looking baffled. She put down her teacup. 'But I don't know why you would bother! Still, it's very thoughtful.'

Rosalind put down the present. It looked very meagre suddenly on the large expanse of the counterpane, but Mother seemed pleased with it. She picked it up and opened it. 'How lovely. What nice handkerchiefs. Did you embroider these pretty flowers yourselves?'

They nodded, smiling with pleasure at her praise.

'They're beautiful. How kind.' She gazed at them, smiling back. 'What good children you are. Thank you. Will you both give me a kiss?' She held up her cheek towards them. 'That would please me very much.'

Astonished but also thrilled, both girls advanced and, one after the other, kissed their mother's cheek.

'Thank you, my dears. Now I'm sorry that I do not have a present for you. But next time you shall have something. I shall ask my nurse to find my purse and you shall have a shilling each. For Christmas.'

'You're very kind but we don't need anything,' Rosalind said politely.

'Now, what refined creatures you are. When I speak to your mother, I shall tell her how well she has brought you up. Off you go now, girls, I must finish my tea and my nurse will be here soon to dress me. I'm not very well, you know, but I'm getting my strength back and soon I'll be able to go home, they tell me. Merry Christmas!'

'Merry Christmas,' they replied, and went out again. As soon as the door closed behind them, they were so overcome with a mixture of delight and misery that they hugged each other tightly and sobbed.

'She let us kiss her!' said Rosalind, tears running down her face. 'I thought I'd never see her again, and she let us kiss her!'

'She's almost well! She must be. Oh, wonderful Mother. If only she knew that she's our mother, everything would be perfect!' Miranda's eyes were damp but shining. 'That would be the best present she could give us.'

Christmas Day was the happiest they could remember for years, certainly since Father had died. The twins held their secret of having seen their mother while the presents under the tree were opened. Everyone was delighted with their gifts: books and a notebook and pen for Miranda, and a sketchpad and paints for Rosalind, while each of the boys had a wooden toy from the attic refreshed and made better by Mr Humphries.

'Use your paper wisely, girls,' cautioned Aunt Constance. 'There won't be a great deal more where that came from, unless things change very quickly.'

'The war won't last another year,' said Grandfather, but with much less confidence than he once had. There didn't seem to be any progress against the enemy, who had pressed into more areas of Europe without any sign of trouble.

'We'll be very careful,' promised Miranda.

When all the presents had been opened, it was time for their Christmas feast. The Fortnum's hampers provided an extraordinary array of delicacies. A capon had been roasted by Mrs Foster with plenty of vegetables and a gravy enriched by port jelly.

When they went into the dining room to see it all laid out, with homemade paper hats at every place, they were so excited by the beautiful table and all the food that they barely noticed Aunt Constance lead a stranger into the room until she said, 'Everyone, this is our guest, Mrs Black. She is joining us for lunch.'

Miranda gasped as she turned to see her mother, dressed in a black silk dress that hung off her slender frame, heels and a little fur jacket. A rope of pearls glowed around her neck and she had put on a small smear of red lipstick. Her fair hair had been brushed out and was held back with glittering clips. She looked so beautiful, as if she had walked from three years before into their lives today.

'Good afternoon, everyone,' Mrs Black said politely, and she was led to her place between Aunt Constance and Imogen, where she sat down carefully and smiled radiantly. 'How beautiful. I do love Christmas. It's most kind of you to invite me.'

Grandfather suddenly scrabbled for his handkerchief and blew his nose. 'You're very welcome, my dear,' he said gruffly. 'Always.'

Imogen, who had seen Mother every day since she arrived from the tower, looked less shocked but still moved. The boys stared at her with wonder, but their eyes were blank and unknowing. They had no idea, Miranda realised. Not yet, at least.

'We shall drink champagne!' declared Grandfather. 'And the best claret from Fortnum's too. Come, my dears, let's enjoy ourselves. Once it's gone, it's gone.'

They stuffed themselves with the delicious food, voting that Mrs Foster could cook much better than Mrs Graham and they were now not sorry that Mrs Graham had gone to live with her sister. Grandfather brought in the Christmas pudding alight with brandy and they all cheered and sang. Mrs Black ate the least and did not sing or cheer, but she smiled quietly and seemed to enjoy herself as an observer rather than a participant. Occasionally she rested her gaze for a while on one of the children, frowning slightly as if to recall something. But just when Miranda hoped she was about to be touched by inspiration, her expression would go back to normal and her gaze moved on.

When the last crystallised fruit was gone, they went to the drawing room to listen to the King's broadcast, which made Grandfather snuffle into his handkerchief again, and to play games by the fire. Imogen took Mother away as she was now quite clearly tired and needed to be quiet.

Miranda felt suddenly very lucky.

The only thing that would be nicer would be if Mr Humphries were here.

She had found, to her surprise, that she missed him very

much. The idea that he might go back to London was a dreadful one. She had learned so much every day from doing his typing and she valued his advice even when she didn't warm to what he was saying.

At that moment, there was a pounding on the front door that echoed through the hall and could be heard clearly in the drawing room.

Oh, he's here, he's back! Miranda thought happily. It had all gone so well today, that would simply top it all off beautifully.

Aunt Constance said, 'Are we expecting anyone?' to Grandfather, who was quite deaf and hadn't heard it.

'Carol singers?' suggested Rosalind, looking up from her paints.

'That must be it,' Miranda said. She thought it was probably not Mr Humphries this late on Christmas Day, though he could have caught a train after lunch perhaps. But carol singers would be lovely, and if they had made the trek up the drive, they deserved to be listened to. 'Let's go and open the door to them.'

They all went out to the hall where the pounding on the door was still going on.

'They're very keen to sing, aren't they?' said Toby brightly.

Grandfather went forward and opened the door, pulling back the great bolt and lifting the latch.

Outside on the step there were no carol singers. It was just one man, and not Mr Humphries. This was a man in a long overcoat and black hat, strands of dark hair emerging from underneath. He was handsome in a sharp way, with

bright black eyes shining under straight brows and a pro-
nounced square chin. As he stood there, smiling at them all,
he scanned the little group, and then saw who he was looking for over Grandfather's shoulder. 'There you are, Dolly!
And there's my boys. Well, well. Ain't it a family reunion!
Most touching.'

Miranda turned to look at Dolly. Her expression was
aghast and her eyes afraid. The boys had moved towards her
and were clinging to her, round-eyed and silent.

'Do you mind if I come in, sir? It's awful cold on this step.'

Grandfather was clearly bewildered by who this might be
but he stood back and said, 'Of course not, my fellow. It's
Christmas. You must come in. But what is your name?'

'Foster, sir. Derek Foster.' Foster picked up a knapsack
that had been just out of sight by the side of the door. He
stepped into the hall, looking around with interest at everything he could see. Then he nodded at Dolly. 'That's my wife,
there, sir. And my kids. I guess the girl's in bed, is she, Doll?
I'll have to see her tomorrow then, I suppose. You wouldn't
expect a man to be apart from his whole family for Christmas, would you? Not when you all are lucky enough to be
in a place this big?'

Dolly spoke up in a quavering voice. 'Now, Derek . . . I'm
sure the colonel can't allow you to stay . . .'

'We'll see what he says,' Foster said, still smiling. 'Aren't
you going to wish me a merry Christmas, Doll?'

'Merry Christmas, Derek,' she said in a small voice.

'Thank you. And to you. Now – a little something would
be most welcome, sir, after my long journey, if you've got it.'

'Of course, of course,' Grandfather said jovially. 'I'll get you a glass of claret, Foster, as it's Christmas.'

'Very kind, sir.' Foster put down his knapsack and rubbed his hands together. 'It's biting out there. I must say, a drop of claret would be just the thing.'

'I'll get the claret, Leonard,' said Aunt Constance, and Miranda could see that she looked very grave. 'Come with me, Miranda, you can fetch the glass.'

Miranda was confused but followed her aunt. As soon as they were in the passage, Aunt Constance said to her, 'Run up the back stairs and go to your mother's room. Tell Imogen not to come down and to lock the door from the inside. She must only open it to one of us. Will you tell her that at once?'

'Of course, but why?' Miranda could feel a growing dread begin to pool in her stomach.

'I can't say. But I have an instinct. Unfortunately I've met some ruffians in my time and that man looks like one. I'll work on Leonard to throw him out, but he has found his way here for a reason. Dolly looks most unhappy to see him, and that is never a good sign, believe me. He must clearly stay the night. But I don't want him to know about your mother and it's best that he doesn't encounter Imogen either. Now run up and tell her, then come back down. Understand?'

'Of course,' Miranda said soberly. She turned towards the back stairs and ran off on her mission.

Like her aunt, she had a horrible feeling that Mr Foster was going to be trouble.

Chapter Nineteen

Present Day

There was no word from Caspar until the third day of his absence. Each day had felt like a week. Georgie had dragged herself through in a morass of utter misery and pain. It felt as though part of her had been ripped out. The grief was terrible and she couldn't eat or sleep. She tried to work to take her mind off it, but everything seemed to set off a chain of thoughts that led to Caspar and her fear that she had lost him for ever. Her wonderful husband, the man she loved.

Hello, Georgie. Sorry it's been so long. I'm going to come home soon and we should talk. I hope you're all right. I'm looking forward to seeing you. I'll let you know when I'm coming. Cx

She felt desperately relieved that he had been in touch – she had been afraid that he would simply never return or speak to her again – and sick with fear. Why wasn't he preparing her for whatever he was going to say? It was almost like he wanted to keep her in suspense and torment her. That felt very familiar. Those tactics of menace and threat were what Patsy and Mike had used all the time. 'You just wait. When we get home, you're going to find out what for . . .'

The horror of the last three days had not just been confined to her pain over Caspar and the terrible mess she had made. It had brought Patsy and Mike back to her as though she had only seen them yesterday. Since Caspar had left, she had been haunted by the voices of her adoptive parents. They seemed to be murmuring in her ear constantly.

When she tried to work, she heard them: 'That recipe looks dreadful. Who's going to want to eat that muck? You're wasting your time. This olde worlde cookery thing is a joke.'

'I suppose this fancy house of yours makes you better than everyone else. You always did have a high opinion of yourself. You need to be taken down a peg or two!'

When she ate her lunch, forcing down a bowl of soup: 'Look how greedy you are. You don't deserve decent food.'

When she thought about Caspar, they told her that he had never loved her and that was no surprise because no one ever would.

The people she hated most in the world had become her constant companions until she wanted to scream to shut out their voices. She went on long walks, crying and talking out loud to herself, begging Patsy and Mike to go away, and trying to explain to Caspar what had happened to her.

She had never told him the whole truth; it was too ugly. And besides, the effort to pull herself free of Patsy and Mike had been so enormous that she dare not let their voices back into her head, even by recounting aloud what had happened.

By the time she was in her teens, she had been convinced that she was worthless and unlovable. She existed in a state of despair, hating her life and yet unable to stop feeling it in exquisite intensity. Pippa was happier and more carefree, perhaps because she had Georgie as a barricade between her and her adoptive parents. But Georgie, alive to all of it and aware of every jeer and insult and manipulation and cruelty, could hardly stand it. She disappeared inside herself to survive.

It was Mrs Arthur, the teacher at school, who had finally seen her and saved her. It took one person to open their eyes and understand what was going on to change everything. She started asking Georgie to help her in small tasks: sorting out the history cupboard or writing up the programme for the school play. In the quiet classroom, she began to win Georgie's trust and get her to open up about what made her so very unhappy. And eventually, Georgie told her about the misery and sterility of her home life, the way she spent her life walking on eggshells, seeking the approval that never came, existing in a state of constant stress and conflict. While the awful physical punishments of early childhood had stopped as the girls got older, there were plenty of other punishments: silence and cold shoulders, snide remarks, insults and criticism dressed up as jokes. There was the way favourite items of clothing went missing, money from Saturday jobs disappeared, how they were kept busy so they missed outings and parties, messages from friends were not passed on. Every day had its tiny attacks, humiliations and deprivations.

Mrs Arthur heard her, and believed her. There was no

question that she believed every word. The relief for Georgie was not just sweet, but overwhelming.

Those were the first steps to freedom, though it did not come quickly. The first thing Mrs Arthur did was arrange for Georgie to see the school counsellor.

In that little florescent-lit, airless room, the counsellor said something to her that she had never heard before. 'Your environment is abusive and you must leave it.'

It was a revelation that left her breathless with shock. She knew when she heard it that it was true. More than that, she knew that she already knew.

Nevertheless, Georgie refused to report Patsy and Mike. 'They'll deny it. No one will believe us. And we can't prove it.'

'It's your choice, Georgie. I can't make you do anything, you know that. You're nearly eighteen, you can leave then,' the counsellor said.

'I can't go without Pippa,' she said firmly. 'I'm staying for as long she does.'

She had learned survival a long time ago, and she would go on surviving until the time was right. The counselling helped, along with the kind, compassionate friendship of Mrs Arthur, who encouraged her to write down her feelings, and who helped her to think about what she wanted to do next. Georgie went from school to study catering and management at a local college, so that she could continue to live at home and be with Pippa while she did her A levels. She found, to her surprise, that as her inner confidence grew along with her determination to leave and start her life properly, Patsy's power simply grew weaker. She stopped tormenting Georgie in the same way. Patsy even became almost affectionate. She started to call Georgie 'love' and to give her more positive attention. It felt peculiar. And it never felt good.

One day, Georgie looked over at Patsy and saw a frightened old woman who could see her power drawing to an end, and the time coming when her daughters would be in the ascendant and able to turn around, look her in the face and ask why. She would be held to account.

She's a bully, Georgie realised. *And bullies are cowards. I never really saw how true that is until now. She's afraid of me. Now she wants to win me back because what is her perfect family worth if her daughters desert her the first moment they can?*

She held her peace, waiting for the moment when she could break free for ever.

When Pippa won a place at university in Exeter, Georgie made her own plans. She enrolled on an advanced cooking course there and that autumn, with the help of grants and loans, they left London together.

There was never a great scene with Patsy and Mike. Gently, irrevocably, the girls broke off their contact. They felt no guilt, and they knew it was right. Patsy and Mike were over, finished and consigned to the past. They no longer existed. The girls looked forward and not back.

And yet, the problem was that they did exist. They had only been dormant, not dead. As Georgie went on her endless tearful walks, trying to shut out their voices, she knew that they had never really gone away. Their legacy was going to destroy her marriage, just as it was destroying Pippa's. Could it be any coincidence that Pippa had married a man who was outwardly amiable but deep down a cold manipulator intent on denying her the love she craved? It couldn't be chance that had led her to a husband who played the same malicious games of thwarting and undermining with criticism disguised as jokes, and whose needs were paramount. Pippa's role was to serve Ryan and play out the life he wanted the world to see, just as Patsy had demanded of her.

'Patterns are familiar,' said her last counsellor, a kind and patient woman who had steered her through the years before she met Caspar. 'We feel safe with what we know. Sometimes, sadly, that is rejection and lack of approval. We are drawn to people who remind us of the treatment we know best. Because that's where we feel at home.'

It was with the help of her counsellor that Georgie managed to work on her own experience to recognise when she was drawn to people because they might reject or hurt her. She learned to look for what would keep her safe: honesty, integrity and trust. That was why she had avoided the bad boys and why, to her great joy, she had found Caspar and recognised his true qualities. But Pippa had not worked on those issues. And she had found Ryan.

'We thought we were free when we got away,' Georgie said out loud. 'But it turned out that we never were.'

When Georgie got back to the house after another long walk, she checked her phone to see that there was a voice message from Sam.

'Hi, Georgie, just to let you know that the furniture is

in like we discussed. Go and take a look. I'm coming back tomorrow or the day after so I'll see you then. The boys are site clearing tomorrow. Speak soon. Hope you like it.'

As she went along the passage, she could hear Sandy had arrived and was bustling about in the kitchen. That meant that the cleaners were in the house as well. She didn't want to talk to anyone, lovely as they were.

I'll go and see the tower, she thought, but without much excitement. Crossing the lawn, Georgie saw that there was no one about, which was a relief. She let herself into the tower. The sitting room looked just as she'd hoped: cosy, unfussy, beautiful. The leaded windows sent shafts of light all over the rug, the lamps made it warm and welcoming. The pictures and books gave it a homely but uncluttered feel. It was just right. She smiled, feeling happier.

The kitchen, especially, was perfect. Bright and modern but with all the charm of the ancient building. On the countertop was a huge bunch of flowers with a handwritten card that said *GEORGIE* on the front.

How sweet of Sam, she thought. *He's even done a card, and I've never seen him write anything.*

She picked it up to open the envelope.

'So it's finished.'

The voice came from the doorway. She jumped and looked up to see Caspar coming slowly into the kitchen. She felt a rush of joy, followed by a punch of anxiety. Her face turned scarlet with the influx of conflicting feelings and she was awkward in a way she hadn't been in years, certainly not around Caspar. 'Is it?' she said weakly, feeling sick. 'Is it finished?'

'It looks finished to me.' Caspar looked around. 'This is fantastic. You and Sam did a great job.'

'Oh! The kitchen! Yes . . .' She almost sagged with relief. 'It was mostly Sam.' She tried to calm herself, wishing she could think of something worthwhile to say, but now he was here, all her great speeches designed to win him back had vanished from her mind. All she could manage was, 'How are you?'

'I'm okay.' He smiled sadly. 'But to be honest, I haven't been great. It's been much harder than I expected. Being away, from the house. From you.'

'Where did you go?'

'To my parents. They have such a peaceful home and the garden is a real place of tranquillity. It was good just to stop thinking about the castle for a while and get some head-space.'

Georgie could imagine him in his parents' garden, his long rangy body in the hammock under the great oak, staring thoughtfully into its branches. 'I'm glad if it helped.'

'It did.'

'And I'm very happy you're home.' She smiled, longing to rush over and hug him as she normally would but sensing that he wasn't in a place to accept that right now. 'I've missed you.'

He looked at her. 'You're sad. I can see that.'

She nodded. 'Very sad.'

'So am I.'

They stood in silence for a moment. Thick misery rose up in Georgie's chest and she looked down at the countertop.

Its grain blurred in her vision as tears filled her eyes but she was determined to hold it together.

'Georgie,' he said softly, 'I'm not going to leave you. If that's what you're afraid of.'

She drew in a sharp breath. 'You're . . . you're not?'

'No. I can see you think I might. But I'm not going to. I love you very much, you know that. I'm angry and upset and I need to understand. If you love me, you'll do that for me. You'll help me to understand. And you'll listen to me too.'

'That's all I want too!' she exclaimed. 'I made such a mistake and I'm so sorry. I don't know how I could have been so stupid! I'm desperate to explain all of it.' She stared at him in an agony of hope. 'Are you really going to let me?'

'I really am. But you need to promise that you'll also listen.'

'Of course I will!'

'Why don't you read the card?' He nodded at the envelope that was still in her hand.

Bewildered, she opened it and read the card inside.

Darling Georgie, you're my family for ever. I love you now and always. Caspar x

She half laughed, half sobbed. 'These are from you?'

Caspar nodded. 'They are. With Sam's help. He sent me a message to say how concerned he was about you.'

'He's a good man.'

'I was coming back in any case, to say the same thing. But

after I heard from Sam, I knew I had to get to you as soon as possible.' He opened his arms. 'Can I have a hug?'

'Yes, oh yes!'

She ran into his arms to press her face against his chest and squeeze him as tightly as she could, happiness bursting inside like fireworks.

'I want to understand. I want to listen,' Caspar said as they walked back across to the house. 'I was so struck by what you said about Ryan, about how he wouldn't listen to Pippa and so could never fix anything. I don't want to be like that.'

'You could never be like that,' Georgie said fervently, holding tight to his arm as they walked. 'There's something faulty in Ryan's wiring. He doesn't listen because he doesn't really care about Pippa, he only cares about himself. So he fixes things like a child would, with a little present but nothing else.' She leaned into his strong shoulder. 'You said *I* was like Ryan.'

He put his arm around her. 'I didn't really mean that.'

'You were right, though. I was not being honest. I suppose my dishonesty comes from a different source from Ryan's, that's all.'

Caspar sighed as they walked. 'I was party to it, though, Georgie. I knew there were things you weren't telling me. I let you evade my questions because it was easier. I never really asked why I hadn't met your parents, why you and Pippa never spoke about them. I've known for years that you're troubled and I've never tried to find out why. That's on me.'

Georgie was silent. She hadn't thought about it that way.

She'd always been glad that Caspar let her keep her secrets. It had not occurred to her that it might be a form of neglect, not to mention something that was so clearly such a huge part of her life. 'You thought it was best for me.'

'Best for me. We often let ourselves keep secrets and tell lies by pretending that it's best for the other person when it's really best for us.' He gazed down at her earnestly. 'You will tell me everything, won't you?'

'Yes,' she said without hesitation. 'It's time.'

They spent the day together, sometimes inside, sometimes walking when they needed to stretch their legs. Sometimes they laughed, and at other times Caspar held Georgie while she sobbed. They talked through all of it and Georgie told him the entire story of what had happened to her. Not always in order and not always coherently, but clearly enough that he very quickly grasped the extent of what she and Pippa had suffered.

Caspar was horrified, outraged and saddened by turns as Georgie described her life up to arriving to live with Patsy and Mike. After that, he was stunned. He could hardly speak as she described the punishments and privations and what they did to her.

At last he said in a shaky voice, 'When I think about how my brother and sister and I grew up in this idyllic place, surrounded by all we could want, with so much love . . . and you, poor, helpless Georgie, were treated in that appalling way. I can't bear it.'

Georgie smiled and shrugged. 'It's just luck. Circumstance.'

'Did you ever want to find your real parents and find out why it all went so wrong?'

'No. Patsy said they were dead, although I don't know how she would know that. Pippa and I never talked about them. Maybe we will find out the truth one day. But to be honest, I don't think I want to find them, even if they are alive. It would be too hard.'

'I can see that. But it seems awful to have no recompense for what you've been through,' he said emphatically. 'It's wrong that a whole lifetime depends on luck. We should all have the same chance for love and happiness.'

'But we don't. That's just the way it is sometimes. Of course people like Patsy and Mike shouldn't treat children the way they do. They were probably mistreated in their turn. I honestly think that Patsy thought she was doing a good thing. On some deep level she knew she was being mean, or why did she hide it from everyone? But on another, she really thought she was a good mother, doing what was best for us. She was fooling herself of course. She was fulfilling her own need to control us, exerting some sort of revenge for how she had been treated, I expect. So how do we stop people being damaged?'

They were in the great hall, where it was pleasantly cool, each lying opposite the other on one of the large velvet sofas. Caspar filled his, while Georgie only reached two-thirds of the way down hers. She pulled a cushion down to raise her head up a bit.

Caspar gazed back at her, puzzled. 'I don't know.'

Georgie said intently, 'We make sure it stops with us.'

She held up a hand, palm out. 'We stop it in its tracks! No more damage. That's why I felt from a very young age that I couldn't risk having children. What if I thought I was being a good and kind mother and I was really inflicting on them what Patsy inflicted on me? I couldn't chance it. And even if I was a good mother, a loving mother, what if something happened to me and the children were taken away, like Pippa and me? What if they were given over to people like the ones who adopted us?' She shook her head. 'No. I could never risk it.'

He nodded his head slowly. 'I understand now. I see. But there is another way to stop the damage, isn't there? My parents loved me and raised me well. I think I would be a good father – I hope I would. But I don't have to fight the damage that was done to me. I mean, they weren't perfect, and I'm sure I would have lots of faults, but the intrinsic love and protection would be there.'

Georgie said, 'I know. This isn't about you and your qualities. I've always known you would be a fantastic father. It's why I've felt so dreadful about my choice.'

'Okay, Georgie. Here is where you listen to me. And I mean, really listen.' Caspar sat up suddenly, as though he had grasped an idea of importance. 'Can't you see that the way to stop damage is not to stop children existing? In fact, if you do that, you perpetuate damage because you won't be able to stop damaged people who are unaware, as Patsy was, from having children and passing on the damage. If you stop the damage by having children but bringing them up without hurting them the way you were hurt . . . then you've made healthy people. Healthy people who can make more healthy children. And gradually, the damage gets less and less. Perhaps it might even, one day, die out.'

Georgie stared at him. She had never thought of this before. It had never occurred to her that she could fight against what was done to her and prevent the same happening to others by propagating health.

Caspar could see she was thinking, and that what he had said was sinking in. After a moment, he spoke. 'I will never, never force you to do anything you don't want to do. If our own children are not to be in our lives, so be it. We've got nieces and nephews and cousins and second cousins by the dozen. There will always be children around us. But just think about it, Georgie. That's all I ask.'

She lay her head back down on the cushion and thought. After a while she said, 'It might be too late for me to change my mind. I've been so adamant all these years. And in a way, I feel as though I have already brought up a child.'

'You mean Pippa? A child can't bring up a child, though you tried your best. It's not the same.'

'No, I suppose not.' She sighed. 'There's a lot to think about. But thank you for listening. I feel so much better.'

'Are you still having counselling?'

Georgie shook her head. 'I stopped not long after we met. I was happy. I didn't feel I needed it any more.'

'Perhaps it couldn't hurt to have an MOT. Bringing all this to the surface might have consequences.'

'You're so wise,' she said with a smile. 'I'll think about it.'

'On another note . . .' Caspar said hesitantly. 'I hope this is okay . . .'

She looked at him quizzically. 'What?'

'Pippa got in touch with me when you didn't call her. She was worried.'

'Okay . . .'

'She told me a bit about what's going on at home. I didn't like the sound of it at all.'

Georgie sat up, anxious. 'What? What happened? Oh god, I should have called her. I've been so selfish, completely lost in my troubles.'

'She understands you have your own life, Georgie. But as I say, I didn't like what she told me. I told her to think about packing up and getting out.'

'What?' Panic whirled in her stomach and out along her limbs. She had a nightmare vision of Ryan losing his temper completely and turning on Pippa. She could just hear him telling a court that she had made him attack her with her ceaseless criticism and arguing. It would all be Pippa's fault of course, like everything else. Georgie leapt to her feet. 'I'm going there right now.'

Casper put out a steadying hand. 'Calm down, Georgie. It's okay. I've just heard from her.' He took out his phone and tapped on his messages. 'She's on her way now. She'll be here tonight.'

'Tonight?' Her mind raced with this new information. 'Thank goodness! But I have to get the rooms ready!'

'There's lots of time. Us first.' He beckoned her over and she went and sat down next to him. He put his arm around her and looked into her face, his grey eyes solemn. 'I've heard what you said. I respect your wishes. But three days ago, you said, "It's not that I don't want to, I don't dare." Will you work on that for me? Because if there's any chance you might change your mind, and that you might dare . . . well, I'll keep hoping.' He paused. 'I want to support you in every way. I'll always love you and be with you no matter what you decide. But . . . can I keep hoping?'

She stared at him for a moment and then threw her arms around him. She realised that he had given her the most incredible gift. Unconditional love. Complete support. A commitment to their future. He was an amazing man. With him by her side, she could do anything, even the things she feared most. She hugged him tightly and he hugged her back. 'Yes,' she said quietly. 'You can keep hoping. I love you, Caspar.'

By the time Pippa's car drew up in front of the house, Georgie had been on a manic mission to get bedrooms ready and sort out dinner for them all. As she frantically prepared, she felt a delicious fizz of joy every now and then as she remembered that Caspar was back and that he loved her and that life would continue after the awful lost weekend of being without him. Those nasty voices, the ones that belonged to Patsy and Mike, had vanished. They had no power over her when she was with Caspar. His love and fidelity were her armour against the snide, criminal, mean-spirited attacks, those attempts to bring her down.

And there was also relief. Pippa was finally out of Ryan's orbit. Caspar had told her what Pippa had revealed.

'Did Ryan hurt her?' Georgie demanded, furious at the thought.

'No.' Caspar shook his head. 'It was much stranger than that. He hurt himself.'

'What?'

'He sort of . . . beat himself up in front of her.'

Georgie was horrified. 'But that must have been terrifying!'

'Yes. I'll let her tell you the story. But when I heard that, I knew that it was time for her to take the girls and go.'

Now she just hoped that Pippa would see that she was wasting her time, energy and health on a situation that could never be resolved. It was like to trying to negotiate peace with an enemy who had all their weapons trained on you and were still intent on victory. There was simply no point.

Georgie and Caspar went out to meet them as the car drew up. Georgie rushed to Pippa, who climbed out looking exhausted, and enveloped her in a huge hug. 'I'm so glad you're here. Well done, Pippa, honestly, well done. It's the right thing.'

Pippa sank into her sister's embrace, her head drooping on her shoulder. 'It doesn't feel like it.'

'Of course not. It must feel like hell. But I promise, you're being so strong. Now let's get Izzy and Sofia out and settled.'

Pippa looked up at the house in tired awe as Georgie went to get the girls from their car seats. 'Wow, this place is amazing. I can't believe you live here.'

'Nor can I,' Georgie said with a laugh. Caspar greeted Pippa with a hug and a kiss and went to get their luggage from the boot. 'But I'm glad we do. We've got all the room we could possibly need for you and the girls.' She looked into the wide eyes of Pippa's daughters, aged five and two, and had a sudden jolt. They had the same mute acceptance of their circumstances that she and Pippa once had.

But they are loved, Georgie told herself firmly as she smiled and leaned in to undo their seat belts. *These girls will be fine, we'll see to it.* 'Come on, sweethearts, do you want to come inside and have some dinner? We've got some lovely pasta for you.'

She reached out her arms for Izzy and lifted out her small warm body. Her niece's arms and legs tightened around her as she lifted her, and Georgie felt the girl's absolute trust in her. She knew she would never and could never abuse it.

For the first time, she recognised something of what Caspar had said to her. Raising healthy people might be better than raising no one at all.

Later, when the girls had been tucked up in their beds, with a nightlight and Pippa's phone acting as a monitor, the adults sat around eating their supper with a bottle of red wine. With the girls taken care of, Pippa seemed to wilt, as though there was now space for her to access her own feelings.

'So that's it,' she said. 'Ryan went off on a golfing week-end with his friends. I packed up all our things. We couldn't bring it all, so I've left most of it in a friend's garage. But at least I had a couple of days to sort everything without him knowing. When he gets back, we're gone. I said in my note that I'm having a break with the girls.'

'That was probably a good idea,' Caspar said. 'Though he'll guess quite fast.'

'Let him.' Pippa took a gulp of her wine and let Caspar

refill her glass. 'Thanks, love.' She sighed. 'I don't want to stay in that house. I've never really settled in Brighton – we only went because of Ryan's job. I made some lovely friends, but it takes so long to be properly accepted. We ended up socialising with lots of his friends from work and their partners. Somehow it didn't jell. I won't miss it if I never go back there.'

'You can stay as long as you like,' Georgie said. 'Can't she, Caspar?'

'Of course. This house is often a refuge for people who need it. You're very welcome.'

'Thank you.' Pippa smiled wanly.

Georgie said, 'So what was it that made you convinced that you couldn't go on?'

'I managed to access his iPad. I'd been suspicious for a while about why he was staying out so much. It turns out Ryan has signed up to a dating site. And he's romancing various women at work. I mean, not sex as far as I know. But you know, flirtations. He is very busy chatting them up with all the same methods he used with me – pretending to be sweet and sensitive and interested in them as people. Quoting poetry and comedy and sending them music to show what a rounded human he is. Getting messages back saying how wonderful he is, what a kind person, what a great listener.' Pippa gave a hollow laugh.

'I'm sorry to hear that, Pippa,' Caspar said. 'And of course Ryan shouldn't act so disrespectfully. But are you sure it was serious? The flirting, I mean? Flirtations can be fairly harmless.'

Pippa shook her head. 'I know Ryan. I know his methods. He was getting frustrated with the way I wouldn't stop trying to solve our problems. I wasn't telling him how wonderful he was, and ministering to his every need. I asked for something for myself: kindness and understanding. All the things he had pretended to me that he had – just as he's pretending to all these other women.'

'Is he really that cynical?' Caspar asked.

Georgie turned to him. 'He's not planning it, Caspar. He's just acting instinctively. I think he's trying to manoeuvre his escape rather than work out the issues in his marriage. He's looking for some other woman to tell him what to do, so that he's no longer responsible.'

'That's it,' Pippa said sadly. 'Exactly. What was always so puzzling to me was that I would point out to Ryan how he was behaving, and he would just look at me like I was talking Martian or something. It meant nothing. He had absolutely no interest. He told me I was just jealous and insecure and controlling.'

'He sounds chronically immature,' Caspar said firmly.

'That's just the start of it.' Pippa drained her second glass of wine. 'That felt so terrible when I found the dating site and all the flirting, but it wasn't the worst bit.'

'Caspar said . . . he hurt himself?' Georgie ventured.

Pippa nodded. 'I confronted him with what I'd found. I was so hurt. I thought he might be sorry, or look guilty or show some remorse. But no. It was so strange. He just lost it. He started attacking himself.' Pippa made two fists and mimed punching herself hard in the jaw, a left hook and a right uppercut. 'Bam! Bam!' She jerked her head back as if she'd taken the blows. 'He slapped himself hard all over his head and arms and chest. He punched himself hard in his own chest. Then he punched the wall, threw a chair and ran out, slamming the door behind him.'

'Oh my god,' Georgie whispered. 'I'm so glad you got out.'

Pippa nodded solemnly. 'It was terrifying. That was a step too far.'

'Violence is violence, even directed against himself. It's a veiled threat.'

'Yes, that's exactly how I felt. It was designed to scare me even while he claimed to be a victim. It was like he was saying, "look what you drove me to do." I knew there was no way back after that.' Her eyes filled with tears. 'But it hurts so badly. Not just because he's behaved terribly but because he isn't that sweet, loving, kind Ryan I thought he was, the one I loved. And I desperately want that man back. Has he gone for ever?'

Georgie reached over and took her hand. 'Pippa, I'm so sorry. I don't know if it helps, but that Ryan never existed. You said it so clearly a moment ago. You're seeing the real Ryan. And you know with certainty you can't love that man. Not just that, but if you try to . . . you'll hurt yourself. Or he will.'

Tears ran down Pippa's face as she nodded. 'I do know that.' She looked up at her sister with trembling lips. 'But it doesn't stop the pain.'

'I know, darling. You have to feel it. There's no other way.'

'Ryan doesn't feel the pain.'

'Because he can't. That's a flaw, not a victory. You can. Because you've got a feeling heart and a functioning soul and you can get through the pain and recover. He can't and never will.'

'But he's my children's father,' wept Pippa.

Georgie squeezed her hand. 'That's why you've left him. That's why you will get better and get strong. Because the damage is going to stop with Ryan. You'll see to that, and your girls will be safe. It will be hard; they love him and need him. You'll need to be strong and tough and fairer than he deserves. But you can do it.'

She looked over at Caspar. He was gazing at her, his own eyes glistening with tears.

'Yes,' he said. 'You're right, Georgie. The damage stops with Ryan.'

Chapter Twenty

1939

As soon as Derek Foster walked into the house, everything changed.

He had a quality that Miranda could not at first identify. She was used to a certain status quo, with her family treated with deference and respect by almost everyone: by the people in the village and surrounding houses, and certainly by the staff and local workers. It was how things were, right or wrong.

And yet, from the moment he arrived, Derek Foster showed none of the deference the family were used to. He paid lip service to it, but there was no doubt that he didn't give a fig for status. Manners, which usually kept people in their place, were now used against those who lived by them.

That Christmas Day evening, he lolled on the sofa in the drawing room, smoking one of the cigars he had taken from Grandfather's box on the side table and drinking whisky he had poured out lavishly from the drinks tray.

Miranda noticed that Dolly Foster looked white and fearful. She had chivvied the boys upstairs instead of letting them stay for the games they had planned, and returned solemn-faced. Miranda guessed her aunt had let Dolly in on the scheme for keeping Imogen and Mother shut away for now. It would surely only be a day or two before Derek went on his way.

The desire to play games had leached away and everyone sat quietly in the drawing room as Aunt Constance, Grandfather and Derek made uneasy small talk. At least, it was uneasy on the older people's side. Derek didn't seem in the least uncomfortable. He had an easy good humour that somehow seemed malicious, as though he was secretly amused by the awkward atmosphere. When Dolly came back, it was only a few minutes before Foster was on his feet.

'Well, now,' he said, dark eyes glittering with whisky. 'I'm bushed. I think we should turn in as well, Dolly. When a man and his wife have been apart for a while, I'm sure you can appreciate that we'd like a private reunion.'

Polite goodnights were said but an unpleasant discomfort remained in the air even when the Fosters had left. The pleasure of Christmas was over and no one wanted to linger.

Aunt Constance looked grim as she turned out the drawing room lights.

'That man is awful,' Rosalind whispered as they went up the stairs. 'He's got the most horrible atmosphere around him. Do you remember Miss Weatherby at school, the games mistress who loved to punish us? She had the same feeling around her too.'

'People who enjoy tormenting others,' Miranda whispered back.

'I don't like him one little bit,' said Rosalind. 'He's not afraid of anyone and he thinks he's magnificent.'

'He knows there's no other man but Grandfather here, and so he's untouchable.'

They stopped on the second-floor landing on the way to their room.

'Is that the wind?' Rosalind asked, her eyes wide.

A weak, wailing sound came floating down the corridor.

'Oh, I hope so,' Miranda said quickly. 'I really do. Come on, let's go, I can't bear to listen.'

She sent up a silent prayer. *Oh, please come back, Mr Humphries. Please come back.*

The next morning at breakfast, Dolly Foster appeared looking exhausted and extremely sad, but refused to say anything at all when Miranda tried to talk to her. Derek did not come down.

'Are you all right, Dolly?' Miranda asked anxiously. She was sure that the wailing had been Dolly's.

'Yes, yes.'

'Are you sure?'

'It's fine, miss. Just have your breakfast, really. I'm taking up a tray to Mrs Black in a moment.' Dolly caught herself and looked around, frightened, and then relieved when she remembered her husband wasn't there.

'I'll come with you.'

Upstairs, Miranda and Mrs Foster joined Aunt Constance with Mother and Imogen behind the locked door of the bedroom. Mrs Foster put the tray of breakfast things down for

Mother, who sat in bed, apparently oblivious of the whispered meeting going on.

'Where's Rosalind?' asked Aunt Constance, looking at Miranda.

'In the nursery with the boys. She's going to stay there with them for now.'

'Good, good.'

Imogen looked tired and harried. 'But what on earth is the problem? Why can't we come out? What is it about this man?'

'Oh, Miss Wakefield,' Dolly said unhappily. 'I'm sorry to say he's not a good man, not at all.' She rolled up her sleeve and showed some vicious bruises on her arm. 'He did this to me last night, and more that you can't see. I ran away from him, see, and didn't tell him where I was going. I thought I'd taken all your letters with the address on them, but he must have seen one and remembered it. It's easy enough to recall after all. He guessed where I'd gone. He didn't hurry after me but let me believe I was safely got away before he made his move. That's typical of him.'

Imogen looked shocked at the bruises. 'Mrs Foster, that's awful. He hits you?'

'I'm afraid many men are capable of such behaviour,' Aunt Constance said grimly. She touched Dolly's arm sympathetically. 'We shall get some arnica on those bruises and any others that you have.'

'Thank you, ma'am.' Dolly looked awkward. 'I'm ashamed to have brought such a man here. I was so glad when the boys were evacuated. He was far too easy with the strap on them when they didn't deserve it. They're good boys. But once they were gone, he put his whole attention on me and the girl, and it was sheer torture. I know plenty of wives take it, and worse. But I just couldn't if I thought there was a way out. And I missed the boys so badly. But of course, he was furious yesterday and gave me a hiding for daring to run away.'

'I suspect that a man of your husband's character and habits has a propensity for violence in the bedroom,' Aunt Constance said. 'Now, don't blush. We have to speak of such things if we're ever to stop them.'

Dolly started to cry. 'Oh, ma'am, I am so sorry I brought him here! You're right to hide the lady and Miss Wakefield from him. He feels he's got a right, see. He feels he can take what he wants. To think how happy I was when he courted me! He was nice as pie then, so sweet you can't imagine. He promised me anything I wanted and I only wanted him. But the day we got married, the day he promised to honour me and told my father he'd move heaven and earth to protect me – that very night he was so cruel! I can't think why.'

Aunt Constance looked at her nieces. 'Girls, I'm sorry you should learn some unpleasant facts of life this way, but perhaps it's for the best. Now please don't cry, Mrs Foster, it's not your fault and no one is angry with you. You have had a terrible time and been very brave about it. But we do need to think about what to do. I'm afraid Leonard is no good at all, being so old. We shall have to outwit him, that's all. From what you say, Mrs Foster, I think we are doing the right thing by keeping the existence of Mrs Black and Imogen a secret. Did your husband say how long he intends to stay?'

Mrs Foster had dried her eyes and now flushed scarlet.

'I think he'll stay as long as he can. He said I'm on a cushy number and he intends to enjoy it with me.'

'As I suspected. I wish Leonard had not been so liberal with claret and whisky yesterday, but there we are. Mr Foster no doubt guessed there would be supplies of one kind or another.' Aunt Constance sighed. 'In this case, I think that it may be best if you and your mother are out of the house altogether, Imogen. You'll be safer in the tower, behind that fence with the gate locked.'

'In the tower? Mother and me?' Imogen said, looking fearful. 'But won't it be cold?'

'It will, but it's only until Mr Foster goes in a day or so, or Mr Humphries comes back. I will feel safer in that case.'

'Of course,' Miranda said with relief. She had been listening with mounting fear. 'Mr Humphries said he'd be back in a day or two. He'll be able to send your husband on his way, Dolly.'

'Well,' Dolly said doubtfully, 'when Derek has made his mind up, it isn't easy to change it. And he likes nothing so much as a scrap. Relishes it, even.'

'I'm sure Mr Humphries will be up to it,' Aunt Constance said. 'Meanwhile we will make sure you have plenty of wood – we'll take the chance on Mr Foster not noticing the smoke from the tower chimney. It's been so foggy lately that he might not see it. And lots of blankets and hot water bottles. I've got an electric two-bar heater you can have as well. It won't be for long.'

'Honestly, Imogen,' said Miranda earnestly to her sister,

'you haven't seen him. There's something very nasty about him. I think you should steer well clear.'

Imogen nodded. 'All right. Mother's safety is most important. She's vulnerable and so beautiful.'

Miranda thought her sister probably didn't realise that she too was beautiful and no doubt extremely attractive to someone like Derek Foster.

'We will allow Mr Foster to drink liberally this evening,' Aunt Constance said. 'And smuggle you out when he's gone to sleep. I think your mother can probably walk this time.' They all glanced at Mrs Black, who was reading in bed, looking as though she had not the slightest interest in what they were discussing. 'Until then, you must stay here and keep very quiet. Thank goodness we chose a room with a bathroom for you. We'll bring you food and drink and you've no need to go out. Take a turn or two around the room for exercise if you need it.' She smiled at her great-niece. 'It will only be a day or two, Imogen, I'm sure of it.' Aunt Constance turned back to Mrs Foster. 'Why hasn't your husband been called up for war service?'

'He's a reserve occupation,' Dolly said unhappily. 'He was working down the docks. As soon as he thought the war was certainly coming, he joined his trade union and got himself voted onto the council. So he's a union official and exempt.'

'Oh dear. He's sharp. Well. There'll be plenty like him, unfortunately, but more of the good sort, I'm pleased to say. Right. We'll go and start preparing for the move. Miranda, can you please go upstairs? Tell Rosalind everything and try and tell the boys not to mention Mrs Black's presence. And remember, you two must also keep out of Mr Foster's way.'

'He doesn't like girls too young,' Mrs Foster said sadly.

'Probably not. But better to be safe than sorry. Lock the doors at night. Keep out of his way.'

Dolly started to cry again, wiping her eyes on her apron. 'I feel so guilty.'

'Enough of that. You're not to blame for his actions. You suffer more than anyone. Tied to him for life.' Aunt Constance's expression softened. 'Poor girl. I'm sorry. Now. On with our scheme.'

They all spent the day keeping out of Mr Foster's way, but he seemed to spend most of it snoozing in the drawing room. For an hour or two after lunch, he prowled about and the twins kept an eye on him at a distance, noting where he went. He showed no interest in the upper floors and the nursery, with no evident desire to see his sons. But he moved around the first floor, trying door handles and looking inside rooms. The twins hid around the corners, using their knowledge of the house to avoid detection, darting down back stairs when necessary, or slipping into dark recesses. They were terrified when Mr Foster finally reached the door behind which Mother and Imogen were hiding, just in case one of them should speak or make a noise while he was outside. Miranda held her breath as he twisted the doorknob but to her great relief, the door was clearly locked and all behind it quiet. Mr Foster moved on, continuing his prowl until he had seen enough and he went back downstairs.

His next stop was Humphries's study. He was in there for some time before emerging again, closing the door behind him and finally returning to the sitting room, shouting at his wife to bring some tea and the remains of the Fortnum's Christmas cake they'd opened the day before.

'What was he doing in there?' Rosalind asked as they stood together in the hall.

'I don't know, but I don't like it a bit,' Miranda said, with a shudder. She hated the thought of Foster pawing through Humphries's things, and all the papers she had typed up for him. The one comfort was that he probably had no interest at all in fossils.

The days were so cold and dark that it was almost hard to know when evening had begun. But when the great clock in the hall chimed six, they all gathered in the dining room for supper. The atmosphere was so different from the good humour and high spirits of the day before; instead, it was strained and anxious with no one daring to say very much, or to even look at Mr Foster. There was an almost primal reaction to him, everyone poised on the edge of flight as though they knew that a wild beast was stalking them with intent.

Only Grandfather was oblivious. He seemed to think that the presence of another male was the main thing, even if that male was of quite another class to his own. He talked away at Mr Foster, who answered amiably enough though without interest and with a certain set of his jaw that indicated he was irritated by the old man not leaving him alone to enjoy his soup and the pie made of yesterday's leftover capon. He was only cheered by the many glasses of wine that Grandfather poured out for him, as if it made up for the tedium of talking to the old man.

Miranda watched him intently, so much so that Foster seemed to sense it, for he often glanced quickly in her direction with slight discomfort but she was always apparently absorbed in her supper when he looked over. She was watching the way he held himself, and remembering the horrible bruises on Dolly's arms and the way she had cried so bitterly about her fate in marrying him.

He's vicious. Mean. I'm sure he's much worse than she's letting on. He might be worse than she even knows. He looks capable of anything.

She wished that Mr Humphries had come back. There was no way to get a message to him. Even if she could get to the post office, she wouldn't know where to send it. They had no telephone number for him and the line was very bad in any case, always going dead if the wires got damaged, which seemed to happen quite often.

She was thinking frantically of what on earth she could do to guarantee they could all be kept safe from Foster. What if he could leave? How could they make him go? The castle, which was so safe from outsiders with its remoteness and its thick walls, was not so safe from insiders. Its advantages quickly became disadvantages.

This is why I need to be clever and head the danger off at the pass. I need to outthink Derek Foster, seeing as we can't outfight him.

*

Foster sat up drinking so long that Miranda had fallen asleep by the time Aunt Constance knocked on her door. She woke with a start and was instantly awake.

'Come on, girls,' Constance said in a low voice. 'Time to go to work.'

'What time is it?' asked Rosalind, yawning. 'I think I nodded off.'

'I did,' Miranda said. 'Goodness, it's after midnight.'

'I'm afraid Foster seems to have a tolerance for drink,' Aunt Constance said. 'Very wearing for all of us. Now, coats on. Did you bring them up as I said? It's bitter outside. I only hope we're doing the right thing.'

'We are,' Miranda said simply. 'I'm sure of it.'

Imogen and Mother were dressed and muffled into coats and hats and scarves and boots, and waiting for them. Mother seemed muted but aware of herself, although she said little.

'I gave her some of her sedation a little while ago – so that she'd be calm and quiet but still capable of walking.' Imogen stood up, helping her mother up by one arm. 'Let's go.'

They all gathered bags and went as quietly as they could out of the room and down the stairs, which seemed to creak as never before under their footsteps. Dolly wasn't with them in case Derek noticed her absence but she had told them that he tended to sleep soundly after drinking whisky and they were sure he'd had plenty of that.

The little party managed to get to the bottom of the stairs undetected and then down the passage to the morning room, where the French windows would give them swift access to the lawn.

The night outside the house was so cold that Miranda's breath seemed to burn in her lungs while her fingers were instantly numb with cold inside her gloves. She was frightened. This scheme, so easy to plan in the warmth of the house, might have real and imminent dangers in reality. She followed Aunt Constance, who led the way with her little torch shaded by black paper, feeling increasingly scared.

But when Aunt Constance opened the door, Miranda saw that the fire had already been lit and the electric heater switched on, and the little sitting room was warmer than she had feared.

'Oh,' said Mother, looking about, frowning. 'We're back here. I know this place.' She looked suddenly mulish. 'I prefer the other hotel.'

'This is only for a short while, Mrs Black,' Imogen said soothingly. 'Just a day or two. They are . . . doing repairs on the other hotel.'

'How inconvenient.' Mother took off her woollen hat. 'I must say, I am terribly tired. I can't think why they decided to start repairs at this time of night. Most strange.' She yawned. 'I think I'll go to bed, Nurse.'

'Of course,' Imogen said.

'We'll go back, if you're all right,' said Aunt Constance. 'And one of us will be over in the morning to check on you. I've put tea and milk and bread in the kitchen, as well as some tins and things.'

'We'll be all right,' Imogen assured her. 'You'd better get back.'

As they went to the door, she said, 'I don't suppose we've heard from Mr Humphries, have we?'

'Nothing today,' said Aunt Constance. 'I expect we'll see him soon.' She smiled at Imogen. 'Don't worry, my dear. He won't have forgotten us, I'm quite sure of it.'

When they had safely returned to the house and the French windows were shut, Aunt Constance said, 'Thank you, girls. It might seem dramatic, but I think we've done the right thing. Now. Off to bed with you both. It's very late.'

'Yes, Aunt Constance,' the twins said obediently.

When they were just by the stairs, Miranda pulled Rosalind into the darkness beyond it, and they waited there until Aunt Constance had gone past and made her way upstairs and they had heard the click of her bedroom door shutting.

The next morning Mr Foster seemed oblivious of all the changes that had taken place overnight, although the tension was somewhat lessened from the day before. Who knew if he'd even noticed that?

The children wanted to go outside in the morning but it was too cold for them to do more than run around for half an hour before they needed to come back inside. Later, the Foster brothers went out with Toby to the stables and came back to report that it was very cold there but they'd put down extra straw against the draughts, and put blankets on the horses and given them warm mash to help them fight the chill. Grandfather said that there was a very old heating system that had not been used in decades.

'Boys kept the furnace in the cellar burning all night and the steam went along the pipes and warmed the stables,' he said as they discussed it at lunchtime. Aunt Constance and Dolly had left, Rosalind flitting off not long after. Miranda felt she must keep watch on Foster. Grandfather went on: 'If it gets too cold, we can think about doing that.'

'Keeping horses warm?' said Mr Foster. 'Let 'em freeze. There's people that need to be kept warm, not animals.'

'We need to look after the 'oss,' Tom said plaintively. 'He can't freeze, that wouldn't be right.'

'Little idiot,' said his father dismissively. 'What do you know? If the horse freezes, all the more horse steak for tea.'

Robbie looked horrified.

'They won't freeze,' Grandfather said hastily. 'They're very good stables and we've not lost any horses there before.'

'I've no doubt that grooms and furnaces and oats helped with all that, sir,' Foster said pleasantly but with the undertone of menace that was ever present. 'But it's colder now than I've ever known.'

'Perhaps you're right, Foster,' Grandfather said, standing up. 'I'll be in my study for the afternoon.'

He went out.

Foster fixed Tom with a steely gaze. 'Come here, boy.' Tom went over obediently and as soon he reached his father's side, Foster hit him with two hard slaps, one over each ear. Tom barely squeaked but the violent red of his ears, the tears in his eyes and the dazed look on his face showed that he had been badly hurt.

'Don't cheek me again,' Foster growled. 'I won't have it, understand?'

Tom nodded.

Miranda opened her mouth to protest, feeling her own face flame with outrage, and then remembered what Dolly had said about Foster relishing the chance to fight. She wouldn't risk it. She didn't dare.

Foster seemed to sense it. He looked over at her, his dark eyes grimly amused. 'Anything wrong?' he asked sardonically.

'No.' She looked away, feeling ashamed of herself. Tom walked back to his seat, biting his lip to stop himself crying. Robbie was staring at his brother with horrified eyes, his little fists clenched, but he also said nothing.

The days followed in the same pattern of the previous ones. It was too cold to go out. The boys spent their afternoons in the stable, caring for the horses and keeping out of Foster's way. Derek drank his way through more of Grandfather's cellar, but instead of subduing him, the wine seemed to make him strangely energetic. His dark eyes were glittering again, fixing on the women. He followed Dolly around with his hungry gaze, looking at her as though she was something he both loved and loathed. Miranda was aware of Dolly moving more slowly, her back more bent and her spirits ever lower. Foster was beginning to get up later, and be more irritable and prone to outbursts when he was awake. He stopped any pretence at good manners and began to deal out slaps at his boys whenever he felt like it. He seemed to take pleasure in thwacking the backs of their legs with his open palm, or landing glancing blows across their heads. Whatever they said or did irritated him, and even keeping quiet got his back up.

A few nights later, Miranda and Rosalind heard a horrible noise coming from the Foster room, which echoed along their passage. In the morning, Dolly stayed in her room with a headache, and when she appeared, she had a nasty bruise on her cheek and a split on her lower lip. She looked so miserable that Miranda could only guess what else she might be suffering that they could not see.

'Girls, keep your doors locked,' Aunt Constance cautioned, looking ever grimmer. An atmosphere of fear and dread had settled over the house, and they all felt powerless against whatever darkness it was that Foster had brought with him.

One morning, in the early hours, when Foster was apparently sleeping soundly, the doorknob on their room turned. It squeaked and Miranda jumped instantly awake and on high alert. She held her breath as she heard it turn, then stick when it hit the lock. The door rattled very slightly as the person outside tested to see if it would open or not. Then it went quiet and there were no more noises except the gentle thump of footsteps going away.

Her heart thudded and fear washed through her. Foster was getting bolder. It was terrifying.

Miranda stayed awake until a fitful sleep took her, but the fear was still with her when she woke up the next morning.

She was first at breakfast. There had been a snowfall in the night, covering everything in white. It looked beautiful, but her heart, which would usually rejoice at the sight of snow, sank. Snow made it more likely that Foster would stay on and that Humphries would not return. She knew that last night Aunt Constance had had a talk with Grandfather, telling him that he needed to order Foster back to London, or anywhere – as long as it wasn't here.

Grandfather thought it was their duty to take in waifs and strays in wartime, and that housing a family was their responsibility. He wouldn't have it that Mr Foster was not a suitable house guest.

Was he afraid? Miranda hoped not. She had always thought of Grandfather as strong and brave. But he was old now. It would be understandable if he didn't want to take on a man like Foster.

'You are simply siding with him because he's a man,' Aunt Constance had said. 'I hope you think better of it, Leonard. The man beats poor Dolly, you must have seen it! She has a black eye and a split lip! He's a bully who hits his children.'

'That's not our business,' he'd said obstinately.

Aunt Constance had clicked her tongue in annoyance. 'I'm sorry to hear you say it. It's wrong and you know it is.'

Miranda found her admiration for her aunt growing by the day. She had thought of her as a pre-war relic, eccentric and somewhat ridiculous. Now she was reconsidering everything she had thought before. Aunt Constance was strong and kind and generous, and she wanted to protect women from the wrath and strength of men. That was a good thing.

Foster came in next. She was not surprised. Although he was no early riser, the others were staying away as much as they could.

'Good morning, Mr Foster,' she said politely as he walked in.

He squinted at her and grunted as he sat down heavily at the table.

'Tea?'

He nodded, so she poured out a cupful from the teapot and pushed the milk jug towards him. He took it, tipped some milk in and slurped from it. Miranda watched him, eating her own toast slowly, nibble by nibble.

Foster did nothing but drink tea, and she refilled his cup twice before he eyed the toast rack and then helped himself to a slice and buttered it. He looked about and said, 'Where's the marmalade?'

'It's finished,' Miranda said.

'Finished? There was plenty yesterday.'

'We ate it for tea with our bread. In the nursery.'

'Gluttons,' murmured Foster crossly. 'What good is toast without marmalade? That stuff is the good stuff too, wasted on you kids.'

'Why not try some blackberry jam?' Miranda asked, pushing the jar across the table towards him. 'I've got some myself.' She picked up her toast and ate a mouthful. 'It's homemade and really delicious.'

Foster eyed it and grunted again. 'I'm not so keen on jam. Too sweet.'

'You'll like it, I promise. Try it.'

He took the jar and looked over at Miranda's toast, which did look enticing with the rich dark jelly swirled over the butter. 'May as well.' He lifted up a good blob of it on his knife and put it on his toast.

'It's best if it's very thickly spread,' Miranda said. She had gone quite pale.

'All right.' He put more on, then put down his knife and lifted it to his mouth. There was a tiny hesitation and then he crunched down on it, taking a large corner into his mouth. He ate for a moment, frowning, and then said, 'You're right.'

'I am?'

'Oh yes. You're right. It is very good.' He took another bite. 'Just as you say. It's delicious.'

Miranda watched as he crunched and swallowed, her fists clenched so hard in her lap that her knuckles were white.

'Derek Foster ate the jam,' Miranda said simply.

Rosalind gave a horrified gasp and clamped her hand over her mouth. Then she released it to say, 'Miranda, you didn't! Please say you didn't!'

'I gave him jam,' she said. 'And he ate it.'

Rosalind went dead white and looked about to faint. They were standing in their bedroom, facing one another, and Miranda wondered if she was going to have to dash forward to catch her sister as she fell.

She said quickly, 'But it wasn't the poisoned jam.'

Rosalind released a tremulous breath. 'How could you do that to me? I thought you'd murdered him! I thought they'd hang you!'

'How could they if they don't find out? I don't think anyone knows he's here. Dolly said he's exempt from war service because he's in the unions, but I think there's more to it, don't you? Why doesn't he need to go back and work?' Miranda threw herself on her bed in frustration. 'Oh, I wish I was a grown-up and could go to London and investigate him!'

Rosalind sank down on her bed, still recovering from her shock. 'But why did you give him jam?'

'To see if I could. If we need to bump him off, we can. He's fine with eating the jam now. It would be easy enough.'

'Miranda, we can't poison him! We can't *kill* someone.'

'You didn't mind when it was Germans,' Miranda said obstinately.

'That's different. They're the enemy, of course we're allowed to kill them. You get a medal for that. But kill Mr Foster and you'll go to prison and most likely get hanged.'

Miranda lay back and sighed with frustration. 'He's a wicked man. He hurts his family. He hits those poor boys.'

'They're all terrified of him. What would we do if he hit Toby or Archie?'

Miranda felt a rush of fury at the thought. 'It's bad enough that Mother and Imogen have to hide in the tower. It's been days now, much longer than we planned.' She sat up again. 'Can't you see why I want to be prepared in case we're in real danger?'

'How can you seriously consider killing him?' Rosalind said helplessly.

'Why did we make the jam if you never want to use it?'

'It's for the war, not for someone we don't like!'

Miranda jumped up, furious. 'We went to so much

trouble! We put the rat on the jar so we knew which was poisoned. We made enough jam to kill half the village! We said we would do it!'

Rosalind stood up, her eyes flashing. 'We will! If the Germans come. Promise me you won't use it to kill Foster, Miranda! Or I'll get rid of it all today!'

Miranda felt her chest constrict with frustration. Why couldn't Rosalind see that the dangers they were all in excused the deed of getting rid of Foster, if that's what was called for? She wanted to tell her sister about the door handle moving in the night, but she didn't dare.

'Promise me!' demanded Rosalind.

There was a long pause and Miranda said, 'All right, I promise.'

Chapter Twenty-One

Present Day

Dear Mrs Wakefield,

   Thank you for your email and your intriguing question! The answer is that there were no dinosaur eggs at Wakefield Castle as far as we know. There were limited dinosaur fossils, in fact. The focus was more on birds and megafauna. I've had a look at the records and I can't see any reference to anything being lost or stolen. Do you have any reason to think anything might have been? We're always keen to find out more about the history of our collections, so do let me know if you're aware of anything that we can add to our archive.

   Thank you so much.

   Best wishes,

   Natalie Spiller

Georgie thought about how much had happened since she had sent off her inquiry to Natalie. She had still been nurturing her secret. Now it was out in the open and nothing had been as bad as she'd feared. She and Caspar were more loving and closer than they had been in a long while, always hugging and kissing, and making love all the time. It was as though they were cementing their relationship after a perilous moment of danger. She felt calm and happy as far as that was concerned.

And now Pippa was here too.

Another orphan finding refuge in the castle. Georgie smiled. Once the sheer capacity of this place had overwhelmed and scared her. Now it was reassuring in its ability to absorb people, to take them in and care for them without any apparent effort. Even Viktoria, who they thought would be such a problem, had been very quiet lately, living in the gatehouse or going off on a jaunt as it suited her. Their panic had been misplaced.

The tourist visits were becoming more frequent during the summer months and in light of Atalanta's publicity, to the point where even Mrs Lambert was looking exhausted. Perhaps it was time to start thinking about formal opening hours. Sandy's little tea area in the courtyard was doing very good business, but they would have to formalise it if it got any bigger. At the moment, it just asked for suggested donations, which meant they didn't have to worry about rules and regulations for serving food, but actually the stables, properly converted, would make a lovely place for a tea room or a small restaurant.

The idea was exciting. For so long, Georgie had hidden behind Atalanta. Her name wasn't even on the cookbooks, despite the fact that they were mostly written by her. Even the small credit at the end of the television programme had made her uncomfortable. Now she was thinking about opening her own place. Perhaps she could even write a book about how to cultivate heritage herbs and how to cook with them . . . A book with her own name on it.

Georgie laughed at herself. Only a few months ago, she hadn't been able to bear the thought of leaving her little flat in London, and now she was contemplating opening the house to the public, running a little restaurant, and doing her own projects.

The other thing that had cheered her was the fact that she had finished the first draft of the book and sent it off, so now she had time to relax and let the whole thing percolate before she received all the edits and suggestions from everyone else.

She and Caspar and Pippa had celebrated with champagne on the lawn on the afternoon that she had sent it off, while Izzy and Sofia had played very happily on the grass, collecting buttercups and daisies and making a tea party with them.

'Well done, Georgie,' Pippa said. 'I don't know how you do it.' She raised her glass to her sister. 'Congratulations.'

'What? I just write recipes! I don't know how you teach thirty children to read and write and all the rest, starting again each year.'

Pippa grinned. 'I suppose what comes naturally feels simple. There's probably some kind of fallacy for the belief that what you can do must be easy.'

Caspar looked over at his sister-in-law. 'It was good of the school to give you leave.'

'I felt bad asking. But honestly, the way things are, I can't work right now. I'm a mess.' Pippa looked suddenly sad. 'The only comfort is that it's not too far off the end of the summer term. But I don't think I can go back there in September, so I've handed in my notice.'

Georgie said gently, 'Has Ryan been in touch since the phone call?'

'A couple of emails.' Pippa shrugged and sipped her champagne. 'I know I ought not to be surprised, but really . . . I still can't take it in.'

Pippa had waited for a phone call from Ryan when he got back from his golf weekend and found her gone. She had expected either outrage or concern. But there had been nothing. Not a word from him, by text, email or phone call. Eventually she had rung him herself. Georgie found her afterwards, crying her eyes out in the drawing room. 'He doesn't give a shit,' she'd said, sobbing. 'He didn't care at all. He said, "If that's what you want, it's fine with me. I can't change your mind if you've decided so what's the point?" I said, "But what do *you* want?" And he said, "Whatever makes you happy." I said, "If you were nice to me and loving and supportive, I'd be happy." He said, "I've tried and I can't seem to fulfil your expectations. I suppose I'll always be a disappointment." But he didn't even sound bothered, or like he cared about being a disappointment.' She blew her nose. 'It's all so hopeless! We never get anywhere. I honestly think he just doesn't care.'

'He's fooling himself if he thinks he's tried. He obviously hasn't. But in another way, he's right. He will always disappoint you because he isn't capable of making you happy – but that's his failing, not yours. You're hearing him blame you but maybe he's telling the truth, that it is his fault.'

Pippa gave a hollow laugh. 'Er, no, he doesn't think it's his fault. He's saying he tries but I won't accept his efforts. So he's blameless.'

'Well, in a way, you won't. And you shouldn't.'

Pippa started crying again.

Georgie said, 'He isn't going to change. Ever. He's been showing who he is for years. You need to accept that, and I think you have accepted it deep down.'

Pippa wiped her eyes and sniffed, but tears kept pouring down her face. 'I just hate to be blamed like this. And even if you're right – and you are right – that doesn't make it hurt less. The tone of his voice is so painful, he made it clear that he doesn't care.'

Georgie shook her head. 'Perhaps he really doesn't. It's just so hard to understand. Does he want to see the children?'

'I asked him that. He said he'd be happy to see them when I can bring them over, as long as I let him know so he can check whether he can fit them in. He's got a busy schedule right now, what with work and golf and cricket. Oh, and some cycling weekends.'

'Oh, Pippa. He's awful. I'm so sorry.'

'I had no idea. I feel like an idiot. How could I have married someone like that?'

Georgie said, 'It's not your fault. He wants you to feel this way. You've left him and he's such an infant, he has to pretend he's pleased. His only weapon is to hurt you and he's doing it brilliantly.' Georgie rubbed her sister's back sympathetically and passed her a fresh tissue. 'I feel so bad because I saw it and I just excused him, as so many others do. I thought the real Ryan was the friendly joker and his lapses, when his mask slipped, were out of character. Now it's quite clear that the reverse was true.'

'You can't take the blame,' Pippa said with a wry laugh. 'I was the one who married him!'

'And now you're out of all that, I think that you should get some counselling. It helped me. Honestly. I think the legacy of Patsy and Mike was more far-reaching and destructive than we realised.'

'Did it really help that much?' Pippa looked up, drying her tears and sniffing.

'Yes, it did. It's not a magic bullet. It takes time. Do you know how long Leonardo took to paint the *Mona Lisa*? Decades. So working on ourselves should take a long time, as we walk around and check ourselves from all perspectives and see ourselves from the outside, see where we can make tweaks and adjustments to fulfil our potential. It's worth doing.'

She had hugged Pippa, hoping to pass on to her some love, strength and hope for the future.

Now, on the lawn in the late afternoon sunshine, Pippa was no longer as poleaxed by grief as she had been, but it was going to be a long journey.

'Have you looked into counselling yet?' Georgie asked, sipping her champagne.

'Not yet. But I will. I think I'm ready.'

Caspar said, 'It's brave to start on that journey, Pippa. But

I think you'll find it helpful. After what happened to you both, it's not surprising you're still processing it.'

'Ryan said I was damaged and that was what ruined our marriage,' Pippa said. 'But I think I married *him* because I was damaged. I couldn't spot him.'

'Exactly,' Georgie said firmly. 'You can be healed. You are already healed in lots of ways. But Ryan will always be Ryan.'

'An arsehole,' Caspar said firmly and it sounded so funny in his patrician tone that they all burst out laughing.

'Glad to hear you're all so cheerful!' said a voice across the lawn and they turned to see Sam walking towards them from the stables. He wasn't wearing his work clothes and looked quite different in smart trousers and a crisp shirt.

'Evening, Sam.' Caspar got up to greet him. 'We weren't expecting you, but what a nice surprise. This is Pippa, Georgie's sister. Can I get you a drink?'

'I won't, thanks, I just popped in. I'm driving in a moment.' He smiled at Georgie. 'How are you, mate?'

She smiled up at him. 'Much better, thank you.'

'Good. So I was driving by and that tower of yours has been on my mind, so I thought I'd just see if you were about on the off chance.'

'You mean the West Tower?' asked Caspar.

'That's right. The one where there was some kind of fracas, or so you might think. Would you mind if I take another look around? I keep thinking about something I noticed, that's all.'

'Of course.' Caspar got up. 'I'll get the keys.' He went off to the storeroom door.

'Let's all go,' Georgie said. 'Do you want to come, Pippa?'

'No, I'll stay here with the girls. I've got some buttercup tea to drink, I think.' She smiled at her daughters who were lost in their game on the grass.

Sam followed her gaze. 'Ah, they're lovely. What are their names?'

'Izzy and Sofia.'

The little girls looked around at their names, wide-eyed.

Sam smiled. 'My girls are a bit bigger than that now. That's a wonderful age. Enjoy them.'

'I will.' Pippa smiled back at him.

Casper came back across the lawn and Sam and Georgie joined him on the walk to the tower. The gate was no longer locked and the tangle of roses had been cut back. Caspar unlocked the front door and they all went in. Everything was just as it was before, in a strange and chaotic jumble.

Sam looked around, frowning. 'The boys want to come in and clear up so we can get a look at it, and there was just something that I kept seeing again in my mind.' He walked over to the sofa, where the floral linen was faded and rotten, springs bursting up through the stuffing. 'Yes. Here. Look.'

Caspar and Georgie went over and inspected the sofa. It was filthy and holey, the pattern hard to make out. 'What?' asked Georgie.

'That hole right there.'

He pointed but Georgie couldn't see anything. 'What do you mean?'

'That hole is surrounded by a scorch mark, and you can see how the filling has burst through it. I think it might be a bullet hole. I wouldn't be surprised if there is a bullet embedded inside the sofa.'

They stared at him. Sam gestured around the room. 'There was a struggle here. And a possible bullet hole. So who knows what happened? But I wanted to take another look.'

Georgie shivered. 'That's awful. I wonder if someone got shot in here?' She turned to Casper. 'Did you hear anything about someone being injured in this tower?'

'No.' Casper looked bewildered. 'But this place was never talked about. We never came in. We weren't allowed.'

'Well.' Sam looked solemn. 'Perhaps that's why. And I doubt we'll ever know what happened here after all this time. But my guess is that it wasn't pretty.'

They walked back across the lawn, where Pippa was chasing the girls around as they giggled and screamed with delight.

'They're a couple of sweeties, aren't they?' Sam said, grinning at them. 'Is their dad around?'

'I'm afraid not,' Casper said. 'It's very sad. He and Pippa have just split up.'

Sam glanced at Georgie. 'You said it was on the edge.'

She nodded. 'And now it's gone over. But it's for the best.'

'The damage stops here,' Caspar said softly and smiled at Georgie.

Georgie gave her husband a grateful look. 'Absolutely.'

Casper said, 'If you're not in a hurry, Sam, are you sure you don't want to join us? We're celebrating Georgie handing in her book. We've got soft drinks.'

432

'Well . . . why not? I'd be happy to. I've got twenty minutes to spare.'

In the night, Georgie woke suddenly, feeling anxious. It used to happen frequently when she suffered the most from flashbacks or when counselling had hit a difficult point for her.

Etti Boule, she thought. *All that disruption in the tower. The fracas. The bullet hole. It's all something to do with Etti Boule. I don't know why I think so, but I'm absolutely sure.*

She thought about the creepy nursery rhyme in Miranda Wakefield's book. How did it go? She could only remember one phrase.

Etti Boule is kind and cruel.

Then something else floated into her mind.

Bad berries kill bad rats.

That was from the recipe for Etti's blackberry jam trifle.

Listen to the voices, Georgie, she told herself. *Listen. What are they trying to tell you? Did Etti kill someone in the tower? Is that what they are saying?*

She managed to go back to sleep after a while, but just before she did, she remembered something, from her earliest days in the castle. She would check it out in the morning.

The next day, Georgie went down early to the kitchen. She made herself a cup of coffee and then went to the storeroom. There were many more things in there now – catering-sized bags of tea and coffee for Sandy to use, packets of shortbread and little miniature jam jars for scones.

Jam. That's what I'm looking for.

She pushed aside a bag and some ancient old rusted tins, and saw what she had been looking for: four jars of jam. She had seen them all that time ago when she'd first arrived but forgotten all about them until now. They had to be very old. Each had a hand-painted label, now faded almost to invisibility. She pulled one down and squinted at it, but it was hard to make out in the dim light of the storeroom. She took two of the jars out and into the brighter light of the kitchen. But even by the window it was hard to make out much on the label except that it seemed to be a cheery scene of mice and berries.

I need a microscope to make this out, she thought, and then an idea occurred to her. She took her phone and snapped a photograph. The photograph came out much clearer than the label was in real life. Now she could see the detail better: yes, cheerful little dormice reaching for plump berries. Very prettily done in the manner of Beatrix Potter.

She took another jar and did the same with its label, zooming into the photograph to make out the detail. Something took her attention. On this label, she could quite clearly see one of the dormice was lying on its back under a bramble leaf. How strange.

She tried to open one of the jars, but after all these years, the lids were too tightly sealed to move. Remembering an old trick Sandy had told her, she took them over to the range and placed them upside down on the lid of the hotplate. The heat would make them expand and they would be easier to turn. After ten minutes or so, she went back to the range and took them off. They were already very warm, and she held one with a tea towel as she twisted at the lid. It came off with a hollow pop and the scent of warm, fruity sugar followed. She did the same with the other. Then she looked carefully at each label to see which one had the dead dormouse on it.

'Oh no! I've spoiled it!' Holding the jars with the tea towel after they had been warmed had somehow blurred the labels so that it was not easy to see which had had the dormouse on its back. 'I should have made another mark on them, to tell the difference.'

She sighed with irritation. She spent a while trying to use her photographs to identify which was which from small differences in the illustration, but it was hard to be absolutely sure.

She looked at both jars sitting on the counter. Picking one up, she sniffed it. She put it down and picked up the other. Both smelled the same. Fruity. Sweet. Perhaps a touch acrid but was that surprising after all these years? When had they been made?

Georgie remembered the illustration of the rat next to the recipe on the scrap of paper she'd found in the recipe book. *Bad berries kill bad rats.*

Berries can't kill you, she thought. *And jam can keep a very long time with its high sugar content.*

On a whim, she dipped a finger into one of the jars and held it up. The dark jam was partially liquified from the heat of the range and it ran down her finger in a large dark blob, like a bead of blood travelling from a cut.

Without thinking, she went to lick it off her finger and stopped just before her tongue touched it.

Could it really harm me? she wondered. She had the sudden urge to taste the burst of blackberry on her tongue and to savour its sweetness. This jam might have been made in the war. She would taste berries from eighty years before, when the world was in its mighty struggle against fascism. It was tempting, to taste history.

The jam stopped trickling and sat on her finger, thick and still glossy.

She put her tongue out again.

Chapter Twenty-Two

1939

The castle was heavy with cold and dread, and the park beyond was permanently white and grey, with icy fog swirling over everything. Winter seemed to have possessed the world so deeply that it was hard to imagine it would ever go away, and all the fun and joy of Christmas was behind them. What was waiting for them? War. Long years of it, most likely, and everything that entailed. The wireless news had said that food rationing would begin next month, with a complicated system of registration and ration books and stamps, and an allowance for each person. Well, they would have to get to the village first, and that looked unlikely for a while in this bad weather. The car was seizing up, Grandfather said, and he was nearly at the end of his petrol ration as it was.

We're trapped here, thought Miranda sombrely. *Trapped with Foster.*

The boys were being very mysterious. They disappeared together for long hours, often to the stables, but at other times flitted about the house, appearing on the back stairs or emerging from the cellar, following their own secret missions. The aim appeared to be to keep out of Derek Foster's way as much as possible.

Derek, though, seemed to be tickled by the boys' attempts to evade him, and he started to hunt them down. He liked to jump out on the stairs with a roar and laugh as the boys yelped with terror and dashed away.

'There's a name for people like him,' Miranda said to Rosalind. 'They like to hurt others. He knows they're terrified of him.'

'Are they terrified?' Rosalind asked. Relations between them were still a little stiff after Miranda's trial run with the jam. 'They seem a bit braver than before.'

'Perhaps they feel there's safety in numbers. I think they're searching for places to hide in case Derek ever loses his temper and comes looking for them with a strap. You see how easy he is with his fists.'

'No wonder they want to stay out of his way. I only wish that poor Dolly could.'

Derek seemed to have lost interest in tormenting Dolly as much as he once did. But Miranda suspected that she was so broken that she was providing less amusement to Derek than before. Dolly devoted herself to looking after Sylvia and keeping herself busy in the kitchen. She was thinner and more haunted. When Miranda came in, she stopped her, grabbing Miranda's arm with unaccustomed intimacy.

'I can't go out to the tower any more,' she said urgently. 'Derek's suspicious.'

Miranda's stomach took a sickly spin. 'He is?'

Dolly nodded. Her hair wasn't properly brushed or styled, as it had been, and looked neglected and oily, as did her skin. 'I've been going out while he's eating breakfast and then getting back in before he's done. But he's like a bloodhound, he hunts out secrets like you never knew. He's guessed we're hiding someone – don't ask me how. So he's watching my every move, listening out for doors opening and closing.' She shuddered. 'And every evening he asks me a dozen questions to catch me out.'

'Does he know who?' Miranda asked.

'No. But he's like a child who wants what he can't have, no matter what. Can you go out there, miss? He doesn't watch you as hard.'

'Of course I will. Give me the basket and I'll sneak it over there.'

Miranda went out the back door and around the stables, approaching the garden out of sight of the house, a basket of fresh bread, eggs, meat, butter and vegetables over her arm. The garden was shrouded in deep fog, which must surely hide her from the house. When she got to the tower, she was icy cold, hardly able to rap on the door and call out to be let in.

Imogen answered the door with anxious eyes. 'Miranda! Where's Dolly?'

'She can't come out, she's being watched. I'm here instead. Please let me in, it's so cold!'

The tower was comparatively warm inside, with the thick curtains shut and the fire burning.

'We need more wood,' Imogen said. 'We're nearly out. Is Mr Humphries back?' She looked hopeful.

'No, not yet,' Miranda said. 'I'll see what we've got and bring some more logs around. Are you all right apart from that?'

'Yes – except for the ghastly tedium. Mother is asleep so much of the time. I read and knit and play cards with myself, and of course there's the cooking and cleaning, but it's very boring. Are you sure we can't come back?'

'Certain,' Miranda said firmly. She described Foster's cruelty to his wife and sons.

'I saw Dolly had been hurt. I hate to think of you all over there with that man in the house!' Imogen looked grave. 'I need to talk to Aunt Constance. We can't stay here for ever. What if he never leaves? Can't Grandfather order him out?'

'He won't do it, and as long as he won't we can't ask for help from anyone else. And I don't know if Foster would go anyway. But surely Mr Humphries will be back soon, and then we'll be all right.'

'I hope so,' Imogen said. 'I don't know how much longer we can cope out here on our own.' She gave her sister a beseeching look. 'Can you and Rosalind come and see me this evening? I'm so lonely!'

'Yes, of course we will,' Miranda said. 'Poor you. Of course you need some company. We'll come later.'

On the way back to the house, as she passed the stables, Robbie emerged like a small wraith and walked with her back to the house. 'Where've you been?' he said, looking at her empty basket.

440

'Just around,' Miranda said. 'Are you looking after Harris and Poppy?'

Robbie nodded. 'We're keeping them warm with their blankets and hot water. Listen, can you hear 'em stamping and blowing? They're proper cold but we're keeping them comfy.'

'That's good of you, Robbie,' she said encouragingly.

Robbie stared at her with eyes of clear, dark brown. 'I know about the jam,' he said.

'What?' Miranda started with surprise. 'How do you know about that?'

'I heard you talking to Rosalind. You said you had poisoned jam, enough to kill the village.'

She stared at him in horror as they went into the cold store, and couldn't stop her gaze going straight to the shelf where the jam was kept. To her relief, the jars were still there.

'Why have you got poisoned jam?' Robbie said in his small yet strangely hard voice. 'Who are you gonna kill?'

Miranda decided not to deny it. 'No one. It's just in case. You know there's a war, it's in case the Germans come. You mustn't touch it, do you understand?'

'Course I do.' They stared at one another, finding a strange companionship with each other.

He wants to protect his brother, even though he's younger than Tom, Miranda thought. *And his mother and sister. He flits around, learning this house from the roof to the cellar. He'd do anything to look after them, just like me.*

'I like it here,' Robbie said at last. 'Or at least, I used to. Before my dad came. It's not been so good since then.'

'No,' Miranda agreed. 'Not since then.'

There was a pause, and Miranda read everything Robbie felt about his father in his face: the hurt and the hatred and the fear. But the little boy said nothing about this. Instead, he spoke confidingly, as though taking for granted that she understood everything. 'We need to stay alert – but I got a plan.'

Miranda stared again, wondering what was going on in his mind. Robbie was just a young boy. Did he understand the world of grown-ups at all? Or was it all a strange and sinister game? In many ways, he seemed knowing beyond his years.

'I got a plan for how we can make him go.'

Now she was interested. 'Really? What?'

'The egg,' Robbie said. 'I reckon we can use the egg.'

Miranda said nothing to Rosalind about Robbie's plan, but she did tell her that Imogen was suffering in the tower and that they should go to her together to relieve the tedium. Rosalind's tender heart was touched.

'Poor Imogen, of course we must see her! She must be so bored on her own. I was concentrating on how lucky she was to be away from Foster and with Mother. Do you think Foster will notice us go?'

Miranda shook her head. 'He's not watching us to the same extent. I think we can sneak out.'

They went just after supper, when Foster was digging into another bottle from the cellar and had started talking with Grandfather about the war and events on the continent, so far as they knew about them. The journey across the garden in the dark felt twice as long as in the daytime, and they arrived with numb fingers and frozen faces.

'We brought logs!' Rosalind said. 'And a game. And some Fortnum's toffee as a treat.'

Imogen was so delighted to see them, she went pink. To their surprise, Mother was there too, sitting on the sofa, well wrapped up in a blanket over her dressing gown. She seemed quiet and not entirely present, but she watched them chattering and laughing and playing their game as they sucked on the toffee. At one moment, Miranda looked up and saw her mother gazing at her with a questioning look and when they caught one another's eye, Mother smiled a small, sweet and knowing smile as though she understood who Miranda was. But it lasted only a moment.

'Thank you for coming,' Imogen said, hugging her sisters as they prepared to go back to the castle. 'It was so jolly. Will you come back?'

'Of course we will,' Miranda said. 'Whenever we can. We don't want Dolly coming here at the moment, though.'

Imogen sighed. 'This has to end somehow. I just hope it's soon.'

'This weather is a worry,' Aunt Constance said the next day to Miranda. They were in her study, with the door locked, and talking quietly. 'Even the newspapers are predicting how bad it's going to be. If the lawn is covered in deep snow, it will be impossible to reach the tower. They'll be cut off.' She looked anxiously at her niece. 'And Foster will be stuck here for the duration of it too. What do you think, Miranda?'

Miranda gazed at her aunt in astonishment. She was being asked for her advice by Aunt Constance. A few short months ago, she'd been an aggravating child, and now she was an adult capable of assessing a situation and offering her solution. She had the task of protecting her family. The whole idea of poisoning jam had been her attempt to do something real that might contribute to saving them all if she had to. Now she was being asked for an answer, a proper grown-up answer to getting Foster out of their house.

Foster had lost that easy air of malicious amusement. He had stopped watching them all with glittering eyes and an unpleasant smile. He seemed ill at ease, and had begun snarling at them, more openly insulting, and was helping himself to the decanter of whisky with greater frequency.

'Can't Grandfather order him away, while there's still time?' Miranda asked.

Aunt Constance looked unhappy. 'I don't believe he will because he knows in his heart he has no power over that man. He will not obey.' She leaned in closer to Miranda. 'Foster has been in here. Money is missing. Small things around the house have vanished. I lock my doors, and the family jewels are in the safe, but there are plenty of other treasures around the house that he could take. I think he may be accumulating items in order to disappear in due course.'

'Why can't we call the constable?' Miranda suggested, outraged. 'If he's stealing?'

'I fear that Lionel's weakness may allow Foster to get

away with it, if Foster claims they're gifts and Lionel agrees. I'm afraid to anger that man. I sense he has very little to lose.' Aunt Constance sighed. 'And then there is the matter of Imogen and your mother. I think we must get them back in the house. One more day. One more day to try and make Foster go. I have one last idea.'

Foster was drunk from lunchtime, swaying around the house as if looking for people to torment. The boys moved around the castle like swift little shadows, always near him and yet never in his sights. They buzzed around him as if purposefully maddening him, while keeping their distance.

'Where are you, you little ruffians?' yelled Foster, running up the stairs. 'Come on, if you want to play some games! Come and let me catch you and then you'll see.'

Miranda and Rosalind stayed in their room, listening as Foster lumbered about. They heard the dash of small footsteps occasionally as the boys ran past. When she heard someone approaching, Miranda opened the door and made a grab. She found herself with a panting Toby in her clutches and pulled him inside.

'What's going on? What are you doing?' demanded Miranda.

'You must know he's drunk, why are you baiting him?' asked Rosalind. She was pale and frightened.

'It's Robbie's idea. He said he had an idea for how to make his father go away.'

'By chasing him round the house?' Miranda said.

Toby shrugged. 'I dunno. Robbie knows what to do.' He

opened the door and said excitedly, 'You girls stay here, we'll take care of him.'

The twins looked at each other, astonished. Then Miranda jumped up. 'I'm going to find Aunt Constance.'

She was in her study, writing letters, and looked up as Miranda came in. 'Hello, my dear. I was about to find you myself. Things are in a very strange state but there has been progress. I had an interview with Foster this morning, and offered him money to leave. He pretended to be insulted, but he took it. I think he may be enjoying his last huzzah before going.'

'What?' Miranda stared at her in relief. 'You really think he'll go?'

'I think he's probably got a bit of cash and a few items hidden away. The money I offered is worth his while and he took it. So he's no doubt having his fun for the last time, draining the whisky decanter, and then he'll be off. Then we can all go back to normal – at least, our version of it.' Aunt Constance allowed herself a thin smile. 'It's a waiting game now, Miranda.'

'The boys are playing hide-and-seek with him. It's very odd.'

'Perhaps they're keeping him occupied. They seem to have a sixth sense about him. Now, I'm writing so off you go. And keep out of Foster's way.'

Miranda made her way down to the kitchen where Dolly Foster was preparing the evening meal. When she looked up to greet Miranda, it was clear she was sporting a large black eye, her whole socket filled with puffy, purple swollen skin and her eyeball red.

'Oh, Dolly!' Miranda rushed over and hugged her. 'What has he done to you?'

Dolly hugged her back and sniffed. 'There, there, don't worry about me. That man thinks I've been talking – though I haven't said the truth about half of what he's done. And it doesn't really matter if I've talked or not, he likes to see me cower and cry. There's not much I can do about that. Better he hits me than the kids.'

Miranda pulled away and said, 'Aunt Constance says there's a chance he'll leave today. She's given him money.'

Dolly looked doubtful. 'Well, he might. But he thinks there's a blizzard coming, that'll trap him here for days. He'll take the money all right. That doesn't mean he's going.'

On the table was a packet of custard and some sponge fingers that Dolly was arranging in a large bowl.

'What are you making, Dolly?' she asked, interested.

'I'm making a trifle,' Dolly said. 'Robbie asked for it specially. It's his favourite, just like his dad. We'll have it later.'

'Delicious,' Miranda said. 'I love trifle. I'm sorry about your eye, Dolly. Is there any steak to put on it?'

Dolly shook her head. 'I've got that arnica, I'll use that. Don't worry about me, I'll be all right.'

Miranda went back upstairs to find her sister and tell her what had happened. 'It all feels very strange today. Perhaps it's the weather.'

Rosalind was curled up on her bed, looking anxious. 'I

think Foster's right and there is a blizzard coming. The air feels heavy somehow.'

Miranda was gazing forward to look out of the window. 'Wait – look down there!'

Rosalind got up and came to join her, staring out over the frozen park below. 'What? I can't see anything. It's not like day out there at all, is it? More like white night.'

'There.' Miranda pointed at a black speck advancing up the driveway. It was nearly at the bridge. She pulled in an excited breath. 'Oh, Rosie, quick! I think it's Mr Humphries!'

'How on earth can you tell?' Rosalind said, staring out. 'It could be anyone!'

'No, no, it's him!' She turned and clutched at her sister, her eyes bright. 'Rosie – we mustn't let Foster see him, not yet. We have to tell him everything first.'

Rosalind stared back, speechless.

Miranda ran for the door. 'Come on, let's get downstairs quick.'

They ran down the stairs as fast as they could, pulling on their coats and mufflers and boots by the back door before slipping out into the thick cold air. Then they raced around past the stables and out over the bridge where they could now see Mr Humphries marching determinedly up the drive with his suitcase, his hat pulled down low against the freeze.

'Mr Humphries!' Miranda ran up and threw herself upon him before he even knew she was there. 'You're back!'

'Whoa!' he said in surprise, his voice muffled by his scarf which was rimed with frost, as were his eyebrows, the felt of his hat and the shoulders of his coat. 'What's this welcome committee for?'

'We're so happy to see you, you can't think. But you mustn't come into the castle,' Miranda said urgently.

Rosalind grabbed the arm that wasn't carrying the suitcase. 'You must get out of sight as soon as possible. We're going to the tower.'

'My tower?' said Mr Humphries, still dazed by the onslaught of the girls' arrival.

'No, no. The other tower. Come on, come quickly!'

As they went, the girls tried to explain as much as they could through freezing lips: that Mrs Foster's husband had arrived, and the menace he had brought with him. The removal of Mother and Imogen to the tower for their safety and the growing threat of the cold, and of Foster's refusal to leave, at least so far.

By the time they had explained this much, while fielding Mr Humphries's questions, they had reached the tower, and Miranda banged on the door with her fist until Imogen opened it and let them in.

It was cosy enough in the tower, at least, and they were still well supplied. Mr Humphries dropped his suitcase and banged his mittened hands together. His face was white with cold, his lips tinged blue beneath his moustache. 'Oh my goodness,' he said numbly. 'It's very, very cold. How do you do, Miss Wakefield.'

'Mr Humphries, I'm so pleased you're back!' Imogen said, relief all over her face.

'I said I would come back and here I am.' He was

shivering, they saw, and the girls pulled him over to where the fire was burning. 'I caught a train just in time. Up north they've stopped running where the snow is too deep. But we got through from the south. It's quite a scene out there. They say it's getting worse as well. They think we'll have an ice storm before too long.'

'Where's Mother?' put in Miranda.

'Upstairs, asleep. This cold weather has acted like a spur to hibernation,' Imogen replied. 'She dozes like a dormouse all the time.'

'How is your mother generally, Miss Wakefield?' asked Mr Humphries. He was unwinding his scarf with cold, clumsy hands.

'She's well, though nothing has changed in her general state, I'm afraid.'

'And I hear you have a thoroughly nasty fellow in the house as well.' Humphries looked at the girls. 'You did the right thing moving Miss Wakefield and Mrs Black out here. Though I'm concerned about the rest of you. It sounds as though I should go over there and tell this man to sling his hook.'

'No, no,' Miranda said hastily. 'Don't do that! You haven't met him. It'll only set him off.'

'Miranda's right, he enjoys a fight,' Rosalind said. 'If he's really intending to go today, then we should give him the chance to leave quietly, shouldn't we?'

Humphries looked bemused. 'All this is most strange. You're telling me that we have a thief who beats his wife and children, and we should hide away and let him go? I think I'll go over there and throw him out right now. I'm sure Colonel Wakefield will be right behind me.'

Miranda and Rosalind exchanged glances. He had no idea what they were dealing with. How to explain the menace of Foster? He was like a smoking, rumbling volcano on the brink of explosion.

Miranda said, 'I think it would be best if you kept Imogen company here this afternoon, and if Foster hasn't left by the evening, you and Grandfather can make him go.'

'As long as we stay one step ahead of the snow,' Humphries said grimly, but Miranda could tell that the chance of spending the afternoon alone with Imogen was something he found rather appealing. 'Very well, I'll go along with it. But the slightest breath of trouble and you must fetch me.'

As the girls huddled together on their way back to the castle, Rosalind said, 'He doesn't have the first idea. I hope he and Foster never meet, that's for sure.'

'My thoughts exactly. Now let's see how the land is lying.'

The castle was quiet when they returned. Dolly was not in the kitchen, but the preparations for the evening meal were set out neatly, a towel covering them. The trifle was nowhere to be seen, though, so Miranda assumed Dolly must have hidden it in the cold store to stop little fingers from tasting it ahead of supper.

'I wonder where everyone is?' Miranda said, looking around.

Rosalind said, 'I expect the boys are in the stable if they're not still dashing around like secret agents. I'll go and see.' She headed back out of the door, over the salted path towards the stables.

Miranda went quietly back into the main body of the house and heard voices coming from Grandfather's study. She crept over to the door and listened. Grandfather was speaking in a loud voice with only a hint of a waver.

'I'm afraid there's nothing for it, Foster. You have to leave. My sister has offered you a substantial sum to be on your way and you've taken it. You've nothing to gain by staying.'

'So you say,' said Foster, and Miranda could hear the slur of whisky in his voice. 'But my family are here. The weather's on the turn. I'm better off here.'

'Please don't pretend you care about your family,' Aunt Constance said icily. 'And the situation with the weather is all the more reason to be on your way. We can put Harris in the trap and take you down to the station now, before the snow comes. The car might not be up to it but Harris will manage. But we must decide now, it's going to be dark very soon. I'm afraid that if you don't cooperate, we'll have no option but to summon the constable and have you removed.'

There was a long pause and Foster said, 'All right. Fair enough. I'll be on my way. Just give me a while to pack my things.'

'Very well,' Aunt Constance said, her voice full of relief. 'Shall we get Harris ready?'

'No need for that,' Foster said.

Miranda heard movement in the room and darted into the shadows. The door opened and Foster came out, swaying very slightly. She heard him mutter, 'I'll shoot that horse before I let them do that.' Then he disappeared off into the hallway, before his heavy footsteps made their way up the stairs.

Miranda stepped out of the shadows and found she was looking into the eyes of Robbie Foster, who had also emerged from the darkness where he had been hiding.

He put his finger to his lips and disappeared up the stairs after his father.

Miranda and Rosalind found their aunt on her way back to her study, and she beckoned them inside.

'Excellent news,' she said, smiling. 'I think we are finally about to be rid of the dreadful Mr Foster. For good.'

Miranda was about to say that she wasn't of the same mind at all, but something made her bite her tongue. 'More good news,' she said instead. 'Mr Humphries is back. He's in the tower with Imogen and Mother. We thought it was best if he stayed out of the way until Foster has gone.'

'Very good thinking,' Aunt Constance said thoughtfully. 'I can see his presence might have been inflammatory. But he will have to come back this evening, as soon as Foster has left, and we must bring the others home as well. It's getting too cold for them to stay out there. We can't risk it much longer.'

'We'll go out and tell them what's happening,' Rosalind said. 'They must be wondering.'

'I expect they might be rather enjoying it,' Miranda said and laughed.

'As long as they are out of the way of that ruffian,' said Aunt Constance, 'then I don't mind. And the sooner we are all safe from him, the better.'

'Considering how cold it is,' Rosalind said with a shiver, 'we seem to have spent an awful lot of time outside today.' She nestled further down into her scarf, following the small beam of light from Miranda's torch as they tramped over the garden towards the tower. The fog was thick and the darkness was coming down quickly. The tower, without lighted windows to spot, would soon be invisible.

'If Foster meant to go, he would have left already,' Miranda said through numb lips. 'He can't go far in this weather, I would have thought. I think Aunt Constance is being a little too optimistic about his going.'

They reached the tower and Imogen let them in, urging them in quickly to prevent the cold air invading the cosy sitting room. Mr Humphries was there looking a great deal warmer, sitting on the sofa with a cup of tea in his hand.

'Well, what news?' he asked, his eyes bright behind his glasses. 'Is that man off the premises?'

'Not yet, though Aunt Constance has tried to bribe him.' She explained what had happened that morning. 'He says he's packing his things and will be off directly.'

Mr Humphries looked sceptical. 'In this weather? Without a car?'

'That's what he says.'

Humphries frowned. 'Let's hope he means it then. He'll need to be off soon. I walked from the end of the drive after getting a lift from the station and that was punishing enough. Like Scott of the Antarctic's final march. If it starts to snow, he'll be in trouble.'

'So we just have to wait!' Imogen said. 'Will Mr Humphries stay here until he's gone?'

'I think so,' Miranda said. 'It's a waiting game now.'

Just then, the door to the tower swung open, letting in a fierce blast of cold air. They all gasped and turned to see Foster, muffled in a dark overcoat and scarf, come bursting into the room, bringing fog and frost with him as he entered. He slammed the door behind him and stood stamping on the mat catching his breath. Then he looked around at them all, an unpleasant smile spreading over his face.

'Well, well,' he said. 'What do we have here? Quite a nice little gathering! I can't think why you haven't invited me to your little house party before now. How very rude.'

No one moved but stared at him in shocked surprise. Miranda felt her stomach churn with panic as she realised Foster was very drunk and, she could sense, delighted to have discovered their secret at last.

Chapter Twenty-Three

Mr Humphries leapt to his feet, discarding his cup of tea, and instinctively stepped forward to face Foster.

'What on earth are you doing here?' he demanded. 'Who are you?'

Derek Foster came further into the room, a flush on his cheeks and his eyes glittering. He looked massive in his dark overcoat, built for trouble. He glanced at Mr Humphries with a sardonic amusement. 'I should be asking the same of you, considering I've been living in the castle for some time and I haven't laid eyes on you.' His gaze flickered over Humphries's head to Imogen. 'Or you, either.' Then he looked at Miranda, who was trying to stand in front of her older sister. 'So you've been the busy fairy flitting back and forth, have you? Keeping your little society a secret.'

Miranda, terrified, stared back at him. She could almost smell the thickness of his breath, heavy with alcohol.

'Well, you minx,' he said, 'your little trick didn't work, did it? I've a mind to give you a good hiding.'

Humphries stepped forward, grim-faced. 'Now listen—'

'You can shut it,' Foster said dismissively, and fixed his gaze back on Miranda. 'You think you're quite something, don't you? You think you're so much better than me, you and your sister and that awful old woman. Your granddad's all right, he talks to me like a human being, shares his grub and his booze. But the rest of you are not worth that.' He snapped his fingers in front of her face, making her jump. 'I can do whatever I want with you lot and none of you can stop me. You just watch.'

Humphries was breathing hard, his fists clenched. 'That's enough! It's pure insolence. How dare you talk to a young lady in that manner? It's cowardly, I tell you.'

Foster drew himself up, squaring his shoulders in return and clenching his own fists. 'Oh, I dare, all right. And I'm no coward. I hurt anyone I please, man or woman, boy or girl. I'm not afraid, it's just that I've got no scruples.'

'That's very obvious,' said Humphries hotly. 'And hurting a woman is beyond the pale.'

'Pah.' Foster half sneered, half laughed. 'You're not married, that's obvious. You try living with one of them and not punching their lights out! Once the romance has worn off, you'll find it's no picnic. They need to be kept in check.' He gestured at Miranda. 'That one in particular is a little menace. She needs to be controlled now before she gets any worse.' Then he looked again at Imogen. 'But this one. She's another matter. She's just how I like them. Blonde. Pretty. Showgirl figure. I'd like a piece of her, if you know what I mean.' He laughed.

Humphries looked as though he couldn't believe his ears, while Imogen's expression was both horrified and scared. Humphries moved forward a step, every muscle tense. 'Do you know who you're talking about? That's Miss Wakefield!'

'She's a woman and she's only good for two things. One of them is receiving a good slap.' Foster leered again. 'I don't need to tell you what the second is.'

'That's it,' Humphries said, taking off his jacket rapidly, then his glasses, and facing up to Foster in a boxer's stance. His face was scarlet with outrage. 'Get out, or I'll fight you right here.'

'Oooh, I'm scared,' mocked Foster.

'Take off your jacket and fight me,' cried Humphries, riled up.

Standing next to Rosalind, Miranda watched as Mr Humphries put up his fists. She wanted to tell him to stop, to not provoke Foster, but she was breathless, unable to speak. It all seemed to be unwinding slowly and yet rapidly at the same time.

'I don't need to take off my jacket.' Foster put up his fists, which looked much larger and meatier than Mr Humphries's. Humphries would be in trouble, Miranda could see that. She tried to shout to him to stop but no words would come. 'Do you think I'm so stupid I can't work out what's going on? That I can't look out of a window and see people leaving the house, or that I can't see from the photographs in the library that one of the family isn't here and isn't ever mentioned? It took me no time at all to work it all out.'

'Stay away from her, from all of them!' yelled Mr Humphries recklessly. 'I'll fight you and if you lose, you leave here right now. Tonight.'

'All right.' Foster smiled again and Miranda thought once more that he was quite handsome in that oddly repellent way. What had made him become this arrogant, dangerous man who didn't mind hurting people weaker than himself? 'Come on then, you. Come and fight me.'

Mr Humphries lifted his fists before his face and started moving like a boxer, back and forth, waiting for a chance to punch the grinning Foster, who turned with every move he made. Miranda held her breath, waiting for the blow to land, hoping that Mr Humphries would cause some damage. Then suddenly, he made a lightning jab with his fist. It was easily parried by Foster, and the fight had begun in a melee of fists. The girls shrieked and moved instinctively to the edges of the room as the two men began to fight in earnest, all boxing etiquette forgotten. As they grappled, they knocked over lamps and tables, and rolled over the sofa before ending up on the floor in front of the fire. Miranda, full of fear, watched as they struggled, saw Foster spot his chance and lift his fist before swinging it into Mr Humphries's temple with all his force and Arthur Humphries, uttering a strange spluttering groan, went limp, his eyes rolling back as he went, and lay there, out cold.

Foster burst out laughing. He got up and pushed at the unconscious Humphries with his shoe. There was no response. 'That was easier than I expected!' he exclaimed, looking about at the girls as if expecting a round of applause.

When there was nothing but three frightened faces, he seemed annoyed. 'What's wrong with you all? He asked for it! He's not dead, he'll come round in a bit. So much for your great protector.' His glance fell on Imogen. 'Come over here, miss. I'd like to see you better.'

Imogen stood on the stairs, aghast. She looked at her sisters anxiously and then at Derek Foster. 'Are you Mr Foster?'

He laughed. 'So you've heard of me. Naturally. Come here. I won't hurt you.'

Imogen seemed to make a hasty decision and she walked towards him, now in full possession of herself. 'Well, Mr Foster, thank you for visiting but I'm afraid I shall have to ask you to leave. I'm very tired and not at all well. I'm living out here for reasons of my health.'

'I'm sure you are,' he leered. 'And what a pretty thing you are.'

Miranda looked at him, repelled. They had forgotten how drunk he was, but now she could see it in the oily sheen to his skin, the way his eyes were simultaneously bright and yet dim with drink. He was almost panting at the sight of Imogen, his mouth open, his fat, dark red tongue visible. Whatever drink did to a man, it seemed to make him hungry for something and this man was hungry for Imogen.

I'm afraid, she realised. *I'm afraid I won't be able to stop him doing whatever he wants. I'm too weak to do it. If only Mr Humphries wasn't hurt.*

She had always thought she could do anything, get out of any situation she might find herself in, but now it felt as though that was just a foolish bit of vanity. She was sixteen, a girl. They didn't have a hope.

She could see that Imogen knew that too. Her back had straightened and her eyes were cool and hard.

She is going to save us, save Mother, by sacrificing herself, realised Miranda. *Please God, let Mother stay asleep upstairs. If she has been sedated, she'll never know.*

'You girls go in the kitchen,' Imogen said suddenly to the twins. 'Go in and don't come out until I tell you, understand?'

Derek looked at them, grinning. 'We'd like a little privacy, children.'

They looked at their older sister, their eyes terrified.

'Go,' Imogen said firmly. 'I'll be all right.'

Their older sister had an authority they had never seen before, and a new firmness and courage in the set of her shoulders. They obeyed, going into the little kitchen and closing the door so that they were left in complete darkness. They clung together behind the door, tears rolling down Rosalind's face, though Miranda was dry-eyed, tense with fear and apprehension.

They heard voices in the sitting room, the clear light tones of Imogen answered by the deeper sardonic ones of Foster. She seemed to be trying to exert her authority over him, to order him out, but it was making no difference. Then they heard her shout, 'No, no! Get back, do you hear me!'

'Oh no, no, no, no,' Rosalind muttered in a high, hurt little voice, her eyes squeezed shut. 'No, no, no.'

'Put that down, you little fool,' said the man in the other

room. 'You can't hurt me, you may as well just get it over with.'

'Don't touch me,' Imogen warned.

Then the sound of a scuffle.

'We have to do something!' Miranda said desperately.

'She said not to,' Rosalind whispered. 'But should we?'

'It'll be worse if you struggle!' exclaimed Foster. 'Keep still, won't you?'

'Let me go!'

'Calm down, you vixen. Ow! Why you . . . keep your nails to yourself, you devil.' A slap resounded through the sitting room. 'There, that's shut you up.'

The twins were both crying now, horrified at the sounds of what was unfolding next door. Miranda thought, *I have to stop it. It's my fault!*

She knew she must go in there and do whatever she could to save Imogen.

Then a sudden noise. Footsteps.

'Get away from her.' The voice rang out clear and authoritative.

An exclamation of surprise from Foster. 'Who the hell are you?'

'This is your last chance. Get away from her.'

'Another of you crazy women to deal with. What are you going to do about it?'

'I'll shoot you, if you don't.'

A shot rang out.

The twins gasped and opened the door. Their mother stood there, pointing a revolver at Foster, who stared back aghast, fear flickering in his eyes. Imogen was pressed against the wall, and Humphries was still out cold on the floor. The smell of cordite filled the room and a large hole in the sofa, where stuffing was now exploding outwards, showed where Mother had sent the bullet.

'Do you understand now? That's my daughter. If you touch her, or my other girls, I will kill you and I won't think twice. You have two minutes to get out of here and to get off this property. Do you understand?'

Foster saw the girls come out of the kitchen to stand next to their mother. The humiliation of it all burned in his face and for a moment, Miranda thought that he would simply step forward and knock the gun from Mother's hand. But she looked resolute and strong, ready to fire again at a moment's notice.

The front door opened again and Robbie Foster slipped inside. He was white-faced with cold, bundled up in a coat and woolly hat, but his eyes were alert and he seemed aware of everything that was happening in the tower. Mother turned instantly to look at the new arrival.

'It's all right, Mother, he's a friend,' Miranda said quickly, hardly noticing that she had not called her mother Mrs Black.

Robbie went up to his father. 'Come on, Dad, come with me. I'll look after you.'

Foster seemed dazed suddenly and he grunted, gazing down at Robbie as his son took his father's large, meaty hand in his own small one.

'Come on, Dad, come with me,' Robbie said again in his high pure voice. 'You'll be all right.'

Miranda sensed a turning point. She stepped forward. 'Yes,' she said firmly. 'You go with Robbie, Mr Foster. He'll show you the best way out.'

Foster looked around at the chaos he had caused. Imogen was pressed against the wall, shocked and fearful at everything that had happened, appalled by his continued presence. The room was a mess, with tipped-over tables and broken lamps and teacups. Humphries was groaning on the floor as his consciousness returned. Foster seemed confused by the woman still pointing a revolver at him, and the watching eyes of the girls, and the tug on his hand of the small boy.

'All right then,' he said at last. 'We'll go then, son.'

Robbie led him out of the door and into the freezing world beyond.

He was gone.

For a moment, they couldn't move and were too stunned to speak.

Miranda looked at Rosalind. She thought her sister would be on the point of collapse, perhaps hysterical, but her tears had dried. Then she looked at Imogen, who still stood against the wall, her hair awry, her eyes huge and shocked. Then she looked over at her mother, who stood there still holding the revolver.

Mother looked down at the weapon in her hand. 'This was your father's,' she said in a surprised voice. 'He said I might need it one day. So I kept it here.' Then she put down the revolver, looked at her daughters in turn, and opened her arms. 'Girls,' she said. 'Come here.'

The three of them rushed to her, each desperate to embrace her.

Miranda pulled away from her mother, her eyes shining. 'Mother, you did it! You saved Imogen!'

'I couldn't allow him to hurt you,' Mother said simply. A look of puzzlement came over her face. 'But what on earth am I doing here? This is one of the towers, isn't it? Where William and I used to come to be alone.'

'Don't you remember anything?' Rosalind asked gently.

'Well . . .' Mother still seemed confused. 'Well, of course. I've been away, on a very long holiday. Or was it a journey? I went away to convalesce, I think. I remember a hospital. And of course you all came to visit me. I think I remember that.'

There was a loud groan from the floor.

'Oh, Mr Humphries,' Imogen cried and they all raced to him where he lay in front of the fire. 'Miranda, get a cold cloth from the kitchen. Rosalind, put a cushion under his head. Are you all right?'

'What happened?' Mr Humphries asked with a groan.

'You did a marvellous job fighting that awful man, and he's gone now,' Imogen said, tenderly inspecting his temple where he'd been hit. 'You're going to have a frightful bruise, I'm afraid.'

'It can't be anywhere near as bad as this headache.' Humphries screwed up his face. 'Ouch.'

Mother walked over to Imogen and put her hand on her shoulder. Imogen looked up and smiled. Mother said, 'Did he hurt you, my dear?'

'No . . . no. It all happened so fast. But he didn't hurt me.'

Miranda went to her mother and gazed into her face, feeling as though the world had suddenly turned on its axis and things had somehow fallen right again. 'You remember us?'

'Yes, of course I do. How could I forget you all?' Mother smiled. 'I'm sorry I've been away for so long. I'd like to see Toby and Archie now, I think. And this poor man needs some help, possibly a doctor.'

'They'll be upstairs now, but you'll see them in the morning, I promise,' Miranda said. Now was not the time for the boys to discover that Mrs Black was their mother. 'But we should get home before it's too cold and dark.' She looked about at the mess in the room. 'I suppose we must come back and clear this up. But let's not think about that now.'

Imogen was ministering to Mr Humphries, asking him if he was up to walking and if he needed his glasses back on. He said he was and he did, and soon they had him on his feet and ready to go, although the pain on his face showed that he was far from comfortable. The twins ran upstairs to put some things in a bag for Mother.

'Do you really think he's gone?' Rosalind asked Miranda as they collected Mother's possessions.

'I don't know. But my guess is that this time, he might see that the game is up,' Miranda said, feeling hopeful. 'And we will make sure that we take the revolver back with us just in case.'

Downstairs, Mr Humphries was sitting in his overcoat and muffler waiting for them, squinting against the thudding pain in his head. Imogen was telling him how Mother had held Foster at gunpoint and ordered him to leave. As the twins came down, Miranda heard her sister say, 'What made you find that gun, Mother, and come down ready to shoot like that?'

Mother looked at her and turned to look at the twins as well as they came into the sitting room. 'It's simple, my dears. No one hurts my daughters. No one. Now. Shall we go back to the house? It must be almost time for supper.'

Chapter Twenty-Four

Present Day

Bad berries kill bad rats.

Listen to the voices, Georgie told herself, as she stood in the kitchen, looking at the dark liquid all over her finger.

She resisted and didn't lick it. Instead, she wiped the jam off and went back to the photographs on her phone, staring hard to make them out. Then she saw it: that wasn't a dormouse on its back under the bramble. It was a rat, paws stiff and curled in the agony of death.

She gasped. The jam had rat poison in it, she was sure of it – at least, the one with the dead rat did. Perhaps not the other, where the dormice frolicked happily among the berries. Of course, she couldn't be certain without laboratory analysis, but it all made sense. It must have been Etti Boule who did it. She conjured up a story where Etti was a cook who had gone insane and tried to poison the family with doctored jam. But that didn't make sense. Any scandal like that would have been known about. And why leave the jam in the larder where it could be found?

Georgie went to the morning room and started investigating on her computer. Rat poison, she discovered, was traditionally made with strychnine.

I've heard of that, she thought. *Isn't it in Agatha Christie novels? A quick way to kill someone off? Or maybe that's cyanide.*

She did a search and found that strychnine was an alkaloid, odourless, tasteless and colourless, that caused death by asphyxiation, and it had indeed featured in Christie novels.

On another site, she read that it killed quickly by convulsions after only a small amount was ingested.

Did that make the jam deadly? Her investigations were not conclusive. The effects could apparently fade over time and then the poison would be harmless if eaten. On the other hand, while instant death might not result, it could still be deadly if built up over time in the body.

Georgie breathed a sigh of relief. It was most likely that she would not have died like a Christie victim if she had licked her finger and consumed the jam, although it was still a possibility.

Then she saw a post on a question and answer site.

Strychnine lasts about a hundred years. But the rat pellets it is soaked in will crumble long before then.

A bolt of fear hit her. Could it last one hundred years? If so, the jam would still be poisonous. The pellets were most probably in it and sugar could preserve the strychnine.

There weren't many results for the expiry date of strychnine and most were highly complicated and chemical, which was no good for her.

I had better just be grateful I didn't eat it, she thought. *And let's hope no one else did either. I wonder who Etti Boule wanted to get out of the way?*

She looked out over the lawn. Sam Locke was back with his boys, clearing the exterior of the West Tower so that they could start repairs. He had said he would be busy for a while at the Manor but he had suddenly found time in the schedule. She wondered if it was anything to do with the presence of Pippa, who was sitting with the girls on the lawn, reading them stories and practising letters with Izzy.

Two of the workmen were standing halfway between the towers, examining the ground and pointing. One bent down and picked something up. It was one of the small cannonballs that often turned up on the lawn. The workmen were talking to one another and walking about in a circle.

Georgie, watching them, suddenly gasped. She jumped up and hurried out of the doors, running across the lawn towards them.

'Don't move anything!' she shouted. 'Don't touch it.'

She reached them, panting, as Sam came out through the fence around the tower. Georgie was pulling a piece of paper out of her jeans pocket.

'What's up, mate?' Sam asked genially, walking towards her.

'Where did you get that?' Georgie asked the workman holding the cannonball.

'Just there,' he said, pointing to the indentation in the grass.

Georgie looked at her piece of paper. It was the recipe for trifle, with the lines about rats and the little diagram of circles and arrows beneath.

The other man said, 'We were just looking at how the cannonballs seem to be in a pattern here. Whereas they're pretty random everywhere else.'

'They match the pattern on this piece of paper, don't they?' Georgie said, showing it to them.

The men took a look and Sam squinted down as well. 'Oh yeah. So they do,' he said. 'And your little arrows there are all pointing into the middle of this circle.' Sam walked into the spot on the grass. 'About here.' He looked down. 'Can't see why. There's nothing here.' He bounced up and down on the spot and then stamped around on the grass. 'Nope, it's just a piece of turf. Maybe there was something here once. You know. X marks the spot.' Just then he frowned and said, 'You know what, I think maybe there is something here.' He bent down and felt carefully in the grass. 'I can't see anything but there's a change in the texture here, like there's a rock underneath or something. Get me a spade, will you, Max?'

One of the young workmen went off and returned quickly with some tools. Sam took the spade and cut down through the turf. He quickly hit something hard. 'Interesting. I'll take it off carefully, don't worry about the lawn.' He started to use the spade as a knife, chopping carefully down through the grass, looking for the hard surface beneath. He worked on until he cut a large circle. Then he got the workmen to help him carefully lift the circle of turf away. It revealed a large wooden lid in the ground, banded and rimmed with iron, with a hoop of iron in the top. The wood was slightly rotten but not as much as might be expected from having had turf on top of it.

'What is this?' Georgie asked, excited. 'Wait, I'm going to text Caspar, I want him to see this.' She quickly typed out a message.

Pippa wandered over, Sofia on her hip, leaving Izzy on the rug absorbed in her storybooks. 'Hello, everyone, what's the meeting in aid of?'

Sam smiled at her. 'We've found a mysterious bit of wood in the ground.'

'And here's a diagram of exactly where to find it,' Georgie said, showing her the paper. 'Look! These large circles must be the towers, and this line is the wall. The smaller circles are the cannonballs, all around this circle, which is the wooden thing we're looking at.'

Pippa looked down at it. 'That's amazing! Where did you find the paper, Georgie?'

'In the old recipe book.' She didn't want to start revealing her discoveries of poisoned jam in front of the others, so she said, 'I think there were some very mischievous children here during the war, from what I've found in the attic and round-about. Oh look, here comes Caspar!'

Her husband was striding across the lawn towards them. 'What's the big find?'

'Come and see,' she called.

'I think it's the entrance to something,' Sam said, testing the wooden lid with his boot.

'Do you know anything about this, Caspar?' asked Pippa. 'Seeing as you're the one who lived here?'

Caspar looked at it, frowning, and shook his head. 'I've never seen it before.' He looked back towards the house. 'I know there are some cellars under the lawn, added in the nineteenth century to store wine and ice and so on. Perhaps this was an entrance to an ice house or something. But we do have an ice house in the park, so I'd be surprised if there were two.'

'Have you been in the cellars?' asked Sam.

Caspar shook his head. 'Out of bounds. We could go in the kitchen cellars, not that we wanted to, it wasn't very nice down there. But the chambers underneath the lawn? No. Locked and bolted.' He frowned. 'Now I think about it I did once hear about a furnace under there, used to keep the stables and the greenhouses warm in winter. But it was out of action a century ago, I should think.'

'What do you think?' Sam said. 'Shall we try and lift this?'

'Of course,' Caspar said. 'We must.'

They started to pull at the iron hoop on the middle of the lid but the whole thing was stuck fast. It took some levering with tools and careful pulling and twisting, with Sam and his men working together, before they were able to heave the lid out of the ground. It revealed a round tunnel heading straight downwards.

'Is it a well?' asked Georgie, curious. 'It can't be a coincidence that the pattern on the paper matched the cannonballs and this entrance. But why hide a well?'

Caspar knelt down and inspected the tunnel. It was dry

and dusty, and on one side a series of iron rungs set into the wall of the tunnel provided a ladder downwards. He looked up at them all. 'I don't think it's a well,' he said. 'My instinct is that it's an oubliette.'

'What's that?' Sam asked.

Georgie remembered something from history lessons long ago. 'Isn't that like a dungeon?'

'Sort of. Even nastier than a dungeon, if that's possible. Oubliette is from the French, to forget. You tossed prisoners down a hole like this and just forgot about them. I suppose someone put some food and drink down if you didn't want them to die too fast. But I think it was a particularly ghastly form of killing someone, essentially – cold, lonely and desperate, like being buried alive.'

Georgie felt herself stiffen. The words of that eerie little nursery rhyme jumped into her mind.

She keeps him deep. She keeps him cool.

Sam said, 'I think there's only one thing for it. I'll go down there with a torch and see what I can see.'

Georgie gasped. They all looked at her.

Caspar said, 'Are you okay, Georgie? You've gone quite pale. What is it?'

'I . . . I don't know how to say this but . . . I think there might be someone down there.'

They looked at her in astonishment. 'What? Why?' asked Caspar. 'Why do you think that?'

'It's something I read in the house . . . nothing concrete.' She flushed. 'I don't know. It's just an instinct.'

'Okay,' Sam said. He put one foot on the top iron rung.

474

'There's only one way to find out.' He smiled at them all. 'Don't forget about me, will you?'

Then he started to climb down into the dark.

'What on earth can it be?' Caspar said, staring at the strange object that was now on the table in the kitchen.

'Whatever it is, it was very heavy,' Sam said, still red in the face and sweating from manoeuvring the object into a makeshift sling so that the others could pull it up.

It was large, oval and putty coloured, and still wrapped in the remains of an old blanket and a lot of straw.

Georgie gazed at it, confused. By the time Sam had reached the bottom, she was sure he was going to say that he had found the body of a man. But he said nothing of the kind. Instead, he said that he had found what looked like an old stone but wrapped in a blanket, so it must have some kind of significance. They had lifted it out and brought it into the kitchen to take a look.

'Could it be a fossil or something?' wondered Pippa.

'That's it, of course!' exclaimed Georgie. 'Why didn't I think of it? It's an egg!'

As soon as she said it, they could all see that it looked very like an egg.

'What the hell lays an egg that big?' asked Sam with a laugh.

'A dinosaur?' asked Caspar, interested. He put out a hand and touched the cool surface. 'Wow. Imagine. A dinosaur egg, hidden here all this time?'

'I don't think it's a dinosaur egg,' Georgie said. 'The

woman at the Natural History Museum said that no dinosaur fossils were sent here in the war.' She quickly explained to Sam and Pippa about the wartime conservation of fossils at the castle. 'But she did say there were avian remains. So this must be some kind of bird.'

'A bird? It must have been enormous! Like something from the *Arabian Nights*!' Caspar whistled softly. 'How incredible.'

'I'll take photos and send them to her,' Georgie said, looking at the egg. 'I asked if anything was missing, but they said no. It's all going to be rather awkward if we say that we've found a fossil that they didn't know was missing.'

'There's not much we can do about that,' Caspar said with a laugh.

'I suppose they'll just be pleased to have it back,' remarked Pippa. 'And whoever hid that egg must be long dead. So we'll never know why.'

Much later, when the excitement had died down and the egg was safely stored in a box in Caspar's study, Caspar and Georgie were sitting together in the morning room over mugs of tea.

'But how do you know so much, Georgie?' he asked. 'How come you asked the archivist if any eggs were missing – and then an egg appears? It's another Georgie moment.'

Georgie smiled at him. 'It was just little things I found around the house. When I went to the attic, I found things that belonged to the children that lived here during the war – including Archie, though he must have been very small. There's not much of his, to be honest – although there is probably more I didn't find. But his sisters, Miranda and Rosalind, seem to have written a lot. I don't know how much is true and how much is fantasy; it seemed very mixed up and a bit of a blend of both. Anyway, I found this rhyme they wrote about someone called Etti Boule. Ever since I read it, I can't forget it. It's very simple.' She thought for a moment and recited it:

'*Etti Boule*
Is kind and cruel
She took a fool
And keeps him still

She keeps him deep
She keeps him cool
Etti Boule
Is kind and cruel.'

Caspar made a face. 'That is quite nasty and very mysterious.'

'I know. And this Etti also has a recipe in the book I found. For trifle.'

'She sounds very unpleasant. I don't think I'd like to eat her trifle.'

Georgie laughed. 'Nor would I. And the recipe isn't very good. But is this Etti even real? She sounds so awful. My only idea was that she was a real person that they disliked so much that they fictionalised her as a villain. When we looked down the oubliette, I thought of that bit: she keeps him dark,

she keeps him cool. It just seemed so apt. So then I thought –
maybe we'd find the fool, whoever he is, at the bottom. But
we found an egg. And also in the notebooks were the lines
Don't forget! and *Where is the egg?*'

'If they know where the egg is, and don't want to forget,
then why are they asking where it is?' Caspar looked even
more bewildered. 'What are they on about?'

Georgie laughed and sipped her tea. 'I know. It's a mystery.'

'Etti Boule,' Caspar said thoughtfully. He went to the desk
and took some paper out of the letter rack. 'How are you
spelling it?' She told him and he wrote it down. He frowned
and wrote something else. Then he turned the piece of paper
around so that she could see:

ETTI BOULE
OUBLIETTE

Georgie gasped.

'Anagram,' said Caspar unnecessarily.

Georgie thought over the rhyme again but this time without imagining Etti as a person but as the oubliette. 'Oh my
gosh! But I don't understand. What does it mean?'

'Children are fascinating, aren't they?' said Caspar. 'My
guess is that they found the oubliette, nicked the fossil for
some reason, hid it down there and then couldn't confess
and ended up playing lots of silly games where they hid clues
about what they'd done.' He shrugged. 'It's the only thing that
makes sense.'

'I suppose so,' Georgie said slowly. She could see how the

puzzle was neatly solved that way, although there were still questions. Why did they take the fossil? Why didn't they confess and hand it back? And why didn't anyone at the museum know it was missing? But the biggest mystery was that Etti Boule had her own recipe in the book and had possibly had something to do with poisoned jam – and how could an oubliette do that?

Etti isn't a person, she reminded herself. *Etti is a hole in the ground.*

The other thing that puzzled her was how the egg could be described as a 'fool' as it was in the rhyme, if what Caspar said was right. She had been convinced that they would find a body in there. And yet, there was none.

'I'll send a message to the Natural History Museum,' Georgie said. 'I suppose they'll want their egg back.'

Caspar was staring at his anagram, evidently pleased with himself for solving it. 'I suppose we ought to,' he said slowly, glancing up. 'Or . . . we could always just keep it. For now.'

'Keep it!' Georgie gave him a look of mock outrage. 'But it's not ours!'

'How do we know that? The museum don't think they're missing anything. It might be ours from some ancestor, some collector. We don't know.'

'I suppose that could be true,' Georgie said. 'I hadn't thought of that.'

'So let's hold off for a little while until we find out a bit more. You said there was a lot of stuff in the attics. We'll go through that and see what we can find.'

'All right,' Georgie said. 'I mean . . . seeing as there were avian fossils here in the war, it does seem quite likely that it belonged to the museum.'

'But not certain,' Caspar replied.

'All right, Mr Logic. We'll wait. I don't suppose it can do any harm.'

Just then the door opened and Pippa put her head around it. She looked unhappy and anxious.

'What is it, Pippa?' asked Georgie, seeing her sister's face. 'Are you all right?'

'Not really. Ryan's just arrived.'

'What?'

Pippa nodded. 'He's turned up out of the blue to see the girls. But before then, we're going to have a talk about things. I'm going to take him into the kitchen, if that's all right. We can have a cup of tea there.'

'Of course.'

'Do you need company?' Caspar asked.

'No, no, he seems perfectly all right.' Pippa sighed. 'I suppose we're going to have to be grown up about this. If it all kicks off, I'll text you.'

'I really don't want to see him,' Georgie said. 'I know that's bad. But of course I'll be polite.'

'I don't think he wants to see you,' Pippa said, 'but probably for different reasons. Wish me luck.'

She smiled and shut the door.

'I don't like to think of him in our house,' Georgie said. 'He gives me the shudders.'

'He's just a bloke,' Caspar said mildly. 'A fairly banal

ordinary guy, with an extraordinary streak of meanness. But you mustn't turn him into some kind of devil. He's just not that important. He might be one of the devil's minions but a very junior one. An apprentice minion.'

Georgie laughed and went to hug him. 'Whereas you, my darling, are an angel, senior level.'

'I'm only human,' he said modestly. 'Although with a touch of brilliance, I can't deny. And you're only human too. That's why you love me.'

He dropped a kiss on the top of her nose.

When Georgie went down to the kitchen two hours later, she assumed it was empty. She had heard Pippa going upstairs and had thought she must be taking Ryan to see the girls after their lunchtime naps, as the kitchen beneath her was silent. So she jumped when she came into the room and found Ryan sitting there, playing a game on his phone.

'What ho, Georgie,' he said when he saw her and she re-membered how he liked his P. G. Wodehouse turns of phrase.

As though that might take the place of a personality, she thought.

'Hello, Ryan.'

'How are things?'

'Fine. You?' She walked over to the sink to put her mug in it.

'Oh yes, very good.' He looked back at his phone. 'Can't complain.'

What an idiot you are, she thought. *Your marriage is over, your children are living away from you. You've just seen your estranged wife for the first time in weeks. And you can't complain, everything is fine. Sitting there playing a game on your phone like a kid.* But she said politely, 'How's your golf going?'

Ryan, who seemed to have been hiding the fact that he was actually rather wary of Georgie, suddenly relaxed and launched into an account of his last eighteen holes at a very good course in Surrey. Georgie blocked him out, unable to bear listening to his smugness, which he clearly thought was self-deprecatory humour but which actually came across as one long boast.

After she'd washed her cup, she turned back to him, feeling she must make a show of being interested. Her eye fell on the table in front of him. There was an empty mug, and a plate covered with crumbs and a dirty knife smeared with purple. In front of it was the butter dish and an open jar of blackberry jam. She gasped.

Ryan stopped mid-flow. 'Everything all right?'

'Oh, yes . . . yes.' She could feel her face flushing. 'Fine. I just remembered an email I haven't sent.' She was quickly thinking of which pot it could be and then remembered that she had left both pots on the side. And both labels had been obscured so that there was no way of knowing which was which – happy dormouse or dead rat. She said casually, 'Did Pippa make you something to eat?'

'Yes, some toast.'

'How was the jam? It's homemade but I don't eat jam and I was wondering what it was like.'

'Very nice,' Ryan said, nodding. 'Very nice. I like black-berry jam.'

'You do?' *So eighty-year-old jam is still edible*, she thought. *Interesting. And he looks fine. No convulsions. No asphyxiation. Thank god.* Pippa would have a hard time proving she hadn't known about the poison when she gave it to her estranged husband. Georgie said lightly, 'I've got these two pots knocking about. One you've just had some of, and another. We won't eat them. Do you want them?'

'Well, the girls don't eat jam but that was lovely so I wouldn't say no. If you don't want them.'

He always did have a very sweet tooth, she remembered. She picked up the other jar from the countertop.

'Please. Have them.' She put the two jars on the table in front of him. 'You can take them with you when you go.'

An hour later, after Ryan had spent some time playing with the girls on the lawn, he headed off.

'This is quite a place you've got here, Caspar,' he said affably as they gathered to see him off in the hall, the girls hanging off Pippa's hands, watching their father leave with solemn faces. 'Any good courses near here?'

'One or two,' Caspar said stiffly.

'Fancy a round or two one of these days?'

'I don't think I'll have time, but thanks for asking.'

'Okay. Let me know if you change your mind,' Ryan said, grinning, as though he hadn't heard the obvious reluctance in Caspar's voice to play golf with him. 'I'll be off then.'

'Don't forget these,' Georgie said, stepping forward with the jars in a plastic bag.

'Oh, thanks. Well, cheerio, everyone.' He waved amiably and set off down the steps to where his Ford Focus sat on the gravel at the front.

'He really is insufferable,' Georgie said as they watched him get in his car. 'I never saw until now what a towering ego he has behind the bumbling exterior.'

Caspar laughed. 'I've never seen someone be such an arse, and be so pleased with themselves for being one.' He shook his head. 'I thought he was harmless, but he's actually incredibly mean-spirited and selfish. He does it very well. You don't see it till you know, and then it's impossible to miss.'

'Imagine how I feel,' Pippa said gloomily. 'I went and married him! I feel like I accidentally married David Brent thinking he was George Clooney.' Then she smiled. 'Well, he's gone and that's something. What did you give him, Georgie?'

'Just some of Sandy's homemade pickle,' she said, crossing her fingers behind her back. 'I thought he might like it. It's got blackberries in it.'

Chapter Twenty-Five

1939

When the party from the tower returned to the castle, they found the house was curiously peaceful. There was no sign of Foster or of the boys.

Aunt Constance came into the morning room at the sound of the group coming through the French windows, opening the thick blackout curtains quickly to dart into the room.

'What is all this?' she said, taking in Rosalind and Imogen helping a wincing Mr Humphries into the room while Miranda was carefully guiding Mother in. 'What on earth has happened? I'd been wondering where you girls were!'

'Foster came over!' exclaimed Miranda.

'He fought Mr Humphries,' added Rosalind, glancing over at him.

'I've taken rather a bad knock,' said Humphries, who was looking pale and ill. 'It was probably a foolish thing to do.'

'Oh dear, oh dear,' Aunt Constance said, looking worried. 'And where is Foster now?'

'Mother did the bravest thing!' exclaimed Miranda as they all moved towards the fire, Aunt Constance making sure the curtains were tightly shut behind them. 'She forced Foster to leave Imogen alone—'

'Imogen!' cried Aunt Constance, looking with consternation at her great-niece. 'Are you all right?'

'I'm fine, honestly. He didn't do any damage, thank goodness, because Mother stopped him.'

'Mother?' Aunt Constance now looked aghast, anxiously looking over to Mother to make sure that she was not shocked by this name. 'Do you mean Mrs Black?'

Mother looked at her bemused. 'What do you mean, Constance? Mrs Black? I think I booked into a hotel under that name once. But I'm sure it was only that once.'

'I see,' Constance said weakly. 'Well, Kathryn, it's lovely to have you home. Your room is ready upstairs.'

Mr Humphries sat down gingerly on the sofa. 'Is Foster here?'

'No, I don't think so,' Constance said. 'It's been very quiet – very. I gave him some money today and he said he was packing his things. We offered him a ride to the station and he didn't return to take it up. I assume he's gone.'

The girls exchanged glances, remembering little Robbie Foster appearing as if from nowhere to take his father away. Perhaps he had led him over the bridge and pointed the way down the drive, letting him go on his way. Someone like Foster, strong, meaty, warm-blooded and fuelled by drink, would make his way to the main road, flag a lift or follow his nose to the station.

'Yes. He must have left,' Miranda said slowly.

'It's the best result then,' Humphries said. 'And the bravery of your mother was the reason.' He smiled over at Mother.

'I did what anyone would do,' Mother said simply. She looked tired, her blue eyes suddenly dim but beautiful. 'We may all be called to do this and more in the war.'

'You must go to bed, Kathryn,' Constance said, going over to embrace her. 'We owe you so much, but you need to rest.'

'I'll take her up,' Imogen said gently. She led Mother out of the room, Rosalind following with the bags.

'Now, Mr Humphries,' Constance said. 'You look most unwell. I suggest you also go to bed, and take the hand bell from the hall with you. Ring if you need me and I will check on you every few hours.'

'That's very kind,' Mr Humphries said, holding the compress to the great bruise on his temple. 'I will do that. I feel rather sick, to be honest.'

As if on cue, Grandfather came into the room. 'What is happening? I've just passed Kathryn and Imogen on the stairs!'

Constance gave him a quick resumé of the past events. 'And Mr Humphries is retiring now, to recover from the head injury. Perhaps you can take him up, Leonard?'

Grandfather looked confused. 'You mean, he's gone? Foster's gone?'

'Yes,' Aunt Constance said decisively. 'He's gone. Just as we agreed. And we can all be very thankful for that.'

Miranda went down to the kitchen to tell Dolly Foster that they were ready for supper now, and found it empty. The food still lay ready to be cooked on the side, but there was the same sense of eerie desertion here as there was everywhere else.

No one seems to want to be in the house tonight, she thought.

Just then, Dolly emerged into the kitchen from the cold store and jumped when she saw Miranda standing in the middle of the room. 'Oh! You startled me!'

'Are you all right, Dolly?' Miranda asked. 'Your eye looks a little better.'

Dolly's hand went to the tender bluish skin around her injured eye. 'Yes . . . yes, it's not so bad as it was.' She looked around and said busily, 'Now, you'll all be wanting your dinner, I think. I'll get on and it will be ready in no time.'

Miranda looked back at the counter. 'And where is your trifle?'

'The trifle! Well now, I came in and found that the cat had been at it so I had to throw it away.'

'That's a shame, I was looking forward to it.'

'Yes, it's a dreadful waste. Never mind, I'll make another tomorrow.' Dolly began to bustle about, pulling out pans and dishes. 'You go on now, Miss Miranda, I'll get the dinner on in a trice. I'll call you when it's ready.'

'All right.' Miranda turned for the door and then looked back at Dolly, already busy with her preparation. 'Have you seen Robbie?'

'Oh yes, he's in the stable with Tom and the others. They came in a little while ago and got some hot mash ready to give the horses. You know how they can't rest if they think those horses need anything. They'll be back soon, no doubt, and I'll send them up to bed as soon as they come in.'

'All right,' Miranda said. She felt uncertain for some reason that she could not understand. 'Thank you, Dolly.'

'You're welcome.'

Miranda did not expect to sleep that night but she fell into a deep slumber as soon as she climbed into bed. The knowledge that there was nothing more to fear from Foster, as well as the exhaustion of what they had been through, helped her to find complete oblivion. It was only when she woke very early that the events of the previous night came back to her.

'Are you awake?' whispered Rosalind through the blackness.

Miranda rolled over and lit her lamp. 'Yes.'

'Wasn't it awful?'

'Awful but wonderful. Mother is back.'

'Yes. She was amazing.' There was a pause and then Rosalind said, 'Do you think she might really have killed him?'

Miranda thought. 'Yes. Why not? She's right. No one knows what they might be called on to do. And she has nothing to lose.'

'Perhaps you're right. I don't really understand it but I can see why you think that. Do you think that man has gone?'

'He's never coming back,' Miranda said firmly. 'I'm sure of that.'

'Good. I suppose I can sleep easily again.'

'It's strange that in all the time he was here, you never

walked in your sleep. I would have thought that the turmoil of it would have set you off. But it didn't.'

'No. But I have no idea why it happens, or doesn't.'

Miranda recalled the doorknob of their room turning and hitting the lock. She wondered if Rosalind had somehow known that she needed to stay safely behind that door and not walk out.

Rosalind said, 'Do you think this means Mother is back? Really back?'

'If it does, then it was all worth it. I know that makes me sound terrible but I don't care. I really don't. Having Mother back is the best thing that could ever be.'

'I think you're right,' Rosalind said in a small voice, and they were quiet until it was time to get up.

Everyone tried to be as normal as possible the next day, for the sake of the children, even though it seemed they were not affected by any of the previous day's events. Although Foster did not, of course, appear at breakfast, the children didn't seem to notice and said nothing, as though they hadn't spent the day before chasing him around the house until he was a bundle of fury.

Mr Humphries appeared at breakfast, looking much better, though he was sporting a huge bruise on his face. After managing some tea and a little porridge, he disappeared off to his study. When Miranda was walking past after breakfast, the door to Mr Humphries's study opened and he looked out, his expression serious. 'Ah, Miranda, can you come in here, please?'

'Of course.' She followed him into the room. 'Yes?'

He turned around, more agitated than she had yet seen him. 'Miranda, my egg is missing!'

'What?' She stared back, her eyes wide. 'The egg?'

'The moa's egg! It's gone!' He gestured at the box which was open, its soft wool lining spilling out. 'Do you know where it is?'

'No,' she said emphatically.

'Come on, Miranda, is this some silly joke to upset me? I would hope you wouldn't be so mean spirited! You know how much the egg means to me and how important it is! It's terribly rare.'

Miranda went to look in the box, staring in as if unable to believe her eyes. She looked up at him. 'I promise, I don't know where it is. I was going to take it – to make you stay here. Robbie had the same idea. So that we wouldn't be left with Foster. I told him it wouldn't work and that we shouldn't touch it.'

Mr Humphries made a disgusted face. 'I would never have left you here with that ruffian all on your own! What do you take me for?'

'Well, I was going to take it. Robbie and I nearly did. But when I saw it in its box, I knew how heartbroken you'd be. So we left it.'

Mr Humphries put his hands through his hair. 'Who could have taken it then?'

'Is the egg worth anything?'

'It has a value on the black market but at the moment, in wartime, it would be impossible to realise anything for it. At least, that's what I think, but I don't know. I never considered selling it. All these exhibits are priceless to me. Look, I'm writing a piece for a journal about it. It's here on the desk.' Humphries swooped up a sheet of paper and read aloud. 'An intact moa's egg is so rare as to be priceless.'

Miranda gazed at him. 'Mr Foster was in here.'

'He was?'

'I saw him come in. Perhaps he read that piece on your desk, and thought that meant he could sell it in London or something. Maybe he decided to steal it!'

'But that's dreadful!' Mr Humphries looked appalled. 'It's so rare, so precious, so important to science. And I'll lose my job. All I had to do was protect the collection. I'll be in disgrace, ruined! Who would want me after this? Do you think he's taken it with him, wherever he's gone?'

'He's the most likely thief. So I suppose he must have.'

'Oh my goodness.' Humphries had gone quite white. 'What a disaster.'

'I am so sorry,' she said. 'But it might still be here. We might find it.'

He glanced at her. 'You are telling the truth, aren't you, Miranda? You don't know where it is?'

'Of course I don't,' she said. 'I double promise.'

'All right. I believe you.'

'I'll keep my eyes peeled.'

'Please do.' Humphries looked ill again. 'If I can't find it soon, I'll have to report it, and goodness knows what will happen then. I can't think why that Foster man couldn't have been happy with some cash and an easy getaway.'

*

After lunch, Miranda waited for Robbie in the passage, knowing he'd come past after visiting the stables as he always did at that time. 'Come with me,' she hissed, leading him to the great hall, which was sunk in darkness and full of the boxes left by the museum.

'What happened yesterday?' she asked urgently, once they were inside, concealed by the mountains of containers.

Robbie stared at her, his eyes glimmering in the dark. 'Dad's gone,' he said.

'Yes, I know. But where?'

Robbie shrugged. 'I dunno. It was cold and dark yesterday, I didn't see what happened.'

Miranda grabbed his arm. 'Oh, come on, Robbie. You know more than this! Where did he go? Did he walk off into the darkness, towards the station? Did he take the money and go? You said to me that you thought you could use the egg to make him leave. Did you? I pretended to Mr Humphries that you'd thought, like me, that its disappearance might make him stay. But you thought it might make your father leave. So what happened?'

Robbie stared at her for a long moment, and then said, 'It was dark. Maybe Dad fell down the hole.'

'What hole?' asked Miranda, confused. She didn't know of a hole anywhere in the garden or in the park. 'Do you mean in the moat?'

Robbie shook his head. 'No. The hole. There's the lid in the ground, by the wall.'

'Oh.' Miranda thought for a moment and then she remembered that there was a strange old iron-and-wood cover in the grass by the wall between the towers. As young children they had tried to yank it up and it had been too heavy to lift, and gradually they had forgotten about it. 'What do you know about that?'

She knew that Robbie had been entranced by the castle. There was barely a part of it he hadn't been into and explored. He probably knew it better than she did.

'I know it's a long tunnel like a well, where they used to put prisoners. Called an oubliette. I read about it in a picture book about old castles. The thing is, you can put someone in there and then forget all about them and it doesn't matter if they're alive or dead. See?'

'Put someone there and forget about them,' Miranda said slowly.

'That's right. And you've got one. Right in the lawn there. See?'

'Yes. I see. I certainly do.'

Miranda went upstairs, chilled and dazed. What was Robbie saying? That somehow Foster had fallen into the oubliette that lay under the lid in the lawn? That was impossible. How could the lid have been lifted? How could he have fallen in, and the lid replaced?

No, she thought, shivering. *It's a story. It's a dream. He's made it up.*

Foster took his money and went, she thought. *He stole the egg because it was easy to pilfer and he believed it was priceless. He headed off to the station and he's on his way somewhere now, thinking he can sell that egg and disappear.*

She couldn't quite imagine any other outcome that wasn't utterly unnatural.

Could a young boy really want an awful fate for his own father? She supposed it was possible, bearing in mind Foster's evident cruelty to the boys and to the mother they obviously adored. She recalled Foster muttering that he would shoot the horse.

Perhaps Robbie thought he really would kill the horse. Would that be enough to make him lead his father to his doom?

Miranda shook her head at herself. Robbie was a small boy. He couldn't do any such thing, even if he wanted to. It was sad and horrible wishful thinking.

She remembered Dolly coming into the kitchen yesterday. She recalled Robbie telling her he knew about the poisoned jam. She thought of the trifle, freshly made yesterday and then thrown away, vanished without a trace.

She felt cold and miserable.

Oh no. Surely not.

A flood of guilt threatened to overwhelm her.

It wasn't us! she told herself firmly. *We didn't do it. We didn't cause it. Foster has gone.*

She had to cling on to the belief as hard she could. There was no other way.

Later there was a conference in Aunt Constance's study. It was the four of them who had witnessed Mother's action the night before. Mother herself had slept soundly and in the morning, Aunt Constance had decided it was best to treat her with sedative, as usual.

'I think it may be wise,' she said. 'Although Kathryn seemed like her old self last night, it may be a mirage. It will surely be a great shock when she begins to understand what happened to her over the last three years. Let us give her time to rest and save her mind from any more torment. As I said, she may relapse. That is by far the most likely outcome.'

But it seemed that Mother had returned. Aunt Constance kept her quite heavily sedated for three days after Foster's disappearance, and then gradually lessened the dose to allow her to become her old self. Miranda guessed that her aunt was doing her best to expunge the memory of the shock in the tower, so that Mother would not risk being sent back to her state of otherness.

No one knew if it had worked. She certainly never spoke of it, or asked any questions. But that didn't mean that she didn't remember. There was no way to find out and so it was simply never spoken of.

Dolly Foster seemed to know that her husband would not be seen again, for, as her wound healed, her happy demeanour returned and she became her old self again, working hard for the comfort of everyone in the castle and looking after her children.

The colonel never spoke of Foster again and never asked a single question about him after the day that Foster disappeared.

The children knew that they were free of him, for good. As the winter worsened and the great storms of snow came, freezing the country into stillness and cutting them off completely, there was little to do in the great house but huddle together and keep warm. The ice storm that came in January sent ice-cold rain sheeting out of the sky that froze as soon as it touched anything. The result was great skeins of ice, like giant spider silk or the rays of a silver-white sun, tethering trees to the ground and pulling down telegraph wires. The wireless talked of communities cut off, walls of snow, animals freezing, no trains, no driving anywhere. Even the two towers at the end of the lawn seemed cut off and distant.

In the cold and dark, snuggled by fires and sticking together through the winter storms, Miranda kept her secret. She wasn't even sure it was a secret as she had no way of knowing if what Robbie had hinted at was true. There was no way to find out either, with the park and garden blanketed in thick snow. All she had were suspicions that played on her mind endlessly. And the fact that when she'd searched for the jars of poisoned jam, she had found four jars together on the cobwebby shelf, although the label on one seemed to now show frolicking dormice rather than a dead rat . . . She toyed with the idea of confronting Robbie and Dolly about it, but when she saw Robbie – so small and innocent, and blossoming in the castle – she couldn't bring herself to do it. And what was the point? Thousands of people were dying every day in the futility of conflict. Who cared if one drunken, violent rascal was never seen again?

If only it didn't hurt her so much to think of it, and cause such nightmares.

In the course of that long winter, Miranda used writing to

rid herself of the fear and tension. She scribbled in her note-books, conjuring up a character, the mysterious Etti Boule. Etti Boule was neither good nor completely wicked either. She killed people, but they were bad people who deserved to die.

'Tell us more about Etti Boule,' the boys would say, round-eyed with delicious terror.

Miranda wrote about her adventures, her crimes and who she was and what she did. Before too long, not quite sure how it happened, even she began to believe in a mysterious cruel redhead, who fed a man a poisoned trifle, and kept his corpse as a trophy for ever.

'As long as he ain't here,' Robbie muttered once, 'I don't care a bit.'

There was no question of Mr Humphries going back to London while they were snowed in at Wakefield, but he didn't seem to mind and neither did Imogen. Mr Humphries spent long hours with her, helping her with teaching the boys and talking to her about London life and all that was on offer there. His own work seemed to occupy him less, and it was obvious how happy they were in one another's company, although no one asked them about it and it was never spoken of.

Miranda and Rosalind spent a great deal of time debat-ing what they were doing and how far it was all going and whether they would get married, but Rosalind said rightly that they would do nothing about engagements as long as they were all snowed in together.

'Imagine if she said no! So awful! He won't ask for ages.

Not while he's here. But I bet they hold hands sometimes and gaze longingly and recite poetry.'

'I should think he's talking to her about extinct mega-fauna,' Miranda said dryly. 'And perhaps she likes it.'

Rosalind laughed. 'If she does, then he should definitely propose! He won't find anyone else as pretty as Imogen who does!'

It was weeks later that the thaw set in, and instead of being frozen, the whole world was sodden. But the relief from that bitter cold was worth it. Mother was almost her old self now; though she had relapses, each one seemed to last a little less time than the one before. Her doctor was hopeful that a full recovery would take place before too long, especially now that the boys knew who she was and showered her with love and affection every day.

Mr Humphries was studying an article about the effect of the winter on bird life when Miranda came in, lugging something in a blanket.

'They say that it will take years for the bird population to recover,' he said thoughtfully as Miranda came in. 'Just think, what if some become extinct! There haven't been many modern extinction events and it would be strange if some simple British birds were affected by one. How interesting.' He looked up and noticed her bundle. 'What's that?'

'I wondered if it could be your moa's egg?' she said inno-cently and put it down in front of him.

Mr Humphries jumped up with excitement. His panic about the lost moa's egg had diminished with the onset of the harshest of the winter. But when the weather changed, he started to fret about it again, wondering where it could possibly be. Now he dashed over. 'Where on earth did you find it?' he asked. 'Where was it?'

He pulled off the blanket. Underneath was a large grey stone, mostly oval in nature but grainy and bumpy. He stared and said, 'Oh.'

Miranda said, 'Are you pleased?'

His face hardened. 'Is this a mean joke? That's not my egg. As you well know.'

'I know.' Miranda gave him a friendly smile. 'But don't be cross. I'm trying to save your bacon. The egg is gone. Perhaps Foster stole it and hid it or . . . or took it with him when he left . . . we don't know. It might be found, it might not. But what we do know is that you'll get into the most frightful trouble if it gets out that it's gone.'

'Yes, you're right about that,' Humphries said unhappily. 'I'm trying not to think about it.'

'So here's an answer. Is anyone else likely to look in the box that holds the egg but you? Seeing as you're the only one who really cares about it?'

'Well . . . I suppose not.'

'So, here's my plan. Let's put in this rock I found. It's about the same size and shape and weight, though of course, it isn't an egg. But put it in the box, nail it up, stick it in the basement and . . . by the time they find out, you'll have found the egg or you'll be retired or something. Or you can claim you have no idea how the egg was replaced. See? No need to confess. No need to worry.'

Mr Humphries stared at her for a moment, taking this in, and then threw back his head and roared. 'You are priceless, Miranda!' he said at last, wiping his eyes. 'It's ridiculous, but why not? I've got nothing to lose, have I? And who knows, by the time this war is over, I might have found the blessed thing. You really are priceless.'

'Just like your egg,' Miranda said, before running out laughing.

Upstairs in her room, Miranda took out her exercise book and wrote down a little rhyme that had been in her head for days.

> *Etti Boule*
> *Is kind and cruel*
> *She took a fool*
> *And keeps him still*
>
> *She keeps him deep*
> *She keeps him cool*
> *Etti Boule*
> *Is kind and cruel.*

Etti Boule would take the blame. Etti Boule would hide their secret for ever. Etti Boule made the jam. Etti Boule was the villain.

It had nothing to do with me, or Rosalind, or Robbie. Or Dolly. It was Etti Boule.

And that's that.

Chapter Twenty-Six

Present Day

In the kitchen of Wakefield Castle was a large crowd of people in black and wearing headsets, vast cameras on wheels that looked like robot cyclops, blazing lights, dangling microphones and, the focus of all the attention, Atalanta Young, in the sauciest bodice she could get away with. While Atalanta flirted with the camera and talked huskily about how gorgeous it was to lard a capon, half a dozen helpers next door were prepping ingredients and selecting dishes and bowls from the huge amount of homeware donated by top stores and designers for the privilege of having it appear on Atalanta's show.

Outside in the quadrangle were trucks generating the electricity for the dozens of cables snaking into the house to power the high-wattage lights and the cameras. There was also a temporary kitchen, with more cooks replicating Atalanta's recipes – or rather Georgie's recipes – as they went along so that she could always pull something perfect out of the oven. A catering bus acted as another cooking venue, this time to provide the meals for the crew, which seemed to be required almost ceaselessly, from early morning break-fast through to coffee, snacks, an enormous lunch, teatime muffins and cakes and then a supper if filming went on past regulation hours. The last truck provided hair, make-up and costume for Atalanta.

'What a palaver!' exclaimed Caspar, coming into the East Tower. 'I can see why you need this place.'

Georgie looked up from the stove, where she was testing a new recipe. 'I wouldn't be able to get a thing done over there. It's organised bedlam.'

'I can see why you'd hate it. Even the new and improved Georgie, with her greater tolerance for people and sound, would have trouble with this.'

'She would. She does.' Georgie smiled at him. 'But at least we have stopped all the tourists for now. I don't think I could cope with that as well.'

'They'll be back, though,' Caspar said. 'All this is causing quite a sensation around here. And once the programme is broadcast, we're bound to get another boost.'

Georgie put down her spoon and made an attitude of prayer. 'Thank goodness for my little tower.' She smiled again. 'But I'm very grateful for all this. Who would have thought the roof would be saved in such a spectacular fashion?'

'And there's Henry and Alyssa,' Caspar put in. 'Don't forget them.'

'How could I?'

'You don't mind them being here, do you? With everything else that's going on?'

'Of course I don't. In fact, they're coming for supper in the garden once the filming has wrapped for the day.'

'Oh good,' Caspar said. 'I'll look forward to that.'

Caspar's sister and brother-in-law had come down from Bath to design and dress the kitchen set and various parts of the house where there would be filming, and had had such a good time doing it that they had set up a small workshop in the stables. They planned to market their homewares in a shop on the premises, living between their house and shop in Bath, and their workshop here at the castle.

'It's really come to life,' Alyssa said to Georgie after their supper in the garden. Caspar and Henry had gone off to examine Henry's prototype for a dresser in the stables.

'That's a bit of an understatement,' Georgie said with a laugh. She topped up Alyssa's wine glass. It was a balmy summer evening, with the sky a deepening velvet blue with a tinge of orange where the sun was disappearing, and a faded silver disc where the moon was rising. The garden was full of the scents of newly opened roses and orange blossom, the aromatic herbs from the garden Georgie had planted, and a lemon verbena candle that burned in the lantern on the table.

'Does Atalanta not stay here in the evenings?' asked Alyssa. 'I thought I'd be hanging out with my new pal, the celebrity chef. My friends were all really jealous!'

'No. The crew stay in hotels but Atalanta is collected by a Mercedes every evening and driven to her own country house, lent to her by a friend and admirer.'

'You know what? I'd have been deeply disappointed by anything else.' Alyssa sipped her rosé wine. 'I am just delighted to discover that she is not a monster behind the scenes.'

'Oh no. She can be tricky, but she's not a monster. She's even asked me if I'd like my name on the cover of the next book – in recognition of this place and the recipe book that inspired the show. She doesn't have to do that.'

'And are you going to?'

Georgie smiled. 'You know what? I am. It's time to come out of the shadows a bit. I've got lots of wonderful plans for the future.'

'You know, Georgie, you've done an amazing job here. Don't take this the wrong way, but I never would have thought you'd be able to do this. You seemed like such a mouse at first.' She smiled at Georgie. 'I underestimated you. I'm sorry.'

'I don't mind,' Georgie said. 'I am a bit of a mouse in some ways. But I'm getting better at venturing out and looking around.'

'Well, whatever it is, you've worked wonders. We're really enjoying it here and so are the kids. It's nice for them to have your sister's children to play with. Is she going to stay long?'

'I don't know. There doesn't seem to be any hurry now that she's moved into the gatehouse.'

'She has?' Alyssa looked astonished. 'You persuaded Viktoria to leave?'

'Not exactly. But she made us an offer we couldn't refuse. Besides, we owe her.'

The week before the filming of Atalanta's show was due

to start, Viktoria had invited Caspar and Georgie for a drink in the gatehouse. They were surprised to receive this first ever invitation but happily accepted. When they arrived, they found not just Viktoria but also a white-haired, rosy-cheeked man in purposefully young-looking jeans, an open-collared shirt and trainers.

'Oh, hello, Johnnie!' Georgie said, taken aback. 'What are you doing here?'

'Georgie! My dear, how are you? Hasn't Viktoria said? She and I are an item!' He kissed Georgie on each cheek with loud, smacking kisses. 'Ever since the auspicious night when you cooked that magnificent feast for us.'

Viktoria came up to him, practically purring and rubbing up against him, and murmured, 'Johnnie, my sweetest, will you fetch the champagne? I'm afraid it's all the way down-stairs in the storeroom.'

'Who is that? He looks familiar,' Caspar said, as Johnnie went off to obey his instructions.

'He was here for the banquet. You met him then, I should think,' Georgie explained. 'He's the head of Bright Eye TV, the company that makes Atalanta's shows.'

Viktoria smiled sweetly. 'He's my new man. And that is why you are having your filming right here in the castle. I persuaded him to do it and I persuaded him to pay a very healthy sum indeed for the privilege. I'll be quick while he's getting the champagne. Here's my suggestion. You give me half the money from the location fee, which should go some way towards a nice flat in London in an acceptable area. You can keep the rest for the roof. And I will vacate the gatehouse and leave you in peace. How is that?'

Caspar stared at her speechless, unable to believe that half of the juicy location fee had just disappeared.

Georgie said hastily, 'Thank you, Viktoria. You've done us such a favour. We'll think about what you've said and get back to you.'

'You'd better think fast,' Viktoria said sternly, 'because there's still time for me to make Johnnie pull the plug. Okay?'

'Okay.'

Just then Johnnie returned with the champagne and Viktoria transformed back into playful kitten and the subject of her payoff wasn't mentioned again. Caspar, though, was furious at the idea. Georgie talked him round.

'We'll get much more out of paying her off than we will out of not. If she gets Johnnie to cancel, we'll lose all the money. This way, we get the show, we get the roof, we get rid of Viktoria and we fulfil the terms of Uncle Archie's will as painlessly as possible. It really is best all round.'

Caspar grumbled but he saw she was right. A bargain was struck – one that included the return of all property belonging to the castle and the Wakefield family – and the gatehouse was vacated almost at once. Georgie had the distinct impression that Viktoria couldn't wait to get out of it, and she had to congratulate her on a well-laid plan to get her own way, excellently put into practice. She ended up feeling that she rather liked Viktoria, whose aura had softened lately, and wished her well living it up in London with Johnnie.

After that, it made sense for Pippa to move into the

gatehouse, particularly after she got a job at the village primary school.

'I loved the castle,' she said, 'but this place is cosier for me and the girls. I don't like running up flights of stairs and using monitors and all the rest. I like us all to be close together.'

Georgie liked it too, the idea that they were separate and yet together.

Now, in the comfortable twilight of the garden, Alyssa asked, 'How is your sister's divorce going?'

Georgie made a face. 'It's going. Slowly. It will take ages. Ryan is not an easy man to negotiate with. Pippa's in counselling and it's becoming clearer and clearer that she mixed herself up with a very tricky character, and they do not tend to be easy when it comes to divorce. Maybe it's slightly easier than the marriage itself – but opinion is divided on that. The only good thing is that, unlike marriage, there is a light at the end of the tunnel.'

'I'm so sorry to hear that,' Alyssa said sympathetically. 'I guess they just couldn't make each other happy.'

'Your marriage to Henry must be a good one,' Georgie remarked with a dry laugh.

'Well . . .' Alyssa laughed too. 'You know – it's good but it's not perfect. He's not a saint by any means!'

'I'm sure. No one is. But you two are a team?'

'Oh yes, we're lucky that way,' Alyssa said. 'I know not every married couple can work together, but we can.'

'And he has your back?'

Alyssa nodded. 'A hundred per cent.'

'And you can talk to him?'

'Of course.' Alyssa looked surprised.

Georgie leaned forward. 'Alyssa, you're really lucky. You don't have any idea what it's like to be in a marriage with none of those things. I mean, none. Zero. That isn't just a story of two people who can't make each other happy. This is a situation where the only thing possible is dysfunction and misery and slowly building despair.'

Alyssa blinked at her. 'You're passionate about this.'

Georgie sat back, a little embarrassed. 'I suppose I am. It touches a nerve with me. You see, a lot of people don't know how lucky they are to enjoy decent human relationships. They think it's the norm. That's not their fault, of course, and I'm very happy for them. I want more people like that in the world. But a lot of people have never known the luxury of loving parents, or loving husbands. And that's not their fault either.'

There was a pause. Alyssa looked shamefaced for a moment. 'I get it,' she said quietly, and they sat in companionable silence for a while. Alyssa looked over. 'I'm sorry, Georgie. I've been really self-absorbed. I know that you and Pippa were adopted. I guess that was not a happy story. And I'm really sorry your sister married a bad lot. He sounds grim and it must have been a nightmare. I think she's doing the right thing, in those circumstances. I just hope she finds a wonderful man next time. And you're right. We got good ones, didn't we?'

'We certainly did,' Georgie said emphatically. 'We certainly did.'

Just then, Caspar and Henry came back from the stables, chatting together as they crossed the lawn towards their wives.

Georgie, watching her husband stroll towards her, was suddenly filled with the most tremendous love for him. *You are my family for ever*, he had written. He had written that at a time when he thought he had lost the one thing he had always wanted: children of his own. Now the house was full of children. Pippa's children, and Alyssa's children. During the holidays, when the tourists came, youngsters came and went all day and Henry was talking about designing a wonderful wooden fort and adventure playground for them in the park.

But the main thing was that when Caspar thought he had lost what he most wanted, he was still true to Georgie. That fidelity meant everything to her. She knew that she loved him from the depths to the heights and for ever. He was her family too. He had listened and tried to understand. He never would completely, but he would always do his best.

Caspar reached them, and bent down to kiss Georgie. He looked over at his sister. 'I hope you wouldn't tempt Georgie with any of that rosé.'

'Don't be silly,' Alyssa said with a laugh. 'I'm not going to give alcohol to a pregnant woman!'

'Just the rose lemonade for me,' Georgie said firmly. 'I'm being very careful.'

'Of course. I'm joking.' Caspar took her hand and kissed it. 'It's still early days. But I have a good feeling about it.'

Georgie gazed up at him. She remembered his utter joy the

day she had told him that she was pregnant. He had been speechless with happiness and could only hold her hands, then hug her and laugh with joy. She had felt so happy not just to give him this gift, but to have this gift for herself as well, if all went to plan. It meant that she was finally free of the horror of her past. It was behind her and she had made her peace with it. She had healed enough to look forward and embrace all the joy life could offer. 'I feel good about it too, Caspar. I really do.'

'Then it's a Georgie moment,' he said with a laugh. 'And that makes me happy.'

She smiled at him and took his hand. 'Me too. The damage stops here, doesn't it?'

He nodded. 'Oh yes. The damage stops here. You can forget all the things in the past that don't need to be remembered any more. This is a fresh page. This is where the real story begins.'

Epilogue

'Shall we turn on the television, Robert?' The nurse bent over him and spoke loudly into his ear. 'It's that programme you like, the cookery one with the pretty red-haired lady.'

She went over and turned on the telly. Robbie sat back in his armchair. He had seen the advertisements for this programme and he had said he wanted to watch it. He was glad the nurse had remembered.

The programme started up with the familiar theme tune, but the setting wasn't Atalanta's usual smart house. Instead, it was an ancient castle kitchen.

'I know that place!' Robbie said to the nurse as she made him a cup of tea.

'Do you, dear?' she said brightly. 'That's nice.'

'I lived there in the war.' His voice, ninety years old now, sounded quivering and unreliable.

'Of course you did! You lived right there, where lovely Atalanta is doing her cooking.'

He sighed. Ageing was difficult and tiring, and it was hard to be taken for a fool because he was old. He stopped trying to talk to the nurse and instead thought about the years of being evacuated, and the great love he had found for the castle. He'd learned everything about it, every nook and cranny. He'd known that there was that secret place. He'd known because he'd put the egg in there, by going through the cellars to where there was a strange old door, very hard to open, that had led into that nasty well. The oubliette. The only other entrance was the hole at the top under the lawn.

He remembered how it had happened very clearly. He and his mother had talked about his father, Derek Foster, a man who had once been in prison for hurting women and young girls, and who viciously beat his wife and lashed out at his sons. His violence to his family was getting worse and Dolly feared that he might one day kill her, and what would that mean for the family?

But almost worse was the idea that he might hurt the Wakefield girls, the women of the family she esteemed and revered.

She would never let that happen, she told Robbie.

He told her about what he'd overhead those twins saying to one another. That they had jam ready to kill the Germans.

His mother had been delighted. 'Well, that's our way,' she'd said happily. 'Quick and easy. And if we can administer justice without anyone ever knowing, then so much the better.'

Robbie had told his father about the egg in Humphries's study. He'd told him it was priceless and that he would steal it for him in case the Wakefields somehow forced him to go. He had showed his father the perfect place to hide it as well, until it was needed. Robbie had sneaked the egg out of its case, wrapped it in Harris's old blanket and some of the straw from the stables, and heaved it all the way to that old dungeon. In it had gone. His father had laughed and been delighted. 'My pension,' he'd called it. 'I'll get it out when the time comes,' he said. 'It'll make me rich.'

Once Robbie had thought that if the egg was gone, then Mr Humphries would have to stay. And if he stayed, then his dad wouldn't be able to hurt them. And Mr Humphries would teach him, Robbie, about fossils and dinosaurs and eggs and crinoids. And one day, when Mr Humphries was desperate for that egg, Robbie would find it and everyone would cheer and he would be a hero.

But then it was impossible ever to find it.

The strangest thing was that in all this time, no one had ever mentioned that missing egg.

But then, they'd never questioned the strange disappearance of Robbie's father either. Derek Foster had vanished, and never been heard of again. And there didn't seem to have been one person who cared, especially not his family.

There were flashes of memory: taking his father to the kitchen where his mother was frying eggs and ham. 'Have some of this, Derek,' she said. 'You look like you need a bit of feeding up.' And after Foster had wolfed that down, she'd offered him trifle. But she sent Robbie out of the room while his dad settled down to his dessert.

Afterwards, the two of them had dragged him along that passageway under the lawn, all the way to the little door whose hinges he'd oiled only lately. The remains of the trifle had gone in with him. The door had been shut tight, the old barrel pulled in front of it. No one but Robbie knew about the egg also being in there.

But Miranda Wakefield knew about my dad. I as good as told her. I knew she'd understood from that look in her eyes: horror. Guilt. And then those stories about that woman who made the poisoned trifle and killed a man.

Etti Boule was Dolly. Finally rising up vengeful and desperate, she had done what needed to be done. She'd known that Foster would never leave. She'd known that he would get meaner and more vicious. She'd known that someone would get hurt and she knew who it ought to be. So she'd sorted it. With Robbie's help. And Miranda told her story over and over, without really telling it at all.

It helped them all make their peace. And the secret would die with him.

He watched Atalanta Young cooking something green and closed his eyes.

I was happy there. At Wakefield. What happy years they were. What a wonderful place for a child.

And yet, no one ever mentioned the egg.

Sam Locke looked in the mirror and straightened his tie. He wasn't usually a tie man but tonight he was taking Pippa out to a smart restaurant in town and he wanted to look the business. She'd seen him in his work clothes and hadn't minded enough to stop her saying yes to a date, but he wanted her to see that he could brush up well.

She was a good woman, and a devoted mother to her two

daughters. She had the same sweetness and vulnerability as Georgie. Bad husbands seemed attracted to women like her, as though they sensed that they'd found a fertile source of love and affection from someone who'd require very little in return. But Pippa had had the gumption to say no and to get up and leave. She knew she deserved better. That took guts.

Sam hoped that the date would go well. He didn't want to let Pippa down, or her sister who had seemed keen on the whole idea. He had a lot of time for Georgie. He liked Caspar but Georgie was the business. The bomb. He didn't think of her romantically but he admired her enormously.

That was why he'd been startled when she'd said that she thought they would find someone down that hole, that oubliette, in the castle lawn. It seemed so left field. But when he'd got down there, to the very bottom, and shone his torch around, he'd got a shiver down his spine. Right there was a pile of old bones in the last shreds of an overcoat and suit, with a rotten hat and scarf on.

He'd gasped. Then got hold of himself. He was not easily spooked, he was a realist. It was a dead body, years and years old. There was nothing to be done about it now. He thought of the police and coroner and news reporters. He thought of all the hard work Georgie and Caspar were putting into the castle and how they hoped that there would be a television series here in the summer. That would all be under threat. The stream of visitors might dry up if the place were known for death rather than cooking.

Then he saw something else. The stone in the blanket. It looked odd. But not dangerous or threatening. It looked interesting. So he picked it up and decided that if he was going to find anything in the oubliette, it would be this: a stone in a blanket. What could be the issue with that?

He'd shouted up for a sling and sent it up.

Down there in the dark, taking a last look around, he'd shone his torch on a small iron-studded door, the only other way into this ghastly place. There must be a passage that led somewhere else, perhaps back into the house. He pushed against it but it was firmly shut. Locked, no doubt. Perhaps even concealed in some way. And then he'd noticed a bowl on the floor of the oubliette, coated with a dark stain. It glinted under the light from his torch. It was glass. How had it stayed intact, dropped from a height like that?

How very strange.

Then he'd climbed up, put the lid on the oubliette and not said a word. One day, he'd go back, get the bones and stick them in an incinerator on some site somewhere. Then Georgie, Pippa and Caspar could look to the future and not to the past.

Not the dangerous past, anyhow.

Sam considered his reflection and then took off the tie. That was better.

He switched off the bathroom light and headed off to meet Pippa.

Acknowledgements

My acknowledgements in every book are heartfelt, but this time I want to emphasise how very much I've appreciated the kindness and support shown to me over the last year. It's an odd thing when one's own life becomes more absorbing and strange than the stories one is trying to create. It has helped to go on this journey with Georgie from dark to light, and from pain to acceptance and recovery.

I owe so much to the people at Macmillan, to their patience, understanding and support. Wayne Brookes, my editor, has been a marvellous champion, helping me to see the way through and get things back on track, and offering editorial brilliance and kindness in spades. I have to thank in particular my brilliant copy-editor, Lorraine Green, who moved mountains to enable us to work together almost page by page on the rewriting, and everything benefited from her perception, skill, sympathy and encouragement. I owe her a lot.

Everyone at Macmillan has been rock-like in their support and I want to thank Lucy Hale, Rosie Friis, Stuart Dwyer,

Laura Carr and Holly Sheldrake. Neil Lang designed another marvellous cover. Thank you to Christina Maria Webb for proofreading.

I couldn't do any of this without the exceptional insight, wisdom and support of my agent, Lizzy Kremer. We have been working together for nearly twenty years and it isn't long enough to appreciate everything she can offer. She is, quite simply, the best. I can't thank her enough for her encouragement and understanding. I want to cheer just as rousingly for the marvellous team at David Higham, especially Orli, Kay and Maddalena, who've all helped me so much.

My wonderful friends and family have been there for me over the last year. I have felt their care and support very deeply. I am endlessly grateful and will never forget it. I also have the fabulous Swans – the novelists of the South West – and many encouraging writer friends who can understand the pleasures and trials of this very strange job. I send you all huge love and thanks, especially to Barney and Tabby, who make it all worthwhile.

I have dedicated this book to three wonderful people who have helped me laugh, create and enjoy the pleasures of life again, while also feeding me the most delicious food (thank you, Amber!). It's been an enormous gift. Here's to much more fun in the future.

A WINTER MEMORY

Forgetting is easy. Remembering will change everything . . .

Now

Years ago, Helen fell for the charming Hamish and was enchanted by his family home, the romantic Ballintyre House in western Scotland. Now, seeking refuge from a scandal that has cost Hamish his job, they are living with his older brother Charlie at the house. Struggling with her own problems, Helen is surprised to find that Charlie's wife has vanished but no one else seems at all concerned.

Then

In 1968, sixteen-year-old Tigs is madly in love with James Ballintyre, her childhood friend and hero. When he marries another woman, her heart is broken. She tries to find her way to a new life and a new love but, somehow, everyone is called back to Ballintyre in the end. Tigs is no exception . . .

For ever

Ballintyre has always been the setting for revelations of love, obsession and betrayal. Now, as Helen seeks the answer to Charlie's wife's disappearance, she is forced to confront her own difficult truths – as the events of the past reach forward to touch the lives of those who still call Ballintyre home, and reveal their secrets . . .

THE WINTER CHILDREN

Some secrets are frozen in time . . .

Olivia and Dan Felbeck are blissfully happy when their longed-for twins arrive after years of IVF. At the same time, they make the move to Renniston Hall, a huge Elizabethan house that belongs to absent friends.

Living rent-free in a small part of the unmodernized house, once a boarding school, they can begin to enjoy the family life they've always wanted. But there is a secret at the heart of their family, one that Olivia does not yet know. And the house, too, holds its darkness deep within it . . .

THE SNOW ROSE

I know they think I shouldn't keep her . . . That's why I've escaped them while I can, while I still have the opportunity . . .

Kate is on the run with her daughter Heather, her identity hidden and their destination unknown to the family they've left behind. She's found a place where they can live in solitude, a grand old house full of empty rooms and dark secrets. But they're not alone, for there are the strange old ladies in the cottage next door: Matty and her sister Sissy. They know what happened here long ago, and are curious about Kate. How long can she hide Heather's presence from them?

When an eccentric band of newcomers arrive, led by the charismatic Archer, Kate realises that the past she's so desperate to escape is about to catch up with her. And inside the house, history is beginning to repeat itself . . .

THE WINTER SECRET

'My dear boy, the place is cursed. It always has been and it always will be . . .'

Buttercup Redmain has a life of pampered luxury, living in beautiful Charcombe Park. Her older husband, Charles, is wealthy and successful, and proud of the house he has painstakingly restored. Buttercup is surrounded by people who make her life delightfully easy. But the one thing she really wants seems impossible.

There are other discomforting realities: her husband's ex-wife Ingrid still lives nearby, although Buttercup has never met her. And it soon becomes clear that all the people who make Buttercup's life so carefree are also watching her every move. Does she actually live in a comfortable but inescapable cage? And what is the real story of her husband's previous marriage?

Xenia Arkadyoff once lived in Charcombe Park with her father, a Russian prince, and her mother, a famous film star. Life seemed charmed, full of glamour and beauty. But behind the glittering facade lay pain, betrayal and the truth about the woman Xenia spent her life protecting.

Now Charcombe Park is calling back people who were once part of its story, and the secrets that have stayed long hidden are bubbling inexorably to the surface . . .

A MIDWINTER PROMISE

The embrace of the past can never be broken . . .

The past

A lonely and imaginative child, Julia loves her family's beautiful and wild Cornish home with all her heart. But, marked by dark troubles, she enters her adult years determined to leave and seek a new beginning in London. It's there she meets the handsome David. They fall in love, but when Julia becomes pregnant, even he can't stop the terrible echoes of the past from ringing in her ears. The only sound to be heard above the noise is the old Cornish house, calling her home . . .

The present

For Julia's adult children, Alex and Johnnie, the house hides the history of their family within its walls. For Alex, it is full of memories of her late mother. For Johnnie, it is the house that should have been rightfully theirs after Julia died but has been stolen from them instead. With their father now lying in a hospital bed, time is running out for Alex and Johnnie to uncover the secrets of what happened to their mother all those years ago. Can they discover the truth before the house closes its doors to them for ever?